SULLIVAN'S ISLAND:

"The setting and the characters are blazingly authentic…
Frank evokes the eccentric Hamilton family and their
feisty Gullah housekeeper with originality and conviction;
Susan herself—smart, sarcastic, funny and endearingly
flawed—makes a lively and memorable narrator. Thanks
to these scrappily compelling portraits, this is a rich read."
—PUBLISHERS WEEKLY (STARRED REVIEW)

"Ms. Frank's evocation of the Lowcountry rivals that of
Anne Rivers Siddons and Pat Conroy both, but this tale of
island life is uniquely her own. A wonderful book."
—BRET LOTT

"Dorothea Benton Frank and I share the exact same
literary territory—SULLIVAN'S ISLAND is hilarious and wise,
an up-to-the-minute report on what it is like to be alive and
female in the South Carolina Lowcountry today. It
contains the funniest sex scene I have ever
encountered." —PAT CONROY

Praise for

SULLIVAN'S ISLAND:

"The setting and the characters are blazingly authentic . . .
Frank evokes the eccentric Hamilton family and their feisty
Gullah housekeeper with originality and conviction; Susan
herself—smart, sarcastic, funny and endearingly flawed—
makes a lively and memorable narrator. Thanks to these
scrappily compelling portraits, this is a rich read."
—*Publishers Weekley* (starred review)

"Dorothea Frank and I share the exact same literary territory . . . *Sullivan's Island* is hilarious and wise, an up-
to-the-minute report on what it is like to be alive and female in the South Carolina Lowcountry today. It contains
the funniest sex scene I have ever encountered."
—Pat Conroy

"Dottie Frank's take on the South Carolina Lowcountry is
tough, tender, achingly real, and very, very funny. *Sullivan's Island* roars with life." —Anne Rivers Siddons

"In *Sullivan's Island*, southern womanhood has found a
new voice, and it is outrageous, hilarious, relentless and
impossible to ignore." —John Berendt

continued on next page . . .

PLANTATION

A Lowcountry Tale

DOROTHEA BENTON FRANK

JOVE BOOKS, NEW YORK

This is a work of fiction. Names, characters, places and incidents are
either the product of the author's imagination or are used fictitiously,
and any resemblance to actual persons, living or dead, business
establishments, events or locales is entirely coincidental.

PLANTATION

A Jove Book / published by arrangement with
the author

PRINTING HISTORY
Jove edition / July 2001

All rights reserved.
Copyright © 2001 by Dorothea Benton Frank.
"The River" by Marjory Wentworth is quoted with
the permission of the author.
This book, or parts thereof, may not be reproduced in
any form without permission.
For information address: The Berkley Publishing Group,
a division of Penguin Putnam Inc.,
375 Hudson Street, New York, New York 10014.

The Penguin Putnam Inc. World Wide Web site address is
www.penguinputnam.com

ISBN: 0-515-13108-3

A JOVE BOOK®
Jove Books are published by The Berkley Publishing Group,
a division of Penguin Putnam Inc.,
375 Hudson Street, New York, New York 10014.
JOVE and the "J" design
are trademarks belonging to Penguin Putnam Inc.

PRINTED IN THE UNITED STATES OF AMERICA

10 9 8 7 6 5 4 3 2 1

FOR PETER

ACKNOWLEDGMENTS

The list of people to remember who helped to bring this story to fruition is wonderfully long and I say *wonderfully* because at each turn in the road there was a new hand extended to me in generous support and friendship.

It was my brother-in-law, Junius Scott Bagnal Jr., who hauled me up and down the rivers of the ACE Basin and regaled me with more information than I could have researched in a lifetime. His superior humor and genuine desire to help never waned. I am now in trouble with my sister, Lynn, for not putting her up front in this paragraph. But, hey, anybody who knows my family even a smidgen knows that Lynn Bagnal's love and support—and not just for me—are legendary. Thank you both from the bottom of my gizzards.

For my nephew-in-law (can it be that he's my *nephew?*), David Oliver of Savannah, the doctor who risked his life, and those of his sons, Steven and Ben, to teach me to shoot skeet and quail with a bona fide loaded gun. I'm happy to report that no clay and no birds died by my hand. You boys can stop laughing now, okay? And to Vicki, his wife and the loveliest of southern women, don't you think it's time we said we were sisters? Thank you to all the Olivers for their hospitality and affection.

Special thanks to Michael Hickman of Jacksonboro for the rescue and the plantation tour. Tall Pines would still be looking for a home without you having trusted the veracity of that lunatic woman you allowed into your truck. And to all the folks of Jacksonboro, you live in one of the most beautiful places on this earth.

A huge dose of thanks for Roger Pinckney from Daufuskie Island, SC. Mr. Pinckney's book *Blue Roots* was an invaluable source and a fascinating read. Anyone interested in the Gullah culture is just a hack if they don't have a copy of this book on their shelf.

To Natalie Daise, many thanks for your correspondence and help on spirituals. Charlotte O. Gordon, my e-mail buddy, is the one responsible for the spelling of *yanh*. She gracefully advised me that the spelling was better than *'eah*. So, yanh it is, Charlotte! I agree.

Billy and Pat Benton of Mt. Pleasant, SC, Ted and Joanne Benton of Winchester, MA, Jennifer and Michael Benton of Irving, TX, all deserve a parade in their honor. Yes, these are my three brothers and their wives, and they've been stellar in their unflinching support. Stacy Hamburger of the Isle of Palms, SC, has a place in my heart forever. I was hoping for a miracle and bingo! I found Stacy, the dream weaver. Greg Marrs, wherever you are, our guest room awaits you and Samantha anytime.

A woman couldn't ask for better friends than Anthony Stith, Larry Dodds, Brigitte Miklaszewski, Shannon Gibbons, Linda Lauren, Dona Hay, Patsy Thomas, Larry Harbin, Pete Dewey, Cheryl and Max Lenker—love y'all!—

Fran Pritchard, Joy Casale, Joe Cupolo, Keith and Chris Stewart, Sparky Witte, Chip Clarkin, and Charlie Moore. My book group—Cherry Provost most especially, for, once again, introducing me around and for believing in me. And to Adrian and Jerry Shelby for their laughter and dependable good wishes.

I bow and scrape to Robert and Susan Rosen of Charleston for their unbelievable generosity and friendship—I love y'all forever! To Catherine Fry of Columbia for her luminous persona, sparkling wisdom, and guest room—thanks, honeychile. And, to Mr. Orangeburg, Dr. Mickey Hay—here it is, bubba, stand-alone proof that you are appreciated by this old island girl for all the wonderful things you continue to do.

Okay. The big guns. Pat and Sandra Conroy—Peter has commissioned a sculptor to do a witty and tasteful statue of y'all for our front yard. Hey, thanks forever. To Bret Lott for his friendship, to Anne Rivers Siddons once again and always, and finally to Josephine Humphreys and to Elinor Lipman for letting me know I was alive. Special thanks to Marjory Wentworth for the use of her extraordinary poetry and her friendship.

Now, the Scud missiles—Leslie Gelbman. Norman Lidofsky. Liz Perl. You changed my whole world and helped me in so many ways which defy words. How can I ever repay your profound faith? Just know that not a day passes without me thinking of y'all and mentally sending you my love and respect. Thank you all. And a special note to all the field reps of Berkley Publishing for their dedication and loyalty. Y'all are the almighty guardian angels of the publishing industry.

To Hillary Schupf and Matthew Rich. I never want to launch a book without either of you. Between the oyster roast and frequent discovery of my unknown cousins, I gave y'all something fun to remember. But, y'all gave me constant thrills. And, Jamie Coulter, if you're out there, thanks again for the spectacular bash!

And to Joni Friedman, my art director, for her superlative vision. Joni, when I first saw my book on the shelves, I wept. You saw what I felt. Thank you.

Speaking of good fortune? How about my fabulous and incredible editor, Gail Fortune? The woman's a genius! Gail pulled me through the dark days of the first draft of this book and never left my side. With her astute eye she gave me more critical advice than Millie could. Gail, thank you over and over for your excellent judgment, your soulful character and for your remarkable saintly patience. Simply stated, it wouldn't be worth it without you. This book makes you an honorary Geechee Girl.

I owe so much to my agent, Amy Berkower, for teaching me the ropes of a new universe and for understanding everything. Thanks, Amy. I hope someday I prove to be worthy of your wing. And, to my cousin, Judy Blanchard Linder, for reading this manuscript and not once complaining but always graciously pointing out the goobers. To Mia and Christian Tudose and Kevin Sherry for their acceptance and compassion.

Finally, I offer sincere gratitude to my family, Peter, Victoria, and William. Better than anyone, you know my heart. As you witness these changes in my life, know that I am so profoundly grateful to you for giving me the freedom it takes to open each door. I rejoice in you and I love you more each day. I am always deeply proud of you and constantly moved by your beautiful spirits in myriad ways. You have always been and will always be the most magnificent part of my life.

River

The river is a woman who is never idle.
Into her feathering water
fall petals and bones

of earth's shed skins.
While all around her edges
men are carving altars,

the river gathers flotsam,
branches of time and clouds
loosening the robes of their reflections.

Her dress is decoupage—
yellow clustering leaves
ashes, paper, tin and dung.

Wine dark honey for the world,
sweet blood of seeping magma
pulsing above the carbon starred

sediment. Striped with settled skulls,
wing and leaf spine: the river
is an open-minded graveyard.

Listen to the music
of sunlight spreading
inside her crystal cells.

Magnet, clock, cradle
for the wind; the river holds a cup
filling with miles of rain.

But when the river sleeps
her celestial children
break the sticks of gravity;

grab fistfuls of fish
scented amber clotted with diamonds,
ferns and petalling clouds,

adorn bracelets of woven rain,
rise with islands of sweet grass
and stars strung to their backs

to wander over the scarred surface
of the earth, like their mothers
simply searching for the sea.

—*Marjory Wentworth*

History of ownership of Tall Pines Plantation,
located on the Edisto River in the ACE Basin of South Carolina:

Original home built on 5,000 acres as a gift by William Oliver Kent on the occasion of his daughter Elizabeth Bootle Kent's marriage to Henry Wright Heyward IV in the year of 1855.

Elizabeth Bootle Kent   wife of *Henry Wright Heyward IV*
(1838–1911)   (1830–1914)

Tall Pines then passed into the hands of their only daughter:

Olivia Kent Heyward   wife of *David Patrick Logan*
(1860–1935)   (1855–1935)

With whom she gave birth to three children:

Male child (1880), died in childbirth
Cassandra Anne (1881–1956),
   married and moved to Philadelphia
Amelia Heyward Logan (1885–1962),
   wife of Thomas Payne Reardon (1860–1947)

Whose hands then inherited the Plantation and with whom she had three children:

Isabelle Marie (1915–1990),
   never married, became a foreign missionary
Thomas Payne Reardon Jr. (1921–1994),
   who practiced medicine in Savannah, GA
Lavinia Ann Boswell (1/29/28),
   wife of James Nevil Wimbley II (deceased)

Who then inherited the Plantation and with whom she had two children:

Caroline Boswell Wimbley	*James Nevil Wimbley III*
(3/22/61)	(7/28/63)
wife of	husband of
Richard Case Levine, M.D.—	*Frances Mae Litchfield—*
parents of:	parents of:
Eric Boswell Levine (b. 1988)	*Amelia* (b. 1987)
	Isabelle (b. 1989)
	Caroline (b. 1991)
	Chloe (b. 2000)

(Dr. Levine's first marriage, to Lois Baum, produced a son, Harry, and ended in divorce.)

CONTENTS

PLANTATION

As seen in the Charleston *Post and Courier*, Obituaries column, August 10, 2000.

Photo of Miss Lavinia in full hunting regalia.

Photo of Miss Lavinia in evening dress entering a party down her staircase, wearing "The Pearls."

Lavinia Boswell Wimbley, widow of James Nevil Wimbley Sr., died at her home yesterday. She was seventy-two years old. "Miss Lavinia," as she was known, was educated at Ashley Hall and The College of Charleston. She later earned a Master's Degree in Art History at the University of South Carolina.

"Miss Lavinia" was an accomplished sportswoman in bird hunting and the shooting of trap and sporting clays. She spoke frequently on the subjects of American painting, the history of rice cultivation, gardens in America, and bourbon whiskey.

A renowned hostess and an avid card player, she is survived by her companions, Raoul Estevez, 31, Peter Greer, 75, a son, James Nevil Wimbley III, 37, a daughter, Caroline Wimbley Levine, 39, and five grandchildren. Visitors may call at the Bagnal Funeral home in Walterboro tonight from six to nine. The funeral is scheduled for 11 a.m. Thursday at Tall Pines Plantation. In lieu of flowers, donations may be made to the Gibbes Art Museum, the Nature Conservancy or the Betty Ford Center.

PROLOGUE

DON'T LEAVE ME NOW!

2000

This story I have to tell you has to be true because even I couldn't make up this whopper. And Mother's wake—packed to the rafters with the well-dressed curious and the well-heeled sorrowful—may seem an insensitive place to begin, but here we are and it's all I can think about—that is, the progression of events that led up to this moment. I'm obsessing and entitled to it too. So would you.

Think about this. You know those pivotal moments in your life that you don't see coming? The ones you wished arrived with a timer going off so you'd know *this is it!* Well, when the phone rang in February, you couldn't have convinced me that six months later, Mother would be in "the box" and I'd be wearing her pearls, twisting them around my finger exactly like she used to do.

Oh, God, here comes Raoul. Excuse me for a moment.

"Mees Caroline, I want to express my deep sympathy

to you in thees torrible time of you troubles."

He took my hands in his. His hands were callused but manicured.

"Thank you, Raoul, thank you for coming," I said, thinking that he was actually rather handsome. He exuded something, I don't know, some masculine whatever.

"She was very beautiful, your mother, and I will hold her een my heart forever."

"Thank you," I said, "I know she was very fond of you."

"*Sí,*" he said, a smile spreading across his face, "ees true."

He released my hands and walked away, back into the crowd. Mother slept with *him?* Well, why *not?*

Where were we? Ah! Pivotal moment! Pivotal moment, indeed. You see, Trip—he's my only brother—called me in New York, in the middle of a cocktail party my husband, Richard, and I were giving, to announce that Mother had flipped her wig and tried to kill him with her daddy's Parker Old Reliable. (That's a shotgun.) He said she was crazy and that he had her power of attorney and was putting her away somewhere where she couldn't hurt anyone.

I knew that was some bodacious bull because my brother was generally accepted as the Second Coming, that is, if Mother's lifelong drooling all over him was an indication of her religious devotion. I guess that sounds like a classic sibling rivalry remark, but you have to know certain things and then you would agree.

First, Trip was the spitting image of Daddy and Daddy was dead—dead and canonized by Mother decades ago. Mother, bereft with her loss, then did a textbook transference of her enormous love for Daddy and heaped it on Trip. Yes, my husband, Richard, is a psychologist and a psychiatrist. We, Richard and I, are . . . well, we'll get to that.

Second, Trip, dweeb that he is, returned her blind-eyed affection with boundless ingratitude. My brother has always been the archetypal rationalization of why I had declined the possibilities of marriage with southern men. It was their relationships with their mothers that always did me in. That, and the archaic sexism. But of course, with the birth of my own son, I quickly realized, and then denied, that I was wrong about that too.

Poor Trip! Mother would say over and over, sighing with the weight of all the problems of the world.

Well, I didn't completely disagree there. Trip was carrying a cross the size of the Brooklyn Bridge with that tacky, low-rent wife of his. Frances Mae and her horrible children! Dear God! What a disaster she was! Gives new definition to the old ball and chain! We'll dissect Frances Mae later, don't you worry about that for a minute.

So, back to Mother and Trip and their Freudian Oedipus *thaing.* I wonder how much Mother would have seen of Trip if our plantation didn't have a dock and a landing so Trip could spend half his life on the Edisto River.

Trip was your basic southern good old boy. Lawyer, fisherman, hunter. Clean-shaven, a good dancer, manly, and with flawless manners. He never came to the supper table without a tiny cloud of aftershave in his aura. He always held Mother's chair for her and found a compliment for her as well. Mother was smug in her reign as the matriarch and that she was well in control of her son's attention.

They shared many things in common. Great regard of weekly family dinners, love of land, sense of place, and the importance of a stiff drink or two at the end of the day. Frances Mae was never going to get in the way of Mother's love for Trip. She didn't stand a chance. Sometimes I would think that he had married Frances Mae just to show Mother that she was irreplaceable. That Frances Mae was some kind of a surrogate who could have his body but would never know his heart.

Unfortunately for Mother, as Trip's family grew, his attentions became less frequent and more disingenuous. When he began to drink a lot, Mother began to whip it on the masses. The gardener, Raoul. The UPS man. Mother spread it around, to say the least. She had a ball—no pun intended. I used to think she did these things to make Trip jealous, but later I decided she was just determined to enjoy every minute of her life.

Mother's affairs pretty well horrified Trip and Frances Mae and helped them build their case that Mother had a loose screw. Well, in the amour sense, she was a loose screw—hell, she left a string of bodies behind her too numerous to count. But crazy? Not even for a second. Our mother, Lavinia Boswell Wimbley, finally laid out in lavender (and blue paisley), was as sane as they came. She offered no apologies.

My heart was completely broken. You see, six months ago I was living in New York and I thought I was very happily married. Richard and I had a great apartment on Park Avenue, our son, Eric, was growing up beautifully, I had a small but successful decorating business, and life was pretty darn good. Sure, we had our issues now and then, but there was no pressing reason for complaints.

No, I never dreamed this could happen. I had spent the last fifteen, sixteen years, or maybe more, building a case for living in New York and against anything remotely connected with the ACE Basin of South Carolina and plantation life. It was horrible to me! *Boring!* The unending repetition of tradition, day after year after generation after generation! *Suffocating!* The ACE was my demon to reckon with and mine alone. And anyone would have thought that at this stage in my life, I was old and wise enough to take it on. So I came home to *see about Mother* for a short visit. I wanted to assess things with my own eyes.

My relationship with Mother and with Trip had been strained for years. The geographic distance between us didn't help things either. But I wasn't going to let Trip move Mother out of Tall Pines and into a retirement community without knowing if it was truly necessary. And that Mother *wanted* to go. I remember thinking, shoot, even though Mother and I had zero in common, she was my mother and I owed her at least that much.

What I found on arrival was exactly what I expected. Mother was playing cards with her girlfriends and talking about men. Millie, Mother's estate manager and friend of a zillion years, was still up to her same old voodoo. Trip was drunk as usual, Frances Mae was pregnant as usual and still turning over the silver looking for hallmarks with her green eyes. And their girls were still full of all the antics of every devil in hell. Everything seemed normal. It was.

I thought it was my mission to open Mother's eyes to Trip's intentions. To make her see that she needed to take it down a notch or two. Surprise, surprise. I was the one, not Mother, who was about to have her eyes opened. It was *my* cage that would be rattled until the fillings in my teeth vibrated. It was *my* complete sense of who I thought I was that would be wrung out to dry. Most importantly, I was to discover who we all truly were.

Over the years, as much as I would vehemently deny my passion for the ACE Basin of South Carolina, its pull on me was an all-powerful force. The ACE is Eden. It's where the Ashepoo, Combahee, and Edisto Rivers join at St. Helena's Sound. The ACE is home to more species of birds, fish, flowers, and shrubs than you could name. Every inch of it wiggles in song; its beauty is stupefying.

No, once the ACE has you under its spell, you are hers for life. You could turn me around, blindfolded, in the handbag department of Bergdorf Goodman on Fifth Avenue and I could point my finger to the Edisto River the same way a compass needle always points north. I was nothing more than an extension of her waters. A displaced tributary.

So tonight we were all here in the Bagnal Funeral Home in Walterboro with Mother's body. There must have been three hundred people who came and went over the hours that I sat with Trip, Frances Mae, Millie, and Mother's closest friends.

People told stories of Mother's crazy theme parties that celebrated Cleopatra's birthday or some little-known Aztec holiday. There was the time she dressed herself as a goddess and floated down the Edisto on our pontoon—decorated with billowing white bunting—to celebrate *The Birth of Venus*. Trip and I were youngsters at the time and humiliated beyond words. I hated her then.

After Daddy died, Trip and I were parceled off to boarding schools; then came the parade of her lovers. She was quiet about her relationships at first, but once she was comfortable with her new way of living, the tempo quickened and the fireworks began. It was then Mother discovered Rod McKuen poetry and found her G-spot in an article in *Cosmopolitan* magazine. There was no stopping her. Back then I despised her flamboyance with every part of me.

Lately, I had completely changed my mind. If Mother was shockingly indiscreet, so what? Everyone adored her. You had to admit that she enjoyed her liberation. She was Miss Lavinia, the ACE Basin version of Auntie Mame. What a gal!

I looked among the crowd for Rev. Charles Moore and spotted him talking to Richard. At least she'd had the good judgment not to sleep with the minister, even though he probably would have gladly hopped in the sack with her. Endowment campaigns did strange things to people. Well, I thought, maybe she's left him something in her will. God knows, he lobbied hard enough for a bequest.

So many people came for Mother, to offer their love and sympathy. It was remarkable. But even though they were all courtesy and protocol on the outside, I knew there was a strong undercurrent. The unspoken gossip was nearly tangible—the wanting to know, Who would inherit the plantation? What of her renowned fortunes? How much was there? Would Frances Mae be the new queen of Tall Pines? Would I, the errant daughter who'd married that odious Brit, a Jewish man, and a *shrink*, come to my senses and renounce him? It was a *situation* I was sure was driving the Lowcountry gentry nearly mad from not knowing.

Situations were what my family called times of indecisiveness and trouble that led to sullied reputations. *Situations* were best dealt with quickly and as quietly as possible. Between Mother's legendary soirees and love affairs, Frances Mae's greed, and my reappearance on the scene, we had enough jaws working overtime to keep the ears of Charleston, Colleton, and Dorchester Counties burning indefinitely.

All the while I shook hands and thanked people for coming, I fantasized that even there, in the funeral home, money was changing hands. Bets were being placed. Until the rumors became facts, gallons of mint juleps would be consumed all over the Lowcountry. The practiced and polished sweet tongues of prediction would wag! The social wizards would convene and foretell our future from imagined signs, fabricated reports, and supposed hints from someone inside the bosom of the Wimbley family.

Well, it wouldn't be me. I had come home to *see about Mother* and I had every intention of executing a dignified farewell for her. So did Trip. In Mother's memory, he and Frances Mae were hosting a fabulous reception—with Millie's oversight—to take place when we left the funeral home. They had truly pushed all the buttons they could find to make it something people would remember. And they would.

"Let us pray," Reverend Moore said.

People became quiet and stood by respectfully. Trip and I had discussed this prayer service with the minister beforehand. All of us were grateful that Reverend Moore had agreed to stick to the standards and not to make a fuss about Mother's character. Her obituary in the *Post and Courier* had caused us some very unnecessary embarrassment. I suppose that there are some people who read them for entertainment—certainly the journalist who wrote Mother's needed to be reassigned to the Used Automobile pages.

At the same moment we bowed our heads in prayer with Reverend Moore, one hundred tuxedoed waiters from Atlanta were over on Lynnwood Drive, popping corks from cases of Veuve Cliquot and arranging seafood and sushi on a sprawling bed of crushed ice. Silver platters were being filled with delicious finger food and a fifteen-piece band with a horn section was going through a sound check. There would be a tasting bar for Mother's favorite bourbons and many pounds of Sonny's barbecue would be hot and waiting in silver buffet dishes to be dolloped on tiny hamburger buns. In my head I could see the hustle and bustle of preparations. Trip and Frances Mae had absolutely done everything they could to give Miss Lavinia the send-off of the century. For once, I didn't have anything ugly to say about Frances Mae.

Millie and I had planned a more toned-down and traditional reception for tomorrow afternoon, after we spread Mother's ashes. But it too would be lovely. All these plans were spelled out in Miss Lavinia's final wishes. We had done our best to comply.

The prayer service ended and people began milling around again, offering condolences to us. Many of them were misty; Mother's best friends had wept openly, holding on to each other. They broke my heart all over again. I had known them all my life and to see them so upset was just awful.

I got up and walked over to Mother's casket. I was out of tears for the moment. Besides, Mother would have wanted me to keep my wits about me at her wake.

Reconciling finding Mother's heart and then losing her so quickly was going to be my ultimate challenge. I prayed she would haunt me forever. Just because she was dead, she had no right to desert me.

I looked down at her in her casket and thought about how peaceful she looked. I was going to need her grit and wisdom to survive, every ounce of it. I wasn't even one-third the woman she was in her weakest moment. I had been a coward for far too long, hiding my emotions behind my Manhattan wardrobe of all black. I brushed back a lock of her hair, thinking how I loved her so desperately and how many years I had wasted mired in anger and resentment. Trip appeared at my side.

"You okay, Caroline?" His eyes were moist.

"Yeah, I'm fine. Lavinia would have loved this, don't you think?"

"Definitely," he said. "She got enough flowers for a senator!"

It was true. The room overflowed with baskets of gorgeous arrangements. Trip and I had ordered two enormous sprays and a blanket of roses for her. The fragrance of the room was head-spinning. Trip looked shaken, so I gave the old boy a hug, and I could almost see Miss Lavinia smiling. He returned the embrace with an honesty I hadn't felt from him since we were children. I guessed he needed me.

Mother may have slipped through my fingers, but not without leaving a sweet residue. She had given me back my love of life, complete with permission and directions on how to live it. I had wasted no time in starting. Across the room, two of my most recent diversions were chatting away like old fraternity brothers. It gave me the giggles because Josh, the old Kama Sutra scholar with dreadlocks down to his waist—the one who could make you twitch in places you didn't even know had nerve endings—stood out in complete contrast to Jack, my doctor friend in the cashmere sport coat. Jack had the most beautiful hands I had ever seen on a man.

Then, over there, was Matthew . . . oh dear, in spite of these *grave* circumstances, I had to admit that my recent liaisons had more than a passing resemblance to Mother's.

I moved through the crowd to the windows and spotted my son, Eric, outside happily playing kick the pinecone with an energetic gang of children. He had never been so happy as he has been here, smack in the middle of the most turmoil I'd ever endured. He was free of stress and filled with alpha energy, truly happy just to be alive and a kid. It was obvious that the ACE was the medicine he needed.

Maybe it was what I needed too. For all those years I told myself there was no life for me here. That I was a city slicker and didn't need them. That I was streetwise.

That I had my own family now and I'd evolved to a woman of few emotional needs.

Sure. When Mother came along, needing me for the first time, that theory exploded with all the insignificant fanfare of the careless dropping of a thin-shelled egg.

Humph, I thought, looking around; for the first time in my life, I had more men in the room than old Miss Lavinia. It seemed that I had a little *situation* of my own. Never be like her? I raised my hand to my throat, twisted her South Sea pearls around my finger, and let loose the longest sigh in respiratory history. Sonuvadamndog, it was in the DNA.

Miss Lavinia's Journal

I don't think I need anyone to tell me that my children are a big, fat pain in my neck. No, I don't. On one hand, I've got my boy, Trip, as lazy as the day is long. Sent him to law school, helped him build a practice, and, Lord, every time I look out my window, he's putting his boat in the water. Doesn't he ever work? No! Does he call me? No! And, if he comes in the house it's always for a cold beer! And my girl, Caroline? Well, I'm sorry to say that she's all but become a Jezebel! Sleeping with her professor! And studying for a master's degree in business! Lord! Where did I go wrong? I just don't know, truly, I don't.

1

RICHARD

1984

When I was twenty-three, I thought I was pretty hot stuff. I enrolled at Columbia University in New York, much to the chagrin of Mother and everybody else I knew. *Why the hell do you want to live in that horrible place? Why can't you get your master's at Carolina? If you want an MBA, go to Harvard! New York City is no place for a girl like you! What do you want a master's for anyway? You're just gonna get married and the whole thing will be a waste of your money!*

I was highly tempted to reply that the reason I was moving to New York was to get away from people like them! But the nice southern girl in me couldn't bring myself to do it. We tried to keep our sass to a minimum. A hopeless endeavor.

Actually, I think the reason I *did* choose Columbia was simply for the experience of living in a major city and I knew the great financial minds were in New York. I had toyed with the idea of becoming an investment banker and a true power broker. But that wasn't what Life's Great Plan had in store for me.

I had signed up for a psychology course as an elective, joking to myself that maybe I'd finally figure out my family if I could understand the machinations of the human psyche. In particular, I wanted to understand why I was so driven to leave South Carolina and why my family was so compelled to stay.

One hundred and seventy-five students were gathered in a small auditorium for class. The first day, lost and frazzled, I arrived a few minutes late. The professor, Richard Levine, was already lecturing. The hall was dead silent when I pushed the door open. He stopped talking and looked at me. So did everyone else. I was mortified.

"Nice of you to join us, Miss . . . ?"

"Wimbley," I said in a low voice, hoping he'd forget my name as soon as he heard it. He had an English accent and he was gorgeous. He looked a bit like Steve Martin and sounded like a diplomat. I wondered if he was married. From where I sat in the top row, I couldn't see a ring.

"Class begins at eight, Miss Wimbley, not"—he stopped and looked at his watch—"not at eight-fifteen."

He was smirking at me! It was obvious he knew I thought he was attractive. I could tell by the smirk.

"Yes, thank you. Sorry, sir." I tried to hide my fascination with his face.

"Whittaker? Kindly pass this to Miss Wimbley." He handed a sheet of paper to a fellow down front and it was passed back to me. I must've looked confused because he spoke to me again. "It's a syllabus, Miss Wimbley, not a summons for jury duty."

The class laughed. My neck got hot. Great, I thought,

this guy is gonna think I'm a dope. I cleared my throat to mark my annoyance. Jokes at the expense of others were not funny to me. I suppose I was overly sensitive. How about I was just embarrassed?

"As the great Freud said, 'What *does* a woman want?' " he said.

Every male in the class guffawed and elbowed each other, agreeing with the professor. He was clearly pleased with himself. I knew that unless I wanted to be taken lightly, I'd better come up with a retort. I raised my hand.

"Yes, Miss Wimbley?"

"And the great Proust said, 'All the great things we know have come to us from neurotics!' "

This took the class to the heights of hysteria while my professor, with the widest smile and cutest dimples, raised his arms over his head as if he were begging for mercy. The women in the class whooped and hollered.

"Dear God! She claims that Freud was neurotic!"

"Proust said it, sir, not me."

He pretended to pull a knife from his heart. The class was now nearly out of control.

"I'll see you after class, Miss Wimbley."

I couldn't wait for the hour to end.

We went out for coffee, and my days as Miss Bon Vivant, cyclone of the dance clubs, screeched to a fast finish. From the minute I saw him and heard him speak, I was so stupid over him, I couldn't sleep. He even made me feel like cooking! The next Monday, I invited him to my tiny studio apartment for dinner and when he accepted, I began to perspire. I couldn't boil water!

I went to Zabar's and straight to the fattest man I could find at the butcher's counter. I figured a fat butcher would know the difference between shoe leather and a steak. I waited patiently for a man who had the name Abe embroidered on his apron.

"How much do you love this man?" he said to me.

"Enough to cook," I said, "and Lord knows, honey, I ain't no Betty Crocker."

"Youse southern and youse can't cook? Don't make no sense."

"Yeah, well, I can learn?"

"Humph." He looked me over like I should've been in the display case on crushed ice with parsley in my hair. "Too skinny," he said to no one in particular, which irked me.

"Well, then, sell me some food, Abe! He's coming at seven!"

"Take the veal chops. Rub 'em down with lemon juice, a little olive oil, fresh rosemary, salt and pepper. Cook 'em three minutes on each side under the broiler. Wrap 'em up in tinfoil for five minutes to rest. Give it to him with a baked potato and a salad with Roquefort dressing. Don't forget bread. You'll have dis bum eating outta da palm of ya hand."

"Thanks, Abe," I said, "I'll let you know how it goes."

"With my veal chops? Dat poor sucker don't stand a chance!"

I walked home to my studio on Ninety-fourth and Columbus, whistling a little tune. Then I realized I didn't have anything to drink for dinner and what the hell went with veal anyway? I stopped at a liquor store and poked around until the salesman was finished with another customer. He sold me two bottles of a pinot noir and I was on my way again, buoyed by false confidence.

When I got home, it hit me. I didn't have a table and chairs! God, was I stupid or what? My first-floor, L-shaped studio was so sparse the occasional visitor couldn't tell if

I was moving in or out. I had a sofa and one huge armchair with a hassock, a stereo, no rug, tons of books on board-and-brick bookshelves, and a bed in the alcove. I had two hours to turn the miserable hole into something alluring. I'd ask the doorman what to do. They always knew everything.

Lucky for me, Darios was on duty. He was from Puerto Rico and, in the true spirit of Latin men, he flirted with me every time I saw him. He held the door for me and took the shopping bag from my hands. I was gonna give him a chance to prove his nerve.

"Good afternoon, Miss Wimbley!"

"Darios? I'm in big trouble and I need your help!"

In the dim light of the basement, Darios and I rummaged through the storage bins of possessions left by other tenants for safekeeping. It could've been the home furnishing department at Bloomingdale's, I had so many choices. It didn't bother me one ounce that these things belonged to other people. Tomorrow they'd go back to where they had been.

"Come over here! This is the Goldbergs' stuff. They're in Hawaii!"

"Perfect!"

He hauled the rug out first. "You wanna see it?"

"Nope. It's a rug and that's all that matters."

We chose a small round walnut table and two ladder-back chairs that were stacked on the side of the chicken-wire pen and within ten minutes my apartment looked one hundred percent better. Darios and I stepped back to observe.

"Needs plants," he said.

"Jesus, Darios, I can hardly afford this meal!" I was living on a tight budget imposed by Mother, probably to make me transfer to Carolina.

"Be right back."

The doorbell rang again and it was Darios with two enormous palms from the lobby. He put them in place on either end of the sofa and I gave him twenty dollars. At the door he said, "I'd rather have just one kiss."

"Go on now, you bad boy, or I'll tell your wife!"

I only felt like a criminal again for a few seconds. My mind returned to the mission, which was, even though I would have loudly and energetically denied it, to seduce Richard.

Naturally, I had no tablecloth. I took an old quilt from the closet and it covered the table to the floor. Flowers? Of course not. But I had books and that would work. I took three small volumes from the shelves, one of Proust, one of Flannery O'Connor, and the last, a book of Elizabeth Barrett Browning's poetry. I used bronze bookends of hunting dogs to hold them upright. I wondered if he would notice the Proust.

Fortunately I had two votive candles, two unchipped plates, and enough matching flatware. Linen napkins? Not a chance. I used clean red dishtowels, which matched the quilt, sort of, and spray-starched them to death on a towel on the floor. In the end, the living area looked pretty darn cozy.

Then there was the matter of the bed. You can't hide a bed in a studio and mine was piled with stuffed animals from my youth. No man in his right mind could feel sexy surrounded by Snoopy dogs and Paddington Bears. I stuck them all under the bed and stood back. An improvement, to be sure, but no den of iniquity either. It was a box spring and mattress on a Harvard frame on wheels. Not even a headboard. Big deal.

Suddenly I wished I had the time and available cash to run to Laura Ashley and cover my bed in beautiful white

linens and lacy pillows. I dug through my linen closet with
a fury, pulling out everything and anything that would
even mildly suggest virginity. This search bore little fruit,
but I did manage to find a set of sheets with scalloped
edges I had forgotten about, and a deep rose, soft wool
blanket. I plumped the bejesus out of my four sorry-ass
beat-up pillows, sprayed them with cologne, and decided
it would just have to do. In a moment of sheer brazenness,
I turned the bed down. Nap, anyone? I laughed out loud
and looked at my watch. Six-fifteen. Forty-five minutes
until kick-off. Okay, shower, shave, and moisturize.

Fifteen minutes later I heard the doorman buzzer. My
hair was wet, I was wrapped in a towel, and Richard was
early. Shit! What could I do? Nothing. I opened the door
and there he stood.

"Am I early?" he said, handing me a bouquet of the
deepest red roses.

"Oh! Thank you! Heavens to Betsy, no! Come on in! I
was just, I was just, oh hell, did we say six-thirty? I'm
sorry." My temperature rose to about one hundred and
seven from embarrassment as I shut the door.

"I don't remember," he said, "forgive me. Caroline?"

"Yes?" We were staring into each other's eyes, my
knees were inexplicably rubbery, and I felt like I was free-
falling into space.

"I never dreamed someone could be quite so fetching in
a towel," he said in a low quiet voice.

God damn. He sounded like James Bond again. Then I
looked down at my bare feet and recovered immediately.
"Doctor? Please allow this Magnolia a few moments to
find her hoopskirts! Better yet, why don't you put on some
music and open the wine?"

"Ah! God knows I love a woman with wit! Where's the
corkscrew?"

"Second drawer on the left of the stove."

I put his flowers in the sink and hopped by him to escape. He couldn't resist tugging on my towel and I yelped and laughed. I did, however, lock the door to my bathroom while I did the fastest makeup and hair job of my life. I threw the proverbial sleeveless little black dress over my head, creamed the hell out of my legs and arms, and slipped on a pair of low-heeled black suede sandals. One gold bracelet, fake diamond studs. No doubt about it, I was going to have my way with him. He probably wouldn't even put up a fight.

When I showed up in the kitchen doorway, he handed me a goblet of red wine and exhaled. We clinked glasses, took a sip, and our eyes never left each other's face.

"I need to cook dinner," I said. My voice was husky and uneven.

"Would you mind terribly if I kissed you first? I've had the shape of your mouth on my mind all day."

I gasped. I couldn't help it, but I gasped in surprise. Some seductress I was. "You have?" Oh, yeah, Miss Groovy strikes again.

He moved in closer until I could smell his breath, which bore the unmistakable traces of toothpaste.

"Yes, I have," he said and put his hand in the crook of my back, pulling me closer to him.

"I smell mint," I said and then chastised myself for saying something so stupid.

He held me back for a moment and smiled. "Are you allergic to mint?"

"Hell, no," I said, opening my eyes wide, knowing that each syllable I uttered made me sound more and more like a perfect moron.

"Do you like mint?" he said. I guess he thought torturing me was fun.

"Yes!"

"Because I have cinnamon gum in my jacket and I could chew . . ."

"Richard?" I pretended to faint, falling backward in his arm. "I'm dying here!"

"Come here, pussycat, Uncle Richard wants to tickle your whiskers."

That was the end of that nonsense. By the time his mouth covered mine we had tasted each other's breath, teased each other's mind, and kicked the ball to the thirty-yard line. To my complete amazement, his lips fit mine so perfectly, it was like kissing my twin. My arms were around his neck and even though I was considered tall, I had to stand on my tiptoes to reach his face with mine. It was the kiss of a lifetime, the kind you read about, not the kind you got. The longer he held me, the more emboldened I became.

When he ran his hands down my hips and cupped my backside he said, "You're not wearing panties."

I said, "Oops. Got dressed too fast."

His tongue traveled my neck, stopping here and there for a nip. "I'll overlook it this time," he said. "Don't let it happen again."

That seemed like a good breaking point to me. If we didn't stop then, we wouldn't stop all night, so I said, "Listen, bubba, we'd better give it a rest. Nice southern girls don't just peel down on the first date, you know."

"Bubba?"

I slipped away from him and led him to the living room. "You stay here while I cook, okay?" I pushed him into the overstuffed chair and put his feet up on the hassock.

"Caroline? What is bubba? And where is my wine?"

I picked up his glass, refilled it, and brought it to him. "In this case, it's a term of endearment."

Dinner was delicious and I thought briefly about Abe the butcher and how I had created this set for *The Love Boat* from the Goldbergs' stash and the lobby plants. Wynton Marsalis played low and moanful in the background. While we drank both bottles of wine, he told me about his childhood. He could've read me the want ads and I would've thought it was poetry.

His story was a tearjerker. He was born in London, the only son of a successful jeweler. He lost his mother to ovarian cancer when he was only twelve years old. His father had remarried shortly after that to a divorcée with three young children of her own. He was sent to boarding school, as he and his stepmother had major differences. He distinguished himself academically and went on to medical school, where he decided he wanted to be a psychologist. Richard was doing his dissertation when he met his first wife, Lois.

Evidently, nothing good came from that marriage except an infant son, whom he adored. As he told me all of this I was lost in his hazel eyes. They had little flecks of green and gold in them.

Between dinner and dessert, Richard's hand found its way to under my dress. We were definitely on the road to Sodom.

"There's something on my leg," I said, feigning fright.

"Don't worry, I can cure your delusion," he said.

"I'm holding out for my wedding night."

"Marry me."

"Okay."

The strange part was that I meant it. I knew, that very first night we were together, that I would marry Richard. All the southern guys I ever went out with were polite and predictable. Not that they weren't just as good-looking as Richard or appealing in other ways. They were truly lovely men. Maybe it was me, that I wasn't ready to settle down. Probably.

But there *was* something else about Richard. He was a little bit dangerous—like there was something in him you couldn't tame. He was so smart and so sexy, I didn't want to spend one day alive without him. I had never felt that way before and I knew I never would again. I had this instantaneous belief that here was a man who could take care of me—if he would. It was absolutely astounding.

That night, he fell asleep on the sofa from grape overdose while I did the dishes. Propriety dictated that I should wake him up to go home. But, not me. I was so smitten and crazy about him, I covered him with a comforter, took off my dress and shoes, and went to bed nude. I rationalized the nude part by telling myself that Fate would rule the night.

If he woke up and went home, he was a gentleman and therefore worthy husband material. If he woke up and got in bed with me, I'd know more about what kind of husband he'd be. If he slept on the sofa all night, he was a horse's ass.

Somewhere around four in the morning, I felt him next to me. No, I smelled him first. Eau Sauvage. Jesus! How perfect was that? I pretended to be sleeping while his fingers traced my side. He snuggled up closer and we were like two spoons. I started to drift back to sleep, thinking in my haze how nice it felt to be curled up this way, how safe I felt. He started to shift his position and it didn't take long to figure out why.

"Caroline?" he said in a whisper.

"Hmm?"

"Sorry to wake you, dear, but I . . ."

"Come here, Richard. I want you too."

That old bed of mine started to rock and squeak, and if

our mouths seemed tailor-made for each other, the rest of our bodies were like Legos. He made me feel so exhilarated, I wanted to scream, but I couldn't have caught my breath long enough for anything more than gasping for air. Making love with Richard was like body-surfing a tidal wave—I had never been so high, so terrified, and so thrilled at the same time. Yes, indeedy, this man was a keeper. When the sun came up and woke us, the bed was five feet away from the wall and the sheets were off the mattress. If not for the Goldbergs' carpet, we would've rolled right into the living room. We laughed our heads off. I had met my match.

Miss Caroline's Journal

Mother's bloomers are all twisted in a knot over Richard and me getting married in New York. She hasn't said so, but I feel it in my bones. What does she expect me to do? Come home and go through brunches and showers given for me by people I haven't seen in a million years? I can see it all now—I'll be unwrapping Tupperware and Corning casserole dishes wearing a hat made from gift ribbons stapled on a paper plate. Somebody will take a picture and send it to Richard and he'll think I'm a total ass and call off the whole wedding. I'm not nervous, really I'm not. I suppose I should call Mother and talk to her about it. No matter what I do, she's not going to like it. Oh, forget it! Richard and I are getting married in New York and that's it! That's what he wants so that's what I want too! But, she hasn't even met him. . . .

2

MISS LAVINIA WOULD LIKE TO HAVE A WORD WITH YOU

1987

"I am not going to New York City! Don't start with me, Millie!"

"Yes, you are! I'm going, Trip and Frances Mae are going, and so are you! We ain't letting Miss Caroline become Missus Caroline without us there to wish her well!"

Millie turned on her heel and flounced out, leaving me madder than a wet hen. "Just where are you going, Mrs. Smoak?"

"I'm going to pack your clothes, and if you don't like it, that's too bad, yanh?"

We had been in the kitchen when Trip called the house and told us that Caroline had called him and asked him to give her away. What was there to give away? She had run off years ago! How can you give away what's gone? I told Trip that if he and Frances Mae wanted to go, that was just fine. I wasn't going to budge from Tall Pines Plantation.

Frankly, I planned to spend Caroline's wedding day dressed in black veils, communing with my dear Nevil's spirit down at the family chapel. I would take a good bottle of champagne, the '61 Dom Perignon, perhaps two, to mark the occasion and toast my daughter from the bluffs over the Edisto River. If she wanted to marry a foreigner she could do it without me. And, the ceremony was going to be in their apartment! Not even a church!

It was no kind of wedding, if you ask me, and they had not. No, they had not asked for my permission, my blessing, or cared one fig if I approved. She had been living in sin with that man for nearly three years, shacked up in that nasty little hovel she called an apartment. Now they're living in a co-op on Park Avenue. How pretentious can you get? And now she calls herself a decorator. Well, la-di-da. All that money we spent to educate that girl at Columbia for her to wind up making some stranger's curtains? My poor girl. If she had only listened to me.

Ah, well, I know she thinks I'm old hat, that I don't know anything about life outside of South Carolina. Well, guess what? Neither does she! She thinks she can just run off to New York and marry the first tomcat who comes prowling around? She thinks she's in love? She doesn't know the first thing about love. Or men! She should've asked me about men. Hell, I could write a book. She's marrying that old man? She's marrying her daddy, that's what.

I needed to talk to Millie. She had to stop this before it was too late. I'd make her put some of her fool voodoo on them or something. I waited until I thought Millie would be occupying herself messing through my things, and then I could go upstairs. Sure enough, by the time I fluffed my hair in the hall mirror and went up the stairs to my room, there she was with half my belongings spread out all over the bed.

"Damnation! Millie? Do you mean to make me fire you after all these years?"

Well, don't you know the old biddy got that heat in her eyes and put her hands on her hips to me!

"Miss Lavinia? It's a good thing Mr. Nevil done gone to Glory, 'cause iffin he see the way you act, it'd kill him."

"Great jumping Jehoshaphat, Millie! You always say that! Think of a new line!"

"Okay. Try this on, Mrs. Plantation Owner of the Whole World. You don't want to go 'cause you're scared yellow that Caroline grew up behind your back and nobody needs you anymore. How's that?"

I sat down on my dressing table bench and all my breath rushed from my chest. "You've cut me to the quick, Millie. How could you say such a thing? First my boy runs off and marries that vulgar trash after he knocks her up, and now my girl is marrying a foreigner. Where did I go wrong, Millie? Can you tell me that?" I felt sick in my heart. I truly did.

"Miss L?"

I didn't answer her. I was checking my nerves to see if I could cry or not. Yes, I could, I decided, and I let the tears roll like a river, wailing like a baby. I did not do this to elicit sympathy from Millie, although it always helped.

"Miss L?"

I didn't answer her again but got up from the bench and took to my bed, pushing the hangers of clothes to the other side and crawling under the spread. She knew it was time to leave me alone. She could pack my clothes later. She left the room, closing the door quietly. That's right. I had decided to go to New York City. After all, how would it look if Millie went without me? And, I knew I couldn't stop Caroline from marrying that man. She was a stubborn girl and I'd just have to let her make her mistakes.

Don't misunderstand me. I'm not saying I was going to New York just for appearances. I knew it was my duty to be there and I have never shirked my duty. Ever. Not once. Okay, maybe once—after Nevil died and I was pretty hard on the children. But I didn't realize at the time that I was in such a deep state of mourning. I was. I probably should have been medicated. But who knew about those things?

Hell, now that we had a—what was he? a psychologist or a psychiatrist? Well, anyway, now that we had some kind of doctor coming into the family, we could probably get all the pills we wanted! Maybe that's why Caroline had agreed to marry him in the first place. The son of a bitch had brainwashed and then drugged her! Oh, merciful God! My poor daughter. I decided to call her.

The phone rang six times. No one home. An answering machine came on with Caroline's voice just as cheery as could be. *Hi! We're sorry we missed your call. Please leave a message and we'll call you back. Thanks.* Why was she always apologizing? She had to stop that. It was a true sign of weakness and one thing the women in this family were *not* was weak. I would tell her so as soon as she returned my call, for which I was not holding my breath.

I closed my eyes again, thinking I might nap. Then, since I already had the cordless phone in my bed with me, I decided to call my dearest friend, Sweetie. She would tell me what to do.

"Sweetie? Listen up! I got trouble!"

"Whatever in the world is wrong, Lavinia? Have you been crying?"

"Certainly not! Allergies! Listen to me, damn it! Caroline is getting married in just weeks to that old man Richard fellow and I'm so upset with her I could just slap her face!"

"Lavinia? You listen to me, darling. Caroline is a grown woman and it's time for you to be gracious about it. If she wants to marry this man, there's not a single thing you can do about it. Not a single thing in this world!"

"He's older than her by eleven years."

"You were a hundred years older than Bob the UPS man and that didn't stop you."

"Well, aren't you the sassy one today? Sweetie? Do you know he's Jewish?"

"Why on God's earth would that matter to a woman who holds Sufi ceremonies and has a five-foot statue of Shiva with ten arms in her bedroom?"

"I use it to hold my handbags and you know it. Nevil and I bought it in Nepal."

"I happen to remember that you bought it from a Christie's auction, dear."

I hated her for her memory. "Whatever. Oh, Sweetie! My heart is so heavy! What am I to do?"

"What *can* you do? You pack your things, put a smile on your face, and get on a plane."

"You know I don't fly."

"Then call Amtrak! You make sure Caroline has everything she needs. You have a word with Richard about his sincerity and commitment and then you wish them well. That's all she wrote, sister."

I sighed so hard into the telephone I probably messed up Sweetie's hair. "Nobody needs me, Sweetie. It makes me so sad."

"Get over yourself, Lavinia, and shape up. I need you

to be my friend—exactly why on occasion, I wonder—
and Caroline needs you to be her mother."

Well, I guess she thought she had laid me out in
lavender. "I suppose I'll get Jenkins to drive me down to
Charleston. Maybe I'll have a facial and shop for shoes.
That always resurrects my spirit. And, I saw in the *Post
and Courier* that Bob Ellis is having a sale." Yes, that
would cheer me.

"Lavinia?"

"Hmm?" Her voice had a sharp edge again and I hated
it when she reprimanded me. I truly did.

"Please don't forget to buy *them* a gift!"

She made me fume! "You know what, Sweetie? Some
days there's just no pleasing you! Good-bye!" I hit the End
button and slammed the receiver on my mattress. Honest
to God! Everybody could just go stew in their own juices.
Yes, they could.

Please join us for dinner!

THE POST HOUSE

On Sixty-third Street at Park Avenue

Friday, February 25, 1987
Eight o'clock

Caroline Boswell Wimbley
and
Dr. Richard Case Levine

Rsvp 212-781-4462

Miss Lavinia's Journal

Millie and I have just checked in to the Pierre Hotel. She's in the room next door. Trip and Frances Mae are arriving at five. My room is very satisfactory. I have a small sitting room and an ample bedroom. There is a lovely view of Central Park and I sincerely hope the muggers stay there. The little man who brought my bags to my room was very nice for a Yankee, although I think he was from somewhere else, like Turkey. Maybe it was Albania. He told me but I couldn't understand a word he said. I gave him three one-dollar bills. He brought me ice. Come to think of it, almost everybody I have seen so far seems to be foreign. It must be sad for them to be so far from home. God knows, New York City is one noisy place! And what in the world are all these people racing around for? Somebody bumped into me at Penn Station and I thought they were trying to grab my purse! Turned out to be a woman my age—all in a dither over who knows what, but at least she had the good manners to apologize.

In two hours I get to meet my soon-to-be son-in-

law. Don't think I'm not going to give him the good "once-over" at least twice! At least there's some Jack Daniels in the minibar. Think I'll have a nip and a nap. . . .

3

MAKE NO MISTEAK!

Millie just called. It was so good to hear her voice and know that she's here! Then I called Mother to see if she was all right and she said she had no complaints. I asked her if I had the wrong number and she told me I wasn't funny. I asked her if she wanted to come over early and see our new apartment and she said she was tired and wanted to rest. I couldn't blame her for that. She had just spent all night on a train.

I splurged and put everyone at the Pierre because then everyone was within walking distance of our apartment. Trip and Frances Mae were due to arrive anytime, and I was finally starting to get nervous. Richard should have been home at three; he promised he'd leave early. Well, I guess something came up.

I called the Post House to reconfirm our reservation for six people. I had extended an invitation to the rabbi, but he declined because he had to hold services on Friday night. Apparently the other rabbi was away for the weekend or something.

Our apartment was spotless. I could just see Mother running her hand over the mantelpiece and finding dust. Not this girl! All in all, I thought she'd be pleasantly surprised to see it.

Richard and I had bought this small two-bedroom coop a year and a half ago, and Lord what a horrible dump it was then! Neither one of us had the money to hire a big decorator, so I took on the job myself. Well, actually, Richard had the money but didn't want to spend it on something so philistine as decorating. Now, if there was one thing Mother taught me—like all normal daughters, I took ninety percent of everything she said and ignored it— Mother taught me never to apologize for trying to make the world a more beautiful place.

I just didn't want to fight with Richard about money. It was something he seemed sensitive about. It was no big deal. Really. I just sat down and figured out how to decorate on a budget just about the size of an Oreo. I knew when Richard saw what I could do with those worn-out rooms, he'd be very proud of me. We spent our nights in unmarried bliss in my tiny studio while the work progressed. He gave up his apartment near Columbia to help cover the costs of the project.

I was focused on the job with all the intensity of a mother pigeon feathering her nest. *They're living in sin!* I could hear Mother's voice the whole way from the Edisto River. My mother's friend Miss Sweetie would say, *I thought they were living in the Village.* Then Millie would say, *Humph! That child ain't capable of sin!* So there was a lot of clucking going on while I renovated and the southern contingent waited to see what would become of our relationship.

Once again the doorman at our new building turned out to be a well of information. Through him I hired a fellow to gut the apartment back to the bricks. I had it rewired, restored the chimney, reinforced the floors, cut through the walls for air conditioners, built an entirely new kitchen, and redid both bathrooms. I bought most of the fixtures from Ikea and the appliances from Sears during their Fourth of July sale. Honestly? They looked almost as good as anything in *Architectural Digest*.

To save money on plastering, the walls of the living room were padded Sheetrock, upholstered in a slubby white rayon-and-cotton fabric that I found on Thirty-ninth Street for seven dollars a yard. The wall-to-wall carpets were textured ivory wool in a basket-weave pattern, found in huge remnants at ABC Carpet. The curtains were white sheers shot with silver metallic threads, looped around pewter finials—fabric from the bridal district of the garment center. If this seemed like a lot of white, it was, but I suppose I had this romantic notion of our life together starting as a blank canvas.

Last month when the major renovations were over, I began scouring the city for houseplants and put them in Chinese reproduction ceramic planters. I took lots of photographs and framed them in red lacquer with tan linen mats. The effect was cool and tranquil. I couldn't wait until he saw it all pulled together. He worked like a maniac at all hours of the day and night and I ran back and forth to the apartment from my office to check on this and that. This had been going on for over a year. We hardly saw each other vertical!

I'll never forget the day I gave him the grand tour. It was just three weeks ago. We hadn't moved our furniture in yet. The only other furnishings were small things I had recently purchased. The carpenters had finally attached all the doorknobs and drawer pulls. The shower curtain was finally pressed and hung. I spritzed all the plants to make them shine and Richard rang the doorbell.

I opened the door and there he stood with a bottle of champagne and two paper cups. As we walked from room to room, we touched the rims of our cups and, smiling, he gave me lots of kisses, saying what a resourceful girl I was, how thrilled he was with everything. We ate Chinese food from cartons on the living room floor. At some point during the evening we christened the apartment by making love. I remember gathering up all our containers and putting the garbage bag outside the kitchen door in the service hallway. We turned out the lights and waited for the elevator. He turned to me and said, "You're amazing, Caroline. Simply amazing!"

Can you imagine how that made me feel? He gave me such courage! Acting as my own general contractor had given me a new career. I learned so much about the practical placement of wall sockets, electrical needs, plumbing requirements, and how to get things done that I decided to become an interior decorator. I knew that Richard thought it was a pretty shallow way to make a living. He never came right out and said it, but I could tell by his tone of voice when he commented as I went over our renovation plans or fabric swatches with him. I didn't care about that because I knew decorating was more fun than being the branch manager of the Bank of New York at Fifty-seventh and Third, which is what I had been doing after I finished my MBA.

Up until yesterday, I was still dealing with the man from California Closets about the way the bedroom cabinet shelves were hung. It wasn't until this morning when the florist arrived and decorated the mantelpiece with flowers for the ceremony tomorrow that I started to get the shakes.

I had been too consumed with organizing the wedding and taking care of the final touches on our apartment to allow myself to face the fact that I was really going to be married. Married to someone not of my family's faith, of another citizenship, with an ex-wife and a toddler son. Someone my mother would no doubt disapprove of on sight. Yep. On sight.

Mother's disapproval was the reason we were being married in New York and not at Tall Pines. I didn't want to deal with it. We were just having a tiny ceremony anyway.

Frankly, I was surprised she made the trip. I knew it was Millie who convinced her to come to our wedding just last week, by train, of course. Mother refused to fly. My brother, Trip, was going to give me away and my sister-in-law, Frances Mae, probably wanted to take inventory.

I looked at my watch. Five-thirty. Where on earth was Richard? The phone rang. It was Trip.

"Hey! You nervous?" he said.

"Hell no," I said.

"You lying?"

"Hell yes!"

We started laughing.

"Yeah, just you wait! That man's gonna put the old leash on you! You're gonna be slaving away for him! That's what Frances Mae does!"

"Yeah, well, we'll see about that. Your room okay?"

"Oh, fine, fine. Frances Mae has got her feet up; says her ankles are swollen from being in the family way. I reckon I'll mosey on down to the bar and see what kind of riffraff I can find to keep me company around here. You want to come over?"

"I'd love to! I've been walking around this apartment

going nuts, waiting for Richard to come home. You buying?"

"Yep," he said. "Leave him a note!"

"Good idea! See you in ten minutes."

I called Richard's office and got his service.

"Do you know where I can reach Dr. Levine? This is his fiancée."

"No. Dr. Levine had an emergency out in Long Island and left his office at two o'clock. Would you like me to call him?"

Long Island? That was where Lois, his ex-wife, and son lived! We didn't have any friends out there and Richard's patients were usually from Manhattan. "No, that's all right. I'm sure he'll be home soon. Thank you."

He had probably gone out there to calm Lois down. She was having a giant temper tantrum because we were getting married. I didn't blame her for that. She was a stupid ass to let him get away in the first place. I never could figure out why either. I wrote him a note, taped it to the front door, and left.

It was freezing outside, low twenties. Just last week we had a snowstorm that left Manhattan covered in twenty inches of snow. After it was shoveled and banked, it froze. The doormen of all the buildings in the city had to cut passageways in the banks so people could get off the curb to a cab without climbing a wall. The cold didn't bother me. In fact, I loved it. I pulled my black coat around me and walked quickly to the Pierre.

By six o'clock, Trip and I were way ahead of Mother and Millie in the alcohol consumption department. I have to say, they made a heroic effort to catch up as quickly as possible. Mother thought I was too thin; Millie thought I looked the same. Mother didn't like my haircut—made me look older; Millie thought it was chic. Mother said she didn't like New York; Millie said she thought it was exciting. Frances Mae sat silently, sipping on orange juice, picking at the nut bowl, and finally, at six-thirty, Richard appeared. I spotted him and got up to bring him over to our table.

"Ooh!" Frances Mae said, "he's a hot one!"

"Yes, he is!" I said.

"For God's sake, Frances Mae!" Trip said, rolling his eyes.

I put my arm through Richard's and whispered in his ear.

"Where have you been, darling?"

"Fighting with Lois, darling," he whispered back. "But, you look beautiful tonight, darling!"

"Come meet my family, darling."

My scowling mother had him in her sights and he went directly to her side, taking her offered hand in between both of his.

"It seems that I have made the greatest mistake of my life, Mrs. Wimbley," he said to her.

"Oh?" she said.

"Yes. I'm marrying the daughter when it's her mother who has stolen my heart on sight."

"Suh? That is one crock if I ever heard one, but you just go on and flatter me to death!" Mother was grinning from ear to ear, fingering *the pearls.* "Do call me Lavinia, won't you? Come sit next to me, you adorable man. Isn't he adorable, Trip?"

"Just precious, Mother," Trip said.

Richard shook hands with Trip, gave Frances Mae a peck on the cheek, and finally turned to face Millie.

Millie looked more elegant than I had ever seen her. At five feet tall and maybe one hundred pounds dripping wet, she didn't look a day over forty, even though she was in

her fifties. Her laser eyes cut right through you and could
see your soul naked. I used to tease her that the long braid
she wore around her head was where she hid her third eye!
She was wearing a pale pink wool bouclé suit with black
trim. It looked just like Chanel and probably was. Yep,
elegant but not happy. Something had come over her like
a bad mood. I knew that look too well.

"Richard, this is Millie Smoak. She's been running Tall
Pines all my life and she's my dearest friend in the world."

"It is a great pleasure, Mrs. Smoak, a great pleasure
indeed."

"So you're the man who's going to marry my Caroline?" Millie said. She looked at him, staring deeply into
his eyes.

"Yes, ma'am, I am the one who is not only going to
marry her, but I'm going to love and cherish her for the
rest of my life."

"Well, you be sure you do!" Millie said and two big
tears splashed her cheeks.

"Oh, Millie!" I threw my arms around her and we
hugged.

"I was there the day you were born, Caroline!" Millie
said and sniffed, trying to compose herself. "The very minute you came into this world!"

"I know, and I love you, Millie, you know I do!" Then
I felt like I was going to cry.

"Well, then," Richard said to the approaching waiter,
"let's have a bottle of champagne!"

"Um, I'd prefer Jack Daniels on the rocks with a tiny
splash? Does that suit?" Mother said.

"Me too," said Trip.

"Make it three," Millie said, "and call me Millie."

"Oh, what the hell, Richard," I said, thinking I hadn't
drunk bourbon since college, "I'll have one too."

Richard turned to the waiter and said, "I'm new to the family. Forget the champagne, I'll have a Dewar's neat. Bourbon all around. And please bring another orange juice for my future sister-in-law."

Richard picked up the check. After that, Richard could do no wrong. We moved on to the Post House and had the most delicious dinner—big steaks, steamed lobsters large enough to give you nightmares, creamed spinach, and cottage fries. We ate and told stories until after ten o'clock.

"Does anyone care for dessert?" Richard said.

They all declined, except Frances Mae, but when no one else ordered dessert, Trip told Frances Mae she didn't need it either. She went into a serious funk. I was a little surprised he spoke to her that way. I would have kicked *my* husband in the shins under the table! But, in all fairness to my brother, Frances Mae was rotund.

"Does anyone want to go over to our apartment for a nightcap?"

They declined again, saying they were tired, that didn't the bride need her rest and so on. Mother had discreetly slipped her American Express card to the captain, so the bill was handled before Richard could even offer to pay it. He got up and bowed to Mother, kissing her hand. We said good night at the door and went our separate ways.

"You were utterly charming," I said as we crossed Park Avenue, "thank you."

"They are very nice people, Caroline," he said, "and, I love you."

"Thank God," I said, "because I sure do love you too."

Eddie the doorman held the door for us and into the lobby we went.

"Eleven degrees," he said.

"Really?" I said, "I didn't feel cold a bit!"

"Aye, that's love for ya," Eddie said and pressed the elevator button for us.

Tomorrow I would become Mrs. Richard Levine. I felt pretty wonderful.

Caroline Boswell Wimbley
and

Dr. Richard Case Levine

Request the honor of your presence
at a reception to celebrate their marriage
February 26, 1987
Le Perigord Park
563 Park Avenue
Six o'clock in the evening

The favor of your reply is requested by January 30

Black Tie

4

GOING TO THE CHAPEL

1987

Our wedding ceremony, which was to be held in our new apartment, was minutes away. I was in our bedroom with Mother and Millie, nursing my nerves with breathing exercises—ujayia breathing, a technique I learned in yoga class to organize my prana. It wasn't working all that great.

"Do you want something to help you compose yourself, dear?" Mother asked. "You certainly don't want to go out there and look like a damn fool all jittering, now do you. Five milligrams of something might be a big help."

I took another deep breath before answering, turned away from the closet door mirror, and just stared at her instead. Why did she say these things? Mother was not going to aggravate me, no matter what.

"Miss Lavinia?" Millie said, jumping right in. "You leave this chile alone! This yanh is her day! You done had yours! You be the fool, not she! Imagine trying to give drugs to the bride! Shame on you!"

"Oh, hush, you old woman!"

"Oh, brother," I said, laughing, "will you two birds quit fighting over this worm?"

The girls loved to bicker—they always had.

I had just finished my makeup and was brushing my hair behind my ears. I could hear our guests outside my door, talking and greeting each other. The ivory crepe dress, just a simple sleeveless sheath, slipped over my head and Millie moved in to zip it.

"You look beautiful, chile," Millie said, "you truly do."

I put the small matching pillbox on my head and attached the tiny combs to my hair. Millie and Mother welled up with tears, and Mother got up from the chaise.

"My hair used to be even more blond than yours," she said.

I thought she was coming over to give me a motherly last placement of a hair or to kiss my cheek. She opened her small beaded purse and handed me something wrapped in an old lace handkerchief.

"Now, Caroline," she said, "before I give you this I want to know one last time if you truly, with all your heart, want to go through with this." I saw her grip tighten.

"Mother," I said, "I know you don't understand me some of the time, but I *love* Richard."

A long silence hung in the air while she searched my eyes for any glimmer of self-deception.

"All right, then," she said, "if you change your mind later, you don't have to give this back. This handkerchief was in the waistband of your great-great-grandmother's wedding dress the day she married Henry Wright Heyward IV in 1855. You do have to give that back. It has been in the hands of every bride in my family for good luck. There's something inside from me."

I took the handkerchief from her. In the true style that only my mother and Martha Stewart seemed to possess, the handkerchief, frail from the years, had been washed and folded like origami into an envelope and tied with an ivory ribbon. Inside was an exquisite diamond pin, obviously very old, in the shape of a bow, its edges trimmed in tiny channeled sapphires.

"Oh, Mother!" I said, holding it in my palm, "it's the most beautiful thing I've ever seen."

"Don't touch the stones," she said, "your body oil will dull them. Here, let me pin it to your shoulder."

"Who did this belong to? I've never seen it before."

"How should I know?" she said. "I bought it from Corey Friedman on Forty-seventh Street yesterday. That's why I was late for cocktails!"

It was clear. She wasn't going to waste an heirloom on a marriage she didn't fully endorse. I didn't mind that, really. She would come around in time. "Mother, thank you so much." I gave her a kiss on the cheek.

"Careful, child, you'll smudge Mother's powder."

I shot Millie a glance. She was wiping her eyes but burst out in a good-natured laugh at Mother's impossible disposition. We just shook our heads while Mother stood back to survey her work.

"Good! Now you have a corsage!" She lifted my left hand to inspect my engagement ring, shook her head in disgust at its small size and modern style, and stood back again. I started to giggle. Nerves, I suppose, but I'd not seen mother so cross in years.

"I love you, Mother," I said, "and I'm not marrying Richard to annoy you."

"Of course, I realize that," she said, "but just remember,

you can always come home if it doesn't work out."

"Why are you so worried, Mother?"

"Oh, Caroline, I don't know. It's just that you're so different from each other! It's going to make everything more difficult."

I looked deep into her fading blue eyes and said, "Mother? Richard and I are cut from the same bolt of cloth. Two peas in a pod—don't worry, we'll be fine."

"Okay," Millie said, "my turn. Take off that shoe, missy bride!"

"What?"

"You heard me! Gimme your shoe!"

"Which one?" I sat on the side of the bed.

"Get up or you'll wrinkle the dress!" Mother said, a little too loud for my already rankled nerves.

"Mother!" I said. Nonetheless, I popped up like toast.

"The right one!" Millie snapped.

I balanced on one foot and slipped off my ivory suede pump. She reached down in her pocket and produced a small greeting card for me to open. Inside was a penny, covered in lace. *Love that man hard,* she had written, *but don't forget to love yourself! Millie Smoak.* I knew instantly the penny was for my shoe. Tradition. As much as I shunned it, at that moment I loved every traditional thing in the world.

"I made that lace, girl," Millie said. "Don't lose it tonight or you have bad juju. And that penny is from nineteen sixty-one, the year of your birth."

"Millie! Thanks so much!" I threw my arms around her and she hugged me back. "Isn't it just like you to be so thoughtful?" God, I loved Millie so much. "I'm so glad you're here. Thanks for coming and bringing Mother."

"What? Me miss all this? All right then, we gone have us a wedding today? Or we gone stand around yanh yapping? I gone directly to your brother to see if it's time."

"Get Frances Mae too, okay?"

"Iffin you say so!" She gave me a wink and closed the door. "Guess we have to." This made Mother and me snicker. Everyone had kindly tried to spare me the torturous company of my sister-in-law again until the absolute last moment, and for good reason. As you already know, Frances Mae was pregnant, but she wasn't pregnant like a normal female of our species.

Last night at dinner she gave us enough material to keep us howling for a week. When she excused herself to go to the ladies' room, she extended her stomach for attention, lumbering across the restaurant like an extra large–size model on a catwalk, holding her lower back.

For some unknown—but surely to be discussed at another time—reason her maternity clothes had revealing necklines to entice all the men with her "ready to lactate with champagne at any moment" mammaries.

Mother said that one night she begged my brother to rub her swollen feet after dinner in the dining room and it had hallmarked the end of Mother's patience and composure with her forever. Maybe Frances Mae thought she was a Trojan Horse whose belly held the Second Coming. Why Trip actually married her and how he could tolerate her was a mystery of karma. Maybe she had washed his leprosy sores in another lifetime. In any case, Frances Mae wasn't pregnant, she was *so so so* pregnant! Jeesch.

By now the apartment was filled. I could feel the vibration of the voices. Some of my friends from the bank were here and a few of Richard's colleagues. Outside in the hall and the living room, their voices were strong and melded together in a dull sound over the music of the chamber ensemble we had hired to play.

I turned to face Mother. Her face was a combination of

resignation and melancholy. I felt my spirits sink a little. "Thinking about Daddy?"

"Yes, how can I not? Our only daughter getting married in an apartment instead of a church? Him not able to be with me and with you?" she said, telling me her sorrows.

"Mother? You're practically an agnostic."

"So what? A church wedding would've been beautiful."

"Small problem. I'm not a member of any organized congregation. It's not like I could have just used the Yellow Pages and made a reservation, right?"

"I know and I respect that but it just seems so odd to get married in your living room."

"Mother? I'm going to tell you something I believe. Even though Daddy's not here in the flesh, I really truly believe he's here in spirit."

"You sound like Millie."

"That's fine. And, we're getting married *here* because we are only having twenty people and because Richard really wanted a rabbi to perform the ceremony."

"Great God! A rabbi?" She sank to the bed, shaking her head back and forth and looking at the floor. "I cannot, for the love of God, believe my ears! Do you mean to tell me that there is a Jewish minister here to perform this ceremony? Your father would spin in his grave!"

"I seriously doubt that. Listen to me, Mother, I don't care where the ceremony is held because I believe God is everywhere. Jesus said that when two or more were gathered in His name, that He was in our midst! Didn't He?"

"He was referring to Himself and even I know that Jews don't accept Christ."

"Mother?" I was smiling now, trying to smooth her wrinkled brow. "God is God, is God. First person, second person, twentieth person, it doesn't matter! Don't you see that what does matter is I'm marrying the man I love and that he loves me and that we're all here together?"

"I suppose so," she said looking at me, almost agreeing. "You always did have an unorthodox view of the world, Caroline. You always did. And the older I get the less sure I am of anything."

I wasn't sure what she meant by that. She just seemed a little lonely, I guess. The afternoon sun was pouring through my windows and the room was warm despite the February chill. I smiled again at her and just as I was about to tell her once more that I loved her, she snapped at me again.

"You've got lipstick on your teeth! Wipe it off!"

"I do?" Just as I looked back to the mirror, the door swung open and Frances Mae and Trip came in. I should say that Frances Mae's swollen-with-life belly came first and that she followed minutes later, but that would be an exaggeration of fact. It just seemed that way. "Hi! How are you?" I said, as though she was my best friend, leaning forward to give her a hug.

"Don't you look beautiful!" she said, clutching her hands to her chest. "Trip? Darlin'? Gimme a tissue! I can just feel the tears coming! Why do I always cry at weddings?"

"I don't know, Frances Mae," Mother said dryly, "why do you?" Mother rolled her eyes to the ceiling and then to Millie, who stood by Trip, witnessing Frances Mae's performance.

"Well, Mother Wimbley, I suppose it's just the innocence of the bride and the hope of the future. Although in this case, Caroline's hardly an innocent child bride, are you, dear?"

"Frances Mae?" I said with a straight face. "See the chandelier over the bed?"

"Uh-huh," she said, dabbing the corners of her eyes,

laden with ninety-two coats of blue mascara.

I whispered now in her ear so only she and Millie could hear, "At night? I press a button and it flips to reveal a trapeze."

"It does?" she said, like the poster girl for blond jokes.

"Yep, but don't tell Mother, okay?"

"Amazing! You can't even see the seams!"

Trip handed me my bouquet, Millie smiled, and, by the time we all filed out, Frances Mae had neck strain and had eaten all the lipstick from her lower lip.

We stood assembled in the hall. Trip took Mother and then Frances Mae to their seats. Millie stayed back with me.

"What? You think I'm gonna run out the door?" I giggled to her quietly.

"No. Just making sure we don't have no uninvited company, that's all."

"Like Lois?"

"Yes, ma'am!"

Lois, Richard's first wife, who up until yesterday tried to talk Richard out of our wedding. I knew all about her campaign of phone calls and letters, but I also knew that Richard wasn't interested in her. She drove him up the wall. On the other hand, Richard hadn't been exactly forthcoming with Lois either. He'd never told her about me or us. She had no idea we were getting married until the invitations arrived three weeks ago at our friends' homes. Some bigmouth told her. Anyway, I doubted that she would try to break in here and stop the ceremony. Even Lois wasn't that brave. She was just a yenta with acrylic nails.

"I think you just want to see me walk in on Trip's arm, right?"

"Right!"

Millie's eyes twinkled in the low light of my foyer. I could see they were misty and she wanted to tell me something she couldn't find words to say.

"Out with it," I said, "we don't have all day."

"Okay," she said, "look in your bouquet. I put a little gris-gris bag in there. I dream about chickens all last night and that ain't good. Keep that man faithful to you! Got everything in there you need, including a piece of Adam and Eve root."

"What?" I dug into the flowers and pulled out a two-by-three-inch red bag with a drawstring. This was too much. "Now, Millie? You think it's right to try to manipulate the fidelity of my husband?"

Trip came to take my arm. "Come on, sister, we gotta go!"

"Yeah, yeah," I said to Trip and then turned back to Millie. "Well?"

"Don't you want him to behave?" She was dead serious.

I had no doubt of the potency of Millie's magic. I had seen it work all my life. So I said, "Millie? I really appreciate this, but no. If my marriage is going to work, I don't want it to work this way. It's not honest." I handed the small bag to her. "But you know I love you for thinking of me, right?"

"Lord, you got a hard head," she said, then gave me a kiss on the cheek and sighed like only Millie could.

Suddenly, I was in a terrific free fall, hurling through the emotional tunnels of my heart. Walking through my foyer would never again be so life-changing. Doubt began to nag at me. *Did* we love each other enough to make a life together? *Did* we know each other well enough? Maybe it was arrogance or maybe it was nerves or maybe I didn't want to appear the fool. I began to tremble from head to foot, thinking I was going to faint from this sudden terror that filled and racked me like a tropical fever.

I was a Wimbley and therefore I would muster the wherewithal to proceed as planned. No matter what. I accepted my bourbon-breathed brother's arm, walked bravely into our living room, where our musicians played Vivaldi with great passion, and married Richard—married him over the gulping sobs of Frances Mae, despite the serious reservations of my mother, and without the magic of Millie.

Miss Lavinia's Journal

All right! Here I am in this infernal city, it's one in the morning, and I can't sleep. Nothing but horns! Don't these people ever go home? It's a good thing I brought my own bourbon—the mini bar's empty! Can you imagine such a thing at the Pierre Hotel? At least they have goose-down pillows, which is more than I can say for Amtrak. That little sleeping car I had was no better than a jail cell! Moreover, now my only daughter is Mrs. Levine. I wonder if she'll raise her children Jewish? He doesn't seem to be religious. At least she's got some spiritual side to her. Well, she'll find her own way with this just like I did. She did look beautiful today. Oh, Nevil! Do pray for her! Pardon me while I pour. . . .

5

SKIRMISH IN PARADISE

1987

Our marriage was divine until our wedding night. I don't remember how it came up or who started the conversation, but it was well after our reception at Le Perigord Park. We walked home; after all, we lived next door at 565 Park Avenue and the reception was at 563 Park Avenue. My arm was looped through Richard's. I think I was making some dumb joke to him about all the money we saved on limousines and wouldn't I be the thrifty wife. I could tell he was a little drunk. That was okay. Getting married was stressful, to say the least. Even I had had three glasses of wine. We were both bone tired. Eddie the doorman greeted us.

"Dr. and Mrs. Levine! Welcome home and congratulations!"

"Thanks, Eddie," Richard said, and handed him a bottle of champagne we brought home for him.

"Aye! 'Tis indeed a night for celebrating!" he said. "When I married Mary Madeleine, we had the whole blooming pub to our family and friends! Twenty-five years and I still recall how we danced! Ow! My feet ache just remembering!"

It was obvious to me that old Eddie had already been celebrating something, probably sundown. But, God bless him, he was so sweet. He followed us to the elevator and pressed the button for us. "So, it was a good party?" he said.

"It was wonderful!" I said. "Now, you take that home and be sure to share it with your wife!"

The door opened and he held it back so we could enter. He looked at the bottle, heaved a heavy sigh of theatrical despair, looked up at us, and winked. "Wedding night!" he said. I knew what he was thinking. On tiptoes, I kissed Richard's cheek and blew a kiss to Eddie as the door closed. Then I got the giggles.

"Well, Dr. Levine? Are you going to ravage your wife?"

"He's a cheeky fellow, isn't he?"

"He's a cheeky fellow," I said, imitating his English accent, and he pinched my bottom. "Ouch! Hey! I asked you a very important question and, as your wife, I demand an answer!"

"Oh, do you now? Well, I prefer to show and not tell!"

With that he pulled me to him, put his delicious mouth on mine, slid my dress up to my waist, and tried to pull down my panties. It was great fun, it just wasn't cool, because when the elevator door opened unexpectedly on the seventh floor, Mrs. Jacobson nearly fainted. She scowled at us in horror.

"I'll take the next car!" she said in disgust.

"You're very kind, Mrs. Jacobson," Richard said, with his usual politeness, and I scrambled to cover my legs.

When the door closed he said, "Come back to me, woman!"

"No way!" We were both laughing now, wondering if Mrs. Jacobson would report us to the co-op board for lewd behavior.

"I'll bet she does," I said.

"Oh, let her and then I'll tell the board that she forages the waste bin on the corner every morning when she walks that horrible little dog of hers."

"Does she really?" I said, eyes wide.

"Of course not, but I'll say on my honor that she does!"

The door opened on nine and we stepped out into the hall.

"Well, Mrs. Levine," he said, "shall I carry you over the threshold?"

"*Absolument!*" I said, using most of my French.

Richard unlocked our door, swooped me up, groaning, and carried me to the bedroom where he unceremoniously dumped me on the bed so hard that I bounced.

"I'm going to close the door," he said. "Can I get you anything?"

"Such as?" I said, twisting my new wedding band on my hand. It was the most wonderful feeling to know I was finally Richard's wife. I was so happy, but he was staring at me with the most peculiar expression.

"I'm going to pour myself a lovely big scotch while you celebrate captivity."

Captivity? It didn't ring right with me. He had been saying things like that ever since we decided to have a wedding. Somewhere along the line I had sort of unconsciously decided to ignore them. I heard the freezer door close and the liquor cabinet door shut and then silence. I waited for a few minutes and when he didn't return I got up to find him. He was in the living room, in the dark, looking out of the window. I went up behind him and wrapped my arms around his waist, leaning into his back with the side of my face.

"You smell so good, sweetheart," I said, "tell me what it is and I'll buy you a barrel of it!"

Silence.

"I love you, Richard," I said, my heart sinking a little, feeling he was troubled, "what's wrong?"

"I don't know," he said. "May I just tell you straight out?"

"Of course! Do you want to sit on the sofa?"

"Sure," he said, crossing the room and turning on a reading lamp. "Come sit by me."

I sat on the end cushion and said nothing, but looked at him, trying to read his thoughts. I reached out to take his hand in mine and he covered mine with his other.

"Caroline," he said, arching his eyebrow, "there are things about marriage that I love. I love having a partner, I love coming home and knowing that someone who loves me is waiting, someone who wants to share my life."

"That's me! I love you forever, Richard. You know that."

"Yes, darling, and I love you forever as well. But there are other issues involved in marriage which, to me, seem pedestrian and unrealistic."

"Such as?" I knew I was not going to like what I was about to hear.

"Well, this business of the wife obeying the husband. It's arcane, don't you think?"

"I don't know. I mean, if you and I had a disagreement over something like, I don't know, health care? And you liked one policy and I liked another, I wouldn't go to the mats over it. I'd do what you thought was best."

"You would?" he said, and took a long drink. His face

was skeptical. "You surprise me! I thought you were, I don't know, more modern."

"I am modern but yes, I think I would support your decision. Richard, I know I married a brilliant man. I have great regard for your intellect and I trust your judgment."

"Humph," he said, getting up and walking toward the kitchen.

I followed him. He opened the freezer and dropped some ice cubes in the crystal tumbler, then poured himself another liberal dose of Dewar's.

"What's this really about, Richard? Money? You know I intend to work. I quit my job at the bank because it was boring. I already have three clients and I've only been in business for a month."

"Well, that's good because I believe every woman should have her own money. You shouldn't have to ask me for everything you ever want for the rest of your life."

"I agree with that. So, Richard"—I took the drink from his hand and put it down on the counter—"what's this really about? It's not about respect or money. What can it be? Fidelity?"

"Ah!" he said, taking the glass back and taking a long drink, "that old nasty bit of ancient lore! Don't you agree that it's rather had its day?"

"No," I said, "do you?"

"Oh, come now, Caroline," he said, walking back to the living room. He kicked off his loafers and untied his bow tie. One by one, he dropped his cuff links and studs into the small Steuben bowl on our glass coffee table. With every clink against the heavy crystal I felt the growing weight of stones on my chest. He put his feet up on the coffee table and looked up at me, smiling. "You can't be serious?"

I stood before him in my wedding dress and bare feet,

wondering if I was making too much of this. "Before I remind you that this is a helluva conversation to be having on our wedding night, may I just assure you that I am very serious about fidelity."

"Darling," he said, lifting his chin to me, "please don't use vulgar language. It demeans you. But you're right, perhaps this isn't the best moment to bring this up."

"Sorry to offend you, Richard, but it's true. And this is the *perfect* moment, because once you harvest the corn it's time to make grits. Or polenta. So let's have it out right now."

"Caroline," he said, and reached out to pull me to his lap. I went along with it and sat down right on him, but then slid back a bit so that we were at opposite ends of the sofa facing each other. "The last thing I want is to scar our wedding night with a silly argument. You are the most adorable woman I have ever known, simply the most divine creature, and I love you with all my heart. There is no other woman I would like to sleep with besides you."

"Good."

"What I meant was, that in the grand scheme, over the next thirty or forty years of our life together, that if you stepped out a little or if I strayed a bit, it would bear no reflection on my feelings for you or about us. Do you understand?"

"Of course I understand, but I would never do such a thing."

"And I'm sure I wouldn't either," he said, pulling me over to his chest. I curled up on him and exhaled. "Shall we make our way to the marital bed, sweetheart?" he whispered to me and kissed the top of my head, stroking my hair.

He spoke with such tenderness that once again I felt stupid and naïve. I didn't know what it was that he had said that upset me so. Probably my own exhaustion, I decided.

When I returned from the bathroom in the beautiful white chiffon and lace nightgown I'd splurged on at Saks, he was passed out cold. Good, I thought, I didn't really feel like making love anyway. Our conversation had annoyed me and, besides, every bone in my body ached. I took off my nightgown, hung it on the padded hanger, and pulled an old white cotton nightshirt over my head. As I had done forever, I brushed my hair up into a ponytail. I covered him up with a comforter and hoped his passing out and neglecting his connubial duty wasn't going to become a habit. He would be so embarrassed in the morning!

I went to the guest room, the room that I hoped would one day become a nursery. My conversation with Richard was kind of a joke, really. Every anniversary I could give him a hard time about our wedding night. He would accuse me of driving him to drink with my schoolgirl innocence and I'd tell stories about how I wound up in bed alone. Oh, sure.

I tossed the bolster cushion on the floor, pulled back the white comforter, and fluffed the pillows as I took them from the cabinet. I loved this little bedroom, with its mirrored walls and economic use of space. It was like the inside of a miniature ship, every square inch used for a purpose. Cozy but crisp because of the white linens and reflections of chrome fixtures. I slipped under the sheets of the trundle bed and turned to the mirrored wall before I switched off the light. God, did I look tired.

I decided I didn't have anything to worry about, that Richard was just letting the alcohol talk. He was just overtired and rambling on. I thought about Richard a little more. Maybe he was right about the business of an occasional fling. Maybe it had nothing to do with the marriage.

After all, I was only twenty-six and he was thirty-seven. He had done a lot more living than I had and he knew things.

I was glad that Mother and everyone else had stayed at the Pierre. My wedding night story would be a secret I could share with Millie, but never with Mother. She would never understand.

Miss Lavinia's Journal

I wish I understood why Caroline's rushing to have a baby. Oh, Sweetie tells me that she should because of osteoporosis or some fool thing, but what does she know? Sweetie's not a doctor! Caroline and I call each other all the time and she tells me little things. I don't think she should have a child yet, but I never could tell her a thing! If she has a baby, what will happen to her little business she's trying to build? What kind of mother can she be if she's running around all the time doing errands for clients! I shouldn't allow these things to put me in a state of agitation, but when I think of the life she could have had! If only Nevil were alive! Maybe Millie will have some advice for me. I just hope that man Richard is good to her.

6

Taking the Good with the Bad

1987

We all know my wedding night failed to produce heirs, but it wasn't long after that. It was just in September, I'll never forget it. Married life had been pretty easy until then. We had found our rhythm and happily life rolled along.

Richard continued to teach at Columbia and was building a list of patients. My little decorating thing was growing like a weed! For some reason, I wound up with retail clients—it was all that gentrification going on in SoHo and Tribeca. If there was a nasty old warehouse available, somebody was turning it into either a home furnishing store, a greenhouse, or a restaurant. My name got around somehow and my phone rang all the time. The constant phone ringing was my first clue that I wasn't charging enough, but I didn't change my rates because I liked being busy. It was nice to have a little money of my own too. My closet bulged with new black this, and new black that, all bought on sale with *my* money. Richard would've died if he knew what I earned or how I spent it. He was a wonderful man in many ways, but like my daddy used to say, he was tighter than a mole's ear.

I was on a job at a new store in SoHo. It was called Om. Yes, another retail outlet for everything on the planet designed to help you relax and contemplate the universe. If you wanted to massage somebody, they had tables with head holes and chairs that wiggled and kneaded your back muscles like bread dough. They even sold bedroom slippers that massaged your feet while you walked around (batteries not included). There were kits to turn your bathtub or shower into Jacuzzis or into steam rooms. Everywhere you turned there was a small fountain designed for indoors. They had produced their own line of bath and body products, curious combinations of flowers and herbs, even sold by the slice! Some days the herbs and flowers reminded me of the ACE Basin and I would wonder what kind of spells Millie could produce with them.

Beautiful music played throughout the store, streaming in from tiny hidden speakers, the kind that causes mind drift. The store's interior and fixtures were all natural blond wood, handmade tiles, natural canvas, and soft lighting. Signage was handwritten in calligraphy and purposely small. It was slick and it was Zen.

By the time all the merchandise was in place and they opened their doors for business, every merchant on West Broadway had been in to see it and had taken my card. I was going to be very busy that fall, which was fine with me.

My job there was really finished, but I stuck around to help them with display. I was leaning over picking up small boxes of votive candles and stacking them on a counter. Suddenly I was so dizzy I felt myself falling.

"Caroline! Are you okay?"

It was William Oliver, the manager, who rushed over and tried to grab the box from my arms. Too late. Thirty-six honeysuckle-scented two-inch votive candles rolled across the floor. The room was still spinning and I saw the floor coming up to hit me. The entire episode lasted less than a minute. Thank God, William caught me before I cracked my head open. He just lowered me to the ground and told me to sit still.

We had become good friends over the last six months. Richard didn't mind if I went out to dinner or to a show with William because he was as gay as he could be.

"What happened?" I said.

"You fainted, girl," he said, looking deep into my eyes.

"No way, I've never fainted in my life," I said, taking the cup of water he offered and drinking it straight down. I was extremely thirsty.

"Well, you did and it's one of two things," he said. I looked up at him, waiting for the kernels of friendly wisdom to fall.

"Number one?" I asked.

"Brain tumor. Do you have any history of brain tumors in the family?"

"No, just my sister-in-law."

"Really?"

"Help me get up, will you?"

He pulled me to my feet. "Is there a possibility you could be in the motherly mode?"

"Help me sit down, will you?"

He laughed like crazy at that and then said, "Well? I know how to find out right now."

"An EPT? Where's my purse? I'm running to CVS."

"Hell, no, honey, we don't need to spend money! Come with me to the bathroom."

The heels of my boots clicked across the floor as I followed him to the employee lounge. We were not alone. One of the girls was washing her hands. I just wanted to splash cold water on my face. William leaned against the ceramic tile counter, blew on his nails and buffed them on his sweater. When she left, he spoke.

"Come here, blondie," he said, "I'm gonna teach you a little something I learned from my dear old granny in the hills of West Virginia."

"What?" I wasn't the least bit sure of this stunt at all.

"It's the blue vein test. Foolproof."

"What on earth are you talking about?"

"You're going to let Cousin William have a look at your ta-tas, God help me, and if they have big old naughty blue veins running down them, your next decorating job will be a nursery."

I started to laugh. "Hold it right there, hotshot. Are you saying that you want me to pull my sweater up and let you see my breasts? I don't believe it."

He faked a shudder that would register four point six on a Richter scale and said, "Buh! Neither can I!" We both laughed and he said, "If you tell a single soul, I'll call you a liar until my dying day!"

"If you want to see them, you're going to have to say pretty please." I walked over and stood close to him. "Do you take an oath that you are a gay man?"

"I swear on my Aunt Freida's red fox jacket that I hope she's leaving to me, so, pretty please, Missy Caroline, lift your sweater in the light?"

"Oh, all right." I pulled my sweater up, revealing my peach lace underwire bra and their contents. He gasped.

"Pretty scary, huh?"

"No, baby, pretty blue would be a better way to describe it!"

I looked in the mirror and, to my complete and utter astonishment, several veins, which were not noticeable yesterday, were as pronounced on my breasts as though they had been drawn with a Bic pen.

That was September. It was now February and sneaking up on our first wedding anniversary. I was feeling like a million dollars after taxes and Richard was very pleased about the baby coming, although this was nothing new to him. For me, it was one daily miracle after another.

Some women get sick and some swell, but I took to pregnancy like nothing I had ever known. I had the strength and energy of an amazon. I'd sleep for eight hours as soon as my head touched the pillow. I'd wake each morning without a single cobweb in my brain. My skin glowed and, most of all, my heart sang.

All day, my hand would rub across my stomach and feel the baby inside respond. Sometimes the baby had hiccups and I'd stop working to watch my clothes jump. When he was restless, I could calm my baby by singing to him or her. I didn't know the gender and didn't care. I was so happy; I just couldn't wait to get my hands on my child.

The only problem was, I gained a lot of weight. I couldn't help it; I was starving all the time. All I wanted was watermelon—nowhere to be found in February in Manhattan—strawberry Häagen-Dazs ice cream, and tuna salad with crackers. I thought I must have been carrying a little girl because everything I wanted to eat was a shade of pink. I couldn't wait until May twentieth, which was my due date.

Richard had almost completely lost interest in our romantic life. We had occasional sex on the run, early in the morning or in the middle of the night. Quick and efficient, nothing worth filming. I just figured that after the baby came, we'd probably go back to our normal gymnastics.

Then he seemed to lose interest in me. I tried harder than ever to please him with beautiful dinners (and you know cooking is a struggle for me) and by filling the apartment with flowers. It wasn't that just our sex life was fizzling; lately, he was distracted and working later too. I was pretty obsessed with my impending motherhood and trying to finish two other stores before the baby came. Rather than have a confrontation, I wrote his attitude off to my hormones and just let everything slide. We bought a Herb Ritts photograph of Bill T. Jones for our anniversary gift and celebrated with dinner at Le Perigord Park. Richard was more and more remote.

On Monday, May ninth, he told me over breakfast he had to go to London to deliver a paper on anxiety, Monday, May sixteenth, at a conference. He was leaving Friday. I got so upset I thought I'd deliver right on the kitchen floor. Anxiety? Perfect. Obviously I didn't want him to go because it was so close to my time. He thought I was being ridiculous. We had a terrible argument, ranting at each other until it got to this.

"Caroline, calm down! You're not going to have that child until the twentieth or after. First babies are notoriously late!"

I hated it when he told me to calm down. It made me feel like my emotions were out of control and what was wrong with me that I couldn't control myself? Naturally, the next thing I did *was* to lose control. "Look, Richard, this is not right. It's not fair to spring this on me! Why didn't you tell me before now? What if something happens?"

"I didn't tell you because I knew you'd get upset just like you are and I didn't feel like dealing with it."

"Oh, that's nice." I could feel my blood pressure rising and the back of my neck was covered in perspiration.

"Now you don't want to deal with me." I started to cry. I don't think I had cried in ten years. I sat there with tears running down my face and he turned away, picked up the *New York Times* from the counter, his coffee cup and saucer, shook his head and walked out to the living room.

"That's not what I said. I said that I didn't want to deal with your anger. God, do you know you become more like your mother every day?"

That was the final straw. I was not like my mother and he knew it. He always said that when he was losing a fight because he knew it would send me to another planet. I took three deep breaths and followed him out. Between Lamaze and yoga, if there was one thing I could do it was breathe. He was sitting in his chair reading as though everything was fine.

"Richard? You go to London and deliver your paper. Have a nice trip. But I want you to know that the things you say to me do not pass right out of the window. They hurt my feelings. They also change the way I feel about you. Worst of all, they show me things about you that I'd rather not believe." He just stared at me, waiting for me to finish. A condescending blank face. "You may be right, Richard, that nothing will happen while you are away. And no one wants you to take this calculated guess correctly more than I do."

He finally folded the paper away and stood up. "There now, darling, that's better. I don't mean to hurt you. You know how much I love you." He started to approach me to take me in his arms but I backed away. "But sometimes . . ."

"I'm not finished, Dr. Freud." He hated it when I called him that and sure enough his face went sour. "You may be *right*, Richard, but you're not *nice*. Being nice is very undervalued in your world but *not* in mine."

"I apologize," he said. "You're right, it was a cowardly thing for me not to tell you of my plans. But Caroline, please, take heart, I will be back in as soon as I can and bring you and our baby something wonderful from the motherland. How's that?"

"It's a start," I said, still feeling pretty glum.

"I have a wonderful idea. This will cheer you up! Let's invite Millie to visit you while I'm gone."

I was stunned once again by his cleverness. It was the perfect solution.

"Richard? That is a splendid idea. Thank you."

I decided it wouldn't pay to be angry with him. What would it change anyway? Nothing, that's what. I called Millie at Mother's that morning the minute Richard left for his office. She answered the telephone on the third ring.

"Wimbley residence," she said.

"Hey, Millie! It's your favorite bad girl!"

"Miss Caroline, what you done now? You had that chile yet?"

God, it was good to hear her voice. "No, but I'm fixing to. I'm as big as a house!"

"That's all right, baby," she said, and I could hear her smiling. "You want your mother to come to the phone?"

"Actually, I called to speak to you." I explained everything to her and she became very quiet.

"Tell me what again, honey. I know I ain't heard you right." Her tone was serious. "Did you say that he's gone off five days before this chile's to come?"

"Well, he has to, and he'll only be gone for a few days." I found myself defending my husband and realizing Millie was right. But somewhere deep inside, I thought it was wrong to criticize your spouse. Besides, I knew Richard wouldn't go if he didn't have to.

"Darlin' chile, don't worry yourself, yanh? I wasn't

gone let you have that baby without me no how. By the grace of God and a long-handled spoon, I'll be there by Saturday, okay?"

"Do you think Mother will mind?" I probably should've asked Mother first, but when Millie answered the telephone, I just let it fly.

"Chile? What's that old lady gone do, fire me?" She laughed and laughed. Everybody knew that Millie was older than Mother. She liked to tease.

When I opened my front door on Saturday afternoon, there stood Millie and Mother. My jaw dropped.

"Well, young lady, have you forgotten your manners entirely? Invite your mother in and kiss her cheek!"

"Mother! Millie! Come inside, of course! Oh! This is wonderful!" I kissed Mother's cheek and my first thought was where would she sleep. I only had one guest room. The other had become a library and office of sorts where I worked during the day and Richard worked at night. I hadn't cooked; I hadn't shopped. There would be the devil to pay for that. Did I even have enough sheets? Well, I'd work it out.

"I brought you a pound cake, honey!" Millie said. "Now, let me take a good look at you!" She held me at arm's length, with her sturdy hands on my upper arms. She was smiling from ear to ear. "You look just fine. Yes, ma'am! And that baby's coming sooner than you think!"

"Oh, Lord, Millie. Please don't say that!" If Millie said it was so, it was so.

"Humph! Now, you and Miss Lavinia gone put your feet up and let me put on some coffee. Then we'll see what."

"Caroline?" Mother said. "Exactly *how* much weight have you gained?"

"Enough to sit on you and make you hush!" Millie called out from the kitchen.

"*You* hush, old woman!" Mother called back.

I could hear Millie laughing and suddenly Mother and I laughed too. She put her hand on my arm and said, "If you think for one single moment that I was gonna let that woman hold this baby before me, you're losing your mind."

I was happy Mother had come; hell, she was my mother, after all. It was probably the shock of her surprise visit or perhaps something Millie put in my coffee that started my labor that night. I had given Mother my bed; I was sleeping in the guest room. Millie had taken the trundle from under my bed and set up in the living room behind the red lacquer folding screen I had found in an antique store on Tenth Street.

I was dreaming I was in the barn at Tall Pines. Someone was kicking me in the back and then that something was squeezing my stomach. I woke up and could smell hay. The bed was soaked; my water had broken. I turned on the light and looked at the alarm clock. Two-fifteen. I didn't know whether I should wake anyone and then decided to wait a little while.

I changed out of my nightgown and put on the dress I had set aside to wear to the hospital. At two-twenty I had a horrible cramp again. Five minutes apart? Okay, wait another five minutes, I thought. I brushed my teeth and put my makeup bag in the little suitcase I had packed three weeks ago and pulled it out to the front hallway. Two–twenty-five, another spasm. I held on to the kitchen counter and breathed through it. The overhead light came on.

"I knew it," Millie said, coming over to me and putting her arm around my shoulder. "Come on, sit. I'll get your mother, you call the doctor, and I'll tell that damn fool downstairs to sober up and get us a cab."

"Okay." That was all I said. What else was there to say?

Richard! I had to call him! I went to the kitchen telephone, took his number from the bulletin board, and dialed. It was seven-thirty in the morning in London. The operator at the hotel rang right through to his room. A woman answered the telephone. I'd have known that voice anywhere. Lois.

"Ha-low? Ha-low?" she said in her nasal Long Island drone.

I replaced the telephone on the hook, mumbled *You sun-uvabitch*, and called my doctor. I buzzed Eddie to get a cab. Off we sped to Mt. Sinai Hospital. Dr. Sheldon Cherry, who had been my gynecologist since I had moved to New York, pronounced me dilated enough to go to the delivery room.

"When they tell you to push, push, you hear me?" Mother said.

"Don't worry, she will," Dr. Cherry said, laughing, "she wants that baby out more than you do!"

"See?" Millie said, "I'm not the only one who can put you in line!"

Mother squeezed my hand and rubbed my hair away from my face. "Good luck, sweetheart, I'll be praying for you."

"Thanks, Mother," I said.

I was going into the delivery room to bring my child into the world. My husband was shacked up with Lois, but I had more pressing issues. Of course I felt betrayed and was outraged, but I had a baby inside me fighting to be born. I'd have plenty of time later to plot my revenge.

The doors swung open and the next thing I knew they were lifting me onto another table.

"I am so sorry y'all have to do this!" I said. "I must weigh a ton!"

"Don't even think about it, honey," the nurse said. "We do this every day."

"I can't wait for this to be over," I said.

"Is this your first?" the nurse said.

"Yeah, I just want to see the baby, you know?"

"Got six myself," she said and smiled at me while she attached a blood pressure cuff to my arm and a heart monitor to my chest.

Dr. Cherry appeared and I hardly recognized him in his green scrubs. He held up my sheet and examined me again. "Got a crown!" he said. He checked the baby's heart monitor and mine too. "Okay, Mrs. Levine, ready to have your baby?"

I was puffing short breaths, trying not to push until he said I could, but the urge to bear down was all-consuming. "Now?" I said.

"Take a deep breath," he said, "and give it all you've got."

I filled my abdomen lower and upper chest with air and concentrated on the light fixture above me. With all my strength I bore down and, in one push, I slowly released the air and the baby's head.

"Got the head, Mrs. Levine, just hold it for a minute." Dr. Cherry was turning the baby a bit or something. I couldn't see. "Okay, once more!"

"That baby looks just like you, Mrs. Levine! He's blond, blond, blond!"

"I think he looks like Dr. Cherry," another nurse said.

I couldn't even giggle. With another push, I felt a huge release, and the baby was born. Then came a thunderous wail, so loud that everyone laughed. Dr. Cherry held him up. He was an exquisite, fat little baby boy with white hair and the reddest face I had ever seen.

"Look who we have here!" Dr. Cherry said and put him right on my chest. "Here's your momma, son."

A son! The first thing I remember is that he was so

beautiful—even screaming he was beautiful. My tiny infant opened his eyes, looked at me, and became quiet. I began to cry. He just stared and stared at me. I wept and wept.

"Oh, good," Dr. Cherry said, "now the baby's quiet and the mother's crying!"

Everyone, and there must have been eight people in there at that point, stopped and looked. My son was just studying me with the most incredible expression.

"Would you look?" the nurse said. "In twenty years I have never seen a baby look at a mother like that!"

His skin was velvet, his eyes were navy, and his eyelashes were thick and blond. He had all his toes and fingers. In my arms was the true love of my life. I didn't have a care in the world. I could've spent the next year just looking at his perfect little face. This child was my miracle. Life just didn't get any better than that.

On Sunday afternoon, Eric Boswell Levine and I were home. I had named him without consulting Richard. I was propped up in bed, nursing Eric, when Millie came in with a tray. His bassinet and changing table were right next to my side of the bed. Richard didn't want to give up his study for a baby's room until the last possible moment. That suited me just fine. I wanted Eric as near to me as possible. Maybe I'd keep him in the room with me and kick Richard out.

"Yanh, you got to eat something," she said. She just stood there with the tray.

"Thanks," I said, "he's asleep now." She took him from me and put him back in his bassinet. "Okay, Millie, what's up? I can tell from your face." I munched on a piece of chicken she had fried that morning. It was delicious.

"Your mother is resting and I don't want her to know we talked."

"About what?"

"Extension telephones. I picked it up the other night without thinking."

She had obviously heard the woman answering the telephone in Richard's room.

"Oh, well," I said, "it's not great, huh?"

"That's all right," she said, "I can fix him iffin you want me to, make the hag ride 'em."

"The hag *was* riding him!" I said. The hag I referred to was Lois; the hag Millie spoke of was another matter entirely. "It was Lois, but if you want to send him another one tonight, be my guest. In fact, make it a double."

Millie winked at me and said, "Drink that tea. It's good for what ails you."

In the ACE Basin, the "hag" is notorious. It's generally accepted that the hags are spirits who exist in a parallel world and the root doctor (someone like Millie) can summon them at will. They come in your house through the chimney, a keyhole, or any kind of opening and ride you while you sleep. Some of them make you have sex with them. All night. And, once they figure out how to get to you, they are not easily expunged. I hoped she could send Richard a big old hag with bad breath and screaming desire. Richard didn't know who he was messing with. You don't cut any fool with Millie's girl or there would be the devil to pay.

When Richard finally arrived home, he was ragged-looking beyond description. Unshaven and hangdog. Millie had fixed him but good. I decided to say nothing about Lois. It would be something I would save and use only if I needed it.

Miss Lavinia's Journal

Never in the world has there been a more loving and wonderful little boy than my grandson, Eric. The dear little fellow sends me articles torn out from the New York Times that he thinks will interest me. I'm going to buy him wonderful miniature trains for Christmas this year! Trip always loved trains when he was little. I'll tell you one thing: he's a lot smarter than those Neanderthals my daughter-in-law brought into this family! And, sometimes I'll answer the phone and hear his dear little voice! I'm glad he calls me because he can't write worth two hoots. But, Lord, he's sweet.

7

ERIC

1995

Like most married couples, Richard and I lived in a reasonably peaceful groove. I had no indication that he ever stepped out on me again. He had been a good husband and a dutiful father to Eric. I wasn't *positive* of his fidelity, but I was pretty sure he wasn't running around. There were no strange matchbooks or numbers written on crumpled paper cocktail napkins. For the most part, I put his one tryst with Lois out of my mind and concentrated on Eric, my business, and being such a good wife that I hoped Richard would never betray me again. In fact, our little family was pretty cozy. Life was all right. At least, it seemed to be.

Raising a child in the city was such a difference from my own childhood on the plantation. When I was a child, the ACE Basin of South Carolina was my whole world. I grew up planting vegetables, gathering pecans, arranging

flowers, riding the Edisto River, and worshiping my ancestors, like a typical Lowcountry girl. I could not even
imagine New York City outside of the images of the
Macy's Thanksgiving Day Parade or the occasional picture
in a magazine of a child playing in water spewing from a
fire hydrant.

From the time Eric could sit up in his carriage, I began
to work a little less, taking on fewer clients. We spent
hours roaming museums, public parks with playgrounds,
and the cavernous New York Public Library. When it was
time for him to go to prekindergarten, I cried like a baby.
What would I do all morning? I'd miss him so much! The
bonding thing had proved itself and there were other by-
products. For example, I learned more about art and history
in those years than I did in the rest of my life. New York
seemed to offer everything and Eric was my excuse to take
advantage of it.

By the fall of 1995, Eric was newly entrenched in the
second grade. His backpack had all sorts of gadgets hanging from it and when he threw it over his shoulder, he sort
of walked with a manly swagger. Four feet tall, as skinny
as a string bean, thick blond hair and dark blue eyes like
mine. He was all energy and simply adorable.

He loved our routine of walking to school together,
meeting again at the end of the day, and going to Central
Park or the Gardenia Coffee Shop on Madison Avenue for
a Coke. We'd talk about the day, go home, do homework
together, and I'd cook dinner while he played Nintendo or
Legos with John Hillman, a boy on the eleventh floor.

He loved building things and my brother, for some unknown reason, was always sending him craft kits and models. Eric would always pick up the telephone and call him
to say thanks. Trip did this on his own, but every time he
did, it served as a reminder that I never reciprocated with

his children. At least Eric's manners were good. The most recent gift was a beautiful remote control sailboat to use in Central Park. Eric was thoroughly thrilled. It made me gasp. I guessed I should have been sending something to Frances Mae's horrible little girls. Trip shouldn't have been doing this. It wasn't like they came to visit or that Eric even knew him. He's seen him twice in his whole life! I had enough stress without pretending to like Frances Mae. Nonetheless, all through September, I took Eric to the park with Trip's boat. At the very least, I had to admit it was a very thoughtful gesture. I didn't know why I was so annoyed.

In the middle of October, I was called to his school for a conference with his teacher. As soon as I sat down, Ms. Daniels started running her mouth. She told me that she suspected Eric had attention deficit disorder and perhaps some other issues. She wanted to put him through a full battery of psychological tests to determine the nature of his suspected learning disabilities and then meet again to discuss our alternatives. She said all this without one visible shred of emotion. My jaw was on the floor.

"I'm very concerned about him," she said.

"Attention deficit disorder?"

"I'm afraid so."

"Are you qualified to make that judgment?"

"No, but I haven't missed a call yet."

I didn't like the way she spoke and I didn't like her. What was she saying? Eric was not a hyperactive child. Energetic perhaps, but very well behaved. I knew Eric's handwriting wasn't as clear as the other children's, and artistically his work was inferior when compared to the paintings and models of his classmates. But so what? He was just a little boy!

On the other hand, if you asked Eric about the history

of mankind, his eyes twinkled as he took you down the timeline from one era to the next. If you wanted to know about dinosaurs, he could tell you everything there was to know. He watched Boyd Matson and the *National Geographic Explorer* endless hours upon end, virtually memorizing everything. Between television, museum visits, and books we read together, Eric's beautiful mind was filled with information and imaginings I'd never had at his age. There was nothing, I repeat, nothing wrong with my son.

I had been warned about teachers like this woman, this Ms. Ice Cube Daniels. They can't teach worth a damn so they blame it on the children, picking away at them, searching for justification of their own ineptitude.

She went on to say he was too easily distracted, had to be constantly reminded to get "back on task." I told her I thought he was probably bored to tears.

She claimed that he had social issues with the other children, that he was a loner. Big deal, I said, Eric doesn't like to play soccer. He is a more cerebral child. That remark set off some kind of pyrotechnics in her miniscule brain.

"Mrs. Levine?" she said, and not very nicely, "I've been teaching for ten years and it doesn't take too long for me to spot a troubled child in my classes."

"Ms. Daniels? Do you have children?"

"That is irrelevant to this discussion."

No children. Probably hadn't been laid in ten years either, from the looks of her.

"Eric's only seven years old! Cut him a little slack!"

"Mrs. Levine, I'm required to bring these things to the attention of the parents and the administration. If you don't wish to accept my recommendations, you'll have to discuss it with the headmistress."

I sat back and looked at her. Who was this horrid

woman trying to attach a label to my son? Over forty, unmarried, graying hair pulled back in a clasp, long denim jumper over a striped turtleneck, huge eyeglasses. As plain a Jane as has ever tormented children. *And* parents. I did not like this woman.

"Test him," I said. "Test him and we shall see what we see." Eric and I would prove her wrong and then I would take out a full-page ad in the *New York Times* insisting her teacher's license be revoked and that she be publicly caned. Maybe I'd cane her myself.

I was suddenly reconciled to testing him. To be honest, I was slightly curious. I wanted to know just how his fabulous young mind was wired. He *was* different from other children, I admitted to myself.

The testing haunted me until the appointed day arrived. What if I was wrong? I couldn't be. When we had hard results in our hands, then his obvious gifts would be revealed and recognized. Most of all, I wanted to see Ms. Daniels writhing in pain in a pool of her own self-righteous, small-minded, and judgmental blood. Every time I thought about her and the heartless way she spoke to me about Eric, I wanted to slap her silly, right across her face.

Eric was the perfect child. Still. I had this nagging feeling that there was more to this than I was prepared to know.

It was a beautiful November morning, typical for Manhattan. It seemed that every taxi horn blared in an off-key chorus. Thousands of cars with commuters raced to their destinations at thirty miles an hour. Great hordes of people rushed by with their briefcases and paper coffee cups, stealing sips at corners. Dog walkers led five to ten dogs each by canvas leashes across the frenzied traffic toward Central Park. Everyone wore their Manhattan Mask—the one that said, *Don't violate my privacy; I might be famous*. Their faces always made me think that there were a lot of cranky people in this town.

I knew that Eric had some anxiety about the whole evaluation process. As we walked up Park Avenue toward his school on Sixty-sixth and Madison, I encouraged him to talk about it.

"Sweetheart, I don't want you to worry about this, okay? These tests are actually kind of fun."

"What if I do bad?" His face was tense and his small hand in mine was moist.

"You *can't do* badly," I said, "it's not that kind of test."

"I wish I was dead," he said in a tiny voice.

I knelt down beside him and looked in his face. He stared back with the most adorable pout I had ever seen.

"Whoa, right there," I said, "don't ever say that."

"Sorry," he said, examining the crack in the sidewalk.

"Look at me, sweetheart. This is what I want you to do. Will you listen to me?"

"Sure."

"Okay, number one. Follow the teacher's instructions. Go slowly, and take the time to reread the instructions." (He was impetuous and always wanted to rush ahead.) "Then, read them again. Number two, when you're sure of what to do, begin your work. Write slowly and neatly. Finally, when you're done, check your work. If you don't understand something ask the teacher. Okay? Pretty simple, huh?"

"You make it sound so easy."

"Just give it a try, okay? For me? You know what to do; just take a deep breath and go for it."

"Okay." His eyes were worried and we continued the short walk to his school. "I'll do my best. Read the instructions twice, do the work, and check it."

"That's all Dad and I ask, is that you do your best. Hey, how about after school? You and me? Chocolate shakes?"

"Deal!"

He seemed a little brighter after that. We arrived at the Smith School; I intended to walk him to his classroom. He dropped my hand and stopped me at the door. The hall was filled with students.

"Mom?"

"Yes, Eric?"

"I love you." He whispered it to me, probably so the other children wouldn't hear.

"I adore you!" I said, smiling.

"I can find my classroom by myself."

"You sure? It's all the way . . ."

"I'm sure," he said. I had always walked him to the classroom. "Mom? I'm big now."

Mom? I'm big now. His words shot palpitations through my heart—not like fatal bullets, but maybe the feeling of surprise you get when the water in the shower inexplicably goes cold for a few seconds. "Okay, baby," I said, understanding his need for self sufficiency. "You go get 'em and I'll see you at three."

All I could think about on the way home was how would I tell Richard about this. No, I hadn't yet told Richard, thinking it wise to keep my séance with Ms. Daniels to myself for the time being.

If Eric's results showed any problems, the comparisons to Harry would increase, by light-years. Harry, Richard's son from his marriage with Lois, was playing violin in a by-invitation-only children's orchestra at Carnegie Hall. Harry was the captain of the traveling soccer team at his school. Harry, president of the fifth grade, Roller-blading wizard, straight A student; and Harry, the once and future Jedi, was a total and complete pain in my ass.

For all of Harry's accomplishments at his young age, he had a smart mouth, was a bully, a practiced liar, and one of the sneakiest, most contemptible children I had ever encountered. And when I tried to discuss his behavior with Richard, Richard became more imperious than ever. If Harry took one of Eric's toys, Richard would say, *Oh, please. Eric has plenty. Why shouldn't he share with his brother?* If Harry picked on Eric to the point that Eric lost his temper, Richard would reprimand Eric, not Harry. On and on. It didn't take long for Harry's visits to become a contest with Eric for their father's love and attention.

The last thing I wanted was for Richard to think there was a bona fide reason to hold Harry in higher regard. So I never told Richard anything. By the time I was finally called in for discussion of the evaluation results, I was doing yoga twice a day and still pretty well lathered in fear and loathing.

The meeting was to take place in the office of the school psychologist. I knew as soon as I swung into the office of Dr. Judith Moore that something was wrong.

"Thank you for coming, Mrs. Levine," she said, rising and extending her hand. "Would you like some coffee?"

Admittedly, she was congenial, but too officious for my blood.

"Sure, just black," I said and shook her hand.

"Please sit here and I'll be back in just a minute."

She indicated that I should wait in the wooden chair in front of her desk. Her small office looked like something from central casting. Old oak desk piled high with folders, beige metal filing cabinets, children's artwork covering a bulletin board, and bookshelves crammed with volumes on everything from ADD and obsessive-compulsive disorder to childhood depression and teenage suicide. I wondered if the other chair would soon be filled by the demoness—

Eric's teacher. She was probably too humiliated to show up. Wrong again. She came through the door with Dr. Moore, chipper as could be. I stood to greet her—after all, may as well be civilized, I thought.

"Good morning, Ms. Daniels."

"Mrs. Levine," she said, nodding her head and sitting in the chair opposite me.

"Well, now," Dr. Moore said, handing me a foam cup of coffee. "We're all here. Good." She went around her desk, took her seat, put her reading glasses on, and opened a manila folder. She looked up at me and sighed. "Mrs. Levine, before we go over the results of Eric's testing, I want to give you some information on how the results and findings were achieved."

"Fine," I said, "I'd appreciate that very much."

"Eric was given a series of tests, which are standard in education, to measure different areas of his general knowledge—mathematics, science, language, reading comprehension, and so on. In the afternoon, he was also given two different psychological evaluations and his behavior was observed and noted." She paused.

"And?" I said, "What did you find?"

"Some very interesting things. Eric is a very bright little boy."

"Thank you," I said, "and a sweetheart too."

"He is a dear little boy," Ms. Daniels said, immediately making me suspicious.

Dr. Moore began again. "He shows particular strength in vocabulary." She handed me a copy of the test to review. "If you'll look at the bottom of page three, his vocabulary is on a sixth-grade level."

The room was silent as I looked at the pages, not exactly sure of how to interpret what I was reading. She spoke again.

"What concerns us is this. Eric, while he is as bright as he can be, he has clear audio processing issues and an obvious fine-motor issue, in that he seldom does an adequate job of transferring data to paper."

"I see," I said.

Dr. Moore looked to Ms. Daniels, who now got into the act. She opened a folder on her lap and produced a writing sample. "This is average work in my class." She handed me a page of written work by another student. "This is Eric's work."

There was no comparison. Eric's work was sloppy and impossible to read. The other child's work was at least twice in volume and easily read, although it did contain spelling errors. Eric's work had no punctuation or capital letters. The other child's work did.

"Well, quite a difference, I agree, but what does it mean?"

"Well, it means that he needs to be seen by an occupational therapist."

"I see." I saw no such thing and she knew it.

"Second, I'd just like to finish going through the results with you. Please understand that here at the Smith School we are not equipped for LDGT kids. We do not have time in our curriculum to offer occupational therapy, social skill workshops, or the therapies that Eric needs."

"What is LDGT?" I said.

"Learning disabled, gifted, and talented," Ms. Daniels said in her smug little way.

I began to breathe deeply, trying to compose myself. The compliment of gifted and talented hardly made up for the learning-disabled part. Dr. Moore could see that I was becoming upset.

"Mrs. Levine," she said, "Eric is a wonderful child.

There are many ways he can learn to compensate for these issues. It's just that the Smith School doesn't offer those services. I'm afraid we do too many children a disservice by keeping them here. They simply fall through the cracks."

"You know," I said, "you'll have to forgive me. I'm not willing to just have him put through one battery of tests at this school and then put him in some school for kids with problems! I'd have to be way more convinced than this."

"We understand, Mrs. Levine," Dr. Moore said, "and we encourage you to have our findings checked out with another professional. Here is a list of colleagues that I've known for some time; they all specialize in children. Or you can use anyone you like."

She handed me a piece of paper and my hands were shaking.

She continued, "I think it would also be important to reassure you that it is not our intention to just ask you to remove Eric today or even this school year. I'd like to suggest that for the present, we find a good OT to work with him."

"That sounds fine to me," I said, not knowing what in the hell an OT did.

"We go one step at a time, Mrs. Levine."

One step at a time. Learning disabled. Fine motor. Audio processing. I couldn't get their words out of my mind. They were telling me that Eric had to leave their school! What if they were wrong? They *had* to be wrong! I'd take Eric to another doctor. Tomorrow!

As I walked down Madison Avenue toward home, I looked into the faces of passersby. Did they have a child like mine? Had they found solutions? The words followed me home and tortured me all afternoon. How in the world would I find the courage to tell Richard? I wanted to take Eric and run away.

Miss Lavinia's Journal

Having children just might be the most thankless job in the world. Trip came to me again for money and made no mention of the other loan. This time it was ten thousand. I can't just keep on handing it to him so I said, Trip, darling, are you snorting cocaine? Now, I know that sounds like an awful thing to ask a person, but I needed to know. He just looked at me like I had two heads and denied it. Something is definitely going on. And Caroline? Something is up with her too. I can just feel it in my bones. Thanksgiving is around the corner and I haven't heard from her in a month.

8

BECOMING MOM

1995

It wasn't enough to love Eric with all my heart. I began to realize he wasn't mine—just that *on loan* thing from heaven they talk about in parents' self-help books—but that I had to help him to prepare to succeed on his own and I had to do a million things to help him leave me one day. Looking ahead to the day that some woman would want Eric for her husband gave me one of those rare moments to pause on the wheel of life. I began to see for the first time how Mother felt about Frances Mae—that she had raised and loved Trip only for Frances Mae to steal him away. That Frances Mae actually slept with him and gave him children must've driven her nuts when she thought about it.

I knew that I had to make Richard see that although Eric had learning style differences, he was every bit as worthy of his father's love and affection and respect as Harry was.

Learning style difference—that's what they called it now—
it was a kinder label. Maybe it was my imagination, but
it seemed like the educational system was salivating to
label children something. So, in the interest of balance, I
planned a family excursion that included Harry.

I arranged for a rental house in the Poconos for the
weekend. The single best feature of living in the Northeast
was the splendor of the fall colors. The following weekend
promised to be the peak of all Mother Nature could offer.

I packed puzzles, games, music, hiking clothes, and
camera equipment. In my own halfway vegetarian style, I
made a wonderful Irish stew with lots of carrots and potatoes and froze it. Then I made two quarts of bolognese
sauce for spaghetti for the boys and one quart of marinara
for me. At the last minute I threw in two quarts of meatless
chili. All of this went into a large cooler with frozen plastic
bricks of ice to keep it and the other groceries cool.

I took Eric to the Gap and bought him great-looking
sweats and jeans to wear and even went so far as to give
Richard specific instructions for Lois to pack for Harry the
same things. I insisted to myself that when I came clean
with Richard about Eric's learning evaluation, it would be
in a setting that would give both of them the maximum
emotional elastic. I was also determined to have the weekend go well.

We packed the rented Jeep with all our duffel bags and
gear and made our way through the Lincoln Tunnel to
Route 80 west. Richard drove; Eric and Harry were to be
the copilots, sharing maps with preplotted routes in yellow
highlighter. I gave the boys snacks of juice boxes, bananas,
and cheese crackers. They were getting along fine.

"When we get to the Poconos, I get to pick my bedroom
because I'm older," Harry said.

"No, you don't," Richard said, "I'm the oldest! I get to pick!"

"Bad news," I said, "the condo only has two bed-rooms—ha! One has a king-size bed and the other one has bunk beds! But there is a pull-out couch in the living room if anybody wants it."

"Not me," Eric said, "I'll take either bunk. I don't give!"

"You don't give what?" Harry said.

"A damn," Eric said.

"Eric!" Richard said. "In this family we do not use foul language." He did not say it in a mean or severe way, but very kindly to minimize Eric's embarrassment in front of Harry. A gentle reprimand. Two points for Richard.

"Sorry, Dad," Eric said, "I should have said that it doesn't matter to me where I sleep."

"Right," I said, "or you could have said, 'I don't attach condemnation to my feelings about in which bed I sleep.' "

"Condensation?" Eric said.

"No, son, condensation is moisture gathered from the air, condemnation is when you damn something," Richard said.

"You cursed!" Harry said. "Condensation! Jeesch! Even I knew the difference!"

"Yeah, well, I'll bet the people in the place of condem-nation would like some condensation!" I said.

Eric started to giggle. Just like my father had done with me, I played the word game with Eric all the time. Richard just shook his head. Harry sucked his teeth and looked out the window.

"Or consideration and compensation!" Eric added and reached over the seat and fingered my shoulder.

"Good one!" I said. We drove on.

We left Route 80 at Tannersville and found Hutch's Real Estate's office. They gave us the keys and a small map and off we went to find the house. It was in a small subdivision, an A-frame cabin on a lake. The small yard was filled with trees in all the color you could dream to see in autumn. Sugar sap maples of bright red and orange, towering oaks with leaves of gold. Every time a breeze blew over the water, a rush of leaves swirled through the air in spirals. It was absolutely perfect.

We unloaded the car and moved in. The boys took their things to their room and Harry came running out minutes later, with his Nintendo to hook up to the television.

"What do y'all want for supper tonight?" I asked. "Spaghetti or stew?"

The boys both voted for spaghetti and I took the containers out to thaw. I had made two things that ninety-eight percent of all American boys eat. And I had brought homemade garlic bread—everyone liked that.

I could see Richard through the sliding glass doors. He was out on the deck, looking over the water. It was truly beautiful in the late afternoon light. I opened a bottle of white wine, half filled two goblets, and went out to join him. He took the glass, smiled, and put his arm around my shoulder, squeezing it. He was still wearing his leather jacket and I had on a thick pullover sweater with a turtleneck. We looked as happy as any couple could, except that I was searching for the moment and method to reveal Eric's test results to Richard. No question about it, I was dragging my feet. Then, in a moment of confidence, I decided to just spill the beans.

"Well, Richard?" I said.

"Hmmm? I wonder if they have a canoe anywhere."

"Probably, and that might be fun! Listen, at some point this weekend, I have to talk to you about something— maybe we can steal a few minutes away from the boys."

Now I had his attention. "What's going on, Caroline? Something wrong?"

"Maybe, maybe not. The Smith School ran some tests on Eric and I'm unsure of how to interpret the results."

"I spoke to them. That old battle-ax called me—Dr. What's-her-name."

"Judith Moore. She called you?" I was flabbergasted! How *dared* she? "What did she tell you?"

"Come inside with me, sweetheart." Richard pulled the sliding door open and we stepped inside. He closed it, stepped around me, and went to the boys' room. "I want you boys to go and gather firewood, okay? Get plenty of kindling!"

In minutes, they were outside with a canvas-handled wood blanket, happily picking up sticks and small pieces of wood. I watched them from the kitchen window; they seemed to be getting on fine. Richard opened the refrigerator and refilled our glasses. I took mine with shaky hands.

"Look, Caroline, I've known since Eric was very small that he had gifts and he had other issues. I could tell by the way he struggled to learn to write his name. I could tell by a thousand things he did and didn't do. I knew it was only a matter of time until it all came out, and here we are."

I searched his face for some emotion but for Richard, it was a fait accompli. If he had known all along, it explained his attitude toward Harry. Harry was his pick of his litter. Eric was somehow damaged and he had neglected to nurture him, the same way a mother in the wild disengages from the runt. I thought my heart was being wrenched in two.

"So that's it?" I said. "You've known this all along and never said a word to me?"

"It wouldn't have changed anything," he said.

I sat down on the couch and was too stunned to say anything! I put my forehead on the heel of my hand and looked at the floor, trying to understand the weight of Richard's knowing and how he viewed the truth about Eric. I looked up at him.

"Richard, you are either stupid or cruel or both!"

"Don't speak to me that way, Caroline. I am not stupid and I am not cruel."

Oh, but you can be, I thought. "Richard, this is classic shoemaker's children syndrome. . . ."

"I don't believe I'm familiar with that one, Caroline."

"It's the one where the shoemaker's children go without shoes. Surely there must have been things we could have done early on that would have helped Eric?"

"Caroline. I guess that, like you, I didn't want to have to face it."

That was easy to understand and yet I wondered why Richard's choice of words always smacked of ice and why I would always rush to anger. Maybe men were more pragmatic and maybe I was overly emotional. We looked at each other and then outside to the yard where the boys ran together. I tried to calm myself.

"It just seems so unbelievable to me," I said. "Look at them."

Both boys were running all over the yard and racing to see who could gather the most wood. It was normal friendly competition, sibling stuff. There was no visible issue or difference between their abilities to perform this simple task, and yet, Harry was much older. Harry was smaller and dark like Richard and Lois. Eric looked like my brother and father—long and lanky and blond. They looked like equals to me.

"I always used to wonder why you didn't insist that Eric

play soccer," he said. "It would've been so good for his grapho-motor skills."

"I didn't know it; that's why." *If you had said something . . .* My thermometer began to rise.

"Or why you didn't find more friends for him. I mean, Lois may be diabolical, but at least she understood that children need to gain social skills, not just vocabularies."

"Richard, you can't possibly be blaming me for Eric's learning issues, are you?" By now it was a struggle not to raise my voice.

"No more than I blame myself for denying they existed. Look, Caroline, Churchill was dyslexic; so was Thomas Edison. So are over fifty percent of the folks these educators and evaluators identify as gifted and talented. If you ask me, there's something drastically wrong with the educational system, not the kids."

"Well, if liking Eric's teachers was a requirement, I'd flunk everything."

"Bottom of the pile. Horrible creatures. We will figure it all out. Don't worry. Come on, let's go and help them carry all that wood. Looks like they picked up half of Pennsylvania!"

Richard went outside and I went to grab my camera. I don't know what was the matter with me. If Richard wasn't stressed to death over Eric, then why was I? I just kept thinking that if I'd only known sooner—*if!* The light of day was beginning to fade, stars were already visible in the dark sky. With the sun at my back I put them all together on the tiny dock with the lake behind them and clicked away a roll of film. In those photographs would be the memories of this weekend and talking to Richard about the truth.

Friday and Saturday, we set the table, made the meals, cleared the tables, washed the dishes. Eric and I did most of the work, Richard read, and Harry spent a lot of time in the yard kicking his soccer ball around by himself. If you asked me what that all meant I'd say that Eric certainly appeared normal, Richard was uninterested, and Harry was not really with any of us in his heart.

It was Saturday night, right before eight, that Eric came down from the attic with an old telescope. He took some paper towels and wiped off the dust, folded it over his shoulder, and went outside in the dark. From the living room, I watched him walk down to the dock and set it up.

Lights twinkled in the distance from homes on the other side of the lake. It was a perfect night to be in the mountains—fifty degrees and clear. I wiped the last of the crumbs from the counters, put on my jacket, and went outside to join him. Two lightweight metal folding chairs were leaning against the shed so I carried them down to the dock.

"I'll bet we're not the first people to do this from this dock," I said, "the chairs were right there by the door of the shed."

Eric mumbled *uh-huh* and continued to focus the lens. "Wow!" he said.

"What?"

"Look, Mom! I can see the moon!" He was very excited and wanted me to look. "I'm going to get Dad and Harry!"

"Okay, you do that!" I said. I watched him running up to the house and all the while I worried how a child so full of life, so curious about everything, who tried so hard to please, could have these troubling issues. I watched Eric through the windows, trying to convince Richard and Harry to come outside and join us. Finally, Richard got up and reluctantly came outside, Eric pulling his arm all the way to the dock.

"Sit here, Dad," Eric said, "I wanna show you something!" Eric adjusted the lens and then stood back. "Look! See the moon?" Richard said that indeed he did. "See that giant dark spot? Galileo thought it was the ocean so he named it *Mare,* which is *sea* in Latin."

"Did you learn that in school, son?" Richard asked.

"Nah. Learned it from the Discovery Channel," Eric said.

"You let him watch television?" Richard said.

"Don't you live in the same apartment?" I said, with wide eyes. "Eric and I watch it every Sunday night."

"And you wanna know why the craters always look pretty much the same?" He didn't wait for us to respond. "Because there's no atmosphere to move the dust around! Hardly any gravity, either, to pull stuff to it! And did you know that the minerals on the moon are the exact same chemical composition as the rocks on earth? Basalt! Yep, all from volcanoes! It's true!"

Richard stood up and put his hands on Eric's shoulders. "Son, that is absolutely fascinating! What do you think it implies? About the origins of the moon and earth, I mean."

"Dunno. That they come from Mars?" Eric was grinning from ear to ear. "That maybe a billion years ago, a big chunk of Mars got loose and hurled itself into space? I dunno. What do *you* think, Dad?"

"I think that's a question for you to answer when you grow up, Eric, that's what I think. Come on, let's go build a fire," Richard said, "it's getting chilly."

"And roast marshmallows?" Eric said.

"Yes," Richard said, nodding his head. "And roast marshmallows."

They each took a chair and I followed behind with the telescope. I felt all at once relieved and warmed by what Eric had shown Richard and by Richard's regard for Eric's enthusiasm. Richard even seemed guardedly proud. Although I hated Richard's games of divide and conquer, he made me laugh when we all got back in the house. Harry was stretched out across the couch, watching television.

"What's a mare, Harry?" Richard asked.

"What?" Harry pretended that he had been oblivious to our presence and used the remote to turn down the volume of the World Wrestling Federation matches.

"Mare," Richard said, "what does it mean?"

"It's an eel," Little Precious said, and raised the sound again. "Who cares?"

"That's moray," I said.

"Yeah, mare means condemnation," Eric said and laughed his way to his bedroom.

"Shut up, rat breath! What do you know?" Harry called out.

For once, Eric had the sense to ignore Harry. He wasn't sure how he had won this tiny battle in the inch wars with Harry for Richard's approval, but he had. I decided we needed more weekends like that.

I went to bed wondering how many stars were visible that night over the Edisto River. I made a guess that the number was in the trillions. There were no city lights to block them, so they all shone on a crisp night like shattered crystals, spectacular droplets across the deep cobalt. Eric would love that. I had a boy interested in the cosmos and made a note to myself to take him to South Carolina more often.

Miss Lavinia's Journal

I never thought I'd see the day that I had to guard myself against my own children. That son of mine is driving me insane. It's not bad enough that Raoul left me for another woman? Doesn't Trip know that I'm upset? He should be happy— he never liked Raoul in the first place. For all the years I was married to Nevil, I was the dutiful spouse, the perfect hostess—and guess what? I've had more fun screwing the gardener than I ever had screwing my husband, although I was very devoted to him. Every woman should have a Latin lover at least once in her life. Legs in the air! Oh, dear me. Trip just made me so mad this afternoon. I am weary of being judged.

9

"Ain't No Way, Babe . . ."

Manhattan, February 2000

"You'll have to speak up, Trip! There are about thirty people in the living room—all talking at once!" Richard, my cranky husband—cranky because he hates it when we entertain in our home—had just handed me the telephone. I pulled the cord around the paneled door into his study to talk to my brother, who only calls me when he wants something. "What did you say?"

"I said, I've *had* it! We have all *had* it with Mother!"

This wasn't good. A telephone call from Trip made my stomach boil like I had just inhaled a whole jar of jalapeños. Reflux. I could feel it already.

"What's wrong?" I said as calmly as I could.

"*What's wrong,* she says to me like I call her every five minutes or something. I'll tell you what's wrong, Caroline. Mother is no longer capable of taking care of herself. She is mentally unstable, cannot handle her affairs, and she needs to be in an assisted-living environment. And immediately."

Well. It had finally come to this, as I knew it would. I knew that one day, my dear brother—the quintessential good old boy—and that horrible wife of his would figure out a way to dispose of Mother.

"I don't think so, Trip," I said, slowly and evenly. I paused to let that sink into one of the many fissures of his cement skull and took a breath. "What's happened to make you feel this way?"

"You know what, Caroline? I wish to hell that you wouldn't talk to me like your English-slash-Hebrew husband talks to his psychotics. That's what I wish."

"I'm sorry that you feel that way. It was not my intent." A bald-faced lie, if I ever told one. "Nevertheless, the solution to your problem does not lie in anti-Semitic sarcasm. If you've got a problem with Mother it's not going to help you solve it if you insult my husband and me. Besides, I'm going to have to call you back."

"I apologize. I do."

"Apology accepted."

"Caroline, she damn near shot my balls off this afternoon."

"What on God's earth . . . ?"

"I was putting my boat in the water and she mistook me for a poacher, or so she said. I think she had been talking to Johnny."

"Johnny?"

"Yeah, as in Walker."

"She drinks bourbon, but never mind. Was the sun over the yardarm?"

"Yes, but still . . ."

"How close did she come?"

"Close enough to scare me half to death."

"Oh, Trip, come on. I may accept the fact that Mother was in the sauce, but I can't believe she wanted to kill you. So why is this such a problem for you to handle? Mother has been a wild woman for years! You should be used to her by now."

"You're overlooking the point, Caroline."

"What's that?"

"*I* don't have a problem with Mother, *we* have a problem with Mother."

There wasn't anything he could have said that would have made me feel more wretched. I needed to sit down or dissolve.

"Trip?" My heart was racing. "I'm going to call you back when our guests are gone. All right?"

"Oh, that's right! You're entertaining! Sorrrry to interrupt your little swarrrray with something so insignificant, Caroline. So you just call me back when it's convenient, okay?"

Now I was angry. "You know what, Trip? You're a pain in the ass. Big time. I have to think about this. I'm not giving you some blanket approval to throw Mother out of her house so Frances Mae can move in with your three girls. I want to talk to you at length and get the whole story. Then I'd like a little time to think it through. That's not unreasonable, is it?"

"In the first place, I don't need your approval. As executor of her estate, I have her power of attorney and down here in God's country, you only need two signatures to have someone committed to a mental institution. The way Mother has been behaving, securing those signatures wouldn't be a problem at all."

No doubt, Mother rued the day she gave him that trust.

"Okay." I realized I was stuck on the phone with him

until he had said what he called to say in the first place. "Tell me what's going on."

"Our mother has broken up with Raoul and is currently sleeping with Jenkins."

"What?" He must have been kidding me. Raoul was a thirty-five-year-old widow's landscaper (read: "stud service") who worked part time—and obviously overtime at the plantation. Jenkins was the African American caretaker of Tall Pines; Mother and Millie depended on him for everything. He lived in a cottage on Mother's property and was practically a recluse. Never mind he was a thousand years old. "Tell me you're lying."

"I only wish. Millie and I saw her coming out of his house very early in the morning. I had gone over to repair some asphalt on our landing and Millie was coming to work. We both saw her, and it wasn't the first time either."

"There must be another explanation, Trip. Did you ask Mother?"

"Oh, yeah, sure. I just went up to her and said, So, Mother, how long have you and Jenkins been burning up the sheets?"

"You have to be a wisenheimer."

"Seriously, Caroline. What would you say? You know how she is! She'd just lie her way out of it!"

"You're right." I looked out the window of Richard's study. If Mother had decided to take it up with Jenkins, she would. The unrelenting sleet was tapping on our soundproof glass. Soundproof glass is a complete waste of money. It was a miserable February night. Perfect weather for a family blowup. Thank God Trip was my only sibling. One like him was plenty.

I had to get back to my party. There were at least ten people over seventy years old and I wanted to be sure to warn them about the icy sidewalks. "Trip, gimme about

two hours and I'll call you back. I just want to say good-
bye to these folks, okay?"

"I'll be asleep."

That was a well-worn family euphemism for "I'll be too
drunk to talk." If I had a spouse and kids like his, I'd be
drunk day and night.

"I'll try to hurry."

"Whatever," he said and hung up in my ear.

And they wondered why I left home. I was half-sitting
on the arm of Richard's tufted leather couch, which stood
flush in front of his desk facing the window. I stared at
the phone. My brother infuriated me. Why couldn't he just
stay out of Mother's business?

Mother sleeping with Jenkins? No way. I could just see
Trip and Frances Mae, plotting Mother's eviction like two
chess masters from the Kremlin. I was doomed and destined to be the peacemaker. I knew it.

Richard and I were hosting a cocktail party for the
Board of Trustees at Bellevue, where Richard was the head
of psychiatrics. It was the only reason he tolerated the in-
vasion—it was the annual customary duty. He took one
look at me coming into the living room and knew I was
upset.

He crossed the room and whispered to me, "What's
wrong?"

"Oh, nothing," I said, "just my brother calling to give
me nightmares."

"Ah," he said, "do you want to go call him back?"

"No, but thanks," I said, "I'll call him later."

"I'll go wind this damn thing up, okay?"

"Thanks."

"Sweetheart? I have to go to the office to pick up some
papers for my morning meetings tomorrow. Okay?"

"Sure," I said.

I watched him walk away. Salt-and-pepper hair, wire-rim glasses, tweed jacket, flannel trousers. The archetypal shrink.

Later, when everyone was gone, the apartment was so quiet it made my ears pound. It was nearly midnight. I called Richard's office. No answer. Probably sleeping on the couch, as he did when he was tired. Well, that makes us even, I thought. We all get tired.

Turning out lights, I looked around at what Richard and I had built in the last thirteen years. We had six rooms of travel memorabilia from our wanderings. Our bookshelves were crammed with learned opinions on every area of psychology and psychiatrics in and out of print. Those were Richard's. They were his library and his weapons. My books were on textiles from around the world, Japanese gardens, obscure religions such as the cargo cultures of West Africa. Sometimes it seemed that he focused on the mind of man whereas I studied the spirit and what man held sacred. Our bookshelves were as good a starting place as any to see the differences between us.

I peeked in our son's room and saw his beautiful head down in his pillow, book on his stomach, glasses still on his nose. Eric was still the true love of my life. And, more interestingly, over the past five years, he had become an A student. I had found a school for him in Manhattan that specialized in gifted children with learning disabilities. He had learned to write beautifully and was doing so well, taking some sixth-grade courses in reading and history but tenth-grade math and science. Even the old curmudgeon himself had to agree that Eric was doing fine. I guess since Richard had achieved his goals through plain hard work in a standard environment it was still hard for him to accept that Eric needed something else.

I reached over and removed Eric's glasses, placing them

quietly on the end table. I lifted the book from his hands. *The Heroes of Ancient Greek Mythology*. Eric loved the stories of Ancient Rome, Greece, and any kind of culture. It made me happy to see that he had his own pursuits, giving me confidence that he'd find his way through the world despite his challenges. We all do, somehow. And, if an adoring mother could possibly make a difference . . . I smoothed his hair, pulled the covers up around him, and kissed his forehead. He sighed in his sleep and said, "Love you, Mom."

"Love you too, baby," I whispered and turned off his bedside lamp.

It was only late at night that I indulged myself with a healthy push of my Me Button. Tonight, I was in the mood to push. I filled my bathtub with hot water, Dead Sea salts, and some oil I had bought from an aromatherapist on Madison Avenue; it promised to soothe and relax my inner spirit and the aching muscles simultaneously. They both needed it.

Trip was on my mind; his story about Mother worried me. Richard was on my mind too. He always made me feel insignificant, unimportant. Then, there was Eric and the way Richard seemed unable to resist comparing him to Harry. Was there any kindness in his criticisms? Or compassion?

I lowered myself into the oily water and crunched some undissolved salt lumps with my foot. Slowly, I ran the big natural sponge across my chest and then up and down my legs. As I thought more about Richard and the way he dismissed Eric, I lost my desire to soak. I rinsed with the hand shower and wrapped myself in a huge towel, draining the tub.

I began my nightly ritual. It seemed unfair that the older I got the more I had to do before sleeping. Unfair because the older I got, the more tired I was at night. But dutifully, I flossed, rinsed, brushed for two full minutes, gargled, used the fruit acid, the eye cream, moisturized my face, neck, chest, elbows, cuticles, and finally my legs. I pulled a white cotton Italian nightshirt over my head and brushed my blond hair up into a ponytail. My hair needed a toner. Big time. It was nearly one in the morning. Richard still wasn't home.

I pulled down the bedspread, folded it, and placed it on the blanket rack. I removed the bolster and tossed the four pillows on our queen-size bed—two European squares and two American standards. The crisp linens felt wonderful and I slid between them feeling more tired than I had in ages. Maybe I would read for ten minutes to help me sleep. Maybe I'd go get a glass of wine. Maybe I'd do both. I did neither, but turned off the light and tried to sleep. I watched the blinking and changing minutes of my digital alarm.

It was almost two when I heard the door open. Red alert—she's mad now! Richard was back. Soon he climbed into bed. I didn't flinch a muscle. I smelled something— the unmistakable stench of Opium. He was snoring in less than three minutes. There was only one woman I knew who wore Opium. Lois. I was too tired to kill him. I'd commit murder first thing in the morning.

Miss Lavinia's Journal

I talked to Sweetie and Nancy about Trip and I told them about the money thing and how he wants me to move to the Century City Resort on Hilton Head. They were horrified and now I realize what a fool I have been. I have let myself be taken advantage of for the last time. He owes me a small fortune and I'll move if and when I decide to. Not when he decides! That fortune is Caroline's inheritance as well. I know I should call her tonight and discuss this. I can't do it. I miss Nevil tonight, something fierce.

10

WAKE UP AND SMELL THE OPIUM

2000

There was no good reason I could conceive why Richard should have been out until two in the morning. His absence served as a stinging reminder of his trip to London with Lois during Eric's birth. Still playing games. The lingering scent of Opium in my bedroom made me so mad that all night, I dreamed of murder.

I dreamed of ways to snuff out the breath of my miserable brother, his phylum Sub-humanis wife, and my husband. And, Lois. Oh, the fun I had in my somnambulistic state! The power I felt! I was Blackbeard—Ms. Blackbeard, if you please—slashing away at their greedy wishes, making them pay for their self-serving ways.

In one dream, I dipped my brother in a huge vat of boiling Velveeta and then turned his hunting dogs on him—his Labs love cheese and would kill for it—in this case, they licked him to death. In another, I tied Richard to his desk chair and tossed his first-edition Jung and Freud books into a fire. He hyperventilated into oblivion. Oh, yes! I was in complete control! Ah!—and Frances Mae, my despicable sister-in-law? I held her hair bleach high out of her reach and watched her roots grow at warp speed. Handing her a mirror, I reveled euphoric as she screamed over and over. For an added measure of macabre torment, I told her that Mother had left all her worldly goods to me and that she would get nothing. *Moo-hoo-ha-ha!* She became a puddle at my feet like the Wicked Witch of the West, calling out in anguish, drowning in her sodium-free tears, disappearing forever.

And finally Lois! I summoned her face and slapped it over and over, her head swinging back and forth like a rag doll. The Dominatrix of the Land of Morpheus, wearing a perfect black crepe dinner dress and pearls. After all, these were my dreams, not theirs.

I woke up surprised, half laughing at my creative and brave self, only to face the reality of Richard and Lois first, and remembering I'd have to deal with Trip and Frances Mae all too soon. Not to mention Mother.

I decided to handle Richard with the silent treatment. Making breakfast for Eric in my robe, I fried two eggs for him and microwaved two pieces of bacon. Eric was drinking his orange juice and packing his backpack at the same time.

"Want more juice, sweetheart?" I asked.

Enter Richard.

"Good morning, everyone! Do we have any bagels?"

He delivered a salutatory peck on my cheek. I said nothing. The spousal chill.

"Something wrong, Caroline?"

"Eric? Would you tell your father that the bagels are in the freezer next to the bottle of Opium?"

"Pop? Mom says—"

"I heard her." Richard sighed one of those sighs that says, *Why me? Why do I have to deal with this? I married her, didn't I? Yes, I suppose . . .*

Eric shrugged his shoulders and took the plate of eggs and bacon to the table to inhale. I stood with the spatula in my hand and rubbed the corner of my eye with the other hand, suggesting complete indifference. I threw in a small yawn to make sure my annoyance was absorbed into his thick sponge of a brain.

"You know, Caroline," Richard said, reaching in the bag of frozen bagels and popping one off, "I think you're a bit paranoid. Would you like to talk about it?"

Paranoid?

"Don't patronize me, Richard. Are you going to tell me that you didn't go to Lois's house last night?"

"No. I went there to see my son—"

"*Other* son," I said, reminding him of how insensitive he was.

"This would be my cue for departure," Eric said and dropped his plate and fork in the sink. "Take cover. Incoming!" he said on his way out the door.

"Wait here, Sigmund," I said to Richard, "I'll be right back." I hurried to the door and found Eric waiting at the elevator. "Eric? Don't mind your father. This is about him and me. Not you. Okay?"

"Sure, Mom," he said, but the familiar pain was clear in his eyes, "I know that. Every time I get around Harry it's always that pack-order alpha-male thing with him. He can't help it. Neither can Dad."

"I love you, Eric, so very much. Wait, I'll walk with you."

"It's okay, Mom. I'm walking with a million people," he said and hugged me. The elevator door opened and he all but jumped in. As the door was closing I heard him say, "You're the best, Mom!"

"So are you!" I said, calling out as the door closed with the bing of a bell.

I turned and faced my apartment door. I should say *our* apartment door, but at the moment I didn't want to think of sharing. I went in and closed it, intending to ignore Richard, because what was the point? He preferred his other son. I knew it, Eric knew it, Lois knew it, and dear, precious, and perfect little Harry knew it and worked it too. They all worked it, including Richard. Harry was a tool and loved it. He was like the little brother of Tony Perkins at the Bates Motel. Harry Bates, just waiting to stab someone through a shower curtain.

I will admit that I tried to sneak down the hall, but good old Richard was waiting for me at the door of the kitchen.

"Shall we talk?" he said, motioning for me to follow him to the living room.

I just looked at him. Not a shred of guilt or remorse on his fifty-year-old face. "I don't have the strength, Richard, to play psychodrama with you this morning. I have a yoga class at ten."

"And I have a very busy morning too. Caroline, I think you know well that I love both of my sons equally."

There he was. Receding hairline, gray at the temples, wire-rimmed glasses, camel-colored cashmere cardigan with woven leather buttons, fresh white shirt, and loose gray flannel trousers. The Jungian King of Denial.

"Nope, I know nothing of the sort," I said, rising to his bait. "And neither does anyone else."

"I can't be held responsible for the opinions of others."

"Of course, but even *you'll* admit it is possible to influence them."

"Perhaps."

"Would it be out of line for me to inquire where you were until two this morning?"

"Was it that late?" He reached in the humidor on the coffee table and began packing his pipe with tobacco.

"Yep."

He cleared his throat, tried to look boyish, and said, "I didn't realize, but with the weather and all, it was impossible to get a taxi."

"Right. That's why you came to your marital bed reeking of your ex-wife's vile Opium. No cabs. Gee, I knew that."

"Caroline, she merely gave me an innocent kiss on the cheek as I left." I wasn't buying that load of malarkey and he saw that when I cocked my head to the side and pursed my lips, blinking my eyes to say, *Right, honey. I fell off the turnip truck yesterday.* I tried to get past him but he blocked my passage. He grabbed me by the arm in anger and just looked at me. The rage was there, right under his civilized surface.

"Let go of my arm, Richard."

He jerked it loose, sending it around the front of my body. "I just want to talk, Caroline. I don't want to fight."

"Then quit lying to me. Better yet, quit lying to yourself and everyone else." Why did he get angry with me when he was wrong? I wasn't taking it this time.

"Just what is that supposed to mean?"

"Look, you want to talk? Let's talk." I pushed by him and sat in his favorite chair. Waiting. He watched me, taken back that I'd have the nerve to take his spot. He then took a seat opposite me. Silence. "So, tell me how you happened to come in so late with that rarest of all fragrances clinging to you like a virus. Nothing like a little Eau de Ex to boost a girl's confidence in her husband."

"Caroline, I know you're jealous of Lois and at some

point you're going to have to deal with that. Ever since she moved into the city, you've been out of sorts. Of course, that's perfectly normal, given the circumstances. But I'd like to assure you that you have nothing to be jealous about. In fact, I'm flattered by it."

"Richard, we're not going there, dear. No, we're not. What we're talking about is your fidelity. And the hour of your return. And the unmistakable scent of Lois, who's perpetually on the prowl to get you back, which is why she moved to Manhattan in the first place! And the way you constantly deride Eric. Words hurt, Richard, and so does a lack of them."

"My fidelity is unquestionable, Caroline. I got home late because I fell asleep on our couch."

"Our?"

"Sorry, her couch. But, I was sitting on it with Harry. We had just finished reading his application essay to Choate, the fire was warm, I had drunk two cognacs, there was an old movie on . . . I guess I fell asleep. Lois had gone to bed earlier, and then Harry turned in as well. I guess he thought I'd wake up. Anyway, at some point, Lois came out and woke me. All very embarrassing, you know. When I left, she gave me a peck on the cheek."

"She probably put melatonin in your drink."

"Perhaps. I wouldn't put it past her. And as to my remarks in front of Eric. Look, I don't want to hurt him. I truly love our son. I do. But you must admit that you baby him and I am left in the unfortunate position to be the tough one."

"I don't baby him, Richard. I show him that I care about him."

"Look, Caroline, let's face facts, darling. Shall we?"

"I'm all in favor of that," I said, thinking any minute I

was going to rise from his chair and strangle him with my bare hands.

"Eric has limits. Harry is rather, well, a superstar."

"What?"

"Harry is going places in this world, and living with Lois is enough to make him fail and never get anywhere. Boarding school would be a blessing for him. I try to step in when I can and lend a hand. That's all."

"No, Richard, that's not all. Eric isn't perfect, to be sure, but he's very bright and happens to have had a fine-motor disability that prevented him from writing all that's in his head. But he's been doing really great and you know it!"

"I'll admit that he is vastly improved."

"Harry is practically sociopathic. He hasn't been here once in ten years when he hasn't tried to hurt Eric and then lied about it until the cows come home. I hope he gets into Choate. Maybe they can teach him how to behave."

"He probably will. His chances are excellent. I have a colleague on their board." He could see me bristle at his Old Boys' Network. "All children lie, Caroline. It's part of their developmental growth of self-protection."

"Richard?"

"Okay, I admit it. Harry can be difficult. But you must admit, he's brilliant."

"So is Eric!"

Richard lit his pipe and examined my face, saying nothing at the assertion that Eric and Harry were intellectual peers.

"Because we have a screwed-up educational system, a kid like Harry will get to go to one of the best boarding schools in the country and Eric is in special ed! It's not right!"

"You wouldn't want Eric to go away to school anyway, Caroline!"

"That's not the point! Look, maybe Eric's not a genius, but he's extremely bright. More importantly, he's also sensitive, loving, and generous, and your attitude is hurting him. If you can't see that, I don't know how you got a license to practice head medicine."

"If you think I'm hurting him then I will try to be more cognizant of that and attempt to be more sensitive. So what else is on your mind? I can see that you're troubled. You have this provincial puritanical belief that you must bear your burdens alone."

Cognizant. I love it when he's cognizant! Provincial? Why was I always wrong? *Puritanical?* It was one of the most maddening features of his personality—this ability to shift blame. He had done it again. But, maybe he was right.

"Nothing," I said. I wanted to say, *Why don't you do something provincial like take your cognizant and stick it up your puritanical ass, buddy?* Obviously, I'd been watching *The Sopranos* too much.

"Come on, Caroline," he said in that voice he usually only used when naked, "tell me what's bothering you. I don't want you to carry your sack of stones by yourself."

I was suddenly aware of the light behind him. It came streaming down through the window and the bleak grayness of the late February morning like razor-thin shards of spring promise. For some reason I believed that he was not fooling around with Lois and that he did truly love Eric as much as Harry. At least it was what I wanted to believe—what I needed to believe. I wanted to tell him everything to lighten my heart and ease my mind.

"It's Trip," I said.

"Ah," he said.

"Exactly," I said, shaking my head back and forth, acknowledging his instantaneous understanding. "And, it's Mother."

"Ah, well," he said, arching his eyebrows and looking way too amused for my money. "What bit of naughtiness has my mother-in-law found her way into now?"

"Trip is such an asshole," I said.

"True," he said, waiting, as if to say, *But that's not the answer to my question.*

"He thinks she's sleeping with Jenkins."

"That's absurd. Interesting, but absurd."

"He thinks she's losing her marbles."

"Who knows? He may be losing his."

"As if he ever had any," I said. "But here's the kicker. He says he's going to have her committed to an institution." I went on to explain how it was possible for him to actually get away with it and Richard was visibly horrified.

"Good God, Caroline," was all he said for what seemed like a long time. "Well, you simply can't allow that to happen. Plain and simple."

"What am I supposed to do about it? I live a thousand miles away, I have a husband, a son to care for, and a business to run!"

He looked at me like the doctor again. "It's perfectly normal for a daughter to resent this kind of imposition, especially given your relationship—or lack of a relationship—with Lavinia through the years. But, Caroline, she is your mother and you are her only other child. You can't stand by and watch her be robbed of her independence without at least looking into it."

I got up and opened the rest of the curtains, continuing the morning rituals, trying to avoid Richard for a moment, trying to anticipate what he would say next. "What are you thinking?" I said.

He got up from the chair and smiled at me. "I'm thinking that you have to go see for yourself," he said. "Besides, you haven't been down there in almost a year."

"Eighteen months," I said.

"A lot can happen in eighteen months," he said. "I can keep the boy . . ."

"Eric," I said.

"Eric," he said with emphasis and a suspicious smile. "Look, it would be good for the two of us to have some time and it would be better for you to be free to spend your time with Lavinia."

"Well, I know you're right. I'll think about it." *At least Eric can keep an eye on you and that tramp ex-wife of yours while I'm gone.* Thank God he couldn't read my mind. "Maybe, just for a few days."

Miss Caroline's Journal

I am so worried about Mother. Something is definitely off-kilter and I know it. I'm haunted that Trip is up to no good and Mother is his target. What can I do even if she is? Sure, I talk to Mother a lot on the phone, but if I try to bring up something unpleasant in the slightest, she doesn't listen to me! She's so stubborn and bullheaded. She won't hear that Eric is anything short of perfection and if she knew half the things I think about Richard, she'd pitch a fit. If she knew about the night at Lois's, she'd burst into flames! Thank God I'm like my father. I'm pretty calm by nature. And, I don't want to get involved in a bunch of sibling junk with Trip. I have enough issues to handle as it is. I'm just gonna go for a look-see and then come home and ask Richard to help me figure it all out.

Miss Lavinia Says Her Piece

I gave life to two children in my lifetime and there was never doubt, not even a tiny shred of doubt in my mind, that they both would be the cause of my death. Death by Annoyance and Frustration. That's how I would go. Let's get one thing straight. I did not try to kill Trip with my granddaddy's Parker Old Reliable. I was cleaning it, he was yelling at me from across the yard, and it fired. The shot landed in the live oak tree next to the house, flushing out a flock of pigeons and wrens. I will admit that the girls and I had been out on the courses, killing clay birds, and perhaps we had imbibed a bit of something to ease the glare of the sun. All right. I know I should never drink and handle a shotgun. But this would've happened if I'd been drinking lemonade. An accident, you hear me?

Trip left the house this evening to drive on back to Walterboro where he lives with that wife of his and three of the most squeaky clean and insipid children I have ever seen in all my days—and just how many days I've seen is nobody's damn business. He has been fussing around here like I don't know what—F. Lee Bailey or some detective looking for evidence, digging into my business. Well, I am going to put a stop to it for once and for all. I just have not yet figured out the course of action to take. But I will.

Why, just this afternoon he started up with me again. We were sitting on the back porch drinking a tall glass of sweet tea in my beautiful water glasses I brought home from Ireland years ago. I remarked to him that it was a lovely South Carolina day and that soon the Confederate Jasmine would be in bloom and how I dearly loved the smell. I knew damn good and well he was itching to put his boat in the river and go fishing but I was determined to make him stay and visit with me for a few minutes. I would not be treated like the harbor captain of a marina. So I decided that he would just have to sit for a short spell whether he liked it or not. He did not.

He was particularly contentious in that he declined to split a brownie with me and I knew they were his favorite. I tried to make light conversation and to be pleasant. So I said to him, "Son, what do you plan to catch today?"

"Nothing if I keep sitting here," he said.

Well! I thought that was extremely rude and unnecessary so I said, "Darlin', I would never dream of holding you here or anywhere against your wishes. I am so sorry if there's someplace you'd rather be. Truly, I am."

Well, that got his goat. He got up and walked the full length of the porch, expelling a sigh from his nose, which by the strength of it, in my mind seemed like a fire-breathing dragon. Gave me a good giggle, but I held my peace. When he came back to where we were sitting he leaned over and gave me a kiss on the cheek.

"Sorry, Mother. That came out wrong."

"Of course it did," I said, "it's all right."

"So, Mother? Would you like to share with me just how you managed to scrape your knees, hands, and face?"

"It is the height of all rudeness, Trip, to comment on another's misfortunes."

"Why did I know you'd say something like that?"

"Sweet boy, I don't mean to frustrate you, but I don't wish to discuss it."

Don't you know that he sat with me for five more minutes and then went straight inside to Millie and she told him the whole story? In all my days! Such impudence! Such betrayal! And no conscience about it either! I never should have allowed him to become a lawyer! It only served to encourage him to be the unfortunate way he had become and allowed him to justify his most ungenteel behavior under the guise of caring about his poor old—so old she's half dead—mother.

They say I am irascible, but I was well within my rights when I called him last night and read him the riot act. He still wants me to consider moving into a retirement community! Oh, yes! He made a grand speech! He went on and on about how beautiful they are and how I'd make new friends. Then he pussyfooted around about how inconvenient it was for his poor pregnant wife to be constantly burdened to check on me and how they would soon have four children and their house was too small. Did he think for one split second that I couldn't see through him? I told him he was completely insane. And that where I lived and how I spent my time was none of his affair. And for good measure I reminded him that it wasn't my fault Frances Mae was pregnant! Again! What nerve!

And this money-borrowing thing of his has simply got to stop. He wanted another ten thousand dollars! I said to him, Dear boy, you must think Mother prints it in the basement! He did not even smile at my clever remark (as we do not have a basement), but, in fact, looked slightly annoyed. When I asked him again what it was for, he became visibly anguished. I don't give a toot. I'm not giving him any more money until he tells me what's going on.

Don't think I didn't take care of Millie's bahunkus either. When I realized she had blabbed on me and the girls, I went straight to her in the kitchen. She was just as calm as could be, humming a little tune and polishing my mother's Strasbourg silver flatware, which had been given to her mother before her by a dear family friend descended from Robert E. Lee himself on the occasion of her marriage. Well, alright, I got it through Neiman Marcus online, but who needs to know that?

"Millie?" My voice sounded shrill. Her eyebrows shot up. There was nothing more offensive than a lady with a shrill voice unless, of course, it was a natural, God-given sound. And then it honestly could not be helped.

"Yes'm, Miss Lavinia?" She continued to work without raising her eyes to meet mine.

"Millie? Is there a reason why you are avoiding my eyes?"

She carefully put down the silver and took off her rubber gloves, placing them beside the pile of forks, knives, and spoons. She took a deep breath, put her hands on her hips, and looked at me square in the face. God's Bible, those eyes of hers could be unnerving, but after all the years we had been together, I had adjusted to her and her ways.

"Well? Say something, damn it!" I said.

"Miss Lavinia? If you don't want me telling your boy the truth, get yourself another woman to run your business! You don't pay me enough to lie before the eyes of God."

"Is this about money?"

It was a vulgar question and I regretted it the very second the words left my mouth.

"No, ma'am, it is *not* about money. If you don't want people talking the story about you then you need to behave better."

Well, we were both plumb, hopping mad. I really didn't blame her, but I couldn't excuse her traitorous deed either. Besides, she didn't scare me. I slammed my hand down on the table so hard that it stung like mad.

"You're fired!" I said.

"I ain't fired and you know it! Who else gone put up with you?"

"I will not have you telling tales on me to my children!"

She put her hands down on the table and spoke to me in a quiet tone, the kind used when trying to talk a madman into coming off the window ledge.

"Then don't give me no tales to tell. If Mr. Nevil were still alive, God rest his blessed soul, he would take a switch to your fanny for using a shotgun and drinking bourbon at the same time. Now you go on and let me finish my work or I *will* quit, and then what will you do?"

She was right. With her whole career consumed by the care of my children, my home, and yes, me, it was plain for any fool to see that I should've been more grateful. I decided to be gracious and let her win this round.

"Oh, Millie! I am sorry. Truly. Can you forgive an old woman?"

"You ain't old, but you're certainly making us all old!"

"Well?"

"Oh, all right. Why don't you go have a nap and I'll call you in an hour."

I just turned and walked away. In my mother's day, her housekeeper would never have spoken to her like that. Anyway, Millie wasn't a housekeeper, but my estate man-

ager. Also, my mother never had a woman like Millie.
Millie would have dressed down the Pope and the President themselves if she thought they needed it.

I climbed the steps to the second floor, thinking a cool
bath and a short nap might be just the thing to revive me.
Millie. She always knew exactly the right thing to do.
Bless her heart.

I just adored escaping to my bedroom. It faced a long
stretch of the Edisto River. From my windows I watched
the sunrise and in the evening I would go out onto my
terrace as it slipped into Mother Nature's pocket for the
night. Nevil had restored the suite of rooms for me years
ago. It had a lovely large bedroom, a very ample dressing
room, and the most beautiful bathroom we could conjure
up at the time.

He always understood my little indulgence for shoes and
had built a special sliding storage area that held all two
hundred pairs in their original boxes and acid-free paper.
Every pair was photographed and the picture was taped to
the end of the box so I didn't have to rummage around to
find what I wanted. Each pull-out shelf was like a pocket
door on rollers and the shoes were stored by color. The
first held all my white and beige shoes, the second reds
and navies. The third held blacks and the fourth was all
sandals, mules, and slippers. Not exactly a Dewey decimal
system, but it worked fine for me.

My collection of shoes was as expansive as my clothes
collection. My mother taught me long ago to buy the very
best that I could afford and make sure it was classic. No
frills or ruffles. Who listens to their mother? I buy one
complete outfit in the spring and another in the fall, and
they are as dramatic as possible. I always have a simple
black dress for each season and I wear my South Sea pearls
every evening for dinner. If I haven't worn something in

two years, I pack it in acid-free tissue and store it. I love clothes and what I wear each day reflects my mood.

The yellow and rose flowered curtains and bedspread of the bedroom were getting old and beginning to fade, but I didn't care a fig about that. The room was exactly as it had been before my darling Nevil left the earth. Oh! What a fabulous lover he was! All right. Maybe not, but oh, he was such an elegant man! When he was in the room my heartbeat picked up and I became giddy with the sheer delight of just sharing the same space with him. Even though Nevil was a perfectionist and a little prissy, being called Nevil Wimbley's wife was the greatest honor I have ever known. I missed him every single minute of the day but I sincerely hoped that he wasn't watching me from above every single minute of the day. I didn't think he would have been too terribly happy about some of the company I had been keeping.

Certainly Trip and Frances Mae weren't pleased about my last boyfriend and I knew it, although they rarely said a word. Was a widow not entitled to a little happiness? Was I supposed to just prune the roses and wait for the Grim Reaper to call for a date? I think not.

When Nevil went to his well-deserved rest and reward, I decided to kick up my heels a little—have a little fun. And if that meant having a younger man at my side, what was the harm in that? Men did it all the blessed time!

My friends thought Raoul was perfectly wonderful. He was as handsome as he was virile. Trip thought he was a common gigolo. Oh, yes! I knew what he thought! Trip and Frances Mae were much more concerned about their *inheritance* than my happiness. Don't think I didn't know that!

Now if he knew the truth about how I had scraped my-self up he would rant and rave until he barked like a fox with a bushy tail. I was wearing those damnable Italian trousers Mr. Armani made and the heel of my new J. P. Todd's got caught in the cuff when I went to jump down from the quail buggy. I hate cuffs! Does anyone think that my son doesn't take a cooler of Heineken on the boat when he fishes? Lord! This double standard! How did a woman like me ever blow breath into such a prude?

Well, we all had our crosses to bear, like my mother used to say. And the opinions and avarice of my son and his disagreeable wife were mine.

At least there was still Caroline, I thought as I filled the tub. She was my only daughter and my other cross. Oh, yes, my Miss Caroline has announced she is coming for a visit. High time too.

I undressed thinking about her and caught a glance of myself in my full-length mirror. Not bad for an old lady, I thought. I could go as far as my slip and no one could tell I was a day over sixty. I made a mental note to myself that if I ever got Raoul back in the sack again to have the room good and dark when I got as far as the slip. My assets were depreciating—taking a trip south, if you know what I mean.

Oh, Raoul! Why did he leave me? Martha Henderson may have more money but I'll bet she never put on a show for him like I did! Raoul loved to watch me undress. I would put on some music, usually Ella Fitzgerald singing Cole Porter, ice some champagne, light the candles, and then set that boy's pants on fire. This was my little secret. In the back of the *New York Times Book Review,* there are all these tapes they sell on how to—you know—be intimate. Let's just say that I was a good customer and a *very* good student. And, I was always as feminine as humanly possible because I know that a man wants to dominate. So I would let him think he did. Gigolo? Of course he was!

But so what? He was worth every penny I ever spent on him.

I poured some tea tree oil into the warm water and tested it with my foot. Too hot. For a moment I considered trying to steal Raoul away from Martha. The thought of his young muscular body and his delicious and never failing—you know—well, it did give one pause. But then I decided to let her have him. I'd had the best Raoul had to offer anyway. At least one hundred times. While the discovery of his infidelity had bruised my ego, I recovered well. Okay, I cried for a week. In all truth, he was an insignificant man, a gardener. He called himself a "landscape architect" and had a truck with the name of his business on the side, but, honey, that was like the garbageman calling himself a "sanitation engineer." We all knew better.

The water was finally cool enough and I stepped into the tub, lowering myself carefully. I would never become one of those old biddies who broke her hip in the tub. How undignified would it be to be carried out by some big burly EMS workers in your birthday suit? Perish the thought!

My thoughts returned to Caroline. For all the money in this world, I could never figure out where I went wrong with her. We just were never close like a mother and a daughter were supposed to be. She was so strong-willed and determined to do things her own way. She must have inherited that all from her father's side of the family.

I squeezed the sponge of warm water across my chest, thinking I would just try to have a nice weekend with her. Maybe I could enlist her support against Trip. But she had never understood me really and it was a terrible loss. When she married a Jewish foreigner, I nearly fainted. I suppose I always thought she would come back here to live.

I never should have allowed her to get her master's degree in business. It was the beginning and end of her. By the time she was twenty-five and had been out of Columbia University for just a short time, she had become hard as nails. Living in New York City did that to even the most genteel and refined people, they always said. Apparently it was true where Caroline was concerned.

And that little fellow of hers! Oh, what a sweet child! There is something so dear about little boys that just makes me want to cry. I declare I wish she had brought him back here to me. How could anyone have ever hoped to raise a decent and well-adjusted child in that awful place?

Lord in His Heaven, I thought as I drained the tub and got out, blotting my bruised and scraped skin carefully. I would just see how it was when she got here and try to take it one day at a time. Maybe I would ask Millie to make a cake in her honor. I creamed my skin with Jergen's body lotion and slipped a crisp white cotton nightshirt over my head. I had three of them, all from Victoria's Secret.

I would venture a guess that my eyes were shut in three minutes. The breeze felt so good coming in through my windows. I could smell Nevil's cologne. I guessed that since Raoul was out of the picture, Nevil was stopping by. I always knew when he was with me. It was a great comfort.

My daughter was coming for a visit. That made me happy. Truly, it did. But if she said one word to me or took Trip's side on this retirement community business, I'd fix her little red wagon and fix it good!

12

"PLANET LAVINIA—RETROGRADE"

The world transformed before my eyes as the Continental Airlines plane broke through the thick blanket of clouds and circled the Charleston Airport. From my window seat I watched the waters of the rivers rise up into view. Turbid on their edges, pristine in their heart. These three rivers flowing together pooled at St. Helena Sound. Morgan Island, Otter Island, Edisto, and St. Helena Island. All of them. Fripp, Hunting, and Harbor Islands. I knew them all better than the birthdays of my best friends.

I took a quick breath in and murmured *Home.* Home! *What?* New York was home! Richard and Eric were home! New York was where I belonged. The ACE Basin had not been home for fifteen years! And it could never be home again.

What it *was,* I was willing to admit, was a beautiful place. A starting place. There was simply no resisting the impact of its majestic kaleidoscope of wetlands, waterways, and salt marshes, all of it breathing and pulsating with life. That much was absolutely true. Its beauty was staggering.

For all sorts of reasons, the ACE frightened me—gave me terrible dreams. I had lost my father there. I had fractured and fragile relationships with Mother and Trip that were easier to handle from a distance. I couldn't bear the company of Frances Mae for more than a short visit. I had so little in common with any of them.

Most of my old friends had moved away to Atlanta, Charlotte, or even California and Richard wouldn't like them anyway. No, I couldn't get involved—the emotional price I'd have to pay was too high. Besides, New York thrived with another kind of energy—an excitement that fed something in me, some kind of need.

Then there was Mother's family's home at Tall Pines Plantation. There are as many stories about my mother's family home as there are about the plantation land itself. Tall Pines Plantation held so much natural beauty that it stunted your own growth. Whatever beauty you possessed was smothered by the blinding sunrises and the sighs of red sunsets, all of them over glistening water—water washing the edges of the habitats of hundreds of birds. The perfection of the ACE Basin and every aspect of its natural purity only served to punctuate your flaws. How could you measure up?

It was a merciless trap—an insidious joke of some horrible devil to make you lazy, boring, lethargic, an imbecile—one I had escaped with wild desperation. And, one where I knew I would never return for any reason other than to visit. No. I was merely here to check on Mother, as was my duty. I would do my duty and return home to New York.

I would be cordial to Trip, Frances Mae, and Mother. I would take Richard's advice and remain calm. Richard had given me an arsenal of chemical weapons—Xanax, Valium, Prozac. I would not need them. I would meditate each day, do my yoga, and tai chi. I was ready. And I consoled myself with the forty-five–minute drive I'd make before I had to face any of them at Tall Pines. It would give me the chance to center myself.

I was feeling sentimental as the plane rolled up to the jet way. I was remembering when the Charleston Airport was a little white building with a tiny tower and one man who announced all the planes over the crackling microphone in his old Charleston accent. *Can'a have yo tenshun, please! Tha plane frum New Yak coming to gayet fo!* Maybe we had exaggerated it over the years, but the retelling of that silly story (and thousands of others like it) was about the only thing that would put a smile on my sister-in-law's face during cocktails. Sweet nuggets of the past—the kind Southerners loved to chew.

My tote bag fit snugly under the seat and my rolling carry-on rested perfectly in the overhead. I never had to worry about someone else taking my luggage. It was too weird. Purple canvas, black leather. T. Anthony on Park Avenue had long been manufacturing a line of canvas bags trimmed with leather. Purple made it easy to spot in the rare event that I did check it.

I got my things together and walked through the small airport to the rental car desk. Along the way I passed displays of sweetgrass baskets and the gift store whose windows were filled with displays of benne seed candy, T-shirts, more baskets, and various pieces of china and trays decorated with magnolias in full bloom. I had to admit that I liked the familiar.

I stepped up to the desk and showed my paperwork to the reservations agent. "I have a reservation," I said, "Levine is the last name."

"Oh, Ms. Levine, we are so-o-o sorry! There are jess no cars left. No, ma'am, not nary a one."

She wasn't sorry in the least. She mistook me for a Yankee.

"But I have a reservation," I said, just as calmly as a clam, "there must be some mistake."

"No, ma'am, there's no mistake. Ya see? This yanh is *tha* weekend of the *Bridge Run*? In addition to the big golf tournament out to Kiawah? They just plum overbooooked and there's jess nuthin' a-tall I kin do about that."

"I'd like to see your supervisor," I said. Hell, I'd fried bigger fish than this little pipsqueak from nowhere with the bad perm. I opened my wallet and pulled out the magic card. The one that guaranteed me a car even in times of nuclear attack. I was something of a big shot with Hertz. It was all that fabric I ordered on my American Express card that got me special privileges with Hertz. At least I was a big shot with somebody.

She took the card, looked at it, sneered just a little, and said, "I'll be *rat* back."

The balding, paunchy supervisor appeared in a few moments, the last vestiges of french fries and coffee covering his breath like a light blanket of toxic waste snow and said, "Well, little lady, I reckon I kin gi-view my Taurus. Givus about ten minutes to clean her up." His name tag read Cephus Jones.

"That will be fine, Mr. Jones," I said, "thank you. I really appreciate it."

"Them's the rules, Ms. Lee-vine."

Whatever, I thought, *you big, fat, stupid, ugly ass.* I always felt better when I cussed people out in my mind.

It was Friday, March tenth. Trip had offered to pick me up but I had declined. I knew he really didn't want to do it. In any case, I preferred having my own car—an escape valve. Mother was less than thrilled to hear that I was coming for a visit, but I think that by the time of our last telephone call, she was almost looking forward to it.

"You're not coming down here to reprimand your mother, are you? It's the height of all disrespect to correct your elders," she had said to me last night.

I couldn't tell if she was kidding or if she knew that Trip was after her. "I hadn't planned on it," I lied, "is there any reason I should?"

"Well, I have my bridge club tomorrow. I'm the hostess."

"Mother, have your bridge club, I'll take a nap."

"Fine then," she had said, pleased that I wouldn't upset her routine. "I'm happy you're coming, Caroline, I've missed my girl, you know."

"Me too," I had said.

Like all adult children returning home, I was filled with a curious mixture of anticipation and dread. But in my case, there was usually good cause for the dread. I loaded my luggage into Mr. Jones's Ford and took off for Route 17 south.

I wondered what I would find. Trip would no doubt get drunk and tell me how it was my job to see about Mother because that's the job of a daughter—an arcane belief if ever there was one. Frances Mae would ask me how much my jacket cost and remark on my haircut and then ask me if I'd brought something from New York City for her spoiled rotten, ungrateful children. Yeah, muzzles, I would love to say. And one for you too. I could see her bony fingers with her French manicure lift a piece of Mother's silver and ask her what she intended to do with it when she was gone. In a bizarre way I looked forward to it all. *When in doubt, retreat to the familiar.* Even if it's a nest of crocodiles?

I cruised around for the Breeze radio station, the one that only played beach music, found it, and rolled down the highway on top of the Swinging Medallions. I definitely needed a double shot, but not of my baby's love. Oh, God, I would just get there, try to stay out of arguments, see what was really happening to Mother, and then I would return to New York.

It didn't take long until I lost radio reception and turned it off. The quiet brought me to a contemplative place. I opened the windows and the old familiar smells rushed in to greet me like ghosts. Pine mixed with the loamy smells of the earth. Soon the car was occupied by more spirits and memories than there were pecans in the grove Daddy and I had planted when I was just a little girl. I began to relive that sweeter time.

We had ten saplings with their roots wrapped in burlap lined up like soldiers on the flatbed of Daddy's pickup truck. We drove out to the clearing and my daddy showed me how to plant a tree. I don't know where Trip was that day—he may have even been there—but in my memory, it was only Daddy and me. He had prepared the land over the past two weeks.

First, he had had Jenkins and four other men clear it of trees and bushes. There were loblollies and some other pines, which were the main population of this chosen acre. Next, Jenkins had disked the land by pulling the blade behind his tractor to turn up the earth about three or four inches, clearing it of grass and small plants. Finally, he used a drag harrow to smooth out the land. Every evening I would ride out with Daddy to check the progress. We had great discussions about where to plant them and how deep the holes needed to be. By the time the day arrived to actually put the plants into the ground, I knew more about the planting of Schley Paper Shell pecans than anybody in the third grade. I knew that one square acre should hold nine to eleven trees, that the holes had to be dug down two and one-half to three feet and that the long taproot had to be planted fully extended. I also knew they were thirsty and that this meant Daddy and I would have many opportunities to go out in the cool of the evening to water them for the first year.

I remembered riding on the tractor with Jenkins as it bumped along the ground. The tractor seat was so high off the ground and I was so small that Daddy had to lift me high in the air for Jenkins to take me from him. I loved the taste of pecans and I envisioned us soon cracking nuts together. I learned that these trees would not bear nuts until I was long gone to college. And it was in those next twelve years that we lost Daddy in a small plane accident.

That thought of Daddy and how we were robbed of him lingered as I drove on toward Tall Pines. It was time to focus on what awaited me. Maybe things would go well. Maybe Mother was fine. Maybe Trip had matured. Maybe Frances Mae was less materialistic. Maybe blonds had more fun. Sure. Dream on.

I was so deep in thought that I nearly missed the turn for Parker's Ferry Road, but caught it at the last second. In minutes, I was passing the Penny Creek Landing, the Shiloh Baptist Church, the New Bethlehem AME Church and the infamous Blue Garden Social Club. On my right were other plantations—Prospect Hill, Wilton Bluff, the Hermitage—and finally, the wall that ran the length of the front of my mother's property came into view.

The foundation was made of bricks, all of them hand-made over one hundred and fifty years ago. Short columns rose up at regular intervals of about twenty feet. In between the columns and resting on the base stood beautiful wrought-iron fencing, each one of its thin spears twisted like taffy with sharp arrowheads on their tops—the kind you shouldn't jump.

I pulled into the private road of Tall Pines and entered the pass code to open the gates. The ancient gates were filled with wrought-iron ducks, turkeys, and pine trees. I used to think the gates were stupid and now I saw them as extraordinary. They swung open and I passed slowly down the avenue of Spanish moss–draped live oaks, bumping along the hard-packed earth. In between the oaks were stands of azalea bushes and palmetto trees and clusters of low-lying camellias.

Mother's whole property was naturalized over the years, planned and executed to appear as if it were designed by God, not man. The only part laid out in a formal design was her rose garden. On either side of the road were acres and acres of beautiful land, old rice fields and cotton fields, now transformed into bird-killing and clay-smashing heaven.

Several ponds sprung up here and there, edged by shocks of the last vestiges of her azaleas, pampas grass with its white plumage, and cypress trees whose roots' tannic acid turned the water brackish. At last my car crossed Duck Tea Bridge and the house came into view.

Tall Pines, the undisputed queen of all antebellum plantation homes in the Lowcountry. She had begun life as a simple farmer's house. Two stories, a classic floor plan of four rooms downstairs and four upstairs. The original kitchen was a separate house in the yard with a walkway leading to the main house. There was a good reason for it to be separate. Back in the nineteenth century they had not yet perfected the fine art of chimney construction, so about once every couple of years the kitchen fires would send hot ashes up the chimney to the cypress-tiled roof and the whole thing would burn to the ground.

By the time my great-grandmother was born, two wings had been added to the main house, one of which included an enormous kitchen, pantry, and laundry facility. Each of the two wings had long windows to match the ones that crossed the front and back of the original house. Wide columned porticos were added all around, which gave the house a new personality, one that said, "I'm big, I'm beautiful, and I'll be around when you're long gone."

Tall Pines's foundation was brick, made from local clay, its walls were cypress, and the roof had been changed from cypress tiles to slate tiles. The entire inside of the house had heart pine floors and my father had added mahogany paneling to his beloved library. Tall Pines was a grand lady. Grand, imposing, and haunted as the day is long. Oh, yes! Haunted!

Tall Pines stood there looking at me as if to say, *And just where have you been, missy?* I got out of the car and looked at her. Once the house got the sense that I appreciated her great beauty and strength, the voice in my head sighed and went away. I'd been back two minutes and I was already talking to the house.

Suddenly, the door opened and Mother appeared on the portico. Her white hair was cut blunt right below her chin and her silk skirt waved in the afternoon breeze. She seemed shorter than I remembered, smaller somehow.

"Hello, Caroline! Do you need help?"

"No, thanks, Mother! I'll come back for my things in a minute." I started up the steps determined to get the visit off on the right foot. "First, I want to have a look at you and give my mother a kiss!" She held her arms out to me and I gave her a hug and a kiss on the cheek.

"Oh!" she yelped.

"What's the matter?" I looked at her cheek again and saw the scrape. "Mother! What happened?"

"Oh, nothing, nothing at all." She began picking up the packages that had come in the mail, which were piled up by the door. "Here, help me bring these inside. You'll have to move your car soon. The girls are coming."

"Mother, tell me what's happened to your cheek. I want to know."

"Oh, it was the most foolish thing. I was jumping down from the quail buggy and my heel got caught in my trouser hem and I fell on my cheek. Scraped the dickens out of my hands and knees too. It could've happened to anyone." She looked at me and her eyes told me to mind my own business.

"Well, you're lucky that's all that happened. Here, give me that." I took another package from her and she continued to stack the boxes high in my arms and she led the way into the house empty-handed. "Mother? What is all this stuff?"

"Caroline? They are life's necessities from various catalog companies. If you think you're coming down here to question me on how I spend my money, you may as well go on back to New York!"

"Good grief, Mother! I just asked a simple question. I'm sorry."

I dumped all the packages on the hall bench. The phone was ringing.

"Fine. Guess I'm a little sensitive. I'm sorry. Didn't mean to bite your head off. Oh, Lord, I'll get it myself," she said and muttered under her breath, "I don't know why I have to be the one to answer the phone all the time. Mrs. Smoak is just too busy and important to do it, I imagine."

"I'll go get my things," I said, but began riffling through the boxes instead. There was one from Barnes and Noble. Another from Saks Fifth Avenue. There were two from

Williams-Sonoma. Under the box from Scully and Scully, I saw an envelope from Victoria's Secret. What was my mother doing ordering from there? Was Trip right? Was Mother going smack off the deep end?

I went out the door to get my things and move the car. The afternoon sun was clear and bright and the air cool and comfortable. It was already spring. The strong smell of pine made me feel like a young girl again. I pulled my luggage out of the car and left it by the steps and then moved the car around to the side of the house where the garage was. Walking back, I found Mother waiting for me on the porch again.

"Do you still play bridge?" she called out to me.

"Not in years, why?"

"Helen has a bad tooth or some such nonsense and can't play. I need you to take her place or else the whole day is ruined."

"Oh, no, Mother! Can't you find somebody else?"

"Not now. It's too late in the day." She smiled at me and I knew my goose was cooked. It was actually a small thing she was asking of me. "You'll have fun," she said. "And I made those little smoked fish sandwiches you like so much. Cucumber too!"

"Oh, fine, bribe me with food. I'll try, Mother," I said, carrying my things up the steps, "but I'm telling you I haven't played since I left home."

She held the door open for me and didn't offer to help. "Just do your best," she said. "Your old room is made up for you. Now go wash your face and put on a nice dress."

"I don't think I brought one," I said under my breath, knowing full and well that I had a dress in my bag.

She ignored me and went back down the hall toward

the kitchen. I climbed the stairs and pushed open the door of my old room and realized that it was still a shrine to my childhood. In all the years that I'd been gone, she hadn't changed a thing.

Miss Lavinia's Journal

It's time for me to dig in my heels and put a stop to all the nonsense in this family.

13

"HUSH UP AND DEAL!"

Airline travel just wasn't what it used to be. It didn't seem to matter if I flew for thirty minutes or twelve hours, I was so tired and felt so completely sticky when the plane landed, all I wanted was to take a shower and go to bed. It was probably all that nasty recycled air. So, it was not on Mother's suggestion but of my own free will that I washed my face like a good girl. I felt better but I wondered just what it was about Mother that made me so belligerent. Hell, I was a grown woman and a mother myself!

Coming out of my bathroom, I looked at my watch. Two–forty-five. I decided to quickly unpack, knowing that Mother was downstairs obsessing over her petit fours and tea sandwiches. I was hanging my jacket when I noticed the photograph of my father and me on the bedside table. I sat down on the side of my old bed with the small silver frame in both hands. The air left my chest in a rush.

I was probably only three or four years old at the time but I remembered the occasion clearly. It was Easter Sun-

day. Daddy was running toward the camera with me
perched high on his shoulders, hanging on to his forehead
for dear life. I stretched out across the bed, kicking my
half-empty suitcase out of the way, and looked at the picture some more. I had his eyes and his chin. I missed him
more than ever. Thoughts of him brought him back to life
if only for the moment. I looked like him and that single
accident of resemblance reassured me I had once belonged
here.

I could've lain right down and gone off to sleep and
dreams but I figured Mother would yank my hair out of
my head if I did. I literally leapt from the bed and decided
to go face the Grand Dame's music. When Miss Lavinia
called for a card game at three, you had better be on time.
Being punctual was at least one thing Mother and I had in
common. Maybe I could find other things and try to build
on them. I put the picture of my father back in its place
and I was feeling so clever and agreeable that I put on a
black linen dress. If that was all it cost to make the old
bird happy, I could live with it.

Before I could get down the stairs, I ran into Millie
coming up the stairs to give me a piece of her mind. The
Sister of Merlin, the Esoteric Empress, the most mysterious of all women—Millie, the Prestidigitator of Tall Pines.

"You don't come to my office anymore and say hello?"
she said, pretending to be insulted. "And yanh I made a
devil's food cake for you? Make it by my own two hand
and you can't come to say hello? Ought to spank your
bottom but good!"

We hugged and started to laugh.

"God, I'm sorry, Millie." She pushed me back to have
a look at what horrors Yankee Territory had delivered in
the last year and a half. "Mother's got me playing bridge

this afternoon and I was rushing to unpack and get dressed."

"Don't call on God like that. Wait till you need him, yanh?"

"Devil's food cake?"

"Yes, ma'am, and ain't that just perfect for a bad girl like you?" She stood now with her hands on her hips and shook her head. "You something else now, girl. You look fine. Even though you can't buy nothing but black."

"So do you, Millie, thanks. And I wear black be- `cause . . . you know what? I don't know why!"

Millie laughed again and said, "Now go on, girl, and help your mother."

Between two minutes to three and one minute after, the doorbell rang twice. I was bringing a platter of food to the dining room when Mother answered the door. I could hear her chatting away. I stuffed a whitefish tea sandwich in my mouth and poured myself a glass of iced tea.

"It's so good to see you! Now where is that darling girl of yours!"

It sounded like Laura "Sweetie" Mahoney and it was. I had known and loved Miss Sweetie to death all my life. She lived on another, smaller plantation and was the most normal of Mother's friends. She, like Mother, was a garden club judge and raised prize-winning roses. She also raised thousands of strawberries every summer and made the best jam I ever tasted. When I was a little girl I used to help her pick them and sort them, eating almost as many as I picked. I'd come home with a red face, sticky hands, and T-shirt all covered with juice from the berries and Millie would give me the dickens. I hadn't seen Miss Sweetie in ten years but I hoped I could depend on her to tell me what was really going on with Mother.

"Miss Sweetie! How are you?" I hugged her.

"Oh, do now! Look at my Caroline! All grown up and so pretty! I brought you something. When your mother told me you were here it was just the best news! I swanny it was!" She handed me a quart jar of strawberry preserves. It had red gingham cloth around the top tied with red ribbon. "Like my label?" The label said, TBDJOTP, STRAWBERRY, MADE BY HAND FROM LAURA MAHONEY'S KITCHEN. "I made it myself on my notebook."

"Notebook? No kidding." And I was expecting a little old lady with a cane. "What does this mean?"

"It means 'the best damn jelly on the planet,' that's what. Don't tell anyone that, though. I wouldn't want it to get around that I use bad words. On occasion only."

"Your secret's safe with me. What kind of computer do you have?"

"Why, a Dell, of course! Got me a LCD screen on my big one at home and so I don't fry these old corneas. And it ain't beige either! It's red! And my traveler only weighs four pounds! Five hundred megs and more RAM than they got in the mountains. It's how I run my business."

"Business?"

"Your mother didn't tell you? When Moultrie kicked the bucket, I said to myself, Sweetie? You ain't going with him just yet, and you need something to keep yourself out of trouble. So I went on down the road to the College of Charleston, took a course in business and another one in computers. This year I'm gonna ship close to ten thousand bottles of jam. That should have been plenty for me, but now I'm thinking pickles."

"Pickles?" My eyes grew wide and hers twinkled. She was thoroughly pleased with herself to be able to shock me with her news.

"Oh, yes, ma'am, there's good money in pickles. Good thing Moultrie is dead 'cause he'd die anyway if he knew how much money I spend on all this technology! Keeps me busy. So tell me everything. How's that precious boy of yours?"

"Oh, Miss Sweetie, Eric's great. Just the love of my life, that's all."

"And Richard?"

"Well, Richard's still Richard."

"Men. I tell you, some days I just scratch my head and wonder just what in tarnation makes 'em tick. Pain in the ass. All of 'em. Let's get us something to eat."

Mother came into the room with her other best crony on her arm, Nancy Cotton, affectionately known as Miss Nancy. She had short blond hair and green eyes, and she looked to be about thirty in her khaki pants and blue shirt. And, she was wearing black Prada loafers with white socks. Very cool.

"Caroline, come say hello to Nancy!"

"Hey, Miss Nancy! How're you?"

"Well, for an old lady I'm still managing to get around. Come give me my kiss, child."

"Miss Nancy! You're not old!" I gave her cheek a light kiss.

"Not so old as your mother!" Miss Nancy said, eyes twinkling with mischief.

"What?" Mother said, "What kind of foolishness are you telling this time, Nancy!"

"*Calm à vous,* Lavinia. A mere chronological tidbit of truth, my dear Lavinia. May I please be fed before I faint?"

"She takes one little trip to France and now she pelts us with her international self every five minutes," Miss Sweetie said.

I offered Miss Nancy the round silver tray of tea sandwiches and she looked suspicious.

"Now, what do we have here?" Miss Nancy said. "Lav-

inia? Are you absolutely determined to ruin my figure? Do
you think I could just have tomatoes on toast? No mayo?"

"Miss Nancy, you can have whatever you want," I said,
"I'll be *rat* back."

"Lavinia?" I heard Miss Nancy say. "How on earth did
an ugly old buh-zard like you give birth to such a beautiful
girl?"

"Hush up and pour me a glass of sherry before she gets
back," Mother said.

"Pour me one too, Mother!" I called out. Hell, I may as
well jump right in, I thought. Did I work for Alcoholics
Anonymous? I didn't think so.

Before long the game was under way. Miss Sweetie was
my partner. Miss Nancy shuffled and dealt the hand, bracelets jangling. I picked up my cards and arranged them.
They were fabulous. I had the ace, king, and queen of
spades, the ace of hearts, the jack, and four others, a void
in clubs, and four decent diamonds. Miss Sweetie opened.

"One diamond," she said.

"Who shuffled?" Mother said.

"I did, Lavinia," Miss Nancy said politely. "It's your
bid, Lavinia, dear."

"Pass," Mother said and sighed hard enough to blow me
off my chair.

"One spade," I said, hoping I was doing the right thing.

"Pass," Miss Nancy said.

"Three hearts," Miss Sweetie said and winked at me.

"That's it!" Mother said. "There will be no signals in
my living room!"

"*Mon Dieu!* Just bid, Lavinia," Miss Nancy said.

"Pass," Mother said and leveled her glare at Miss
Nancy.

Mother's mood had gone sour. I could not believe that
she was actually so competitive and a poor sport to boot!

Needless to say, we kicked their butts to Kalamazoo and by the time five o'clock rolled around, Mother was thoroughly annoyed. It wasn't my fault. I played dummy half of the time anyway and I thought she had won enough hands to save face.

"Will we see you in church Sunday, Caroline?" Miss Sweetie said at the front door.

Mother and Miss Nancy were there too, chattering and giggling, for which I was grateful. Miss Nancy had always been able to shift Mother's moods.

"Oh, yes! Wouldn't miss that sideshow for all the world," I said.

"We have a cute new preacher," Miss Sweetie said, whispering behind her hand to me. "I think your mother's sweet on him! God knows, she hadn't been to church in ten years until this cute young thing showed up!"

"Hush your bad mouth, Sweetie!" Mother said.

"How old is he?" I asked.

"What's the difference if he's willing and able?" she said and stopped on the steps.

"Il est un hot-tay!" Miss Nancy said, wiggling her eyebrows up and down.

"Good Lord, Nancy," Mother said, "I sure hope you don't go to China!"

"Hottie? You girls are bad! Probably wants endowment money," I said, under my breath.

"You don't know your mother well at all, do you?" Miss Sweetie said.

"He's already well endowed," Mother said, mumbling under her breath to her friends.

"Mother!"

"Honey, you can tell by a man's body language what he's got, don't you know that?" Mother said, eyebrows arched.

We all burst out laughing.

"Mother!"

What in the hell was going on here?

"They all want money, Caroline, we know that!" Miss Nancy said. "But we have a list of what we want too! *C'nest pas?*"

I shook my head wondering what my mother and her friends had been up to, while they giggled like a bunch of schoolgirls. We all waved good-bye to Miss Sweetie, who kicked up the dust when she peeled out of our drive in her red Mustang convertible.

"She had to buy a red one?" Mother said.

"Strawberries? Get it?" Miss Nancy said.

"And when she goes in the pickle business I imagine that she'll buy a green one?" Mother said and they began to cluck.

"I imagine so," Miss Nancy said and walked down the drive to her navy BMW.

"Cool," I said.

"Indeed," said Mother with all her attitude and we went inside. "Caroline? Better get some rest. Trip and his gang will be here at seven."

Oh Lord, I thought, what next?

"Prepare for the worst," she said.

"Mother? May I ask you something . . . personal?"

"Maybe. What?"

"Is it true that you had an affair with the gardener?"

"Caroline! Of all the crust!" She looked at me with narrowed eyes. "All right, I'll tell you so you hear the story from the horse's mouth and not from your brother's jaded perspective. Yes, I did. And it was fabulous! For six months Raoul Estevez and I tripped the light fantastic. He wasn't the first and he won't be the last!"

"Mother! You shock me!" I leaned against the living

room door for support. So what Trip had said, at least part of it, was true!

"Caroline! Wipe that look off your face this instant!" She crossed her arms and shook her head. "Child? Haven't you ever read the Constitution?"

"What's that got to do with this?"

"We are *entitled* by our forefathers to the *pursuit of happiness*! Think about it!"

"You're *entitled* to sleep with a man half your age by the *Constitution*?"

"If it makes me happy? Yes! Since when did you become so anal, Caroline? Life's short! Live it, girl! Now, I have to go rest before they arrive."

She patted my arm, gently raised my jaw to meet my upper lip, and went upstairs. I watched her. She had more spring in her step than I did. Pursuit of happiness. Entitled to it. I'd have to give this my full focus. It was a strange but interesting concept.

Miss Lavinia's Journal

Oh, my, it's good to have my daughter here with me! And I think it's going to be good for her too! Lord knows, she's way too serious! That girl needs fun!

14

COCKTAIL TIME

If my daddy had drawn air long enough to know Frances Mae, he would've held his hand to the Bible and declared that Trip would surely die a drunk. If he'd lived to witness the shenanigans of Amelia, Isabelle, Caroline, and Frances Mae combined, he would've recommended plain old murder. That's what Daddy would've done. Because after all, there were just certain kinds of people who could lead you to dive right in the bottle, especially if you were a peace-loving sort of fellow.

That was what Daddy and Trip had in common. Peace-loving good old boys, who knew their place, when to speak, and which topics were considered polite in mixed company. They revered generations of tradition—these things were their Bible. Hunted for sport, never killed more than they could carry. Never overfished. Never broke an oyster bed until it was the season. Mended their own casting nets, cleaned their own guns. They followed a code of honor on the river and in the woods, living like they had the game warden on one shoulder and Jesus on the other.

They stood when Mother or any lady entered the room, held her chair at dinner, and opened every door for her. They never discussed money or the affairs of government in front of ladies. And they never made a vulgar reference with a lady present. For all their refinement, they were as masculine as a man could be. They were gentlemen and gentlemen were expected to marry ladies. What the hell happened to Trip's judgment when he brought home Frances Mae was anybody's guess.

Even Millie had been horrified. Mother, Millie, and I became the Unholy Triumvirate. Behind her back we called Frances Mae everything from *sine nobilitas* and *rapacious* when we were feeling superior, to *hairball* and *mucus* when we had been overserved and the hour was late. We had many names for the Idolater of the Dollar, the Pernicious Peroxided Pretender to the Throne, and the alliterated Jabbering Jacksonboro Jaguar.

In the old days, gentlemen of our family were supposed to marry ladies from another, more sophisticated and worldly society. And ladies of our family did the same. But not Trip and not me. Nope. Richard's résumé may have been bizarre to some, but Frances Mae's was downright scary.

The first time Trip brought her home it caused a major brain spasm in Old Lavinia. For the only time in her life she was without words. It was the summer of 1986. Trip had finally graduated from Carolina Law School and was studying for the bar.

Trip was tooling around town in the new convertible Chrysler Le Baron Mother had bought him as a gift. I was home for a weekend visit from New York and weeding in the garden with Mother when his car came screaming around the front drive.

"What?" Mother said, looking up from the rose bed.

Mother was wearing a huge straw hat to shield her face from the sun and a sundress with an open back so she could tan. I looked up then and saw Trip hop over the side of the car and run around to open the passenger door. It was just like Troy Donahue and what's-her-name from the fifties movies—Sandra Dee or someone.

"On my mother's grave! He's got a young woman with him!"

"I'll be damned," I said.

Trip was not successful with the ladies unless they looked and smelled like Labradors. That car was an apparent asset.

We stood and watched her get out and look at the house. Actually, she took inventory of our family's home, smiling. A chimpanzee with curled-back lips—it was all I could think. You would have thought he'd tossed her the keys to the joint. Next, she threw her arms around Trip and kissed him so hard he fell back against the car, most likely bruising his pelvic bone in the process. He had his hands on her round little backside, rubbing it. Mother turned so red, I thought for a minute she would burst her carotid artery. I was coming undone with surprise and giggles. I knew her. She was the waitress from the coffee shop in Jacksonboro. The waitress with *the lips*. Mother held her hand to her chest. Trip finally had the presence of mind to quit tickling Slut Bubba's tonsils and look up to where we stood. That was the first hello. Some opener!

Mother and I stood rooted in the garden like a couple of overgrown tulips, slack-jawed and burned. Nothing Sherman ever did frightened a woman in our family as much as Frances Mae Litchfield in her tight jeans, white high heels, and tube top. Except for her hair. Bleach! Bleach! Bleach! No! No! No! Women of Mother's family never bleached! Highlight, perhaps. Enhance, maybe. Clorox, never. It was going to get worse before it ever got better. Or get better before it got worse.

Mother started walking toward them and I followed on her heels. I would rather have taken a bullet in my head than miss a syllable.

"Mother!" Trip said, calling out. "Come and meet Frances Mae!"

Even from the back of Mother's head, I could tell her jaw was locked in her Greenwich Grin.

"Hi!" I said, stepping up to them and extending my hand, which hung in midair while she inspected it like a fish on ice. "I'm Caroline."

She finally figured out she was supposed to shake my hand and snapped back to earth. "Hey!" she said. "Yew juss as purdy as your bubba say-ed. Yes, ma'am, yew sho nuff is."

She smiled wide and tossed that mane of layered pseudo Farrah to the left and to the right. She was all of five feet one to Mother's five seven and my five eight. Her accent was so thick it could have had us evicted forever from the Charleston Yacht Club. Her arms never left Trip's waist. "En, yew mussy be Mizz La Viniea," she said to Mother, not realizing that among our friends, her behavior would have been considered having sex in public.

"Let's go inside, shall we?" Mother said. Chill of major magnitude.

"Why not?" said the miniature Barbie, who now took my brother's arm, snuggled up to his side, and made the fatal mistake of taking the front steps before Mother.

I could see Mother's nostrils fill and collapse. Her jaw remained firm and resolute. She would not let this crimsonnecked slut from nowhere steal her baby. That was the first of our many miscalculations about Frances Mae.

Frances Mae Litchfield and James Nevil Wimbley III were married by a justice of the peace in Florence, South Carolina. Mother did not attend. Mother was not invited. Mother took to her bed for two weeks in the greatest of all southern swoons. Even Millie disappeared for a day or two. Trip took Frances Mae to Bermuda.

I was back in New York with Richard when Millie called to tell me I had a sister-in-law. We thought it was a perfectly scandalous event and decided to get married too. What the hell, I thought, after Frances Mae, Richard would look like a prince to the family. Wrong again.

The fact that time flew the Concorde did not escape me. Frances Mae and Trip with their three daughters from hell were coming for dinner. Where had the years gone? And, Frances Mae was pregnant *again*. I looked at the clock. Six-forty-five. In fifteen minutes, their arrival would shroud Tall Pines with the first act of classic southern family dysfunctional drama. It was inevitable.

I opened the French doors in my old room and let the breeze come in. The river smells rushed in on a magic carpet and I took a deep breath. I sat right down on the floor in the lotus position in full view of the Edisto. The Edisto, majestic and musical as it slapped the riverbanks, made a little song for me as it had when I was a child. I closed my eyes and tried to empty my mind. It was good. I saw rushing waves of purple and green pulsating larger and then shrinking away only to be replaced by more floating waves of color. I was alone, in a beautiful breeze without a care in the world.

Somewhere in the distance I heard the door close, like the great jaws of Jonah gulping down a snack. And, like old Ahab, we would all bang around the belly of familial indigestion for the next few hours. I would rise to the occasion and not allow any of them to unarm me. Unarm.

What an odd choice for my expectations of the evening! Boy, was I conflicted or what? Who knew? It could be fun. Maybe Frances Mae had had a lobotomy since I saw her the last time. Meow.

From the hall stairs I could see Trip pouring drinks in the living room. Frances Mae was shrieking in the hall powder room that one little witch of hers had put gum in another little witch's hair.

"Tell her to go to the kitchen and get some ice from Millie," I said. "Freezes it and then you can chip it off."

"Ah, Caroline! Just in time!" Trip handed me a glass of white wine. "Let the healing begin."

We clinked glasses and I sat on the sofa opposite Mother in her chair, taking a small sip.

"Thank you, brother, it's good to see you."

"And you as well, sister. Don't you think Mother looks particularly lovely tonight?"

I looked at Mother and she rolled her eyes. "Freshen my bourbon like a good boy and don't try to fill my head!" Mother said. Despite her feigned annoyance, she smiled at him. He was, after all, the family's Christ child. He took her nearly empty tumbler, offered her a bowl of nuts, and she picked through them for the cashews.

Trip poured and Frances Mae burst in, her baby demons hiding behind her.

"Caroline! How lovely to see you!" she said, and I watched the muscles under her face twitch. Nerves. Who could blame her? I got up to greet her.

"Hey, Frances Mae! How are you feeling?"

"Oh, as well as can be expected, I imagine. My ankles give me such a fit! And my breasts are killing me! Girls, come kiss your aunt!"

Mother coughed at Frances Mae's reference to her breasts.

As if on cue the girls ran away, out the front door and down the steps, slamming everything. Giggles and screams.

"They are so bad," she went on. "I try, but your brother here just won't switch 'em. When I was a little girl, my daddy beat the stinking slop out of me if I didn't behave! I'll go get them." She smiled and left to fetch her, as she would say, "younguns."

"Stinking slop," Mother said in a faraway voice. "How utterly picturesque."

"What you mean, Mother, is how lacking in gentility, how unrefined?"

"Hey, y'all, let's cut her some slack tonight, okay? When I go back to New York, y'all can autopsy me too," I said.

They stopped and looked at me. It was an uncommon moment of support for Frances Mae. I felt a little sorry for her. She had gained at least thirty pounds and her outfit, from a garage sale in a tacky neighborhood, teetered somewhere in fashion maternity hell. And, as usual, she had neglected to blend her lip liner, so that her mouth gave the appearance of a mackerel. I knew my thoughts were unkind, even mean, but, God in heaven! She stood out in such loud contrast to everything around her, I truly had a struggle to hold them back. I glanced at Trip, who read my mind. He took a long drink and turned to pour another for himself. He raised it to me and suddenly I was a little annoyed with him and with Mother.

"I'll be right back," I said, "I want to see my nieces."

I opened the front door and looked across the yard. It was one of those Carolina nights that makes you glad to be alive. Low humidity. Beautiful intermittent breezes. The smells of flowers. I walked around the gravel drive to the left side of the house and toward the river, following the sounds of their voices. From the distance I could see Frances Mae straightening Amelia's hair and retying her bow. I stopped to watch for a moment. All three girls wore tea-length sundresses. My two little nieces, Isabelle and Caroline, had puffed shoulders and sashes. Amelia's dress was different because she was, after all, thirteen. Nonetheless, the little girls had perfect blunt, chin-length haircuts, parted on the side, with a hank of their hair rubber-banded and tied over with a large satin bow. Except Amelia, who wore a headband. From where I stood, they looked like three lively angels, all innocence and light. I knew better.

The crickets were clattering away in the woods and lightning bugs glittered all around. Frances Mae had sunk into a lawn chair and put her feet up. She was trying her hardest, she always had. It wasn't her fault really that she always said the wrong thing or did the wrong thing. And, to her credit, her English had improved and her accent softened. A little. Trip wasn't complaining so why should I? No, Trip was just a challenge to his liver, that's all.

"Frances Mae!" I called out, "I thought I'd come out here and watch Three Mile Island burn off a little steam."

"Oh!" She looked puzzled but glad to have the company. "I declare, Caroline. You look so thin and elegant. I just feel so fat and ugly."

"You are not fat and ugly," I said, "not even a little bit." I put my hand on her shoulder and I saw her eyeball my wristwatch.

Exactly like Mother, she released a long sigh. "Is that a real Cart-tee-ay watch?"

"Yes. Actually, I bought this for myself for my thirtieth birthday."

She looked longingly at it and then at me. "I don't believe your brother would ever do something so grand for me."

She sounded so sad that I almost fell for it. "Frances Mae? You're missing the point."

"Oh, Caroline, I'm sure I am not missing the point. You may have bought it for yourself because you have a job. You have your own money. My job is to be a good mother to Trip's children, a loving wife, and a good daughter-in-law to y'all's mama. I love my job but the pay's scarcer than hen's teeth."

"Well, we'll have to put a bug in Trip's ear for Christmas or something." It was the first time I looked at the world from her point of view in maybe ever. But, I also knew that women who played the victim usually chose it through some passive-aggressive desire to illicit pity and admiration. At least that was what Richard always said. Maybe I'd been married to a shrink for too long. It annoyed me that she still hadn't asked about Richard or Eric.

"Good luck, honey, he's a wonderful man but he could squeeze the balls off a buffalo nickel."

I winced at the thought of bovine genitalia. "Trip? Cheap?"

"Are you serious? He squeaks! Look at me! Do I look like the wife of a rich man? Why, Trip Wimbley spends money on three things—hunting, which includes dogs, fishing, which also includes dogs, and betting on football. If the washer breaks down . . . oh, Caroline, I know I shouldn't talk ugly about Trip. He's a wonderful husband and I love him with my whole heart, but we are gonna burst out of our house when this baby comes. I can't bring home a toothpick and find a place for it."

I hadn't been to their house in Walterboro for several years, but I could imagine that she was right. She obviously spent whatever money Trip gave her on the girls and their clothes. Their house had only three tiny bedrooms.

"Come on, Frances Mae"—I offered her an arm to pull

her up—"we'll call California Closets tomorrow. Tell Trip I made you do it."

"Oh, my! Bless your heart! What a wonderful idea!"

"Thank you," I said, "now, let's get those little torna-does of yours up to the house and ready for Millie's dinner and Miss Lavinia's table."

The girls came when we called them away from their game of swing the statue and followed us like ducks in the twilight. Frances Mae continued to coddle them, fuss-ing over their appearances. Suddenly, I realized she was probably petrified of Mother. And, of Trip. And not too sure about me.

"Let them go on ahead, Frances Mae; I want to ask you something."

"Why sure, Caroline. Y'all girls go on now and wash your hands. I'll be there directly."

The girls slammed the door behind them and we stood on the porch. In the evening light she didn't look or seem so dangerous. I only had one question for her.

"Frances Mae? If I ask you a question, will you give me an honest answer?"

"Why wouldn't I?" she said, a little defensively.

I ignored that and plunged ahead. "What's really going on around here with Mother? Why do you think that my brother wants to put her in an assisted-living community?" She stared at me and then the horizon, which was blazing red with the final light of day. I could tell that she had waited for this moment.

"Why, Caroline, what on earth are you talking about? I never heard such nonsense in my whole life!" She looked hard at me and all the old feelings of anger and hatred flooded her face. She turned to walk into the house, leaving me alone outside.

"I'd like to see him try it," I said.

Hearing my threat, she stopped, turned back to face me, and smiled the knowing smile of an enemy. Then, like the serpent in the garden, she slowly slithered through the door.

Miss Lavinia's Journal

Just a quick note—have to go to dinner—Nevil, can you hear me? Pay attention!

15

DINNER IS SERVED

I suppose because I was home, Millie was serving dinner. As a general rule, Millie would cook something for herself and for Mother and then go home to her cottage on the property. Or, Mother would cook for her. She had ceased to act as household help years ago and had become the estate manager, directing Mr. Jenkins's attentions to the never-ending renovations and repairs required to keep Tall Pines in good shape. Millie had a lady originally from Mexico, Rosario, who cleaned house. Rosario's daughter, Paula, did the laundry. Millie was also the Almighty Possessor of Mother's checkbook, paying the bills and balancing her accounts. However, only Millie was allowed to dust Mother's Meissen collection or polish certain pieces of silver. That wasn't because Mother said so, but because Millie trusted no one else to do it right.

Millie ran a tight ship. She earned seventy-five thousand dollars a year with a package that included housing, a car, car insurance, full medical benefits, a golf cart, and cash bonuses. She was worth double every nickel she earned. I worried because she was obviously near retirement and then what *would* Mother do?

When Millie appeared at the living room door and announced dinner, we left our drinks and followed Mother to the dining room. I went last, taking Millie's arm, whispering to her.

"Millie? We gotta talk."

"Humph. Plenty, yanh? See me later, girl, hands too full now," she said and disappeared into the kitchen.

Mother stood at the head of our enormous mahogany table, waiting for Trip to seat her. After Mother was seated, he helped Frances Mae take her seat at Mother's left and then I was seated at Mother's right. Trip sat Amelia to my right, then Isabelle. He took Daddy's seat after he seated Caroline next to Frances Mae.

We all waited for Mother's cue.

"We need more men in this family!" Trip said, trying to be humorous about the amount of women he had the burden to seat.

Trip's humor would never give him the opportunity to give up his law practice and go on the road. No, it teetered somewhere in between corn and sarcasm, sort of like Chris Rock in a real bad mood.

"Bread! Gimme a piece of bread!" Caroline said, in a loud voice.

"Caroline!" Trip said, "you know we wait for Grand-momma to begin."

Caroline crossed her arms and pouted. Silence. Mother looked down her nose at her, raising her eyebrows and lowering her chin. Classic "Miss Lavinia," to show her annoyance. Mother took her napkin from the table, snapped it crisply, and draped it across her lap. Then, she shook her head sadly and with an audible sigh. The gesture spoke of Mother's faith that anything springing forth from her daughter-in-law's womb was just a hopeless case.

"Who would care for gumbo?" Mother said, lifting the lid from the tureen in preparation of filling the stacked soup plates before her. The steam escaped all around her and the dining room was filled with the rich smells of tomatoes, onions, and seafood.

"Aren't you gonna say a blessing, Grandmomma?" Isabelle said.

"What did you say, child?" Mother said, the lid still in midair.

"Hush!" Frances Mae said.

"I said, we need to bless the food before we eat it, don't we?" Isabelle said.

"Miss Lavinia's Theater" was now officially open for business.

"I do not believe that I have just heard, with my own ears, my granddaughter correct her grandmother! Is that possible?" Mother said. Mother's face was incredulous and she spoke in a low and even tone, similar to the one I use when preparing to throw a major tantrum. She continued to hold the lid of the tureen high.

Silence at the table again. Frances Mae blushed hard as she bit her lips to hold back her tongue. Trip cleared his throat. Even I was surprised that Mother took issue with such a small faux pas.

"Isabelle," Trip said, "I know you did not intend to be rude, but you should never correct your elders, sweetheart."

"We always say a blessing at home," Frances Mae said, in a small disingenuous voice.

She defied Lavinia to take on Jesus. Mother declined.

"I see," Mother said, her voice dripping fury. "As you are entitled to do. But I do not wish to be reprimanded by a child. Is that beyond your understanding, Frances Mae?"

"Isabelle?" Frances Mae said.

"I meant no disrespect, Grandmomma," Isabelle said.

She spit the apology out so quickly and articulately that I knew she had done this many times. I looked at her and her face was flushed with embarrassment. Another fun dinner with Lavinia was under way. So far Amelia and I were the only ones who hadn't taken a bullet.

"Mother? Not too much, all right?" I said.

"As you wish, dear," she said, and passed my bowl to me.

The gumbo was thick and rich, the same recipe Millie always used. She'd start with bacon, frying it crisp, then use the grease to fry onions and bell peppers. She added tomatoes, some water, tomato paste, a little salt, and a pinch of sugar to take the acidic edge from the tomatoes. Then she'd add lots of chopped okra. Close to serving time, the shrimp, chicken, and sausage were added. The whole stew was served over fluffy, steamed white rice. It was one of those dishes I could eat until I rolled off the chair. Even though I had been something of a quasi vegetarian for years, I'd eat whatever Millie cooked, except a big steak or venison. Elsie and Bambi. No can do.

While every plate was served, we waited. No one dared lift their fork until Mother lifted hers and had taken the first bite. She looked all around the table to be sure no one had defiled this ancient reverence for her position and southern gastronomic ceremony. Satisfied, and with her dinner fork in hand, she said, "Shall we begin?"

And we did. It was mouth-wateringly delicious. Millie appeared from thin air with a sweetgrass bread basket, lined in antique linen, and moved in silence around the table offering hot biscuits. When she got to me, I could tell from the enlargement of her eyeballs that she had heard every word of our conversation and did not approve of Mother's attitude.

"Don't mind me, Millie," I said, "I'm just sitting here masticating."

"Make you grow hair on your hands, too," she said and giggled. "You bad."

"My stars! The children!" Frances Mae said.

"It means 'to chew,' " I said. What I meant was, *It means "to chew," idiot.*

Trip rolled his eyes and refilled his goblet with white wine. It was an inside joke. When Daddy was alive, we had "word of the day" at dinner in his relentless efforts to educate his knuckleheads. *Masticate* cracked us up. Anything naughty, no matter how remote, cracked us up, especially body parts.

Trip cleared his throat loudly. "So, Caroline! What's new in the big city?" He added, "Would you like some wine?"

"Yes, please," I said, hoping it would help me relax.

He rose from his seat and poured for Mother and then for me.

"Thank you, dear," she said, "yes, Caroline, what's new in the big city?"

"Y'all know what? I think there's more going on here than in New York!"

That pleased everyone to no end, because if there was one thing my family loved to believe, it was that they lived in the true center of the universe.

"Oh, come on now," Frances Mae said, trying to bait me, "what about all those museums and Broadway shows and shopping?"

"The museums are incredible, true, but Broadway is about half dead from revivals and I only shop twice a year," I said, revealing next to nothing. "Fill me in on the local gossip, Frances Mae. How's your family doing?"

Flattered, she said, "Well, my mommer's fine and Diddy's fine—he just got new plates . . ."

"Plates?" Mother said. "You mean he bought your mother some new china? How lovely!"

"No, ma'am, uppers and lowers. You know, teeth to mas-tuh-cate with?"

"Touché," I said. "How about your brothers and their wives and children?"

"Well, they's fine, 'cepten Johnny, who won't be home till the fall."

Johnny was her ne'er-do-well, sad sack of a brother who made a living working part-time at a gun shop in Goose Creek.

"Oh?" Mother said. "Is he away on business?" Clearly, Mother wasn't paying close attention.

"No, ma'am," Frances Mae said, whispering behind her hand so the girls wouldn't hear, "he's up the river."

"Meaning?" I said, quietly.

"He wrote a rubber check," she whispered. "A big one. He's so stupid. Even I know you can't be doing that, 'specially when you paying back taxes!"

Mother and I nodded our heads as though it was perfectly normal for our family to have an in-law in the pokey.

"And, his children?" Mother asked, unsure of how to continue.

"Erline's got her hands full with them four wild thaings." Frances Mae just shook her head in sympathy for her sister-in-law.

"I imagine she does," Mother said, her voice drifting off.

I watched Trip pour more wine for himself. Who could blame him?

"Trip, if there's anything left, I believe I'd have a splash of that," I said. And they thought Mother was a scandal?

"Regretfully, dear sister, it seems to have disappeared. I shall uncork another right away," Trip said in his fake English accent.

Trip was always English when he got in the bag. I used to think it was to make fun of Richard; now I recognized it as simply "the bag."

"So, Amelia? Isabelle? What's going on at school? Are we making good grades?" I asked.

"Yes, ma'am," they said together. "You are not either!" they then said in stereo, each accusing the other of lying, and then broke into a fit of giggles.

"I see," I said, amused. "Do you still like to dance, Amelia?"

"Uh-huh," she said, bobbing her head up and down.

"So does Isabelle! And our Caroline has just started up at dancing school at Miss Ginny's, isn't that right, sweetheart?" Frances Mae said.

Caroline, who had a milk mustache and tomato stains on her dress, also said, "Uh-huh."

"You should say, 'Yes, Aunt Caroline,' not 'Uh-huh!' We love the English language in our family, don't we, Caroline?" Mother said, trying to rescue her granddaughter from a certain plunge into a life of Frances Mae–speak.

"Oh, yeth!" I said, mimicking a good little girl voice, "we have a love affair going on wiff it!"

This made Amelia and Isabelle laugh and diffused another one of Miss Lavinia's zingers for Frances Mae and her children. Even Mother had to take a deep breath, knowing she was being mean.

"Oh, I know what y'all think of me," she said, and looked around the table at the girls, who were now on the edge of control. "Go ahead and laugh!" Mother smiled at all of us. Trip returned and refilled our glasses.

"We think you are a rare bird, Mother! A rare bird," I said, and toasted her.

Frances Mae arched her eyebrows and raised her water goblet. "Yes, indeedy do, Mother Wimbley, you have your own feathers!"

"Here, here!" Trip mumbled from his end of the table.

"Now, after dinner . . ." Frances Mae started to say, then shot the evil eye to Trip to slow down his alcoholic consumption. *"You have to drive, you know,"* she whispered to him.

"Not!" he said, suddenly reduced by his excesses to one- and two-word replies.

He raised his glass to Mother again. I watched her smile and return the toast.

"Well, I'll drive, then," Frances Mae said and Trip nodded his head, "but after dinner the girls have a special show for their grandmother and aunt! Isn't that right, girls?"

"Yes, you are quite correct, Mother dear," Amelia said with a smug grin.

What a little smart-ass! "Having a love affair with the English language?" I said.

"Just dating," she said, "I'm too young for an affair."

"Amelia!" Frances Mae said.

"I think this meal is finished," Mother said. "Let's have dessert in the living room."

The girls kicked back their chairs and scampered out of the room. Trip filled his glass and stood, swaying slightly, and went out on Frances Mae's arm. Mother still sat in her place and turned to me as though I had a solution for their behavior.

"She makes him happy on some level, Mother," I said.

"I cannot fathom," she said. Then she snickered, placed

her hand on mine, and said in a sober voice, "She wants
my house, you know. She wants me to move to a retirement community so they can have my house."

"Over my dead body," I said. And I meant it.

The "show" my nieces had orchestrated required music.
Frances Mae had brought along a CD of *The Four Seasons*
and put it on to play. We sat on the sofa and the chairs,
and waited, surprised she had heard of Vivaldi.

Millie appeared with hot coffee, decaf of course, and a
pitcher of half and half, placing them with the silver service on the butler's field tray. The tea service was one of
Daddy's last gifts to Mother. I remembered for a moment
the Christmas he gave it to her. It came in robin's egg blue
boxes wrapped with white ribbons. Tiffany's. Each piece
stood on tiny elephant's feet, including the oversized tray.
Mother's initials were engraved by hand on everything in
an elaborate script. We all held our breath as she opened
each box. I remember that I thought it was the most amazing thing I had ever seen. I could see my face in the tray,
its patina was so flawless.

"Look in the teapot, Lavinia," Daddy had said.

Mother had looked first at Trip and then to me, as if to
say, *What wondrous thing could be in the teapot?* She
removed a pale blue velvet sack, which when opened, revealed the biggest, whitest pearls I could have imagined.

"South Sea," he said.

Mother burst into tears from his generosity. Daddy fas-
tened them around her neck and she wore them at dinner
every day to this day.

Thinking about that, I poured for Mother and sat down
again. Unconsciously, she fingered her pearls. Trip helped
himself to a cup of coffee, lacing it generously with co-
gnac. He fell back into an armchair with a hassock and
looked like he might zonk out at any time.

My three nieces waited in the hallway until Frances Mae
cued them. When Frances Mae gave her signal, the three
little destructo-cons came into view on their tiptoes with
their arms over their heads like ballerinas. Amelia was
first, followed by Isabelle and, finally, Caroline, who wore
such a serious expression of concentration that it made us
smile and elbow each other.

"Pretty hands, girls!" Frances Mae said. "Pretty hands!
Middle finger to the thumb!"

The girls immediately checked their hands, adjusted
their fingers, and began to twirl into the living room. They
paused for a moment, lined up in a row. First, Amelia
began to move, doing quick spot turns to the far opposite
corner of the room. Next Isabelle followed her, determined
to outdo her sister by spinning even faster. Then came Hell
in a Dress, at warp speed heading full throttle to disaster.
Crash! Crash! Crash! The floor was covered in splintered
Waterford crystal. Frances Mae stood horrified. Trip
winced and I waited.

"Turn off the goddamn music, Frances Mae," Trip said,
quietly, finding his tongue again.

Frances Mae blanched and the stereo became silent.

"Now, Trip, don't curse at your wife, son," Mother said,
"she's expecting a blessed event and besides, that was
from *your* share of my estate. Merely one less thing to
remind you of me someday. One less burden."

I knew that Mother was kidding but Frances Mae did
not.

"What are you saying? Are you saying that you have
already divided your property between Caroline and Trip?"
Frances Mae said, at a volume seldom used to speak to
someone you respected.

Well, Mother had her on the hook now and as Millie

appeared again and began to sweep up the pieces into her dustpan, Mother tortured Frances Mae.

"Lord, yes, child," Mother said, "my worldly possessions have been legally designated on paper for years!"

"You girls go wait in the car. Move it!" My nieces ran like all hell for the front door and slammed it behind them. Frances Mae turned back to Mother. "So, even though I drive you all over the place and visit you once a week and my children make cards and gifts for you, you would penalize us? What has your daughter done for you lately?" Frances Mae blurted this all out, waving her hands and gesticulating like a crazy person. The entire room, including Millie, stopped breathing. Mother just looked at her. She was completely aghast that Frances Mae had taken her seriously. Miss Lavinia possessed Mother again, and Miss Lavinia was pissed off in purple.

"Time to go home, Frances Mae," Trip said, suddenly sober and up on his feet. "Sorry, Mother. We all have our crosses to bear. You have klutzy grandchildren and my dear wife has a wild mustang for a tongue." He kissed Mother on the cheek and said, "Thank you for dinner and I'm sorry about the bowl. I'll replace it tomorrow."

"You can't. It was my great-grandmother's—Elizabeth Kent's—given to her by General Robert E. Lee himself on the occasion of her wedding to my great-grandfather Henry Wright Heyward IV." Mother was completely straight-faced.

I knew she was lying through her teeth. She had won it in a raffle at the garden club when I was a girl. I had a clear memory of the day.

"Great," said Trip. "I'll be in the car, Frances Mae."

"Oh, no, you don't!" Frances Mae said in a shrill voice. "We ain't moving till this yanh is settled. Mother Wimbley, I have been insulted enough by this family to last me for a million years. I know you thaink I ain't good enough for this family. I don't care what about yew anyway. If you want to give everythang to Missy, go on! Do it! Just don't be expecting thaings to be the same between us."

Mother, "Miss Lavinia," was ashen. No one had ever spoken to her that way in all of her life. The air was so thick you couldn't hack your way through it with a machete.

Mother fingered her pearls again, took a long look at Frances Mae, and said, "Good night, Frances Mae. Drive carefully."

With that Mother left the room, followed by Millie. Trip had disappeared to the car, no doubt, and there I stood with the queen of Beelzebub's Bubbettes.

"She was kidding you, Frances Mae," I said, in an attempt to calm her down, but she was off and running so fast there was no telling what she would say or do next.

"Yew thaink yew're so smart, don't chew? Don' chew? I have given three and soon four chillrun to this yanh family and all yew been able to *pro*-duce is one pitiful child who's a moron!"

"What are you saying?"

"What everybody already knows, Caroline. That your boy is, that he's, well, as thick as a post!"

"You know what, Frances Mae? If you weren't expecting a child, I would beat the liver out of you. But your pregnancy, added to the fact that I know you are a stupid hillbilly from nowhere, will spare you your yellow teeth tonight."

"Ooooooh! Scarrrry!" she said, laughing at me, like she believed what she said was right. But for all her defiance, I could see she was shaking. Her lip quivered, she had difficulty swallowing, and I thought she might faint, she was so white. "You cain't be putting bad mouth on my chillrun and my kin when yer own chile is *dee*-formed in the brain!"

"Frances Mae, God help your unborn child and God help my brother. You must be the most mean-spirited, uneducated, greedy, jealous, no-class piece of trash I have ever had the unhappy luck to come across. If you want to know what a moron is, look in the mirror, Frances Mae, look in the mirror. There's an ugly one there with fat lips like a flounder waiting to see you. And, you can say whatever you want, but you don't have the wherewithal to hold your own for five minutes in polite company without disgracing my father's name."

"Yew go to hell, and yer mommer too!"

"Frances Mae? As long as I am in a room with you, I'm *there* and so is Mother. Why don't you just go home, Frances Mae, before I take you apart?"

"Go ahead. You ain't nothing but a snobby bitch anyway! You ain't got the guts to cut grass much less my ass!"

"Get out of *my* house," I said.

My house. Major rattle to the enemy. Big time. She sputtered, shook all over, and her breathing took on new dimensions. She didn't know what to say.

"Yer mommer ain't dead yet, is she? Is she? Is she? Answer me, goddamnit!"

"Frances Mae, my son is not a moron, and until you take it back and apologize, I'm not speaking to you." I was so furious with her, that I knew I had to get away from her immediately or I was going to do something I'd no doubt regret.

Then, I heard something trickling, like water. When I looked at the floor, there was a pool of urine between her feet!

"Yew kin clean it up too, Miss Hot Shit! It's yer fault fer getting me so upset."

"Good night, Frances Mae." My God! I didn't wait to see what she would do. I turned and left the room. Lord! She had actually wet the floor! Mother's pastel Aubusson! If she went into labor tonight, and there was anything wrong with the baby, I'd take the blame.

Walking slowly across the hall to the dining room, stopping to turn off the hall lights, and then the dining room lights, I heard the front door slam almost off its hinges. When I pushed in the kitchen door, I almost knocked Mother and Millie off their feet.

"My girl!" Millie said, slapping me on the back.

"Victory!" said Mother, "now shall we have a little something to help us sleep?"

"Mother?" I said, thinking about Mother's fragile Aubusson rug, the stench of Frances Mae, and the fact that I, who rarely drank, had already consumed, with enthusiasm, two large glasses of wine. "Make mine a double."

Miss Lavinia's Journal

Nevil had some nerve to die first and leave me with all of this to contend with. I surely hope there's justice in the next world, because heaven knows, there's none in this one! And, Caroline? She's too good for her own good. We almost got to talking after dinner and then . . . oh, my stars . . . well, I think she sees what I see. This nearly depresses me. Truly.

16

MILLIE'S MAGIC

Millie and Mother looked like two naughty girls. They had been waiting silently, in the low light of the cleaned kitchen. The hum of the Sub-Zero refrigerator and the dishwasher was the late evening background music.

"Well?" Mother said.

"I can't discuss it," I said. "The Dalai Lama says we should love our enemies. They are our best teachers. Besides, it's too upsetting."

Mother turned up the side of one mouth and gave me a suspicious look. "Good grief." She was drinking bourbon on the rocks and handed me her glass for a sip. "Want one?"

"God, that's good! I haven't had a bourbon in years!"

"Bourbon and branch," Mother said, "it's the only thing I wouldn't want to live without." She poured a drink for me.

Millie, who was leaning against the sink with her arms folded across her chest, stared at me like I had lost my mind. "That and your cigarettes. I'm going to get the coffee service," Millie said. "Love your enemies? Humph. What kind of fool is that?"

"I'm going to bed," Mother said.

"I'll help you, Millie," I said, and kissed Mother on the cheek. "I'll be up shortly."

Mother nodded her head, stubbed out the remains of her cigarette, and said, "Good night, all! Millie, thank you for a wonderful dinner! I don't know what's wrong with a daughter and a mother confiding in each other! I truly don't!"

"Oh, alright. Did you hear everything?" I asked them.

"If I had, why would I ask you?" Mother said.

Millie was quiet.

"Well?" I said, looking at her.

"I think she's got a bad accent that ain't worthy of the worst redneck in the state of South Carolina," Millie said.

"She peed on the rug," I said.

"Great God!" Mother's face was stunned. "On my Aubusson?"

"Don't worry. It'll come out. Club soda," I said and looked from Mother to Millie for further comments, but my sister-in-law whizzing on the family heirlooms pretty much locked their jaws into rigor mortis. At least for the moment. At last, Mother spoke and said what she always said when she was exasperated.

"Well, I'm glad your father didn't live to see this. It would've killed him."

"No doubt," I said.

"Nothing else? Did you cuss her out?"

"Do you think I'd give her the satisfaction of hearing me use a cussword? That would imply a relationship and God knows, we ain't got no kinda relationship!"

"That's my girl! Never curse in front of the enemy.

What else happened?" Once Mother's interest was piqued, it was piqued.

"Mother, I am exhausted. We can talk tomorrow."

"Well, all right," she said, "you've had a long day." She reached out and patted my arm. "Good night, Millie, thank you for everything."

I was too upset to do an autopsy on the evening. My heart was still pounding and sleep was the furthest thing from my mind. The whole scene with Frances Mae was like something from Kafka. If someone picks on your child, it's impossible not to take it personally. All those tidy maxims like "consider the source . . ." don't apply and don't help. My blood pressure went off the Richter scale whenever anyone took a shot at Eric.

I turned to Millie. "Come on, Millie. Where's the club soda?" I took the roll of paper towels from the chrome dowel stand and then searched under the counter in the butler's pantry where Mother had sodas stored. Millie stood waiting for me. I found a small bottle and followed Millie to the spot where Frances Mae had wet the floor.

"You know what she did, don't you?" Millie said.

"I was a witness, Millie. She was so upset that she lost control of herself."

"Maybe, maybe not. I'd say she was marking her territory."

"Whoa! Like a hound dog? I don't think she's that smart."

"I think her hate and her anger are so natural to her that she did let it go without even thinking about it. She wants you to know you're taking her place and she don't like it."

"Good Lord, Millie," I said. "If that's true, we'd all better guard against her other natural urges."

"You said it, honey. And that's just what we gone do."

I poured the contents of the bottle on Mother's rug and

watched it bubble. I knew Millie was conjuring up a root cure to protect us from Frances Mae's anger. Then I laid six paper towels over it, caught them up by the edges, and put down another layer. I looked up and there was Millie by my side with a plastic garbage bag and another small bottle of club soda.

"Better do it one more time," she said, "then we go out to the garden and fix Frances Mae good. We don't need no negative fool coming 'round yanh and messing with us."

"Yeah, we'd better do something. For all I know, she could show up with one of Trip's hunting rifles."

Millie's eyebrows shot up at the thought of it. So did mine.

"Don't even think it!" she said.

"No kidding. Come on, let's get out of here."

I knew we were heading for Millie's house and her magic garden. When I was a young girl, I had always loved it when she let me in on her herbal and spiritual practices. Okay, it was a form of voodoo. I admitted that to myself. But, when we did a little ceremony together to solve a problem, that was when I adored living at Tall Pines the best. I had nearly forgotten the excitement I felt when Millie and I would make gris-gris bags and bottles of remedies for various ailments. Oh, yeah, Frances Mae was about to get hers.

"First, let's go get us some goofer dust," Millie said, "we can take my golf cart."

Goofer dust! Out the kitchen door we went. It was eleven-fifteen. The night had turned a little cool, but the millions of stars and a nearly full moon shed plenty of warmth. Millie turned the key and the golf cart kicked forward. We rolled our way across the lawn, passing the boat landing, her cottage, the barn, the windmill, the ice house, the kennels, and the greenhouse. At the tiny road, paved with gravel and oyster shells, we turned and crunched along slowly until we reached the family chapel and graveyard.

The family's chapel had been built by William Oliver Kent in 1860 and was used by several plantations, for worship, weddings, and baptisms. It was eventually abandoned when the Baptists built a large church in Jacksonboro.

I played in it as a girl—knowing it was haunted like anything. It was a sign of juvenile bravery, a condition for club membership to spend fifteen minutes inside alone. Sometimes the old organ would groan or the wind would whip through a cracked window, scaring my friends out of their skin. Not me. The dark stained glass fascinated me and the old musty smells led to imaginings that would have given most adults nightmares. But I was a sucker for the other world and invited my dead ancestors to talk to me anytime. I believed in everything.

After Daddy died, Mother, being much more practical in nature, cleaned it up and used it for dinner parties and small concerts. Basically, she ruined my clubhouse.

My whole family was buried in the small graveyard outside. My great-great-grandmother Elizabeth Bootle Kent Heyward had buried my first American ancestors—her parents—in an elevated crypt, high on the bluffs of the Edisto River. When and if their spirits took the time to rise and look, they had the most incredible views of sunsets over water. There were many graves, some so tiny—babies lost to yellow fever and smallpox; others, handsome carved headstones describing the heroics of the deceased—patriots lost in the wars. A low brick wall of coping surrounded each plot and then another surrounded the entire area, with pillared corners and wrought-iron pickets.

Millie and I climbed the three brick steps and opened

the wrought-iron gate which, honoring all the historic pain
of every family loss, screamed something horrible.

"God, Millie, think this place is haunted? We should've
brought three-in-one oil."

"Humph. Them haints are what I'm counting on. Come
on, we gots to pay Mr. Nevil a visit. You gots to ask him
what he thinks."

I rubbed my arms and kept walking past the many
graves until we reached the site of my father's plot.

JAMES NEVIL WIMBLEY II
1927–1974

BELOVED HUSBAND AND FATHER

> *"Sunset and evening star,*
> *And one clear call for me!*
> *And may there be no moaning of the*
> *bar,*
> *When I put out to sea."*
> *—Tennyson*

Sobered, I sat at the end of Daddy's grave on the low
wall and read the tombstone several times. In the blue light
of night, to sit at the edge of my father's resting place, the
raw smells and sounds of the river just over the bluff—
these things made me think and feel deeply.

Millie left my side then returned to me with a conch
shell from the golf cart. She walked away again, to the
edge of the bluff in the moonlight, where she stood in
silhouette against the night sky. She was protection and
powerful magic, all at once.

I knew in my mind that my father would hear whatever
I needed to say to him. And, that he would answer my
heart. I had not done this in years, but I fell back into the
ritual as though it was just yesterday that I had called upon

his spirit. I got on my knees and began to pray in my own way.

"Please, God of all, Mother of all, bless my father's soul, his family, and all who knew and loved him. Please let my father speak to my heart. I need his counsel."

I concentrated and waited until I could have sworn Daddy was beside me. "Daddy, you're not going to like this. Mother is being tormented by Trip and Frances Mae. They want Mother to leave Tall Pines so they can have it. And, Millie is getting close to retirement, I think. Anyway, I had a horrible fight with Frances Mae tonight. I don't know what to do. Please help me. And, please, show me the way with Richard and Eric too. I love you, Daddy, and I miss you. I pray for you every day, but you know that."

I felt a heaviness in my throat as I concentrated. I tried to quiet my mind so I could hear him. Over and over, I could hear these words: *Be my daughter.* That was all. I opened my eyes and sighed, half expecting to see him there. I scooped some dirt from over his heart in his grave into the conch shell. Millie came to my side and took it with one hand, giving me something with the other.

"Yanh," she said, "give him this to taste. No man ever love my gumbo like Mr. Nevil."

It was a very small Tupperware container with three or four tablespoons of gumbo. I opened it, dug a little hole with my finger, poured in the stew, and covered it up, patting the cool earth. I looked up to see her sprinkle something over the dirt in the conch shell.

Smiling, I looked up at Millie. "If I know Daddy at all, he'd rather have a bourbon! What are you using, salt?" Salt was mixed with the dust to keep it alive with the spirit.

"No, sugar. You're right. Next time we bring him some Old Crow. It's past midnight now. Let's get us on home before your Miss Lavinia come running in her nightgown to find us in the moonlight and your brother for sure carry her off to the crazy house. I got the goofer dust; you got the answer?"

"I'm not sure, Millie, I'm not sure."

"Well, you think on it for a while."

On the way home, we stopped at her cottage. It was a clapboard bungalow, with a small front porch. The old wicker rockers with blue-and-white flowered cushions and the hanging plants of full, dark green ferns that decorated it were inviting. It was small, just six rooms, but beautiful. Millie turned the lights on in the living room and then pulled the overhead light on the ceiling fan when we entered her kitchen. She filled her kettle with water and lit the flame beneath it. I was in the mood for tea and she knew it.

"How's your garden this year, Millie?"

"You mussy be joking with me, girl. You want some tea?"

"Sure, thanks. Warm up my bones!" I knew that come June, she'd have bumper crops. She always did.

"Sit yourself down. You gone tell me what Frances Mae say to upset you so bad or do I have to beat it out of you?"

I sat at her immaculate kitchen table as I had at least one thousand times in my life. All those times I had come here to unburden my heart—just like now. Her table still held the white Popsicle stick napkin holder I had made for her years ago at summer camp. Twenty or so paper napkins stood there all neatly folded in half. I fingered them; she watched me and finally my eyes met hers.

"You gone tell me for three reasons," she said. "Number one, iffin you don't, you ain't getting none of my special tea I been saving for you. Number two, I want to stop this fool mess with your brother and his wife just as much as you do. And number three, somebody in this family needs to start learning what I been knowing all my life 'cause when I go, a library gone be going with me! Now, you gone be my partner or what? Come on!"

She got up, giving me a moment to consider what she had said.

"Like I have any choice," I said.

Although she faced away from me, I could see her smiling by the way she cocked her head. When she pulled back the red gingham curtain to her pantry, there were the herbs. For the first time in so many years, I saw Millie's arsenal of herbal weapons. There were gallon-size Mason jars, all of them lined up on the three shelves and filled with whole and crushed ingredients. She put the shell of goofer dust on the counter and paused to consider what she needed, removing several jars from the shelves. She scooped out handfuls into separate small bowls.

Her kitchen window, the one over the sink, was a greenhouse—an extension shelf with large panes of framed glass for heat. It was filled with old clay pots that held carefully tended herbs, waiting for the warm weather to find their place in her garden. She reached up and snapped some lavender from a baby bush and let it drop to the drain board. "Now, where's my chamomile?" She leaned over to another bush and snapped off some branches. "Thank you, Mother," she said.

She opened the back door of her kitchen and indicated with a nod that I should follow her. We went across her back porch and down into her garden.

"Millie!" It took my breath away. She had a rosemary hedge on one side that gave a fierce fragrance to the night air, only to be outdone by the smells of tea olive trees. Sweet. Pungent. Hyacinths bloomed in beds with daffodils and tulips. And everywhere were camellias. I picked a bloom from a bush and held it in my hand, thinking what

a miracle flowers were. Its petals were white with stripes
of deep pink. It looked too perfect to be real. Then I leaned
down to the ground to smell the hyacinth blossoms. "God,
Millie, it smells so outrageous out here, I don't know
whether to eat or take a bath!"

That made her laugh. "Oh, do now! I'll give you some
alligator root to soak with before we go. Come yanh, I
want to give you a piece of tea olive for your bedroom.
Come. We got work."

We went back inside and Millie continued talking like
it was the middle of the day. My head was floating in a
cloud of spring's near arrival.

"March weather makes me think about all I got to do
to get ready for summer! I don't know why I bother anymore with basil and dill. Come June, the monarchs come
to town and eat up every scrap!"

"Yeah, they're like locusts! But June means all the jasmine is ready to pop."

Her kettle was whistling, so I moved it to the front
burner. She moved the small bowls and the shell of dust
to the table. Before she would mix the herbs, she poured
tea.

"Yeah, God, and it also means your mother will be
having fits over her roses for the next six months!"

I shifted in my chair and she put a cup and saucer in
front of me.

"Chamomile, orange peel, Saint-John's-wort, and pep-
permint." She poured the steaming water over the herb mix
in the bottom of her teapot. "Make you feel wonderful." I
picked it up and it warmed my hands. "Soon's we drink
our tea, I need to find my Red Devil lye and some ten-
penny nails. Next we have a little service and then we can
go on home and fix your mother's house against Frances

Mae and any kinda bad thing. So talk to me. We ain't got all night."

"Promise me you won't go crazy?"

"I ain't making no kinda promise till I know the story."

"Okay. She said Eric was a moron, Millie. I wanted to hit her. I've never hit a person in my life and I was ready to beat the hell out of her."

Millie jumped up from the table and she put her hands on her hips. When Millie was angry, she reverted to Gullah and it frightened me as I watched her spin and pace. I was about to let the tears roll.

"He say what? Fuh true? Dat woe-man gone better watch she mouth! That kinda talk ain't no good fuh dat chile she carry. Bring bad juju, yanh? Ain't no right! I got a mind to . . ."

"Millie, Eric's not a moron. He's a bright, energetic, sweet . . ." I held the cup to my lips and my eyes filled up with tears. Tears, big old crocodile tears, slipped down my face.

When she saw me cry, her rant ceased. Millie took a deep breath and put her hand on my shoulder and said, "Hush now, Caroline, ain't nothing wrong with your boy. He's perfect. She ain't gone say nothing like that to you ever again and if she does, just tell her we'll see where we all land in time, ain't that right? Damn. I'd like to whup her behind. But no use in that. Life's a river and the water keeps moving." She dug in her pocket and handed me a tissue. "Yanh. Blow your nose and talk to me. What'd your daddy say, chile?"

"He said, *Be my daughter.* What the hell is that supposed to mean? I *am* his daughter!" The tears kept streaming down.

"I don't know, but it will all show itself in time. Let's try to stop now, all right? Come on, baby. Let's hush."

I looked up at Millie and her lips were set so hard against each other that they were nearly white.

"Hate's a terrible thing. We shouldn't let her get to us, but picking on a child ain't right."

"She's a bitch."

"Yes, she is, and a stupid one besides. And, she gone get hers by-and-by. Now come on. Dwell on it a little while. I knew from the day you were born with a caul that you had the second sight. Well, no visions so far, but at least you can hear!"

I sat there with my forehead resting on the heels of my hands, sniveling like a schoolgirl. The caul. They all said it was true. I was delivered by a midwife at Tall Pines. Millie was there to help. They were surprised to see the caul over me, the thin membrane, that Millie swore meant I had some psychic powers or potential or something. All I know is that she kept it, spread it out on cardboard and dried it. It sounded disgusting to me, but I never doubted Millie's word. And the tiny chips she used of it, when she did a ceremony for my safety or protection, must have had some strong luck.

"Lord, chile, you got too much worriation in your head." She looked at me and saw that I was reasonably calm. "Let's do what we come to do; it's getting late."

I felt better—relieved. It was so good to be able to talk to her. All my life I'd told her things that I never told Mother. Giving my trouble to Millie's heart nearly solved my problems. But not quite. I was still as angry as all hell with Frances Mae.

I followed Millie with the bowls and shell to a closet in the living room that, in a normal home, would have held coats. Not in Millie's house. When you opened the door there was an altar dedicated to her orisha, the angelic deities of her Yoruban religion of Ife. Needless to say, Millie was a high priestess. It was no secret. For decades, people had come to her from all over the Lowcountry for cures and for advice.

The altar was a curious collection of plaster and wooden Christian statues and clay statues of African deities. Jesus, Mary, and Joseph were there in various representations from the Holy Family to Jesus alone as the Infant of Prague or the Sacred Heart. A large plaster Madonna held the center on an elevated surface covered in pristine white linen, edged in lace that, no doubt, Millie had tatted. Photographs of our family and Millie's family and friends were propped against candles in various glass containers and of various colors. There were small clay statues of Ori, Obatala, Eshu, Oshun, Ogun, Oya, Shango, and the rest of the sixteen angels, or odu. I had played with them as a child, like dolls, while Millie told me their stories. Each one stood for a particular ethic and served to remind the devotee to find the highest good in everything and everyone.

I knew that each candle represented a deity and that each color held a special meaning. Strings of cowrie shells, and rattles made of gourds and decorated with feathers, were placed among the other objects. It had been fifteen years or more since I had seen her altar and what used to make me giggle, I now accepted and respected as serious.

First, she sprinkled a little water on the floor. Next, she lit the red candle dedicated to Eshu Elegba. When she did this, she rattled the gourd and said, *"Iba! Elegba esu lona!"* (Praise to Elegba who owns the road!) Without a pause she dropped and touched her right hip and elbow to the floor, and repeated this with her left side. The gesture was very much like a genuflect, but it also meant she was going to send her prayers to a female orisha. But first, she appeased Eshu, because he was the prime negotiator with the other ancient elders.

Then she lit a candle for Oya, the goddess of the cemetery, the departed, and of rebirth. Much like eastern religions, Ife held that some things must die so that others can be born. Oya was invoked for protection, as she was known to be a great warrior. She was recognized as the wind and possessed great psychic abilities. Millie called to her in Yoruban and mixed the dust in the mortar with the herbs. Then she rattled the gourd several more times and rang a small handbell twice. She blew out the candles and turned back to face me. She put the ground herbs and goofer dust in a Ziploc and said, "Now, come on, let's get you back to the big house before the sun starts coming up." Then, she put something in my hand. "This is a piece of Saint John the Conqueror for you to carry wherever you go and this is alligator root for your bath. Make you sleep good."

"Thanks," I said, knowing it would work. The last thing I wanted was to spend the night wide awake, thinking of ways to kill my sister-in-law.

Rolling back across the uneven land, Millie's conjure ingredients rattling in her pockets, my roots in mine, I felt completely at home. I could not believe it, but I felt that I was exactly where I belonged on the planet. Why had I condemned this place? In the blue night air, in the fullness of pine and floral suffusion, in that moment, I could not remember.

I hopped off the golf cart and we went around to the front of the house. She put the lye under the front steps along with the herbal mixture and a can of nails.

"That will have to do until tomorrow. Millie's pooped."

We walked around to the back porch where we said good night. I stood on the back steps and watched Millie drive off in the direction of her home. As though she had eyes in the back of her head, she threw her arm up and waved to me. I waved back and, sure enough, I saw her bob her head in recognition.

What a night! I hadn't even been home twelve hours!

Miss Lavinia's Journal

I saw them go off in the night together, Millie and Caroline. That Millie makes my nerves act up with all her hocus-pocus. But I do so hope they figure out a way to fix that Frances Mae. What a disgrace she is! I'm sure my rug is all right, but what in the world is the matter with that woman? Am I obliged to give a shower in her honor? Heavenly days. I imagine I'll buy diapers for the new baby and diapers for her as well. Wait until I tell Sweetie and Nancy this one! What a night!

17

GONE FISHING

Morning came with an early sunrise, the sounds of hundreds of baby birds begging to be fed and their mothers squawking for them to just wait a minute. I drifted off, waking again soon at the sounds of Trip hollering at his dogs for yelping at the birds. It was time to go see what hazards men had heaped on the Edisto. If I still owned anything around here, it was a piece of that river.

I gave in to Saturday morning and got up to stretch, surprised by how well I felt. I had slept so soundly! The bed was barely wrinkled! Then I felt pretty naïve—after all, I *had* drunk tea with Millie. Only God knows what was in it. *And,* I had taken that quick soak with freaking alligator root, for God's sake. Richard would have laughed himself sick over that.

I pulled on my jeans, a white T-shirt, and a chartreuse cotton cardigan. One brush tamed my bed head, and then another scrubbed away the sleep from my teeth. I was pulling my hair into a rubber band when I went looking for

Mother. Taking the steps two at a time, I found her with Trip in the kitchen. Still in her robe, she was reading the newspaper intensely and having a cup of hot tea. Her ever-present cigarette, Benson & Hedges 100, menthol please, waited. Its smoke rose in soft spirals with the same patience evil uses in baiting human souls. Some things would never change.

"Morning!" I said, kissing Mother's cheek and giving Trip the hairy eyeball.

"Caroline," he said, putting his mug down on the table, "I want to thank you for not knocking Frances Mae's teeth out last night."

"She's a piece of work. Don't *menshone eet*," I said, pouring myself a glass of orange juice. "That's French for 'don't mention it.' I learned that from Miss Nancy."

"Nancy is a veritable wealth of information," Mother said, to no one in particular.

"Although I must admit, it was tempting," I said.

"Well, thank you for exercising your excellent personal discipline. Wanna go out in the boat?" Trip asked. "Tide's perfect. I'll even let you drive."

He *must* have been feeling guilty to let me drive.

"I get to drive?"

"Yep."

"Okay, deal. You must be desperate for company." I grinned at him, raising my eyebrows in a dare. Poor bastard. Frances Mae was more color and drama than he deserved.

"Must be hard up as hell," he said. He got up and slapped me on the shoulder. "Let's go, missy."

"I do believe my children have scales on them some-where. God knows they'd rather be on the water than the land." She wasn't snide, but it was another tiny dart to the neck from her quiver of guilt weapons—said smilingly, meant seriously.

Mother looked up from her place at the kitchen table and did, in fact, smile at us. She was reading the obituaries. At least she seemed pleased that my sister-in-law's incontinence couldn't rattle our cages to the point where Trip and I would fight with each other. I mean, it was pretty humiliating to have a wife who did those things.

I wrapped one of Millie's biscuits in a paper towel and put it in the microwave for ten seconds. Then I slathered it with some of Miss Sweetie's strawberry jam and ate it as fast as I could get it in my mouth.

"For heaven's sake, Caroline, put it on a plate and sit at the table! You're eating like you were born in the trees!"

I swallowed the last bite, drained my orange juice, and put the glass in the dishwasher. "It's okay, Mother. Trip will have me back in an hour and we can plan the day. Alright?"

"I imagine it has to be alright! What say do I have in the matter?"

"Aw, come on now, Miss Lavinia, I'll be back in an hour." I gave her cheek another light kiss and she smiled around the corners of her mouth. She loved it when I called her Miss Lavinia. Sometimes.

"Oh, go on and leave me my peace. Oh, my! Look at this! Dale Clarkin has gone off to Glory!"

She busied herself with the details of his death, brows narrowed and lips pursed. Trip and I stopped at the back door and waited for her to say more.

"Who's he?" Trip said, looking at me like he'd never heard of anybody named Clarkin.

"Just someone I used to know, that's all," Mother said, sighing. "My, my. He was such a wonderful dancer!"

"Old boyfriend, hmmm? Come on, Mother, 'fess up," I

said, by the open door. Reading aloud to us was a tactic to delay us. Trip slipped out to the back porch and was getting impatient.

"Well, you go on with your brother, dear. I don't want to bore you with stories about old lovers."

"Lovers?" Now my eyes got wider.

"Come on, Caroline! Are you staying or coming with me?"

Mother looked around to face me and just smiled. "Don't keep your brother waiting, Caroline. It's terribly rude."

"Right," I said, and closed the door. Classic Lavinia. Bait and switch. *Oh, go with your brother! No! Stay with me!* Jeesch. I opened the door again. "You can manipulate me as soon as I get back, Mother!" When she saw me laughing, she squinted her eyes and shook her head.

"Take a jacket!" she said.

I ignored her and hurried down the back steps. Trip was already twenty yards in front of me, talking to Millie. I ran to catch up to them.

The early morning pungent fragrance of damp pine and earth gave me a start. I had nearly forgotten how smells defined the time of day. Soon the sun would burn away the dew and this part of the world would smell like something else. What would it smell like at noon? Before a summer rainstorm? How funny, I thought to myself, that I had nearly allowed those memories to drift away, so easily, that familiarity with my past. But the ACE was powerful. I thought I'd discuss that one with Richard when I went home. He'd wax volumes about the meaning of remembering smells, while I sat like an adoring idiot. Maybe I'd be better off just to look it up on the Web.

"Mornin'!" I called out to Millie. Trip's dogs came bounding toward me. They were gorgeous animals, sleek and healthy. I scratched their heads and behind their ears. Trip had kept dogs for years. Sometimes he brought a brace of golden retrievers for bird hunting, but today he had Labs. Anybody who loved animals couldn't be all bad.

"Mornin'!" Millie called back.

The dogs followed me as I walked and Millie drove her golf cart toward me. She stopped, took off her jacket, and handed it to me. "Don't you know better than to go out in the morning air without a jacket?" She looked stern as she said it.

"Thanks," I said. "Whatcha doing up so early?"

"Shoot, girl, don't you know I got powder to spread?" She dropped her jaw in a snap to jar my memory. "Last night?"

"Right," I said, pointing my finger at her, "see you later."

Trip had untied the cleats, boarded his boat, started the motor, and was getting ready to cast off from the dock when I hopped on. His dogs sat on the dock, where they would wait for his return.

"New boat?"

"Yeah, I took this one out of the hide of an investment banker. He used to live in downtown Charleston on the Battery. Now he lives in a one-bedroom apartment in Atlanta."

"Probably costs the same. I hear Atlanta's got some high-tone apartments."

"Not that high. There's beer in the cooler," he said.

I looked at my watch. Eight o'clock. Good grief.

"Nah, that's okay," I said, "but thanks. So did this little puppy put you in the poorhouse?"

He coiled the ropes on the floor of the boat and pushed away from the dock with a paddle.

"In the thirty neighborhood by the time she was all fitted

out. Hand me a Heineken, will you? You girls behave! I'll
be right back!" he said to his dogs.

"Sure. Well, she sure is yar." I waited for a response.
Silence. "I heard Katharine Hepburn say that once in the
The Philadelphia Story. Yar? Get it?"

"Yar, I get it."

He laughed and I shook my head. I dug around in the
ice of the cooler, pulled out the coldest can, and gave it
to him. Trip's drinking seemed pretty excessive to me. I
mean, I knew it was Lowcountry tradition to drink beer
on the boat and I knew that cocktails were a part of life
and that wine with dinner was a sign of sophistication
and . . . what was I doing but justifying his behavior? Hell,
I wasn't such a prude just because I didn't drink that much!
I just didn't like anything that made me foggy in the head.
The first minute Richard could see that any alcohol was
beginning to make me tipsy, I'd hear about it. But, if I
didn't have Richard to make sure I didn't overindulge,
would I? Was I being an enabler to Trip? God, perish the
thought.

I watched Trip from the side as we made our way down
the Edisto, past old Hope Plantation and all the others. His
thirties had brought him good looks; I had to admit that.
God knows he was gawky in his teens and twenties. But
his chin was filled out and all his outdoor sporting adventures had given him a nice tone. And, he was probably
lonely. It couldn't be easy in his shoes. Something about
lonely men was appealing.

I looked around at the riverbeds, and the old rice gates.
What marvelous inventions they were. I could almost see
them rise and fall and hear the voices of men speaking
Gullah calling out to each other. After rice was planted in
the fields, the gatekeeper would raise his panel gate, allowing freshwater in on high tide to flood through a trunk—

usually a hollowed-out log. That freshwater allowed the seeds to germinate. When the heads of the new plants peeked out from the water, he would wait for low tide, open the gate on the other end first, and the water would rush back to the Edisto. If the incoming water contained the smallest amount of salt, the entire crop would die.

The scene was from another time, all of it built by the ingenuity of slaves to make the white man rich. It made me sick to think about it. I knew more about slavery than the average white person because of Millie, and because I was descended from rice planters.

The entire concept of owning someone baffled me all my life, although women were certainly treated like property until recently and still were in many places.

The river always did that to me—made me think about things I ignored day to day.

The Edisto River was a trickster with many personalities. One was her freshwater area that supported certain fish, crustaceans, and vegetation. It was so clear you could drink it. And, if you didn't want to drink it, you surely wanted to run your hand through it as the boat made its way downriver. That's exactly what I did.

The winding estuaries on its sides were home to everything from oyster beds to alligators, fiddler crabs, and osprey. When you looked at the riverbanks, they reverberated with small creatures, birds and fiddlers, busy with their day. It was another world in miniature, except for the alligators. Some of those suckers were huge!

When you arrived downstream to the salted water, everything changed again. You caught different fish, heard different birds, and saw different vegetation. At that moment, I was filled with awe by the incredible beauty around me. Then I remembered Trip, Frances Mae, and Mother—the reason for my visit.

I was on a fact-finding mission; so far I knew several things. One, my sister-in-law was a horror show. The fact that she was a crass and gross individual from a family of scum was not nearly as offensive as her ambition. Two, Mother seemed fine, aside from her entitlement issues and all her dinner table hoo-ha. Why Trip thought she needed to live in a retirement community was beyond me. She obviously had the means to support herself and, although Millie was getting on in years, I'd prefer one Millie to a thousand younger caretakers. And, three, why *did* Trip put up with Frances Mae?

Over the years, Trip had become the most successful divorce lawyer in Colleton County. All a woman had to do was leave Trip's business card on the table and her husband instantly became the benchmark of perfection. *Divide by two.* That was Trip's motto and no man wanted to do that. Better to take up hunting and fishing more regularly and ignore the wife. That was what Trip himself appeared to be doing, in addition to drinking his ass off.

"Hey, Trip!"

"What?"

"Gimme the wheel! I know these waters just as well as you do!"

"Oh, fine!"

I took the wheel and pushed the accelerator forward, causing the front of the boat to pitch up high.

"You're gonna scare the gators if you don't kill us first!" he said under his breath. Trip had a habit of mumbling his opinions.

"What?" I pretended not to hear him, but pushed the accelerator forward again. I could see him smiling from the corner of my eye. We both liked to race the river. It felt like flying, like you never had to stop, like it was yours. The river air was thick and delicious and it was going to be a beautiful day. "So, tell me about Mother, Trip. What's really going on here?"

"She's getting old, Caroline, that's all there is to that."

"She seems the same to me. I mean, she's getting older, sure. We all are."

"Yeah, that's true." He looked down the river as we headed toward St. Helena's Sound. He was deep in thought.

"Talk to me," I said.

"Okay. Here's the story. Believe what you want, but Mother did, in fact, try to shoot me. She knew damn good and well it was me in the yard. Who the hell else would it be? I'm here at least four times a week! She said she was cleaning the gun. Well, she probably was. But, by pure coincidence, I had just had a discussion with her a few days before about what her plans for her future were. She was plenty pissed about that too. Old Lavinia ain't fond of taking advice from nobody, no how."

I thought about what his words implied. That he was here all the time, that he wanted Mother to move out, that he wanted, and Frances Mae wanted, to move in. It made me sad, to think that Mother would be so angry that she would do something so foolhardy. Neither one of them had told me what was literally said, but it must've been pretty bad. Greed was a horrible thing. Fear was worse. I decided to remain silent and to see what he would say. We drove on for a while, nothing but the wake behind us and the sound in front of us. Soon, he spoke again.

"Caroline, you're not here, so you don't know how it is. Mother has worn me out with her games. You saw her last night at dinner, how she went for the girls like a bull-dog? She's mean as shit. And, Frances Mae might be a royal pain in the ass, but she is my wife and I wish Mother wouldn't treat her like dirt."

"I thought she overreacted about saying grace. It wasn't the nicest thing I ever saw her do. Seems like she doesn't have much patience."

"Patience? Let me tell you something, Caroline, when she was screwing the *landscape architect,*" he said, with plenty of sarcasm, "it was embarrassing enough. But when he dumped Mother and took it up with somebody else, she went nuts for weeks!"

"Hell hath no fury . . ." I said.

"Right, but even Mother knows you don't drink booze on the quail buggy to the point where you fall off on your face." He paused and looked at me, shaking his head in disgust. "If she can't act right, then she shouldn't be allowed to handle guns."

"Look, Trip, I sure don't disagree with that. And, I've been thinking about Millie. If something happened to her, Mother would surely have to make other arrangements. And I think she realizes that. But I don't think we have the right to discipline Mother. She isn't crazy; she's angry. Very different. And, if I were you, I'd call before I showed up, just to be on the safe side."

Now why had I said that? Because Trip's side of the story had some merit? Or because my old anger toward Mother was so dark that it kept me from standing up for her? The tangle of issues that came with aging parents was something I had never considered. I didn't want to deal with Trip and Frances Mae. Or Mother, face-to-face. But, it was what I had come home to do.

"And this business with Jenkins is just another indication that Mother's completely off the deep end."

"I'm still not sure of that, Trip. I'm just not."

"Ask Millie if we both haven't seen her coming out of his cottage at the crack of dawn." Trip spat over the side of the boat, a symbol of his disgust.

Judging people made me nervous. I had lived a long time in a world of considering others and trying to overlook or to understand others' frailties. If anyone looked that closely at me, God only knew what they could find.

"This ain't easy," I said. It was the smallest of all olive branches I used to cool his smoldering. But it would buy me a little time. "Let's go on up to the Bait and Tackle in Skeeter Creek."

"For what?"

"I gotta get me a Moon Pie and a cold RC if you want me to figure this out."

18

ON DRY LAND

Trip and I rode the waters for another hour. I was ready to go back home then. He wasn't telling me what he was really worried about. Maybe Mother would tell me what was really happening here. The end of our morning excursion came about naturally when he decided to drop his hook in the water.

"I'm gonna see if I can catch some fish," Trip said, "wanna come?"

"Nah, thanks, though, just drop me off at the dock," I said.

Be my daughter. The words were ringing in my ears as I jumped off the side of his boat and his dogs jumped on. I walked across the yard. Obviously, I was his daughter. Then I knew what Daddy meant was that I should act as he would if he were still here. In the flesh, that is. What would Daddy do? I asked myself this over and over.

Well, for starters, he certainly would not have been proud of the precise words I used on Frances Mae last night. That's for damn sure. Daddy never looked down his nose at anyone in his whole life. That was Mother's sin. And mine. I would try hard to change that, but Lord! Frances Mae was so déclassé!

Change! I heard him in my brain. Okay, I'd make every human attempt to do that. Just my luck I had a dead father who spoke in sound bites. *Change!* There he was again. Alright, already! Jeesch. It was broad daylight and I was walking to the kitchen from the dock. Well, if my daddy intended to haunt me, I could live with head noises. But if he showed up in a body, forget about it. I'd be home in New York before they knew I had left. The very thought gave me the shivers.

Daddy would've approved of the boat ride. It was good. I needed to find out what was on Trip's mind and how he saw things. Everybody always had their own perspective on things. Before I left my goal was to try to make everyone share one version of the truth. I would enlist Millie and Richard, and try to keep Daddy's spirit going to monitor my progress.

It was nine-thirty, according to the kitchen wall clock. Trip wouldn't be back until lunch. I thought I'd find Mother in the kitchen, but she wasn't there. I immediately assumed she was probably fussing around somewhere in her shoe closet. That stinking shoe closet still gave me nightmares. When I was little she spent more time there than with me.

My own shoe collection was another Zen experience— all black. Loafers, one pair. Low pumps, suede and leather, one pair each; mules, black grosgrain; flat boots, one pair. Tennis shoes, one pair, white. Period. Good girl.

It dawned on me suddenly that perhaps my minimalist approach to shopping was the result of some episode of maternal neglect. And, whether it was real or imagined, it shouldn't matter anymore. Suddenly, it didn't. What a joke! How many other things in my life had I embraced because I thought Mother would choose the opposite? That was too scary to consider.

I reached for the kitchen wall phone and saw the first line was lit. That meant she was working her jaw with somebody, probably Miss Sweetie or Miss Nancy, telling the tale of her Aubusson.

It was a good moment to have a private conversation with Richard. I went upstairs to use my bedroom telephone to call him. On the way up the steps, it also dawned on me that at the first blush of self-realization, I ran to Richard. He answered on the first ring.

"Hi! What are you doing? Sitting on the phone?"

"Well! Sweetheart! Yes, I suppose I am! How are things down south?"

"Richard, you ain't gonna believe what happened last night."

I told him the story of dinner and the unfortunate dance recital and then, saving the best for last, the bit about Frances Mae's bladder and Mother's rug. Thinking it wise to do so, I left out the late-night visit to the graveyard, bringing Daddy back to life, and conjuring up spells with Millie. I also skipped the part about her remarks on Eric, half in fear he would agree with her.

However, we did discuss Millie's eventual retirement and my ride on the Edisto with Trip. I could tell he was thoroughly appalled by Frances Mae's behavior.

"What a foul person your sister-in-law is!"

"Excuse me, your family ain't exactly rampant with royalty either, you know."

"Sorry. Well, what's to be done, Caroline?"

"I don't know, I called you for your sage wisdom."

"Hmm. Well, there's no point in Trip and Frances Mae

attempting to run Lavinia out of her house on the grounds of insanity. She can change her power of attorney with a one-hour visit to her lawyer, which I would certainly advise her to do."

"Excellent point! Why didn't I think of that?"

"Being brilliant is how I keep you loving me."

"No, baby heart, that's only one reason."

"Good girl. And, I think it would be propitious to have a conversation with Lavinia about gun safety and make her promise not to drink and shoot."

"Right. Propitious. Love that word. I think I'll do that as soon as we hang up. So, Richard, do you miss me?"

"Passionately. When are you coming home? I need a woman."

"Tomorrow afternoon. And, Richard?"

"Yes?"

"I would prefer if you would say, I need *you.*"

"I need you, Caroline. I want to throw you down! I ache for you. I want to rip off your panties! I die for you. I pine for you! I weep . . ."

"Oh, for the love of God, lemme talk to Eric."

"Not home. Over at that kid's apartment."

"Okay, tell him I called and that I love him? He can call me tonight."

"I'll tell him."

We hung up and I kicked off my shoes and crawled back under the covers of my unmade bed. I let my mind float while I mused about Mother, about Richard and the life I had chosen for myself. I used to think that I could never be happy anywhere but New York, away from Mother's politics and protocol, away from Trip and Frances Mae. I began to fret that maybe those choices had robbed me of something larger.

The sheets were cool and my pillows were so soft, I

could have slept again, except that Mother was at my doorway. She didn't make a sound, but I knew she was there. I could feel her.

"Come on in, Mother," I said, through closed eyes.

"If you need to nap, that's fine. I just was hoping you'd talk to me."

I patted the bed beside me and instead, she sat carefully on the end.

"So, Miss Lavinia, what's going on with the Queen of Tall Pines?"

She loved that title and the corners of her mouth turned up in amusement. "Oh, Caroline, I don't know. Golly. Let's see." She began by counting on her fingers. "I've got Daniel Boone for a son, that is, when he's not being Perry Mason, an incontinent gold digger for a daughter-in-law, a huge house, an old lady with a sassy mouth for a manager, and I'm no spring chicken myself."

"Not too bad," I said, and smiled at her. I propped myself up on my right elbow to show her I was interested. "There are worse things. So Mother? Wanna tell me what's really going on around here?"

She looked at me long and hard, understanding that she needed me as her ally and unsure of what had transpired on my boat ride with Trip.

"I was out with Sweetie and Nancy on the courses. We got a little tipsy and I tripped and fell off the quail wagon. I know it was irresponsible of us to drink and shoot and we have all made a pact to never do it again. Raoul and I are no longer seeing each other, but I want you to know I have not one regret about my affair with him. He was good to me, Caroline. I had fun. Period. I was upset when he dumped me for Martha, but I got over it."

"Trip said you moped around for weeks."

"It probably appeared that way to him, but he is always

here snooping around, and it irritates me. I feel like they are plotting my demise, he and that horrible wife of his."

"I won't let them do that, Mother. Tell me, how is Jenkins?"

"May I let you in on a little secret?"

I held my breath and waited for her to confide that she was now sleeping with him. "Sure, I love secrets!"

"I'm teaching him to read! I go over to his cottage every morning and we practice. Don't tell Millie, though. She thinks he's literate because he's handled all the money she gives him for feed and seed all these years. I don't want her to know. Jenkins has been too good to this family to have him embarrassed. Wait here just a moment, I'll show you his workbook."

Relief waved through me like a flash flood. She was teaching him to read! Thank God. Hell, when I got my hands on Trip, I'd kick his butt. Mother came back in and opened the spiral notebook for me.

"Look, here is what he could do last fall." She showed me a sample of his handwriting that was all jagged and sloppy. She flipped to the end of the book. "This was how he was doing in February. Remarkable, isn't it?"

"Mother, you are remarkable!"

"Thank you, Caroline. I must say I'm pretty proud of Jenkins. It proves that an old dog is never too ancient to learn a new trick, doesn't it?"

I couldn't help but lean over and hug her. "You are some girl, Lavinia, do you know that?"

"That's Miss Lavinia to you! I'm still your mother!"

We smiled at each other. In that moment, I forgave her everything and just wanted to help her secure her future.

"Hey, what about dinner tonight?"

"Would you believe they are coming back?"

"No!"

"If I were Frances Mae Litchfield, I'd have my husband drop me off at the Hess station and I'd wait there! But, she called. Very penitent. Just a few minutes ago."

"Every word! I want every word!" I kicked off the covers and sat cross-legged, facing her. "Unbelievable."

"Caroline? Were you under my sheets in those jeans?"

"What?"

"Don't you know they could have fleas or any number of unsanitary things on them?"

"Sorry, Mother. Just tell me about Miss Thing's apology and I'll change the sheets later."

"Where was I? Oh! Yes!" Mother stood up and put her hand over her heart and looked up to the ceiling. "Well, she called and in that sickening little goo-goo, redneck voice of hers she said, 'Mother Wimbley? I am calling to offer my most sincere apology for my behavior and my children's behavior last night. I don't rightly know what come over me but I sure enough did make a big old jackass out of myself and I am truly, truly sorry for it from the bottom of my heart! Can you find it in yours to forgive this poor sinner? If y'all will give us a second chance we will bring dinner to you tonight, so's y'all don't have to drive that dark road!' What could I say? So, I said, 'Bless your heart, Frances Mae, don't think another thing about it!' "

"Like Eric says, I'm gonna hurl chunks!"

"My grandson talks like that?"

I nodded my head.

"He's just like my Nevil! What a devil your daddy was!"

"Gosh, let's hope not." She looked at me, obviously not understanding what I meant.

"Call her back and suggest something simple like a bar-becue on the grill. Y'all can eat on the verandah. The girls can run around like nuts and they're not stuck at a table."

"What do you mean, 'y'all'? We can have a round of sporting clays." She was mentally filling a thermos with mint juleps.

"No cocktails until the guns are put away, okay?"

"Yes, you're right, of course." She narrowed her eyebrows at me. "You're not saying that because of what happened with Trip, are you?"

"Let's just say that my husband had some advice for you to keep the hyenas at bay." She waited for me to continue. "Gun safety, and, most important, change your power of attorney immediately."

"Oh, do you think so? Caroline, that really disappoints me. Truly, it does. Do you think they'd actually try to steal my house out from under me?"

"No, but I think you need to send them a message that this is your house and that you're in charge of your life, not them. And, by the way, I'm not speaking to her, so if she comes here trying to act like everything's okay, count me out." I rolled over and put the pillow over my head so I wouldn't hear the lecture that would spew forth from Mother's lips any second like a geyser.

"What?"

There wasn't a pillow on the planet that could drown out Lavinia when she wanted to be heard. She jerked the pillow from my hands and threw it on the floor.

"Now, you hear me, missy, we have forgiven her!"

"Correction. You have forgiven her."

"Caroline Wimbley! You listen to me!"

"Levine?"

"Whatever. You're still a Wimbley. I do not like to think that we can't have this tiny family of ours together once a year without a world war. I am sure that whatever she said to you, she's sorry now. And, Caroline, she's pregnant."

"Mother, she's always pregnant. Her ovaries do not excuse her tongue."

"Out with it! Tell me what she said! Immediately or I'll go in the yard and cut a switch!"

I just stared at her, debating whether to tell her, knowing she'd use it against Frances Mae as a weapon the next time she got under her skin.

"I will do it! I'll cut a thin little thing from the chinaberry tree and sting the back of your legs with it, if you don't tell me!"

What was the use? If we were all going to share the same truth, I had to be a part of it too, not judge and jury.

"She said Eric was retarded and everybody knew it."

Dead silence. Mother was flabbergasted. We just stared at each other until Mother finally said, "We know no such thing and she will apologize to you or she will never come in this house again."

"Good luck, you're the one with the keys to her conscience, not me."

"I'm calling my attorney this minute," she said, leaving my room in a great flourish.

I hoped she would.

I waited for Millie to come around to help me set the supper table, which the rest of the world called the dinner table. Trip went home to Satan's sister and Mother napped. Lunch, which we called dinner, had been another feast. The entire house smelled like cloves. Millie had glazed and baked a fruited ham, slow-cooked collard greens in onions and fatback, fried okra in cornmeal, and stewed tomatoes, onions, and baby lima beans, and served it up on a nest of steaming, fluffy white rice. Every time I took another bite of meat, I scooped up a spoon of Mrs. Sassard's artichoke relish with it. Needless to say, there was a basket of fresh corn bread on the table, which Millie refilled three times. I drank three glasses of sweet tea and ate so much I thought I might explode while Trip and Mother gave me the gears about being a vegetarian.

"Yanh," Trip had said, "have some more ham, missy, and tell me again how long you've been a vegetarian?"

Mother giggled and so did he.

"Shut up, you big creep, and just pass it, okay?"

"Trip?" Mother said. "Be a good boy and pass the pepper vinegar to your sister for her collards. There's not much fatback in there, Caroline. Just to flavor." She giggled again.

If Mother had called her lawyer, she never mentioned it. But her mood was so light, I assumed she had. Trip was busy bingeing and suspected nothing. Thank God for that.

After lunch, I had time alone and walked the grounds, thinking. Okay, so it became apparent that maybe I wasn't a devout vegetarian. Ham! Fatback! In a mere twenty-four hours, I'd realized that maybe I wasn't a devout anything!

Hated home with a passion? How come I called the bedroom where I slept *my* room? Why was I running the Edisto with Trip and bragging? About the purity of the water? The wildlife and vegetation? Rejoicing at the smells of the earth? Who forced me to marvel at the sunset last night?

Student of yoga and Eastern religions? Hell, last night I was out with Millie on her golf cart practicing voodoo! Loving the memories of playing with her statues! Remembering the power of her herbs and spells! Agreeing to carry on her traditions!

Happily married? Listen, I knew that in my mind I had been castrating Richard every chance I got. But I ran to him to hide from myself! I didn't want to feel! I wanted to stay numb! What was the episode or series of incidents that had brought me to this?

Normal? I was normal? Excuse me, did anyone hear me talking to the walls of Tall Pines or to my dead father? It was that lousy caul, that's what. Maybe I had been duped by a membrane, tricked by the city lights of New York, held captive by a brain repair specialist. No, maybe, just maybe, I considered for a moment, it wasn't Mother who was so bad. Maybe I was just afraid. Afraid I'd have to choose.

By the time Millie arrived to help with supper, I had worked myself into a world-class snit. I had even jogged around the plantation instead of doing my yoga.

Millie was outside wiping down the table. That table and all the furniture out there had been one of the smartest things Old Lavinia had ever hauled home. For years, we sat in the dining room in sweltering heat. When Daddy died, Mother redid the verandah with ceiling fans and the old wicker, which had belonged to some dead relative, was repainted white.

Each piece of the wicker collection, a dozen or more in all, weighed a ton. They were heavily detailed with spirals and finials and where there was wood, it was hand-carved with ducks and marsh grass. The cushions on the sofas, chaises, and chairs were dark green to match the shutters of the house. The whole side of the house looked like something from a cover of *Southern Living* magazine.

I brought out a tray of glasses and plates and put them on the glass top of the table.

"Miss L laid up in the sack?" Millie said.

"Yeah, God, and she's snoring so loud you can yanh her all over the house!" Back for one day and I was already saying *yanh* this and *yanh* that.

"She's happy to have you home, girl. You know that?"

"Nah, she's just resting up to cut Frances Mae's fat ass, that's all."

Millie's eyebrows shot up to heaven and she stopped in her tracks to look at me.

"This I gotta see, yanh?" she said, smiling from ear to ear.

Miss Lavinia's Journal

When I called my lawyer he gave me all sorts of excuses why he couldn't make a house call. I said, Frederick? You be here in one hour or I'll tell what I know about you all over Charleston! He likes to wear ladies' undergarments. I found his personal profile at the Love@aol.com Web site! I sent him an e-mail as a joke and oh, Lordy, I thought the man would have a heart attack! Men are so stupid! Why in tarnation would a sane person put that kind of thing on the World Wide Web? Well, anyway, he came right over. . . .

19

HAVE A NICE TRIP

At four-forty-five, I looked out the window to see a man driving a car pulling out of the driveway. I had not seen or heard him arrive. Outside, I found Mother on the front porch, waiting for Trip and Frances Mae to arrive, pacing back and forth, smoking. I went out to join her. It seemed to me that Trip spent a lot of his day driving back and forth to Walterboro.

"I am not happy," she said, tossing her cigarette into the hedges, which was not something she ever did.

"I seldom am," I quipped. I knew she was thinking about Trip and what Frances Mae had said to me. My remark caused her to give me a long stare, which I tried unsuccessfully to duck.

"Well, then, shall we join forces? Misery loves company, you know." We just looked at each other for a minute, mentally bonding, and then she spoke again. "I have made a decision."

"Well?"

"We are going to have a little family meeting, Lavinia style," she said.

"Oh, Lord." I shook my head.

When Mother made a decision to stir the pot, others made soup; she made stew. Deep inside, I knew another wild night was about to unfold. I looked up at the sound of a car and, sure enough, here came Trip's Ford Expedition loaded with dynamite—that is to say, his family. I started to go inside.

"You stay put, Caroline. Never run from the enemy."

"Mother, I just don't want another confrontation."

"Who are you afraid of, Caroline? Frances Mae or yourself?"

I swallowed hard and watched them pull up to the front and pile out. Time to face the bogeyman.

"Mother Wimbley!" Frances Mae called out. "You look so pretty! I swanny you do! Is that a new dress?"

The girls tumbled out, all in matching pink sweat outfits with matching satin bows in their hair, except Amelia, who wore a headband.

"That will do, Frances Mae," Mother said. "You girls go play in the yard! I want to talk to your mother and father for a few minutes."

Frances Mae's insipid smile dissolved when she looked at us, and she shooed her girls away. Trip got the cooler of food they had brought and with his other hand he took Frances Mae's elbow to help her gestating rotundity up the steps.

Mother turned and went in the house. They followed her and I took up the rear. We entered Daddy's study. Trip, arriving last after dropping the food off with Millie, plopped himself into Daddy's cracked leather wing-back. Frances Mae lowered herself to the couch, every gesture a demonstration of her discomfort and self-sacrifice to populate the family. I sat on Daddy's desk chair and Mother stood.

"Now see here," Mother began, "there has been too much innuendo and bad blood in general going around this house and I won't have it. I am not dying, I am not crazy, and I am not incompetent. Also, Trip? I wish to inform you that I have changed my power of attorney temporarily and perhaps permanently."

Trip slapped his hand over his forehead. "Jesus Christ! Why, Mother? What has Caroline been telling you?"

"Mother Wimbley! I just cain't believe—"

"Hush, Frances Mae," Mother said, "I'll get to you in a minute."

"I haven't been telling her anything, Trip." I was on guard now. Mother had changed her power of attorney through her own volition. I had never called her lawyers. She had.

"Oh, sure," Trip said. "How are you going to manage Mother's affairs from New York, Caroline? Answer me that."

"Caroline doesn't have my power of attorney," Mother said, "her husband does."

"Good God, Mother! You brought Richard into this?" I was stunned.

"Yes, indeed I did. It was all accomplished by fax machine this afternoon. One thing I have to say for Richard, Caroline, is that when called to task, he was more than willing to help me. Besides, after fifteen years, I'd say it was a pretty compliment to pay him, a way of making him feel like a full family member. He may not have been my choice for you as a husband, but at least I know he won't throw me out of my own house."

"Good Lord," I said, not knowing what else *to* say.

I glanced around the room. Frances Mae seemed conflicted over whether to wither, die, or remain silent. Trip just stared at his knuckles. Mother looked smug and very in control. She had just lit a cigarette and she slowly blew smoke as she gave Frances Mae the dowager queen stare. Mother was having no problem choosing her words.

"Now, Frances Mae," Mother said, and after inhaling her cigarette twice, she stubbed it out in the bottom of her Waterford ashtray, "it seems that when I forgave you I didn't have all the facts. You owe Caroline *and* me an apology for what you said about Eric last night. Trip? Are you aware that your wife called my only grandson a moron? That she said he was damaged in the brain? Thick as a post?"

"Jesus Christ, Frances Mae, why in hell do you run off at the mouth like that?"

"Because it's *true,* that's why!" she said. "He's retarded and you know it."

Frances Mae had made a great mistake in underestimating Mother's loyalty to me.

"I ought to slap your face, Frances Mae Litchfield," Mother said. "Someone should. Between your behavior last night and your unconscionable meanness—you are a disgrace."

The room was dead quiet then. Mother had taken away her name and rebranded her with her maiden name. The ultimate insult. Score: Dowager Queen—one, Pretender to Throne—zero.

Frances Mae started to cry. In one movement, Trip reached to the desk and shoved the box of tissues in front of his pathetic wife. No one breathed. We listened to Frances Mae for a few minutes and the more she wept, the more outraged I became. Suddenly, everything became clear to me so I crawled out on the sturdy limb of the family tree and spoke.

"May I say something?"

"Of course, Caroline," Mother said.

"First of all, Frances Mae?" She looked up at me. "Shut the hell up, okay? No one sympathizes with your tears. We all know you can turn them on at will, so why don't you just turn them off." So much for Millie's voodoo keeping Frances Mae's anger at bay.

Frances Mae blew her nose and looked at me with a white-hot hatred. I ignored her and shifted my attention to Trip and Mother. "You know, I came down here specifically to see how you were doing, Mother. Trip had told me this crazy tale and I half believed him. But in twenty-four hours, I am seeing something entirely different. This is not Communist China, Frances Mae."

"What the hell is that supposed to mean?" Frances Mae said.

"That when you see something you need, you can't dig around plotting and scheming to justify taking it for yourself, by saying your need for the thing is greater than the rights of the person to whom that thing belongs!"

"Like I said, just what the hell is that supposed to mean? Trip, darlin'? What is your sister saying with all her fancy talk?"

Before Trip could answer, Mother spoke up again. "What she is saying, Frances Mae, is that my demise, real or manufactured, will in all likelihood not coincide with your need for another two bedrooms. And, although this plantation has historically been run by women, there's nothing to say I can't change that tradition. I might just give it to the Historical Society of Charleston! Furnished!"

"Well, I guess that's pretty much that!" Trip said.

"No, it isn't," I said, "you and Frances Mae have to stop looking at Mother as the source of all your problems. Mother has never denied you anything, Trip, and you know it. But if your house needs enlarging, you could fish a little less and work a little more!"

"I could, huh?" Then, he started to laugh. "I reckon my big sister has just dressed me down, y'all," he said to us; and then, to no one in particular, "I reckon she has." He looked at Frances Mae, who was obviously bewildered by what had occurred. "You just don't get it, do you?"

"What?" Frances Mae said.

Trip took a deep breath. As far as he was concerned, Frances Mae was hopeless and the meeting was over. "Why don't you go round up the girls, honey? My sister and my mother have promised to let me shoot some clay birds with them and I want to make sure the girls are safe inside."

"Sure, honey," she said, lifting herself up from the couch by pulling on Trip's extended arm. "See y'all later." She was about to leave the room when Mother stopped her.

"Frances Mae?"

"Yes, ma'am?" She looked all innocence.

"You seem to have forgotten that you owe us an apology for your unkind remarks about Eric. Eric is not retarded, Frances Mae, and if I ever hear you say anything remotely like that again, you will not be welcome in this house."

Frances Mae's jaw locked and her face flushed. Taking her time, she looked from one of us to the other, the corner of her lip raised in a sneer. Finally, she said, "Caroline? Mother Wimbley? I am not sorry one damn bit for what I said about little Eric the retard."

"What?" Mother said. "How dare you?"

I couldn't help myself—I flew into her and slapped her across the face with all my might. "You stupid bitch; you go to hell!"

Frances Mae screamed, "Ow! Why you . . ." and tried

to hit me back, but I caught her arm in midair. Trip jumped up and pulled me away. I was seriously going to kill her with my bare hands. He got between us and held her back.

"Caroline! Stop this instant!" Mother said, panic in her voice.

"That's right and I'll tell you another thing!" Frances Mae said, sputtering and spitting saliva.

"Shut up, Frances Mae, just shut up!" Trip said. "Mother, I'm sorry. I'm taking her home."

"Oh, no, you're not. I'm not finished," Frances Mae said.

"Oh, yes, you are!" Trip said.

"No!" Frances Mae said, nearly screaming. "Y'all listen to me, damnit!" Mysteriously, we all became silent and allowed the buffalo to say her last words. "I am only saying what's true. I am sick to death of being treated like dirt by this family. I have tried and tried to make y'all love me and my children and they know the truth too—that their grandmother hates them and their aunt could care less about them. I'm tired of being hurt by you and tired of my children being hurt by your sarcasm and criticism. Y'all are the ones who owe me an apology. I'll be outside in the yard with my girls. Anytime you want to start acting like family to us, let me know."

If they had given an Academy Award for Biggest Balls, Frances Mae would've won it. She shot me a smug look, then turned on her heel and waddled out.

"Sometimes the truth *is* ugly," Trip said.

"There's not a word of truth in what she said," Mother said.

"Mother, she may not be as refined as you'd like, but she's not stupid when it comes to her children," Trip said.

"But it's okay for her to be completely insensitive when it comes to *mine*?" I said, my heart still pounding. "She is the meanest person I have ever met! I am *never* speaking to her again!"

"Mother? There's room for regret on all sides," Trip said.

Mother shook her head and sighed. "Well, I guess I'll get on out to the barn and ask Jenkins to hitch up the buggy. Maybe I'll take my granddaughters for a ride."

Trip and I were left to face each other.

"Yeah, she'll ask him to hitch up the buggy and for a roll in the hay too!" Trip said.

"You're a total asshole, do you know that? Would you like to know why Mother goes to his cottage every morning?"

"Please, no details. The whole thing is repulsive."

"She's teaching him to read and write, you big dumb ass."

"Well, Caroline, I can see your little Jew-boy husband has taught you a thing or two. Like how to make your own family feel like shit? Let me ask you something, are you really happy with that pompous ass?"

"Are you really happy with that lowlife?"

We stared at each other until our rage subsided into a simmer. I went back and sat on the couch and looked at him standing by the door.

"Look at this room," I said.

"What about it?" He stepped back in, went to Daddy's desk, and stopped. Then he ran his hand across Daddy's desk, picked up Daddy's horn-handled magnifying glass, and held it. "We used to use this to examine bugs."

"Trip? Don't you think that while we are in the confessional of Daddy's office we should at least try to absolve our anger with each other? It's not like we have that many spare relatives, you know."

He looked at me for a few minutes, took a deep breath,

and finally nodded his head. "You're right. Come on, girl, let's go shoot the ass off a mess of clay birds."

"Just two more things."

"Name 'em."

"You call my husband a Jew-boy ever again and I'll kick your jewels clear past your tonsils."

"Understood, and two?"

"If that piece of feces wife of yours ever makes another unkind remark, no, even implies anything unkind about my little boy, who by the way is the sweetest child on the planet, she's a dead woman."

"Truce. But hey, try to get Mother to cut the girls a little slack, okay?"

"Make her apologize."

"Look, Caroline, my wife's a jealous woman. That's all it is and you know it."

"I know no such thing."

"You get Mother to lighten up and I'll get her to apologize."

"No guarantees, but I'll try."

"Okay, me too."

It was how we established a temporary peace, by coming clean. But that peace was fragile and we both knew it.

Hell, I understood Trip's reluctance to work more to please Frances Mae. If I still lived here, I'd be on the river all day long too! What would a sane person rather do? Work to satisfy the needs of a redneck, mean-ass bitch by practicing law in the world of the anger and grief of divorce? Or spend the day on the mighty Edisto, fishing, drinking beer, thinking, and forgetting about the world? Was my meditative practice so different? No, it was like fishing. It was also the powerful urge Trip and I recognized in each other—our need to escape into our own world. It was probably one reason why we could try to forgive each other.

From the back porch, I could see Frances Mae down on the dock with the girls. They held bamboo poles and were lined up like three pink Popsicles, watching the water for their corks to bob from the weight of a croaker on the hook. Frances Mae went from one to the other, encouraging them, recasting their lines. I had to admit, she was a decent mother to her girls. At least she tried her best. It was true, that Mother and I had never given her any quarter. But Trip didn't either.

I decided to go outside to speak to her, hoping to make some peace. I needed to make her understand the truth about my son. I'd squeeze an apology from her. She saw me coming and even in the distance I could see her bristle. I didn't blame her. Never mind Trip. This was between me and Frances Mae. I'd get my apology from her now come hell or high water. If we were going to have some family reconciliation, she had to do her part as well.

"Frances Mae!" I called out to her.

She turned to face me and then turned away again. So she wasn't in the mood to make up? Well, we would see about that. I got to the dock and my shoes clacked down the ramp, and still, she ignored me.

"Frances Mae, I want to talk to you." I walked toward her.

"Stay away from me," she said, backing away.

"I think we need to settle this, Frances Mae," I said, continuing toward her.

She backed up one step too many and tripped over the bait bucket, falling backward from the dock into the water.

"Oh, my God!" I said, screaming. I may have hated her guts, but I never wanted her to fall off the dock seven months into her pregnancy! "Isabelle! Amelia! Go get your

daddy! Get Millie! Bring towels! Run! Hurry!" I got down
on my stomach and held my hand out for Frances Mae to
take. "Grab my wrist!"

She was coughing and crying. "This is your fault!" she
said. *Hack! Hack!* "Oh, God, it's so cold, help me, god-
dammit!"

She caught my arm and I tried to make a quick judgment
for her safety. "I can either pull you up or you can swim
around to the other side and use the ladder. The ladder's
probably safer for you." She let her nails scrape my arm
as she let go.

"You fucking bitch!" she said, and moved through the
water about five feet. "You're a fucking murderer!" She
moved along another ten feet, muttering and spitting.
"God!" *Hack! Hack!* "Damn you, Caroline! Damn you to
hell! If there's anything wrong with this baby, it's all your
fault!"

"Try to calm down, Frances Mae, the girls will be right
here with towels. I came down here to talk to you to try
to settle this." I was angry all over again. "You backed
away from me. I didn't push you. You tripped, you stupid
sow."

She came up the ladder, mascara dripping, hair matted
in clumps with river grass, dress sticking to her like Saran
Wrap over a watermelon, two cantaloupes, two hams, and
a giant rump roast. She was a veritable Sunday buffet waiting to be served.

"I hate you," she said, under her breath.

"There has never been a question about your affection
for me or about mine for you. Now . . ." I turned to call
out to Isabelle, who was running toward us, arms filled
with towels, Millie on her heels. "Pull your ugly ass up
and if you say another word to me, I'll push you back in

the river and you can float away to hell. Look at you! My
poor brother!"

"What happened?" Millie said. "Honey, go find your
daddy quick!" she said to Isabelle. "Frances Mae, turn
around, here." She put the towels over her, warming her
arms and back. "You all right?"

"I feel like I'm gonna faint," Frances Mae said, rolling
her eyes.

"Let's get you up to the house," Millie said. Saint that
Millie was, she put her arm around her shoulder and led
her away. Isabelle and little Caroline followed, chanting,
"You okay, Momma? Momma? You okay?" I was left
with Amelia on the dock.

"Guess we should put this fishing stuff away," I said.

"You're in trouble," she said. When I looked at her all
I saw was a miniature Frances Mae. "Momma thought you
were gonna push her, that's why she backed up and fell.
It's all your fault. I'm telling."

I could not believe what I had just heard come from the
mouth of a thirteen-year-old girl. "Don't get involved,
Amelia."

"You don't scare me, Aunt Caroline, my momma says
you're bad. I know what I saw!"

"You go right ahead and do that, Miss Amelia, and
you'll find out all about grown-up anger."

"I'm telling my daddy!" She started running toward the
house. "Daddy! Daddy!"

"You do that," I said. I turned around and leaned on the
railing. *Great. This is just great.*

Frances Mae went to bed and slept.

Before Frances Mae reappeared for dinner, Trip,
Mother, and I had another chat over cocktails outside as
the grill heated up.

"Do you know what my daughter told me?" he said.

"I can only imagine," I said.

The sun was beginning to set and the sky was deep red and bright purple against the fading blue. I turned away from it to face Trip and Mother.

"Trip, surely you don't believe for a minute that . . ." Mother said.

"Of course I don't," he said. "Caroline has grounds to push her, but she doesn't have that kind of desire to endanger anyone. After all, she's got the soul of a vegetarian now."

"Oh, fine, knock it off, okay? I'm glad she's all right," I said. "Hell, Trip, *you* know she's crazy."

"Crazy is a big word, Caroline," Trip said. "I wouldn't say she's crazy. Every time she's pregnant, she acts up. I'm sorry for what she said about Eric. I know it's not true."

"I have a suggestion," Mother said.

For Mother to have a suggestion and not a solution or to give an order was certainly a gentler, kinder Mother than we had known.

"Tell it," I said.

"Why don't we just pretend that everything's all right and be a family tonight?"

I looked at Trip; he looked at me. We both hated the pretend-thing, but the price we'd have to pay to settle all our differences with each other at this point was just too high.

Frances Mae was properly subdued at the table, Trip served up fabulous steaks, Millie brought out a huge salad and steaming baked potatoes with freshly snipped chives from her garden. Yes, I ate steak and loved it too. We drank two bottles of California special reserve cabernet sauvignon from the Stag's Leap cellars. We watched the girls twirl and dance in the growing evening light until they were mere silhouettes against the trees and water.

None of us had the desire to fight or compromise. Frances Mae's fall had jarred us into a reprieve. So we pretended things were all right to get through the night. The truth would reveal itself in its own time.

Miss Lavinia's Journal

*Dear Nevil, Dear Diary, Dear Caroline, and
Dear God, this is sounding like a letter, isn't it?
Well, it's just that I don't know if anybody listens
or if anyone will take the time to read this. If
anyone does, it will be Caroline. So, girl of mine?
What a show! Old Frances Mae went for a
swim. You should've drowned her, except for the
fact that she's carrying my boy's baby. That's
exactly how I feel. If there's one thing that I
despise, it's vulgarity. It's not your fault, Caroline.
Oh, I don't feel so well tonight. I could hardly
swallow my dinner. I'm a little dizzy too. Well,
maybe a good night's sleep will pick me up.
Tomorrow, we'll go to church together and I think
this time I'll say a prayer or two. It can't hurt
and, who knows, it might help.*

20

SHOULD BE GETTING BETTER, BUT IT KEEPS GETTING WORSE

Sunday morning, as I dressed for church, I was feeling all out of sorts. All at once, going back to New York meant living in confinement. I had never looked at New York that way. It also meant, and this was the larger issue, that although I had Richard, good friends, and even some clients who cared about me in New York, they weren't from my blood. No one I knew in New York gave a moment's regard to my soul. For the first time in many years, I thought about my own longings. Millie, Trip, and Mother. All of them confided in me, needed me, and cared about how I felt—not just on the surface, but deep inside.

I knew also, and I would never admit this, that I lavished Eric with nearly all my focus and ever since Richard went to London with Lois something in me was suspicious of him. I was trying to figure out why I guarded my heart with him and thought that maybe, it was because he was always judging me. I was always coming up short, somehow. In all the years we had been together, he could never specify what it was that I wasn't enough of to thrill him. Instinctively, I knew there was an underlying current of general dissatisfaction. Frankly, I didn't have the desire to know either. What did that say about my marriage? That it had run its course?

Mother came in the room with a glass of juice for me.

"Well, Caroline, you must say that you got your money's worth out of your plane ticket." She leaned against the dresser, smiling victorious.

"You could sure say that." I stopped folding and packing and took the glass, draining it in one long gulp. "Thanks. I needed something to drink. You look nice." I put the glass down on the end table. Mother was wearing a pale blue wool crepe suit with matching pumps. She smelled like gardenias.

"Don't do that. You'll make a ring."

"Sorry," I said, and quickly put a tissue under it even though it was dry as a bone. *Once a mother, always a mother,* ran through my brain. In the next moment, a swell of emotions filled me and I felt myself choking up. "Mother?" She was looking at pictures of all of us that decorated the dresser in little silver frames.

"Hmm?"

"I don't know, I just . . ." I couldn't help it. I started to cry.

"Caroline! What is it? What's the matter? Come here, child!" She came and put her arm around me! I was so surprised by that, I wept and wept. We sat on the end of my bed. "Whatever has happened?"

"Nothing! Everything!"

I cried the tears of a thousand years of holding back, of denial, of feeling unloved, out of place, out of sync, of things I couldn't identify. I stretched out across the bed and she rubbed my back until finally I got a hold of myself.

The next thing I knew, Millie was in the bedroom doorway.

"You been gone too long, girl, that's what's the matter with you," Millie said.

"Yeah," I said, "you know, we might be a screwed-up family, but we are still a family. And I do love y'all. Except Frances Mae. Mother, am I required to love Frances Mae?"

Unknown to me, Mother had cried silently with me. I hadn't seen her eyes wet since my father died. But my question made her smile and even laugh a little. "No, Caroline, you don't have to love Frances Mae and neither do I. She is—what is it the young people say? Ah, yes, pond scum!"

"Mother! Pond scum? Oh, my God!"

"Now, let's dry our eyes and go to church and pray for forgiveness for the wretched things we say about her." She stood up, took the tissue box from the dresser, and offered it to me.

I took one, wiped my eyes, another to blow my nose, and almost laughed. "Mother? This is all highly unusual, you know. I know how you feel about church and religion."

"Wait till you lay eyes on the reverend!" Millie said. "I hear tell he looks like one of them fellows on *Baywatch!*"

I turned to Mother, who was reapplying her lipstick, gauging the depth of her lascivious grin.

"He's hot, all right. Who knows? Perhaps I'll find religion."

"That's how we know she's old," Millie said in a whisper to me, "getting worried about Judgment Day."

"What's that, you old fool?" Mother said.

"She said you want to take him down to the river for a baptism," I said, giggling.

"All right, you two. That's sufficient! What time is your plane, Caroline?"

"Six this afternoon," I said.

"Well, wonderful! Perhaps we can squeeze in a round of clays after all!" She stopped and looked at me. "Brush your hair, darling. You look frightful! I'll be downstairs waiting for you."

When she left the room, Millie turned to me and said in a whisper, "I think this one's over fifty."

"Well, thank God for that."

In my opinion, the reverend in question was no more than a peacock. Every widow in the congregation had shortened her skirts for him. I sat in the back row with Mother, Miss Sweetie, and Miss Nancy, listening to and watching them remark in gestures and giggles about his various attributes. His sermon about sins of the flesh couldn't have been any more useless than it was on those three. No, they clucked like schoolgirls and preened like bathing beauties. After church, in the yard, I was introduced to him by Miss Sweetie, who dragged me to his side.

"Reverend Moore? I'd like to introduce you to Caroline Wimbley, Lavinia's daughter from New York City!"

I reached out to shake his hand. "Levine," I said. "It's nice to meet you, Reverend. Great sermon."

"Thanks. Please call me Charles. Did you say Levine?" he said, raising his chin to look down at me. "I'll bet there's a story there!" He smiled at me and I glared at him. Just what in the hell did that mean? Stupid ass.

"I'm sorry, that didn't come out right. I meant that you were living in New York! It must be wonderful and filled with exciting adventures."

In his defense, he flushed a deep scarlet with embarrassment at sounding anti-Semitic. Suddenly, Mother was at my side.

"Won't you join us for brunch, Reverend?" Mother said.

"Oh, I would love to, Miss Lavinia, but I'm afraid I'm already committed. Another time. How long are you staying, Caroline?"

There was no mistaking the look in his eyes. Boy, was he barking up the wrong tree.

"I'm leaving this afternoon," I said, adding, "Charles."

"And you'll be back soon, I hope?" he asked, much in the same tone the Big Bad Wolf would have used on Red Riding Hood.

"Yes," I said, hurling him the practiced New Yorker eye that said, *You must be kidding yourself!*

"Come along, Caroline! We've taken enough of his time. Another time, Charles—we'll call in advance."

We said our good-byes and all the way home Mother went on and on about the reverend's obvious attraction to me. She didn't like it one little bit.

"He liked you, Caroline. Did you see the way he stared at you?"

"He's too old for me, Mother—and too young for you! Plus, he's an ass! Plus, I'm married!"

"I know, but I'll bet he's hot in the sack!"

"Jesus! I'll bet they ran him out of his last church for chasing skirts!"

When we got home, Trip's car was there.

"How was church?" he asked as we pulled up to the front of the house in my rental car.

"I'm never stepping foot in there again!" Mother announced as she hopped out to offer her cheek to Trip for a kiss.

"Why not?" he said.

I slammed the door and came around to join them, laughing to myself.

"Because that minister's a philandering pedophile!" Mother said as she flounced up the steps and into the house.

Trip stared at me for a translation.

"Flirted with me, not her," I said, deadpan.

"Ah!" he said and burst out in a great laugh.

We stood out there guffawing and punching each other for a few minutes until Mother reappeared.

"There's not one damn thing funny about it either!" she said from the front door. "Come on in and let's have Bloody Marys and omelets! Caroline has to leave by four!"

Her announcement caused another round of laughter. Finally, Mother laughed too.

"He's a skunk," she said, "now, for the love of God, Trip, mix the drinks!"

He limited the vodka to a mere dash across the top of the glass. I took mine into the kitchen to help Millie.

"Mother says we have to shake a leg, so I came to help you."

"Your mother's always saying something. If she doesn't like the way I'm doing things, she can cook it herself! Now, how about that minister?"

"Major loser," I said.

"Go set the table, girl, and I'll have this out in two shakes."

I set the table with Mother's Herend china, the Victoria pattern, my favorite. We ate our meal in a hurry because we all wanted to get outside. During lunch, Mother and I inquired about Frances Mae.

"She okay?" I said.

"Yeah, seems so," Trip said.

"Good," Mother said.

I didn't say we belabored the issue of Frances Mae's welfare, I said we *inquired.*

Millie was in the kitchen when I brought in the plates and silver.

"Great brunch, Millie. Thanks. Trip says Frances Mae's okay. What do you think?"

"You're welcome. That all depends," she said, giving me a look that spelled out the arbitrary nature of Frances Mae.

"On what?"

"Yesterday, I made her some comfrey tea. That should have calmed her down. But that woman got it in her mind that you try and hurt her and that's all." Millie stood with her arms crossed across her waist, shaking her head. "She has a sickness of the spirit, Caroline, something like evil. They say the devil protects his own, but he sure enough let her fall in the water."

"Millie, I don't want to take the blame if she has early labor. I did not try to hurt her. She backed away from me when I went to her to try and find a solution to our troubles with each other. She tripped over the bucket and fell. Here, look what she did to my arm. God, Millie, you know me! I would never do anything like that!"

Millie examined the scratches on my arm and sucked her teeth.

"Caroline? You got trouble, yanh?"

"Millie! I didn't—"

"No, chile, that ain't the trouble. The trouble is you don't know where you belong. Nobody yanh knows your boy. People love bad talk. They love to say something bad about you when you seem so lucky."

"Ah, come on, Millie."

"Girl? You done gone on and become a fool? You was born with a silver spoon, no, a *gold* spoon and that's a curse! People gone hate you and don't even know you. So they gone hate your boy or try to hurt you through him. Frances Mae's spirit is eaten alive with jealousy, like a cancer working on her every waking minute."

"How am I supposed to deal with that, Millie?"

"Be your daddy's daughter and claim your rightful place. Show your mother who you are. Better yet, show yourself who you are!"

"What in the hell is that supposed to mean?"

"Don't you cuss at me, girl, or I'll spank your bottom! You ain't too old to turn you over my knee!" Millie's eyes flashed.

I said, "Sorry, Millie, but just what would you do?"

"I think I'd take a long look in the mirror, and think about the woman you want to be. Not the one you are today, but who you intend to become. Then, I'd bring my boy down yanh as much as I could. Children can help grown-ups heal, you know? Yes, they can. I think I'd be taking stock of my whole life, Caroline."

She looked at me as if she knew everything, all my fears and doubts about Eric, my insecurities with Richard, my avoidance of questioning the direction of my life.

"Well, you're probably right, but looking too close is also a loaded weapon, Millie. You taught me that."

"Yes, it is. But wasting time is a sin. You can live your life like an ostrich in the sand, but I don't recommend it. No, I don't."

"Maybe I should call Frances Mae."

"Leave her be and go find your brother." She raised her eyebrows to me.

Suspicious? Of what? Ah! I saw! Without Millie telling me anything in words, she was suspicious that I had only chinked the iceberg. Good Lord, I thought, how much more could I take?

It was one o'clock. Mother and Trip and I were dressed and ready to go out on the courses. Well, actually, Mother and Trip were. They both wore the classic Lowcountry shoot-a-gun ensemble—olive trousers, cotton turtlenecks, and hunting vests. Twins except that Mother had wrapped an Hermès scarf around her neck. I had on jeans and a chambray shirt. We walked over to the barn and stables together. This would be the first time I'd shot a gun in years.

When Mother opened the door of the hunt room, it sent me tumbling back in time. I stepped inside the tiny room and looked around in amazement. The walls were a virtual gallery of framed photographs from years ago. Me on my first horse, holding a trophy I had won at a show, grinning with no front teeth. Pictures of Trip, me, Mother, and Daddy, all of us decked out in English gear and other pictures of us dressed in Western. Strings of ribbons, cracked with age, stretched across the paneling above the pictures. My paint-by-number renditions of Flicka and Black Beauty were still there, hanging next to each other by the door. The old couch had the same upholstery it had when I was a girl and used to nap there under an afghan while Daddy worked at the desk on the opposite wall. Sometimes, he would be reading the latest issue of *Field & Stream* and I would fall asleep. Another memorial to our past. It pulled my heart and a sentimental sweetness consumed me.

"Caroline? Go say hello to Jenkins. He's probably in the tack room."

"Of course! I can't wait to see him!"

Trip looked sheepish. Mother and I shot him a look with the psychic message that he was still a big dumb ass to even think that Mother would sleep with Jenkins.

"Honey, he's as spry as ever! Just last week he was out

spraying all the fescue for mold. Week before that he was planting sorghum like a madman."

When Mother starting talking fescue and sorghum, she became Miss Lavinia. She was in her milieu when she got around the barn, possessed with a heightened vitality. Maybe because she felt Daddy's spirit lurking in the shadows. God knows, I did.

Their last project had been to convert the old rice fields into eighteen rounds for sporting clays and bird hunting. They had adored going out there with friends to whoop it up. Maybe she thought that riding the buggy with her girlfriends paid tribute to Daddy in some way.

I had to admit it, Buddhism aside, shooting sporting clays was a lot of fun. Skeet was for sissies. I mean, you stood in one spot, yelled *Pull!*—and the pull boy would release a clay disc into the air from either the left or the right. You would aim your gun slightly ahead of the arc of the bird and fire. Pull! Pow! Crack! Big deal. Now, trap was a lot more interesting because the clay birds flew away from you just like real birds would—a much greater challenge overall.

But sporting clays was the ultimate of all nonkilling sports that required a gun. The rice fields had now become a golf course of sorts. Instead of eighteen holes, it had eighteen rounds. Each round was designed for either trap or skeet, but the fun of it was that you were never sure where the trap house was, and Jenkins moved them from time to time so that even Mother was surprised.

In between the rounds were areas planted with specific plants to attract quail and turkeys. Quail nest on the ground in sorghum and bicolored hespediga, whose pink blossoms held seeds that quail love. The problem was that the deer loved it too, so there was this constant battle to keep them out.

I opened the door to the tack room and the perfume of leather and saddle soap hit me full force. It was a drug. Jenkins wasn't there, so I went through to the barn. Old Jenkins had fitted out the quail buggy with a pair of mares and was just waiting like always for someone to arrive and say how great that was. And, it was.

He stood there with his back to me. White hair, slightly stooped, wearing the same type khaki pants and shirt he had worn all my life. Starched and pressed. No one would mistake Mr. Jenkins for anything less than a gentleman.

"Mr. Jenkins!" I said. "How are you?" My heart filled to overflowing, remembering episodes with him from when I was a child.

"Better now that I see you, Miss Caroline, better now."

"How are my pecan trees doing?"

"Chile? We got more nuts 'round yanh than we know what to do with!" He smiled wide, revealing his strong teeth, and his dark eyes twinkled with merriment.

"You mean my sister-in-law and her brood or the actual fruit of the pecan trees?"

He laughed now, and picked up the reins to lead the horses and buggy outside.

"Yeah, good to see you, Miss Caroline! You bring some life with you!"

Jenkins helped Mother and me onto the buggy and then climbed into the driver's seat with Trip. We were all settled on the red leather benches and soon we were on our way out to the first round. When we arrived minutes later, Trip jumped off and offered me a twenty-eight gauge, over- and underbarreled shotgun. "This will save your shoulder," he said.

"Hang on, Hoss, you got a twelve-gauge!" I said. "An unfair advantage, suh!" The smaller the barrel, the smaller the shot, the harder it was to hit the target. I hadn't forgotten everything. "Bubba? Lemme remind you that a ding is as good as a kill!"

"She is slick!" Trip said.

"Worry about your own shoulder," Mother said, and jumped off the buggy like a teenager at the first stand. "I go first. Rank has its privileges."

"Is the target sequence marked?" I asked.

"Hell no, that would take all the fun out of it. Jenkins mixed them up between dove, quail, pheasant, and even rabbit. You never know what's coming!" Trip said this, clearly getting excited himself at the prospect of killing clay. Man, he had some serious aggression issues to work through.

"Be quiet, you two! I'm trying to concentrate!" Mother said.

We stood back and waited. Mother took her first shot at the clay disc, which released from her left, and shattered it. She shot four more, one overhead, two from the right, and one low one. Five for five.

"As you can see, son, if I had wanted to blow your brains out last week, I could have. Your mother is still a crack shot!"

"Somehow, I don't feel all that much better," he said. Trip took his turn. He got three of five. "Damn. Sorry, Mother."

"It's all right, I'd say damn too if three out of five was the best I could do," Mother said.

I stepped up to the stand and held my breath, fixing my aim through the sight. I got two out of five. "Tell me again why we're doing this?" I said.

"Tradition, Caroline, it's what we always do," Mother said.

I wasn't sure I liked this particular tradition, but I was positive I understood the value of ritual. Everybody was entitled to a space of their own in which they could shine. This was Mother's and she had proved her point well.

"Yalk! Yalk! Yalk!" Trip said, making a turkey call as we walked back toward the buggy.

"Give it up, bubba, even I know you can't shoot turkey until April first."

"Can't take the Lowcountry out of the girl," he said.

I waited until I was sure Mother couldn't hear us. "Hey, Trip!" He turned back to face me. "Kiss this, bubba," and I pointed to my backside. I let him think he was right.

Miss Lavinia's Journal

Well, my girl's gone home. And, she is my girl again. Isn't it funny how you don't know how much you miss someone until they are about to leave you again? What I would give to have her here with me! Hell, I'd even give her the pearls. . . .

21

DR. BLUES

We all had a good laugh and many hugs and promises passed among us before I finally tore myself away from Tall Pines to return to Richard and Eric. Trip hung around the house to say good-bye, on the excuse that he was going fishing in the late afternoon. Even Miss Sweetie had brought me two jars of strawberry jam to take back. She hugged me with a ferociousness I wouldn't forget. *Come and see your mother more often, girl. You hear me? She needs you! I will*, I had promised, *I will*.

Millie gave me her famous look as I packed my car. She stood by the back fender with her arms crossed, feet apart in a stance of defiance, her eyes boring a hole right through the side of my head.

"What're you doing, Millie? Putting the plat eye on me?"

"Why? You feeling guilty?"

"Should I?"

"Should you?"

Now, what that was all about, I wasn't quite sure. I just hugged her and finally she said, "Go on back and do what you gotta do."

All through my plane ride back to New York, my thoughts were of my family in South Carolina. I had been so off the mark about everyone. Trip was obviously unhappy with his marriage, when I thought he was okay with it. Somehow, our argument had renewed our relationship. He was too much of a coward to show the full measure of his contempt to Frances Mae, so he had set me up to do it. I had complied with probably more gusto than he had hoped for. But, it was good. At least Frances Mae would keep her villainous tongue still for a while. I just hoped she didn't go into early labor.

And Mother? It was the first time I had felt any warmth from her in decades. Or seen her demonstrate any need. In retrospect, she *had* been worried about Trip's capacity to bounce her from Tall Pines to wherever. I suppose it had always been hard for me to see past her little barbs, but once I did, I saw them for what they were—a bad habit and nothing more.

But, even his *grab for the throne* was some kind of a weird cry for her to save him from himself. Surely, he could not have seriously thought that Mother would allow him to unseat her. Old Frances Mae had obviously exhausted herself licking her fat lips at the prospect of becoming the Queen of Tall Pines, but I knew it would be a freezing cold day in hell before Mother let her within an inch of her tiara. Still, there was something going on with Trip.

My visit had given them confidence. How perverse! Moreover, it had reminded me of who I was. Like I didn't know? *Be my daughter!* Well, Daddy? Was that good enough for you? *Change!* Oh, fine, I thought, and resolved to change. That change would demand acceptance of a lot of complicated issues. I knew that.

Mother was only asking for a closer tie with me. Was that too much? No, of course not. What Trip was asking was that I understand his situation and help him deal with it. Then I knew why he had been sending Eric all the gifts—we were all he had, all he had that he wanted, anyway. If all it took was to give that thing he married a verbal blast from time to time, well, I hated to admit this to myself, but I could actually relish it.

What of Millie? Good God! Did she truly mean to turn me into a voodoo priestess? Nah. All that hocus-pocus about *the caul*. On the other hand, who knew? When I had teased her that her spell for Frances Mae was impotent, she had reminded me that the magic had found its place in me when I exorcised her evil spirit with my words. Whatever.

I had to laugh at myself, remembering the way I had told Frances Mae what I thought of her the night she wet the rug, and how the next day I had told her not to just shut up, but to shut *the hell* up! And, Mother wanting to give her matching mother and child diapers when her new baby arrived. Oh, what a wicked thought!

At Tall Pines I had emerged as the Deliverer? How bizarre! Me? God! It felt good! It had made me feel really alive! Then it occurred to me that in my marriage I was a bit of a mouse.

If Richard and I had an argument, I *never* raised my voice to him. It wasn't civilized to raise my voice, he said. But back at home (did I say home?) I had rediscovered this other part of my personality that I'd kept on ice way too long. Well, I thought, now I'm going back to where my life isn't so crazy. I don't need to expend all that energy every day, I thought. Suddenly, the prospect of that seemed dull and dreary. But, I missed Eric. Maybe I'd take him down to the ACE to go fishing with his uncle. It would probably do them both some good.

I was still considering my next visit on the cab ride into Manhattan. May was so beautiful in South Carolina. Maybe I'd get tickets to the Spoleto Festival. If I could convince Richard to come, he would enjoy that. I couldn't really blame Richard for his lack of enthusiasm for my family. They had all but ignored him for years. But maybe now, with Mother's trusting him with her power of attorney, he'd feel more inclined to give them another try. I hoped so.

It was nearly nine when I finally reached our building. Phil, the other doorman, rushed out to help me with my bags.

"Welcome back, Mrs. Levine!" He took my carry-on luggage and I followed him down the marble entrance hall to the lobby.

"Thanks, Phil. Is Dr. Levine at home?"

"No, he went out around eight. Eric is at the Hillmans' apartment."

"Phil?" I pressed the elevator button.

"Yes, ma'am?" The elevator opened and he put my bags in on the floor.

"You've got a tracking beam in that cap, don't you?"

"I guess I do!" He laughed and the door closed.

I took my things into the dark apartment, turning on lights as I went from room to room. Maybe I'd take Eric out for supper somewhere in the neighborhood. I was just about positive that Richard hadn't been to the grocery store. I opened the refrigerator door and confirmed it. Chinese food cartons. Well, maybe they had fun together, watching an old movie or something. I went back to the study to thumb through the mail and picked up the telephone to call the Hillmans. There was voice mail, so I dialed in the number and code. Two messages. First message: *Hi, Mom! I'm up at John's! Call me when you come home!* I hit three to erase it. Second message: *I thought I told you Tenth and University at eight! Where are you?* The voice of Lois.

I left my luggage in the hall and decided to call Eric when I came home. Why exactly was Richard having dinner or drinks or both with Lois when I was coming home? I couldn't wait to hear the reason, and my intuition told me I was not going to like what I heard.

Phil hailed a cab for me and the next thing I knew I was on Tenth Street and University Place, standing outside of Alberto's, an Italian restaurant Richard and I used to frequent years ago. We stopped going there because every time we did, we had an argument. We decided Alberto's had great pasta but bad karma.

The outside of the restaurant was windowed, covered up to table level by green curtains on a brass rod. Huge trees by the windows partially concealed the view into the dining room. I didn't see Richard from outside, so I took a deep breath and went in.

My whole world was about to tilt as the door revolved and I knew it as sure as any premonition I had ever had. I began to shake. The maître d' greeted me—"Buena sera!"—and handed my coat to an unemployed actress to check.

"Do you have a reservation, signora?"

"No, no! I'm just surprising friends! I won't be but a moment, but I'd love a glass of champagne!"

"And the name of your party is . . . ?" He was checking the reservation book and I walked right past him toward the back of the restaurant where I remembered there were booths. I was a nervous bundle of determination and mi-

raculously I smiled at the waiters and other patrons as
though I owned the place. What I wanted to do was faint.

Two booths away from where I knew I'd find them, I
stopped for a minute to breathe. What would I say? The
first voice I heard was Richard's.

"You're a naughty girl, Lois, and I shall have to spank
your bottom later!"

"Promise? With the hairbrush?" she said, but it sounded
like *Oy! Dew ya praamiss? Wit tha haaaairbrush?*

Shit, now what? I turned to see the captain fast on my
heels with my glass of champagne. I stepped in front of
Richard's booth. He was on the outside and Lois was next
to him on the banquette. Her hand was under his napkin.
His hand was under her backside, or at least in that relative
vicinity.

"Caroline!"

Busted. The look on his face and on her face was a
combination of horror and giddiness as he tried for a split
second to feign innocence.

"Hi, honey. What's up?"

In one movement, I reached down and jerked the napkin
from his lap. There it was. Exhibit A. Lois's nasty hand
wrapped around Richard's rapidly shrinking one-eyed
friend. Ick. The captain caught up with me and I took the
glass from his tray, toasting Richard, who had quickly covered himself with the edge of the tablecloth. I almost
wanted to laugh at them. But in a moment of strange fix-
ation, I became calm instead. Seeing them doing this . . .
whatever you called it, to each other in public was so absurd to me! How old were they? Gross! It was like watching a train wreck. Part of me wanted to look away and the
other part couldn't stop staring.

"Will you be joining your friends for dinner?" The captain said, obviously not realizing a thing was out of line, *or* that a thing was out.

"No, I think not," I said, "but you can put my drink on Dr. Levine's bill."

The captain mumbled something like *Very good* and went back to the kitchen.

"So! Here we are at the Mutual Masturbation Society!" I said. "Will someone make a motion to approve the minutes?"

"Caroline, sit down. I can explain," Richard said, sweat beading his brow.

Lois said nothing, but leaned toward the wall so Richard could remove his hand from her bottom, which he carefully did as though it had never been there at all. I wasn't sitting down; I was still watching the train wreck. After what seemed to be a time that hung in space, moving neither forward nor backward, I took another sip of champagne, put the flute down in front of his goblet of red wine, and spoke.

"This is not good, Richard," I said. My voice was even and low.

"Come now, let's be civilized," he said.

"Civilized? You *perv!* You call your public display civilized?"

"Please don't make a scene, Caroline, you're getting hysterical."

"Really?" I said, a little louder.

A busboy was passing with a tray of glasses and a water pitcher. I reached over his head and took the pitcher. It was nearly full. The busboy just kept going and I turned to face Richard.

"Caroline, don't, please . . ."

"Seems to me, bubba, that you're the one who needs to cool off."

Lois backed up as far as she could and I emptied the ice water all over Richard's head. I slammed the pitcher down on their table, then picked up my champagne and threw it in Lois's face. While she shrieked and tried to catch the river of mascara running down her collagen-implanted cheeks, I said, "You whore, you nasty, nasty whore! I've been wanting to do that for a very long time."

I turned away from them and walked reasonably non-chalantly to the front of the restaurant and out the door. I was all the way to Fiftieth and Madison before I realized I'd left my coat. I said nothing to Eric about his father that night, but I knew my marriage was over. The telephone rang every fifteen minutes until I finally turned it off at midnight.

Richard never came home. I assumed he was with *her*. Jesus, and I thought Frances Mae was a badass.

Miss Lavinia's Journal

The house is so quiet tonight; I just hate it. Trip asked me for more money! Fifty thousand! He owes me an explanation or else my wallet is closed to him. I'll take him on the carpet tomorrow. I'm too tired now.

I made tomato sandwiches for Millie and myself and we ate them in the kitchen. One thing we both agreed on was that seeing Caroline was good for both of us. I do wish she would call. She left her sweatshirt here and I found myself burying my nose in it to find a trace of her. I guess everyone would think that's pathetic. Everyone except Nevil, that is. I slept in his shirts and pajamas and everything of his for years. No one knew. Well, I hope she got home to New York alright. I would've heard if the plane had crashed, I suppose. She'll call eventually, won't she? Of course she will! So wonderful to see my girl again. . . .

22

FAMILY LAUNDRY

I don't know how, but the next morning I managed to get out of bed and fix Eric's breakfast. I had barely slept at all. Images of Richard and Lois together tortured me all night. I knew what I had to do, I just didn't have the wherewithal to get on it first thing Monday morning. I was going to leave him.

It was cold and drizzling outside and a raw day all over town. The skies were gray like my mood. Eric kept asking, "What's wrong, Mom?" I hadn't figured out what to tell him yet, so I was vague saying, something like, "You don't worry, sweetheart, everything's fine. Mommy just has a lot on her mind today." And, when he asked where his father was, I lied and said he had left very early for a patient in crisis. *Physician, heal thyself.*

We hurried up Park Avenue to his school on Seventy-fourth Street, and I watched from the corner with my hands tucked under my arms as Eric ran to the building, neck scarf flying and backpack bouncing. He liked going in by himself. In fact it had come to the point that he hated me to walk with him. I always found an excuse, though—cash machine, deli, something. He was growing and becoming more independent in spite of me. Okay, I admit it. I over-protect Eric like a mother bear and it's obvious. But, hello, we live in Manhattan! I did not want to get a phone call that my only child was missing.

Meandering back down Park Avenue lost in my thoughts, my eyebrows tightly knitted and my jaw clenched, I relived what had happened, how I had been convincing myself of his fidelity, how stupid I was. More than that, I went way back to the unforgettable discussion we had on our wedding night and his trip to London when Eric was born. How many other betrayals had there been? Was he sleeping with her the night I smelled the Opium? Probably! I just knew it the same way you know anything you feel in your bones before it happens.

I wondered what it was that he still saw in Lois, or what she did for him. She was hard-looking. Her taste in clothes was vile, her body was overexercised, her hairdo was about twenty years too young for her, and her makeup bordered on something from *The Rocky Horror Picture Show*. She looked like a Halloween rat with spiked hair and my hus-band was willing to betray me to have her. I hated her guts. Surely there had to be enough old geezers in this town who liked the feel of her two-inch-long nails and the taste of her lip gloss! Enough old farts who loved her ac-cent and the way she chewed gum? Jesus!

The more I thought about her the more angry I became. Did she think she could just waltz in here and take my husband? I don't think so! Then I remembered him saying that he was going to spank her. And there they were, get-ting it on in a restaurant like a couple of porn dogs at a skin flick with popcorn boxes.

Well, that certainly explained why he always called me provincial. He wanted something that wasn't on my menu. I mean, I never would've done what Lois was doing in a restaurant, but maybe I would have been willing to try other things, if that was what he wanted. Like talk dirty in bed or something. He had never asked.

Hell, everybody knew that British men were a little to the left. I knew that I should at least talk to Richard. I decided to call him when I got home. It wouldn't have been right to just call a lawyer and change the locks. Not after fifteen years of relatively happy cohabitation. I was so hurt and so angry. What would he say for himself?

There was no doubt, I was utterly and completely shocked. I couldn't even cry. And my anger was growing with each breath. How dare he do this to me? How *dare* he? He always said he loved me! Weren't words and vows supposed to mean something?

The telephone was ringing when I entered the apartment and I answered it in the kitchen, knowing it was Richard.

"Caroline? Are you there?"

"Yes, I'm here, Richard."

"Listen, Caroline, I know you're upset and I don't blame you for that."

"Well, that's nice." I hadn't even taken off my coat, which was dripping tiny pools of water all over my kitchen floor. My hair was a mass of damp tangles and I didn't care either. My eyes were all glassy from lack of sleep. I must have been some sight. "I mean, that you don't blame me. For once, that is."

Long silence.

"I suppose we have some issues we need to work through. Caroline, you know I love you."

"I thought you did." I knew my voice sounded empty of almost everything, including love and forgiveness, but

I was fatally wounded. There could be no denying it, but suddenly I realized that nailing him and fidelity weren't the point, at least, not where he was concerned. He had been living two lives—one with me and one with Lois, doing God knows what. I didn't want my imagination to go too far.

"I do love you," he said, "and, darling, I am so sorry if I have hurt you."

Here came the tears, just bubbling over and pouring out, hot and stinging. When he heard me crying, he got upset. Then he started to cry.

"Jesus, Richard, why don't you come home and let's talk. Where are you?"

"Right outside the lobby on my cell phone."

"Well, then, for God sake's, let's not air our family's dirty laundry all over Park Avenue. Come upstairs and I'll make coffee or something."

I opened the front door of our apartment and raced back to the bedroom, kicking off my sneakers and sweats as fast as I could. I ran the brush through my hair and bit my lips to bring some color to them, knowing I looked pasty. I barely had time to zip my black trousers and pull a black turtleneck over my head before I heard him in the hallway. I brushed my hair once more and went out to face him.

He looked like holy hell. His hair was a wreck, he hadn't shaved, and suddenly he looked aged. I could see that his eyes were red. He sniffed loudly.

"Do we have any tissues?" he asked.

"Here, Pee Wee," I said, in reference to the comedian who'd been arrested for public masturbation, and handed him the box.

"Oh, great. Big joke. Can we be serious, please?"

"Sure," I said, and poured out two mugs of coffee. "There's no milk."

"I don't care. Isn't there Häagen-Dazs in the freezer?"

Ice cream in coffee was something we used to do in the early years. If you threw in brandy, we had Irish coffee. Seemed like a reasonable thing to do now, except that it wasn't even nine in the morning. I scooped some vanilla into our mugs and handed him one. He followed me out to the living room.

I stood by the window, looking out, waiting for him to say something.

"Caroline, I want to try to explain."

"I'm listening." I took a sip, blowing the steam away, and continued to stare out of the window at the buildings across the street.

"Look, within the range of sexual behavior between consenting adults, many different preferences exist. That's normal. At one end of the spectrum are men who cannot perform unless they climb out on a ledge, or unless they feel they are in real danger, or . . ."

"Or they think they will get caught."

"Yes. I imagine so. But there are worse things. Some men beat their wives, some want ménage à trois, some want a different race, some like to tie up their partners. What Lois and I did was something that was very spur-of-the-moment and I never dreamed you'd be there. I never wanted to hurt you. We had a lot of wine, and two cosmopolitans before dinner, and hell, Caroline, she started it."

Hell, Caroline, she started it! I finally turned and looked at him. "Oh, well, then, that explains everything."

"No, I suppose it doesn't." Richard stared at the floor and ran his hand through his hair several times before he spoke again. "Look, I'm sorry and I am begging your forgiveness."

"Richard, when Eric was born . . ."

"When I was in London? What about it?"

Was he going to lie again? "You were with her then, weren't you?"

There was a long pause while he examined the carpet.

"Yes. I'm so sorry, Caroline. I mean it. I never wanted to hurt you like this."

"Are you still in love with her?"

"God, no."

I knew I could forgive him then, but I wanted to know the truth and we weren't quite there yet.

"Richard? This is what I don't understand. Why, if you wanted to have sex that was a little out of the ordinary, why didn't you ask me?"

"Oh, ho!" He burst out laughing. Then he laughed and laughed. I did not join him. He was not funny. "Caroline! Caroline! Ask you? You spend an hour scrubbing up each night and come to bed like a nun in one of two thousand white cotton nightshirts with your hair in a ponytail, for God's sake! Ask you to do it on the floor? In a cab? In the shower? In a costume?"

"Costume? What kind of costume?"

"Hell, I don't know! A nurse? A French maid? Something leather?"

"That's silly, Richard!"

"My point exactly! The reason we don't send each other to the moon anymore is that I need fantasy. Lois, bitch of the world that she is, understands fantasy. Look, I don't love Lois. But Lois *understands*! This is about sex, not love!"

"I see." The ice in my voice wasn't for special effect. He viewed me as small-minded and pedestrian. It was true. I was. There wasn't enough wine in the Oak Room Bar at the Plaza Hotel to make me feel sexy in a nurse's outfit!

"Why did you never . . . I mean, is this a regular thing with you and Lois?"

"Oh, hell, no. Look, sometimes we just have a drink at a bar downtown or a club and chat about Harry. Then we go our separate ways."

"So, you've been meeting her for a while? I mean, what's been going on here?"

"Caroline. Listen to me. When I married you, you were practically a child. I was entranced by your youth, your beauty, and your fragile southern nature. You were the Melanie of my dreams!"

"Gone With the Wind?"

"Exactly! But no fantasy lasts forever. I realized you were innocent of any kind of alternative behavior . . ."

"Alternative behavior?" Outrageous!

"Call it what you will. I didn't want to spoil you. You've always seemed so happy in your role as Eric's mother and my wife. I didn't want you to think ill of me and I didn't want to frighten you."

What was this side of my husband I knew nothing about? I believed him; in fact, I knew in every part of me that he was telling me the truth as he saw it.

"Richard, you treating me like *the virgin* is a tired and sorry excuse for what you did. How do you know what goes on inside my head? I have my fantasies too, you know. And I am older now—old enough to start lying about my age."

"You're not understanding this at all."

"What? Explain it to me, Richard, because, more than anything, I want to understand."

"Oh, God, Caroline. Listen, you're a nice girl, a stupendous girl. But you are not like me. As much as you have always wanted to think that we are the same . . . what's the point? Here," he said and reached into his pocket, producing ads from the personals of *New York* magazine, "look and see for yourself."

I took the crumpled pieces of paper and tried to focus on what they said and what it meant. *SWF wants SMBD Master for pleasure. Write Box 11-CM.* Another one read: *SBF seeks SMBD for whipping up fun.*

I didn't need to read any further. *Sado. Masochistic. Bondage. Discipline.* No, I didn't. Richard had ceased to be my husband when? The day I married him? When I became pregnant? Who knew? It was finished and with no proclamation required. There was nothing to say, except that I became angry, angry like I'd never been before.

I was incensed to think that I would have to leave my marriage because I was a conventional girl. My home of fifteen years was splintered down the middle like a photograph cut in half because I didn't want . . . what? He was trapped or addicted or possessed by some carnal beast who had no interest in me. Thank God.

His desires were so completely self-centered; where was his spiritual nature? Where was mine? Beyond the fact that I felt in my heart that his behavior was truly sinful on some level, what made me think it was? I didn't practice any particular religion, but I had studied enough to know that life was about service to others, not about serving yourself. Whatever God had created us surely didn't want us to seek to be victimized, or to dominate. That whole scene with Lois, and whatever else he was engaged in, went against what I knew on instinct to be right and wrong. It was like playing with the devil, if there was one, and I had always thought the devil was a myth. Now I wasn't so sure.

Of course, I thought, I could stay with him and let him just carouse around the West Village with Lois from time to time. But that would be living a lie. I would remain the dutiful and faithful wife while he and Lois played out whatever fantasy they wanted? Nope. Not a chance. Or, I could take a lover on the side, but that wasn't my style. As ridiculous as it seemed, at that moment, I felt embarrassed and small-town for wanting a traditional marriage, missionary sex, and fidelity.

We should have stopped and talked about all of this. I could envision it. Richard would hold his high ground and I would concede to his sophistication and worldliness. He would never admit I had a moral or spiritual point. Not because he couldn't admit false pride, but because he was morally bankrupt. He really didn't know the difference. I was appalled.

So I read his clippings and it was all I could do not to vomit. Two could play that game. "Great," I said, dropping the papers on the table, "and you like this life?"

"Yes," he said, searching my eyes for forgiveness. "It's what I need."

I gave him nothing; he gave me nothing.

"Fifteen years is a long time," I said. The sun was streaming through the living room windows, marking the beginning of what was destined to be an historic day. I pushed the large blue and white Chinese jar with the ficus tree into the light. Richard watched—watched me struggle and did not help. "It's been dropping leaves; probably needs more light."

"Probably," he said. Now that he had confessed, he seemed to lose interest in the conversation I was trying to provoke. In fact, his *probably* carried a trace of annoyance. He picked up the morning edition of the *New York Times* and began flipping through it.

"Most of them have been good, don't you think?"

"Most of what?" he said.

"The years, Richard, the fifteen years we've been together."

"Aside from your abhorrence of this issue, I think we have a reasonable marriage, Caroline, is that what you want to hear?"

I became quiet. Was that what I wanted to hear? No. If it had been true, I would've loved to have heard it, but he made a mockery of marriage and of my life with him. It was one thing for him to protect me from his cavorting with Lois. It was another for him to admit his proclivities and then ignore the fact that I was shaken, in truth, devastated by them.

"Richard, I don't know how else to say this. I love you. I always have and I always will. But, I have to leave this marriage and I think I'm leaving today. My body and my things will be here until I can arrange for a mover, but my brain has left the building. I can't take it, Richard. I don't want what you want. In fact, what you want is so far from what I want that there's not a bridge in the world that could bring us together again."

"Oh, fine, Caroline, blame me! Blame me that you are so pathetically provincial!" He was going to take the posture of anger. Anger I could deal with, it was whips and chains I had the problem with.

"It's not your fault; it's not my fault."

"I see." He came close to me by the window and put his hands on his hips. "Then, what is it?" He practically hissed and for the first time in all the years I had known him, he looked ugly to me. Really ugly. Like a gargoyle. What used to be beautiful in his face had changed. He was thick-lipped, with hooded eyes and stained yellowed teeth. His paunch was pronounced under his sweater. Between his politics, his verbal and psychological abuse of me and of Eric, and his entire demeanor, I had a real problem at that moment remembering what I had ever seen as attractive in him in the first place. Even his breath was sour.

"Richard, I don't like you anymore."

"Is that all?" he said.

"That's enough," I said. "The very fact that on some level you think that you can explain away your infidelity and relieve yourself of the impact of it by treating me like a child and calling me pedestrian—well, Richard? You can't. I'm just not that understanding."

"I see."

"It will be a long time before I'm able to look at you in the face and not think about this. You'd better get a lawyer."

Things were strained for the next few days, as I made preparations for Eric and me to leave. There had not been a single argument over Eric coming with me. I had two outstanding decorating jobs; the final details of both could be completed by e-mail and fax to New York. Eric's school gave me the work he needed to do to complete his academic year and I filled out the forms to homeschool him. I wasn't terribly confident I could act as his teacher and his mother, but I decided I'd get tutors if I needed them.

When I told Eric we were going away for a while, he was remarkably calm about it.

"You and Dad are splitting up, aren't you?"

"We're going to try living apart for a while, that's all. Your grandmother needs us and I want to see if we can help her."

"Oh," he said, looking at the floor. "You can tell me the truth, Mom, I'm almost twelve. Fifty percent of all marriages end in divorce."

"Dad and I have some serious differences, Eric. This has nothing to do with you."

"He told me that Harry got into Choate."

"Bully for Harry." I took his face in my hands and made him look at me. "You are every bit as bright as Harry and one helluva lot nicer. Don't you ever think that he or any-body else is better than you. Do you hear me?"

He smiled at me and threw his arms around my waist. "It's all gonna be all right, Mom. I don't want you to worry. You know I love you, right?"

"And I love you! Now, go pack!" God in heaven, he sounded like a little old man. "This is a great excuse to clean our closets!"

"Whatever!" he called over his shoulder, and then out loud for his own benefit he said, "They must think I was born under a rock!"

The kicker was my call to Mother. I was dreading that and put it off until the last moment. I should not have.

"Mother? It's me, Caroline."

"Well, hello! I thought you'd gone and dropped off the earth! Is everything all right?"

"Mother? Remember what you said to me on my wed-ding day?"

"Did you lose that pin? Dear Mother of God, do you know how much that cost?"

"No, Mother, I still have the pin. What I wanted to know is if Eric and I can come visit for a while."

There was a long pause and then she cleared her throat. "Get on the first plane you can, Caroline. I'd love to see you and my grandson. Stay as long as you like."

And that's how it was. When the movers came, I had tagged the furniture and household objects we were taking. Our clothes went into wardrobe boxes and the rest of our life went into cartons and crates. Richard had said, "Take what you want. I don't care." So I did. I had engaged a lawyer to draw up a separation agreement, and Richard immediately agreed to the terms. He would pay a generous amount of alimony and child support. His visitation was limited to one month during the summer and any weekend he wanted to visit us in South Carolina. He would pay for all of Eric's tuition and tutors and whatever other medical or physical therapy he needed. I knew he would honor the agreement. He honestly felt pretty bad about everything—bewildered is probably more accurate, since he couldn't fathom that I still didn't understand the difference between love and sex—and he surely didn't want the world to know what he was up to after hours. Not that I would have exposed him. I wasn't feeling vindictive. Just deeply saddened. I understood what he meant about love and sex, I just didn't agree. One bit.

I had thought Richard might come to the apartment to say good-bye. He did not. Did shame keep him away? Or had he simply cut us out of his heart again? When we were waiting for the cab to arrive, Eddie the doorman, practically bursting with the need to say his piece, finally spoke.

"Mrs. Levine, I know I'm just a doorman, but if I can ever do anything to help you and the boy there, you can call on me. In this world, we all are having hard times. We are all needing our friends."

The cab pulled up and he turned to take our luggage. I choked back a burst of tears and hugged Eddie's shoulder. How sweet! I had hoped that Richard would appear at the last moment, but still he did not. His absence reinforced my resolve.

On the taxi ride to the airport, Eric turned to me and said, "Don't worry, Mom, I'll take care of us." I squeezed his hand and kissed his dear, precious forehead. I had enough love in me for two parents. I'd give it all to Eric. Even though I still couldn't bring myself to name the disease, we were going home to heal.

23

I KNEW IT WOULD COME TO THIS

Now, don't tell me how to handle my daughter. Caroline Wimbley has always had a head like a pile of bricks. And I don't know where she got it from either. I told her not to marry that man, but no child of mine ever listened to a damn thing I had to say. But, she can't say I never warned her. I knew it would come to this one day. It had to. They had nothing in common. Nothing! You can't put a field horse out to stud with a purebred Arabian mare! It's a crime against nature! Unnatural!

The first thing I did after she called was to take a deep breath and a shot of Jack Daniels. Then I called Millie at her cottage.

"Millie? Get out of bed, you old fool. Caroline's coming home and we have work to do!"

"I already made up two rooms yesterday, Miss Lavinia. Now, leave me alone and let me sleep!"

"I swear to God, Millie, sometimes you spook me!"

And do you know that she had the nerve to hang the

telephone up in my ear? I should have gone right over
there and thrown cold water in her face! If I hadn't had
so much to do, I might have done just that!

Next, I called Sweetie and Nancy on conference call.

"Y'all? Something's gone wrong in Caroline's marriage
and she's coming back to Tall Pines for a long visit. I
think she's leaving that skunk, but I'm not sure."

"She didn't say?" Nancy said.

"You didn't ask?" Sweetie said.

"She did not say and I did not ask. If she wants to
confide in me, she will," I said. "But, I know this, she's
pulling Eric out of school and I don't know how she's
going to handle that. I mean, the boy has to go to school!"

"I can't believe you didn't ask, Lavinia," Nancy said,
"that's not like you at all."

"When are they coming?" Sweetie said.

"This morning. Their plane lands in Charleston at
eleven."

"I just made up some chicken casseroles," Nancy said,
"want one for y'all's lunch?"

"And I made strawberry bread yesterday," Sweetie said.
"I'll bring a loaf over right away."

"Now, see here," I said, "if y'all come over, you all are
not to say anything. Is that clear?"

"Jesus, Lavinia," Nancy said, "I wouldn't dream of it!"

"Don't mind her, Nancy," Sweetie said. "Lavinia's just
excited."

And, I was excited. I couldn't wait for her to arrive. I
fussed around the house while Millie gave instructions to
her staff, to recheck the bedrooms for hangers and drawer
space and things like that.

"The cable television man will be here by ten," Millie
said, "and the phone company will be here this afternoon."

"Whatever for?" I asked.

"Miss L? Don't you think that boy wants to watch the World Wrestling Federation? And don't you know Caroline needs a modem? How else is she gone do her business?"

"Well, you just think of everything, don't you, Miss Smarty!"

"Your green eyes are showing, Miss Kitty!" Millie said and started laughing. So did I. By golly, she was right!

Oh! This would be wonderful! I stopped and called Trip.

"Get over here and make sure you have gas for your boat, boy! You need to take your nephew fishing!"

"Mother? What are you talking about? I have to be in court this afternoon!"

"Your sister is coming home with Eric. I have to hang up. Gotta cut roses for their rooms. Come for lunch!"

I took my largest basket and my best clippers and went out to my garden to see what I could find. Lost in thought, I gathered up roses and small magnolia branches and filled my basket to capacity. When I looked at all the materials I had cut, I had to laugh. I had enough to fill every room in the house! Maybe I should cut some camellias and float them in the toilet bowls like they did on those silly house tours! Oh, I was having such a good time, planning Caroline and Eric's visit.

I walked the whole way to the bluffs by the chapel. I put my basket down on the chapel steps and went to check on Nevil. Dear Nevil! Lord, I missed that man! I wondered what he would say to Caroline about her trouble.

She hadn't sounded heartbroken to me. I hoped she wasn't because I didn't have the strength to listen to a lot of babble about that man. Richard! Dear God! He had my power of attorney! Oh, hell! I'd have to change it again.

Well, I was sure that Trip had told Frances Mae that Caroline was coming home with Eric. Ever since Caroline had put Frances Mae in line, she had behaved better. Meek, in fact. But, Lord! I hated a meek woman. Especially when I knew it was an act. No one could act like Frances Mae. I hoped she wouldn't come around for at least a few days.

I wiped off the dust from Nevil's headstone and had a little chat with him. "Nevil? Do you hear me? That girl of yours is coming home with our grandson. Do you think you could help me figure out what I can do to help her? Dead, you say? Now, Nevil Wimbley, I'll have none of that. You wake up, you old slackard, and think!"

Satisfied that I had put him on notice, I left the grave-yard. I leaned over the chapel steps to gather up my basket and garden shears, and don't you know a wind came out of nowhere and blew my Kaminsky straw hat clean off my head. That was my Nevil for you. My hat sailed right back into the graveyard and landed on his plot.

"You don't scare me, you old devil!" I said, and picked my hat right up. I knocked the dirt off of it and thought for a moment. Either he didn't like my hat, or he wanted to let me know he was around. Either way, Nevil appar-ently thought he'd have the last word. Not so. "Nevil? Lunch is at noon! I expect you to be there and to behave! Is that too much to ask?"

My wristwatch said ten o'clock. The sun was climbing the sky and I went home, singing a little tune and thinking about where I'd put all the beautiful flowers. No one could spoil my good mood. Not the living or the dead. Caroline needed me and this time I wouldn't let her down.

24

ACE IN THE HOLE

Friday, March 17, 2000

I took the aisle seat and Eric sat by the window. We were
headed for the only place I could logically think of to go—
Tall Pines. In between us, our mountain of carry-on—his
backpack, my purple sack, magazines, newspapers—
seemed like a statement of a long trip ahead. It was. He
stared out the window. I tried not to appear unsettled
should he look in my direction. I was.

I flipped through a magazine and tried to rehearse what
I would say to Millie, to Mother, and to Trip. Maybe they
wouldn't ask until I offered to tell. Sure. I wondered if
anyone would meet us at the airport. In spite of my nerves,
I was feeling brave and had nearly convinced my emotions
that this was not a permanent move. But there was no
question that it was. At the same time, intellectually I knew
our marriage had taken the ultimate swan dive. I couldn't
see any conditions under which Richard and I could ever

honestly reconcile. I was thoroughly repulsed by what he found to be perfectly acceptable and irresistible. And I wasn't about to apologize about being a normal conservative person. I had married an imposter. On one hand, I felt pretty stupid that I had never realized this was how he was. Plain and simple, I had been tricked. Or maybe I had tricked myself.

I may have felt stupid, but I had tried to be a good wife to Richard. I had also loved taking care of Eric. I had married the Prince of Darkness and, by the grace of God, given birth to a cherub.

At least I had Eric to show for all those years. Sure, maybe I had my MBA from Columbia, and I had worked as a decorator and had some success. But my most important job had always been as Eric's mother. I was profoundly grateful for that assignment. I knew that boys needed their fathers and I prayed that Richard and I could work that out. I didn't have a lot of hope that Richard would give Eric the emotional support he needed right now, because he never really had. I would have to discuss that with him at some point. And, I would have to give Eric extra reassurances.

At the moment the thought of Mother flashed through my head, along came a slice of guilt. Maybe all mothers tried their best. Maybe mine had too. She had warned me that marrying Richard was dicey. I wondered how she had known that fifteen years ago.

I reached over and took Eric's hand from the armrest.

"Wassup, Mom?"

"Just thinking, that's all." I held his hand up to mine, palm to palm, and measured the difference in their size. "I remember when I first saw this hand, you know."

Eric just smiled at me. "Bigger than yours, now."

"Yeah, that's true." I took a deep breath and looked at

him, "Eric? Everything's gonna be all right."

"I know that, Mom, I'm not worried a bit. I just thought it was so weird that he didn't come tell us good-bye. Didn't you?"

"Yeah, but you never know, baby. He might have had an emergency. We can call him later just to let him know we arrived safely. How's that?"

"You don't think he's, like, furious at us for leaving?" Eric's eyes searched mine and I knew I had to deliver some kind of truth or he would know I was placating him.

"Eric, he might be a little bit angry, but you know what? It's okay for him to be angry. Any judge in the country would agree that you belong with me. And, I'm going to take the responsibility from your shoulders of worrying about it. Worrying is my job. Dad and I need some time apart to think, so I want you to view this as an extended vacation. How's that?"

"Vacation?"

"Sort of."

"I would've picked Disney World."

I knew his feelings were confused. Hell, mine were. I also knew I had to keep his spirits up. I would find the moment to tell him about the separation papers.

"Did you know that Disney World is only six hours away from Tall Pines by car?"

His face lit up. "You're joking! That's the first good thing I've heard in a while!" He looked out the window again. "Hey! That's Charleston, isn't it?"

I leaned over and looked. "Yep, it sure is!"

"Boy, what a quick trip!"

"It's a quick trip, baby, but it's a million miles away."

Eric nodded his head and the bell pinged, followed by a flight attendant reminding us to replace our carry-on bags and all the usual landing instructions. That accomplished,

I looked over to Eric again. "Hey, know what? This could be a real adventure. You're going to become a Lowcountry boy! I'll bet Uncle Trip can't wait to teach you to cast a seine net!" Sure. Well, who knew? Maybe!

The plane rolled up to the jet way and we gathered our things. It occurred to me that not one week ago I had considered coming back for another visit for fun. Now I wondered how long I would stay. Was I moving home permanently? More truth? I really didn't know *what* I was doing! For now, I was just going to spin a cocoon around Eric and myself and try to recover from our trauma.

To my utter astonishment, Mother, Mr. Jenkins, Miss Sweetie, and Miss Nancy were in the baggage claim area. What a reunion! We ran to them and hugged them, raising such a ruckus in the airport that I thought we would get in trouble for disturbing the peace!

"We thought y'all would have a lot of luggage!" Miss Sweetie said, smoothing the arm of my jacket.

"*Oui! Mais,* not just that! We wanted to see y'all!" Miss Nancy said, giving me a hug.

"No, we all wanted to see if y'all were all right, Caroline. Now let me have a look at my grandson." Mother looked right past me and took Eric's chin in her hands and examined him. Then she turned to her friends and said, "Y'all? I want you to meet the finest boy in all the world!" Miss Sweetie and Miss Nancy cooed and smiled but, to our surprise Mother put her arm around his shoulder and walked away with him, saying, "All right! *Now* I've got my *boy!* It's been far too long since I've seen you, sweetheart! I am going to show you things you've never *dreamed* of! There's a whole *world* in the ACE Basin! A whole new world just waiting for *you!*"

Well, Miss Sweetie, Miss Nancy, and I exchanged looks of panic. Mother sounded like Rosalind Russell in a live audition for *Auntie Mame*. I didn't know if she meant to resurrect that old pontoon boat and start her river parades again or if she meant to teach him to drink bourbon and shoot trap! At least she had shown up looking normal, wearing a blue cotton sweater set and navy trousers. I thanked the heavens that she had not shown up in one of her costumes. That was unfair of me to think that. In fact, she hadn't done anything like that in years.

She apparently wanted Eric to see her as normal, warm, and grandmotherly, of which I hoped she was capable should the occasion arise. I turned back to our welcome committee, the two well-wishing mother hens and Mr. Jenkins.

"Welcome home, Miss Caroline," Mr. Jenkins said, extending his hand, which I took and shook soundly.

"Thanks, Mr. Jenkins, thanks a lot." I looked around at Miss Sweetie and Miss Nancy, who stood by, waiting for me. "Let's go get the bags. Well, y'all were right. We have about twenty suitcases!"

Jenkins loaded most of our things in the back of the van and Eric helped. Mother watched Eric laughing with Mr. Jenkins over the strategy of packing the van. Jenkins pretended not to know what to do, scratching his head. Eric began giving instructions like a diplomatic drill sergeant. Mother turned to me, saying, "Caroline? The time has come to start concentrating on that boy's gifts! I can tell you in one look that he's a brilliant child!"

"Mother, you are so right!" For once, we were in perfect agreement.

In minutes, the convoy to Tall Pines Plantation was under way. I rode with Miss Nancy in her BMW, Mother rode with Miss Sweetie, and Eric rode with Mr. Jenkins.

"Caroline?" Miss Nancy said, backing out of her parking

space. "Your mother is so happy that you came to her, you can't imagine. Do you want some music?"

That remark revealed that Mother had told her friends that I was leaving Richard. Who was I kidding? With all this luggage? Hell, most of the world probably knew. Gossip traveled the Lowcountry at the speed of light.

"Life is weird, Miss Nancy."

"You can say that again," she said. "I always say, if you can live long enough, you'll see just about everything."

I wanted to say, *You don't know the half of it,* but I opened the console to look for tapes instead.

"Sorry, hon, my music's in the CD changer in the trunk. Just mash that button and then the next one and you can cruise through 'em."

Mash it! That was the first time I'd heard that term in eons! The next thing I knew, Shania Twain was singing "I Feel Like a Woman!" and we were tearing down Highway 17 south, blasting by Mother's and Mr. Jenkins's cars, waving and laughing our heads off. She must've been doing nearly one hundred miles an hour. My heart was in my throat. When Miss Nancy was sure she had them far behind her in the distance, she slowed down to around sixty-five.

"You don't know Lavinia like I do," she said. "That old biddy will read our lips and we won't have a moment's privacy! So tell me, you all right?"

I had no doubt that she was right, but she didn't have to scare the hell out of me to make her point. "I'm fine, Miss Nancy, I *swear,* we're both fine." What was I supposed to say?

"Okay, enough said. If you need anything I expect to hear from you, okay?"

"I need a little time to get organized, that's all. I guess for the time being, we'll be staying with Mother. But eventually, I'll have to find a place for us. I think we would enjoy living in downtown Charleston, or maybe over on Sullivan's Island. What do you think?"

"Real estate prices are through the roof! Wait till you see! But I have a niece who's a broker. I'll give her a call over the weekend. If there's anything decent on the market, she'll know about it."

"That'd be great. Meanwhile, I've got a lot to do to get Eric situated."

"School?"

"Nope, I'm gonna homeschool him. I'm really looking forward to it."

She dropped her head to one side and got quiet.

"No good?" I said.

"Caroline, I'd be the last person on the planet to advise someone on raising their children, especially considering how mine turned out." That made me giggle. Her son was a forest ranger living in Colorado, alone in the woods, writing a book on the secret life of screech owls. Her daughters, both of them, lived in a commune in Vermont and had multitudes of children, with different partners, without the time-honored tradition of a marital ceremony. Growing up, I remembered their escapades were bizarre. "But, it occurs to me that it might put extra stress on your relationship with your boy. I stressed my kids to death and it didn't pay. They all took after Houston, my dearly departed husband. There wasn't a thing I could do to change them."

"I don't want to change Eric, but I don't want to stress him out either. I'll have to give that some thought. Tell me something, Miss Nancy. What's your opinion of Mother? Trip seems to think she is having trouble keeping things going."

"He's as crazy as hell too, yanh? *Excusay moi*, but they

could both be a lot nicer to Lavinia, if you ask me."

"I'm asking."

"You stick around awhile and you'll see. It's not all that subtle."

"Well, last weekend she seemed fine to me."

"She is. Don't you worry about Lavinia. She's got better beans than Boston!"

I smiled and sat back and listened to the sounds of her car's engine as we roared down the highway. Suddenly, out of nowhere, a state trooper appeared at our side, indicating we should pull over to the shoulder of the road.

"Shit, shit, shit," Miss Nancy said, "I hate this! They always pick on me because I'm a senior citizen!"

I thought to myself, yeah, a senior citizen with a lead foot *mashing* the hell out of the gas pedal! She rolled down her window and started fishing around in her wallet for her driver's license.

"Afternoon, ma'am," the trooper said, and took off his aviator glasses. I recognized him! Who was he? I had gone to school with him!

"Don't I know you?" I said.

He looked at me and some major pheromones passed between us. This man had the greenest eyes and the most beautiful smile I had ever seen.

"No, ma'am, I'd remember you if I did."

"Where'd you go to school?" I said, more convinced than ever that I knew him.

He pulled off his helmet and I took off my sunglasses.

"Caroline? Caroline Wimbley?"

"Yes! Matthew? Matthew Strickland?"

"My God! I thought you had run off to New York City and you were never coming back!"

Miss Nancy was visibly relieved and allowed us to continue our reunion, hoping it would save her points on her license and a big fat fine.

"Matthew, can I have a word with you?"

"You surely can! I'll be goll-derned."

He even came around and opened my door, just as he had when we dated each other in the Dark Ages of high school. I got out of the car and stood next to him, brazenly appraising what the years had wrought. We had burned it up together, dancing at the Merchant Seamen's Club in the wee hours of the hottest summer on record. He was still one of the finest specimens of male composition ever to walk the woods. It had troubled me that he never wanted to go to college. It had troubled him that I *did* want to go to college. Ambition broke us up, and serendipity had brought us back together—for the moment. What in hell was I thinking? Naughty, naughty. That's what.

"Matthew? How's your family?" I checked out his left hand. Naked.

"Sheila left me five years ago. All my kids are grown and gone."

"That's just *awful*," I said, as insincerely as I could.

The wind was blowing his hair back from his face. He squinted and I could see he had tiny lines around his eyes. They did not detract. I imagined that unlike Richard he did not have one ounce of flab on him. The guy was a brick.

"How's that sumbitch you married," he said, "that head doctor?"

"Frankly, Matthew, I've left the sumbitch. I'm going to be staying at Mother's with my boy, Eric."

"Is that a fact now?" He looked at the ground and then back at me.

This was no time to be coy. "That's a fact. We'd love to have you stop by."

"Yeah, Gawd, I always heard your husband was a few bricks shy of a load."

"That's one way to put it."

He put his helmet back on, opened the car door for me, and as he closed it he put on his sunglasses. "I'll come by some evening, Caroline. It would be fun to catch up. Y'all have a nice day!"

I looked at Miss Nancy. "I used to date him."

"I gathered as much," she said.

In the time it took to drive halfway to Tall Pines, I had ripped off and wadded up my mourning clothes, thrown off the mantle of sorrow, and flirted my guts out with a state trooper. Nice work! Down south when we ran short of men, we recycled.

Miss Lavinia's Journal

When Sweetie and I got in the car, we carried on like girls. I think the old gal was almost as excited as I was to see Eric and Caroline, but Sweetie's always been a gusher. I pride myself on restraint. But, Lord! Eric has grown so! What a beautiful boy and what a vocabulary! Nevil would've eaten him up! God, her disaster has brought me such happiness! Did I say that right?

25

ON MY SHIELD

My daddy always said that when soldiers went to war, they came home either carrying their shield or on their shield. I guessed I was on mine, and feeling pretty darn defeated. In everyone else's favor, they didn't hold it against me.

Millie came out to greet us when we arrived and hugged me until I thought she'd crack my ribs. When she hugged Eric she began to cry.

"Come on, Millie," I said, "I can't take it if you crash!"

"I been saving these tears for a long time, Miss Caroline, and they got to flow now. Can't hold them back no more!"

"Get a hold on yourself, you old fool," Mother said, hurrying by her, "we need to get dinner on the table! My grandson is starving!"

Millie dried her eyes and started laughing. She released Eric to Mother's outstretched arms. As they walked away, Millie said to me, "She is one cantankerous old bird, you yanh me?"

I nodded and said, "Come on, I'll help you." I linked

my arm through hers and we walked into the house together.

Dinner was filled with small talk and anything but questions about what had actually happened between Richard
and me. *Y'all have a good trip? Cold in New York? Isn't
it a beautiful day?* In one way, that was a relief and in
another, it was waiting for the inevitable. Millie called
everyone to the table at noon and we all assembled in the
dining room—me, Eric, Miss Sweetie, Miss Nancy,
Mother, and, at the last moment, Trip arrived.

The buffet was arranged with Mother's old Sheffield
covered dishes filled with a sausage and shredded chicken
dish in one, steamed rice in another, and fresh corn and
tomatoes in a third. They were practical as well as beautiful, each one having a well in the bottom to hold hot
water, designed to keep the food warm throughout the
meal. I hadn't seen them in years.

"Oh, Mother! I remember these casserole dishes!" I put
my plate at my place and helped myself to a biscuit.

"I'm not sure I'd refer to them as *casseroles,* Caroline!
They are hardly Pyrex!" But that remark lacked its customary sting, as Mother was honestly teasing me.

"They are *ex-quis-eete,* Lavinia!" Miss Nancy said.

"Lavinia? Aren't they the ones given to your mother by
Senator Sanders and his wife when she married your father?" Miss Sweetie said.

Senator Sanders's family had saved their plantation,
Beech Hill, from Sherman's torches by calling out, *"If you
burn the house, you burn me!"* Unlike the live oaks of Tall
Pines, it had an avenue of palmettos. The Sanders family
had quite a history, but they had not given Mother that
silver. Daddy had bought it in New York for Mother when
they celebrated her fortieth birthday with a vacation there.
I remembered the day she unpacked them and I played

with all the pieces like a puzzle, fascinated by their detail.

"Why, yes, I believe you're right, dear!" Mother said.

Trip shot me a glance—a straight face with arched eyebrow. I giggled. Mother never passed up any opportunity to distinguish her reputation—honestly or otherwise. We all served our plates and found our places, Trip giving Eric the first of many lessons on protocol.

"Come on, boy," Trip said, "help your uncle seat the ladies!"

"Sure!" Eric said and followed Trip's lead until we were all seated.

This caused the eruption of many little remarks on how Eric had grown and my, my, what a little gentleman, and aren't you proud of him, Caroline? Yes, yes, I said, I certainly was. Eric grinned with the realization that this wasn't Kansas at all, while we all waited for the Great and Terrible Oz to lift her fork.

"This smells so good, Mother!" I said, famished from our trip.

"Good, darling!" She slowly unfolded her napkin and draped it across her lap, smiling at everyone, knowing they waited. Then, in a dramatic sigh, she finally picked up her fork and took a small bite.

"I made it this morning!" Miss Nancy said.

Eric looked at me. "What is this stuff?" he whispered.

"Young man, it's the food of the gods! Chicken Pilau and fresh vegetables! Try it!" Trip said.

Eric wasn't a picky eater, he was a plain eater. We were always watching our weight, so he wasn't accustomed to sauces, spices, and gravies. Chicken Pilau had a reputation in our kitchen for as long as I had lived. Every time anyone passed the stove, they sprinkled more pepper in the pot.

It was a wonderful dish for a crowd and indeed there were many family stories where it played a leading role.

Daddy loved to tell the story of Louise, his mother's cook. His mother would say, Louise? I'm having company! Let's make Chicken Pilau (pronounced *perlow*). How many? Louise would ask. His mother would say, Twenty. Louise would pause and say, Get me four chickens then. If his mother said *fifty* were coming for dinner, Louise would pause and say, Well, then get me four chickens. It was the Biblical loaves and fishes. Easy to make too. You just boiled the four chickens with celery, onions, and a bay leaf in plenty of water. When the meat fell off the bones, you strained it and used the juice to cook the rice. When the chicken cooled, you shredded it and added it to the rice with cooked sausage. With pepper. And more pepper. And still more. Extra juice was used for thin gravy.

All eyes were on Eric as he piled his fork with suspicion and chicken. He ate it, then blew a little air from the spiciness and grabbed his iced tea, gulping it down. He began to devour it with the typical gusto of a starving boy. "Damn, Mom! This is awesome! How come you never made this?"

Everyone burst out laughing that he had said *damn*. On any other day, the table may have held back breath while Mother chastised the offender, but not today. I began to view this lunch as a celebration of sorts. Not a celebration that said Mother was right about Richard, but one that showed the affection we all felt for each other.

"How's Frances Mae?" I said, thinking I should at least be polite enough to inquire.

"Big as the broad side of a barn and looks like she's due to pop any minute," Trip said. There was more than a trace of disgust in his voice.

I felt sorry for Frances Mae, but only for that moment. I was not looking forward to seeing her any more than she probably wanted to see me.

"I'm sure she's ready for that baby to come," I said.

"To be sure. Does anyone care for a glass of wine? Trip?" Mother said.

Everyone declined, including Louie the Liver. "Have to be in court at three," he said.

"What for?" Eric said.

"Well, son, I got me a case this afternoon, all right. Seems this fellow got lost in the middle of the night and wound up crawling through the window of his own house. Said he lost his keys or some such fool. Well, his wife, my client, got scared at the noise and shot him with his own pistol right in the jewels."

"Mercy!" Miss Sweetie said.

"Tomcat. Serves him right," Miss Nancy said.

"You don't know that, Nancy!" Mother said.

"Well, she's right. We all know he had been running around with every kinda loose woman in Colleton County—got pictures to prove it. Anyway, he says she tried to kill him. She says she thought he was a robber. Now, they're getting divorced."

"Heavens! No wonder!" Miss Sweetie said.

"Yeah, this fellow says he's broke but we know better. Got copies of his bank statements from the Cayman Islands." He looked at Eric with his serious face. "You don't want to know how I got those."

"Cool! It's just like television! Judge Judy!" Eric said. "Can I come with you? Mom?"

I looked at Trip and shrugged my shoulders. Trip wiped his mouth carefully and put his napkin on the table. He took a long look at Eric, who waited for his verdict.

"Why not?" Trip said. "If we get back here at a decent hour, and if you behave yourself, maybe I'll take you fishing!"

"Cool," Eric said. "Yes! This is very cool."

"Okay with you?" Trip said to me.

"Sure, it will give me a chance to unpack our clothes and get settled."

"Can I get y'all some lemon meringue pie?" Millie said, circling the table, collecting plates. "More tea?"

Eric got up without being asked and began helping Millie to clear the dishes. As soon as they disappeared into the kitchen, Mother, Miss Nancy, Miss Sweetie, and Trip remarked on Eric's conduct. "He's such a fine boy!" "Isn't he an angel?" The pie was quickly eaten and our first meal at Tall Pines was at an end.

"Well, girls," Mother said to Miss Nancy and Miss Sweetie, "are we still playing cards this afternoon?"

No wonder Mother had been anxious for lunch. She wasn't going to let our arrival interfere with her bridge game!

"Unless the sky falls! I made strawberry muffins this morning," Miss Sweetie said. "You can ride with me, Lavinia."

"Let me just get my sweater," Mother said.

"That's just what we need is more food," Miss Nancy said, in my direction.

I walked them all to the door, and stood on the porch as each car drove away. When I closed the ancient front door behind it, its thud and clank seemed heavier than usual. And more complete. I had closed the door on Richard and I was back where I started. Tall Pines.

I went to find Millie to do a little self-indulgent moping, but the kitchen was empty. Looking out the back door, I saw her golf cart rolling down the lane toward her house. She must've cleaned the kitchen by wiggling her nose, I thought.

That seemed like a good time to take a walk around the

yard and maybe visit the rose garden. The afternoon sun was warm and my legs were in need of a good stretch. I threw my sweater around my shoulders and left from the back door. I wasn't twenty feet from the house when I had this urge to turn around. All at once, I realized that I was alone. In every sense of the word.

Why had I come back here? I could have rented an apartment in New York and just gone on with life, but to tell the truth, I was completely over the pace and the energy of the city. Life there had a black hole where its heart should have been.

Was Mother less happy to see me than her friends were? It certainly had seemed so. Maybe that wasn't fair. I was being a baby, but I had to say to myself that some part of me wished she would have stopped her life for me. Maybe she was smarter than that. Maybe she wanted me to settle in at my own pace, give me some time to come to her.

Trip had certainly taken a shine to Eric. That was wonderful because maybe he could help take up some of the slack of Richard's absence. Mother had definitely shown some sweet affection for Eric too. Depending on Trip and Mother made my alarms go off. Could we coexist without some kind of mutual dependency? No, or else I shouldn't be here. Tall Pines was not a boardinghouse. I had come here with my son for refuge. If I had found any kind of resolve in me it was that I wasn't going to live any lies. Leaving Richard was just the first step in changing my life. Our lives. I hoped Mother wouldn't disappoint Eric as a grandmother in that way she had hurt Trip and me when Daddy died. Would I spend my entire life trying to please parent figures? Wasn't Richard more than that? There were so many issues and I had so many questions. As much as

I hated to, it was best to go back to the beginning and examine it. The next thing I knew I found myself sitting in a lawn chair, staring at the Edisto River, smelling the jasmine and remembering.

26

DADDY

1974

I had just graduated from Carolina Academy in Walterboro and was spending the summer getting in gear to go to Ashley Hall in Charleston. Ashley Hall was where Mother had gone to school and she announced I would go there as well. Daddy wasn't too keen on the idea of me leaving home so early, but he understood that the options in our neck of the woods were limited. We were sitting in the kitchen, sharing a Hershey bar—plain chocolate, my favorite.

"You can take me out to supper on Wednesdays," I said.

"And I'm going to do that too, so you had better not be making plans without me for Wednesdays!" he said, his eyes filled with mischief, then suddenly they clouded, and his face became solemn.

"Daddy? Why are you looking at me like that?"

"To remember, Caroline, to remember your face just

like it is now. You are the spitting image of my mother. She was a beautiful woman, a heart-stopping head turner. You will be too. You had better tell those boys in Charleston that your daddy will rip the legs off the first one that tries anything funny with my daughter."

"Daddy! I'm almost fourteen! And, in case you forgot, it's an all-girls school!" I smiled at him and watched him relax, letting out little puffs of air, him trying to hide the fact that he had actually been concerned. That he had realized in that flash of a moment I no longer wore pigtails, that, good Lord, someday I'd have a sex life. It made me want to apologize for growing up without his notice or approval. In another way, I felt myself swell a little as though my possibilities had been discovered. I *was* growing up. Boarding school a whole thirty miles away! I could come home on weekends and there was nothing to stop Daddy and Mother from visiting me during the week.

I had some anxiety about going away, but I figured all those other generations of girls went there and didn't kill themselves; neither would I. I'd be fine.

Trip was going to have his eleventh birthday that July and Mother was planning the party. All it took was anticipation of a party to watch the energy surge in Mother. Party? She was the tree in Rockefeller Center, and somebody flipped her switch. God only knew how overboard it would be. I heard her talking to Mr. Jenkins about creating a western town from plywood cutouts and something else about costumes. She was probably gonna fly in Roy Rogers and Dale Evans from somewhere and have a rodeo in the old rice fields. Pigs would die, there was no doubt of that. Mother just couldn't help herself. She was born to dream up and give the fantastic parties she wanted to attend.

We all knew that Trip wanted a horse for his birthday.

The campaign had nearly coincided with his birth. His entire room was swallowed alive with horse mania—posters, sheets, magazines—you name it. If it had a horse on it, Trip owned it.

I was a sympathetic partner. I got my horse when I was eleven. Seemed fair for him to expect the same. But Daddy worried that Trip wasn't mature enough to be responsible for such a large animal. I rode my horse, Ginger, every day, fed her and groomed her too. Of course, Mr. Jenkins helped me, but I stood on a stool when I was Trip's age and worked the knots from Ginger's mane with my fingers. Ginger knew all my secrets and that relationship was carrying me through the jungle of my adolescence.

And, we all had our indulgences. I had Ginger, Mother had about a billion pairs of shoes, and Daddy had his little airplane. It was a little red and white, single-engine Piper, prop job. Mother always said it wasn't any better than a nasty old crop duster, and refused to fly in it. But Daddy would preen like a peacock when you asked him for a ride.

One Valentine's Day when Mother was entertaining a group from the Charleston Historical Society out on the lawn by the river, Daddy buzzed her party with a long flag, slapping the breeze behind the plane that said, LAVINIA IS THE QUEEN OF MY HEART!

Another time, on her birthday, he drove it almost to the front door. We ran outside to see what the noise was and there stood Daddy, in his World War II pilot's uniform, complete with white silk scarf and a huge bouquet of flowers. He claimed to have a date with a certain young Lavinia Ann Boswell and Mother was completely charmed.

"Who are these beautiful children?" he said, and produced Hershey bars from his pocket for us.

"Why, sir? I'm not sure, but they appear to be ours!"

He and Mother drove all over Tall Pines, drinking champagne.

Naturally, Trip and I thought their dramatics were stupid and embarrassing. I mean, did the whole world have to know they probably still had sex, even though they had children? Jesus! Did they give our personal humiliation a second thought? Not on your life. They were so stupid over each other that the only time Mother and Daddy ever even remembered they knew us was at meals, and when we had "family hour" after supper.

Family hour was another one of Daddy's inventions of conscience. Every night after supper, we would continue our dinner table discussion in the living room. Daddy would make each of us read something from the Charleston newspaper and then we'd have a great discussion about it. Sometimes the articles we chose were about sports and sometimes they were about politics. Every now and then Mother would use Dear Abby's column to give us a lesson in morality, Lavinia style. Even though Trip and I groaned about the forced feeding of the state of the outside world, we adored it. There was something reassuring about those hours that made me believe that even though we were a wacky family, we were a family nonetheless.

It was hot that summer, more steamy than usual. All day long the heat would build and deep in the afternoon violent thunderstorms burst forth like it was the end of the world. The rain came down in torrents, the lightning crackled and flashed all around, and then, in minutes, it was over. Afterward, we'd sit outside, eat watermelon, and watch the steam rise from the earth. Hell couldn't have been that hot. Some nights Trip and I would run down to the dock and jump in the river. Mother had us pretty well terrified of alligators, so to say we took a quick swim would be an understatement.

Anyway, it was the hottest summer I could remember. I was in the kitchen with Millie, sewing name tags on socks and underwear to take to school. It was July twenty-first, a week before Trip's birthday. He came in the back door in a state of excitement.

"Guess what?" he said.

"What, fish breath?" I said.

"Shut up, dog face. Mr. Jenkins has been cleaning out the old stall! Don't you think that's a good sign, Millie?"

Millie stopped sewing and looked up. "It's not a bad sign," she said. "How's the sky look?"

I looked out of the window across the river. "Dark and crazy," I said, "gonna rain. Jeesch! Five minutes ago the sun was shining!" Shadows fell across the room as the sky became more and more ominous.

"What else is new?" Trip said, peeling a banana and eating half in one bite. "Bet I'm getting my horse!"

"Seems likely," Millie said, and came to the window to see for herself. "Where's your daddy?"

"Don't know," I said. "Down at the barn?"

I didn't like the look on Millie's face. I'd never seen her quite so serious.

"I was just there," Trip said. "I think Mr. Jenkins said he was going up for a ride."

"Come on, boy," Millie said, "he's got better sense than to fly when there's a storm coming!" Her breath became raspy and short.

She went out to the hall and called for Mother to come downstairs. Mother heard her and, annoyed, called back to her.

"Stop screaming like I don't know what, Millie! If you need me you can walk . . . what?" She stopped on the landing of the stairs and a huge clap of thunder boomed all around us. The chandelier in the foyer flickered. We stood behind Millie, glued in place by fear. I knew it before it happened. In my mind, I saw a plane in flames. Daddy was inside, unconscious, and his khaki trousers were on fire. I started to scream. Over and over I screamed until I felt the sting of Mother's hand on my cheek.

"Stop it! Stop it right now!" she said, screaming at me, just as loudly.

I shook all over and began to cry. "He's dying," I said. "I can see him . . . Fire! Mother! Millie! Oh, God, please! Do something!" I ran out the front door into the storm. Sure enough I saw the smoke in the distance. We ran, all of us, slipping on the wet grass, stumbling through the bushes, to the place he had crashed. By the time we got there, we were all hysterical and soaked to the skin. The rain had slowed to a drizzle. Mr. Jenkins was on his knees, on the wet ground, with his arms folded around his head, hiding his face.

"I tried, oh, God, I tried to get to him! To get him out! He was gone, but I didn't want him to burn up! Oh, where is God this day?" Mr. Jenkins's anguish was quickly spread among us.

I tried to cover Trip's eyes so he wouldn't see Daddy. We held each other, staring at the wreckage and sobbing. Trip screamed over and over. *No! No! No!* The engine on the front of the plane was burning and smoking and I could see over Trip's head that there was nothing left of Daddy but a blackened cadaver, nearly burned beyond recognition. Little fires burned all around, like patches of death.

I couldn't stop staring. Millie held Mother back as she screamed over and over. Then the worst happened—what was left of the plane exploded, hurling pieces of jagged metal high in the air. We fell to the ground in fear, screaming louder yet until I knew we had all gone insane. Where was Daddy's body? Who would find it and put it back together? We were as horrified and hysterical as I imagined anyone could be.

There was no one to blame and no way to make it end. I was facedown on the ground; water puddled all around me. Oh! The grief and anguish of us all! Everyone weeping, sobbing. *Where was God this day,* Mr. Jenkins had said. Senseless. Horrible. My tears rolled to the ground along with raindrops, a tiny river of loss, flowing away with all I had cherished. How could this be real? How could God let this happen? Ashes fell in my line of vision, ashes of my father, falling on me, in my hair, in my tears. I watched this shower, on my stomach, face to the side, tears rolling. Ashes falling in spirals. Me sighing then gulping again, wounded, permanently damaged in a ghoulish sense of disbelief. My salt, Daddy's ashes, the rain. Trip crawled to my side, trying to talk through his crying.

"Come on," he said, "get up. We gotta get up."

I couldn't move. I heard him, but I couldn't answer. I knew he wanted me to be his big sister. I didn't want to be anybody's anything. Maybe I'd never feel again.

"Come on," he said, over and over, "come on!"

Finally, I felt Millie's hand on my shoulder. The rain had started again and then it had all but stopped but I felt like I was sinking into the earth, part of it then, impossible to pry loose. I didn't care. I grew roots. My daddy, my wonderful daddy, he was dead.

"Come on, Caroline, Millie's gone help you to your feet," she said in the most impassioned voice I had ever heard her use. "We gots to take care of many things now. Many things." She put her hand under my arm and Trip did the same on my other side and they pulled me up to my knees.

"Oh, God," I said, "oh, God." I started crying again. The whole accident, the smoldering wreckage, I was so

unable to steady myself, to calm down—it was too much.
Now I was afraid to look, that Daddy's arm or leg might
be hanging in a tree. I didn't want to raise my head. Millie
just put her arms around me and Trip did too. We stood
and cried together, making sounds like inconsolable babies, small animals in pain, soaked, muddy, wailing against
this unthinkable catastrophe. We cried until we couldn't
cry anymore, each of us stroking the other's hair, back,
arm, cooing and then breaking down again until we had
worn ourselves out.

Mother had disappeared; Millie said Jenkins had taken
her back to the house. They were calling the fire department and the police and only God knew who else. I was
dumbstruck that she had left us with Millie. Seriously!
How could she have done that? It made me so angry I
wanted to hit her! She had never reached out for us, not
once in the time we had been witnesses to the fire, the
explosion, the elements. What had she been thinking? We
were just children! How could she?

What I remember of that day, that horrible day we lost
Daddy, is a mosaic of moments—the largest tile, the explosion—the others, small details. I was cold and covered
in mud; my hands were freezing. I was tired, I had never
felt that kind of weariness. I ached all over, my throat, my
stomach, my shoulders and back. Too tired to lift my feet,
my head, or my arms. My throat hurt from crying. I could
only sigh and sigh.

At about the same time we arrived back to the house,
men began arriving in official vehicles—the coroner's station wagon, the fire chief's truck, a team of men from the
fire department and police department with dogs to search
for pieces of my father's body. Mr. Jenkins directed them.
We went upstairs, filthy and bedraggled.

Mother's door was closed. Millie took Trip and me to

our rooms and started hot showers for us to wash away the nightmare.

"Use shampoo and wash your head good, yanh?"

"I will."

In the shower, I sat on the floor of the tub and let the water run and run. I watched it go down the drain and saw my happiness slide away with it. I would never be happy again. I had loved Daddy too much and God had punished me for it. I knew then that it was a sin to love like that—so completely. If you did, you got robbed.

I went to Trip's room in my bathrobe, hair in a towel, and he was just sitting on his bed, wearing boxer shorts and a T-shirt, staring out the window. His face was wet, his eyes almost swollen shut from crying.

"You okay?" I went over and looked at his face. I sat down beside him and put my arm around his shoulder. His bloodshot eyes searched my face and he tried to talk without sobbing.

"What's gonna happen to us now?" he said, and then his voice cracked from the weight of our uncertain future. He was so young to me then. Boys needed their fathers more than girls, I thought then.

"I don't know. I'm gonna take care of you. We are all gonna take care of each other. Come on, baby, don't cry. I love you, Trip."

"I know," he said, "but Daddy's dead and I can't stand it."

"Me either," I said, "me either."

We sat for a while and then I got up and walked to the window. The Edisto River was there, still flowing, no doubt with Daddy's ashes, a witness to what had happened, rising and falling, moving toward St. Helena's Sound, carrying our pain, the same way it had carried the pain of others for all time. I felt like I was a thousand years old; I had seen everything.

"Trip? Let's get dressed and go help Millie."

"Okay."

I felt a little guilty that I didn't go to Mother's room and see how she was. But I was going to be angry for the rest of my life. Angry that she hadn't come to us. How could her grief have been greater than ours? Or more important? Seething with hatred for her, I walked silently by her door, into my room, and dressed to go help Millie.

Millie sang in the kitchen, low and serious, as though her songs would cleanse us of how we felt. They were a solemn plea for mercy.

> *Gone down to the river,*
> *The river flows with life!*
> *Gone beg my god to help us all,*
> *Help us through our strife.*
> *Take this pain away, God!*
> *Oh, take our pain away!*
> *Heal our hearts so we can live,*
> *To praise You one more day!*

I took a tray of sandwiches from Millie and put them on the dining room table.

"People gone be yanh all day and into the night," she said. "Tell Jenkins to come see me. I got work for him."

"Okay," I said. Normally, I would have stolen a sandwich intended for company. That day I would've been swallowing rocks. I couldn't seem to think or stay focused on anything.

The doorbell started ringing.

Miss Sweetie was the first to arrive, with Mr. Moultrie, her husband. Soon the living room was filled with people, coming and going. Miss Nancy, her family, Miss Ellen and Mr. Jimmy. Miss Marian, Mr. Charlie. Everyone from the area came, strangers I had never seen who must've been friends of Daddy. Everyone was consumed by the shock of Daddy's death. Their faces were frozen in masks of denial, sorrow, and grief. The truth was terrible to comprehend.

Mother appeared and sat in her favorite chair and the guests would kneel and speak to her, holding one of her hands in theirs, trying to console her. I saw Trip staring out the window and went to his side.

"Come on," I said, "come with me. I gotta find Jenkins for Millie."

"I don't feel like doing anything," he said.

"Come on, bubba, I know this stinks, the whole thing stinks, but we gotta get ourselves together. We can't not help Millie."

His vacant eyes met my face and we left the house together.

We walked, my brother and I, toward Mr. Jenkins's cottage. The door was open. We knew what we would find. And there he was, at the table, head in his hands. From the back we watched his shoulders rise and fall as he wept silently and alone.

It struck me that I was alone now too. Daddy had been my link to Mother. And Trip's. Who would hold us together now? Mr. Jenkins loved Daddy and had worked for our family for almost as long as Mother had been alive. Although he had always worked at Tall Pines for Mother, he was a man's man. He loved to tell the stories of how he taught Daddy to ride a horse, to burn undergrowth, to shoot wild turkeys and how to clean fish. He had loved my daddy, all right. Loved him like a son.

"Mr. Jenkins?" I said, "I'm sorry to disturb you, but Millie sent us to get you. She needs you."

His eyes, red from crying, tortured by grief and shock, scared me for a moment.

"Tell her I'll be there directly," he said, pulling his white and wrinkled handkerchief from his back pocket and wiping his whole face, as though it would make everything the same again, the same as it had been that morning, before the storm.

"Okay," we said, and closed his door quietly behind us.

Without even the suggestion from each other that we do so, we ambled our way down to the river dock. Watching the water move was something we had done together all our lives. We stood side by side, leaning on the railings, watching the moon rise and the water rush below us in tiny silver caps, in its southern flow, moving in arms that joined into others, always moving. The voice of the water was great, singing a song to soothe us, telling us that though we paused now, and it was right that we should, life went on. Our challenge was not to make sense of Daddy's death, but to make sense of his life and to be strong enough, smart enough, old enough to hear what the Edisto was trying to tell us.

"Caroline?"

"Yeah?"

"Where do you think he is?"

"Daddy?" Trip bobbed his head, and I tried to think of what Daddy would be thinking now. "I don't know, but I know this. If he could talk to you, he wouldn't say that you have to be the man of the family. He'd say to just be a good boy and that he's sorry he left us like this."

"Yeah."

For another few minutes, or maybe for a while, we stood together watching the movement of the water and trying to find Daddy's voice in our hearts, our minds. I thought that I could feel Daddy's regret that we had been witnesses to the explosion, regret that he couldn't repair things for us. I could have sworn I could smell his breath. Then I realized it was the smell of the river. Always the Edisto.

27

THE MERRY WIDOW SPEAKS

It was the shock of Nevil's death. Looking back now, I can tell you plainly that I was in a state of shock that lasted far too long. If I had realized it at the time, things would have been very different, I assure you. For the first and only time in my entire life, I was at a loss for words. I don't mean to say that I couldn't speak at all, it was that I couldn't think of what to say to the children. So I said nothing. I know now that it wasn't right, that they were absolutely split in two by what happened to their daddy. But, so was I.

The day before and the day of the funeral are still a blur. There was no wake because there was no body to mourn. That was the first thing Nevil's death deprived us of—a body. It wasn't fair. The coroner's men had gathered what they could find and put it in a bag, but I knew in my heart that there were still pieces of Nevil out there in the rice fields. How on God's earth was I to explain to my children that they shouldn't play there? I was filled with a

kind of fear you cannot imagine that they would come
across something the dogs had missed. No, they could not
play outside. There would be so many sweeps of the fields
until we were satisfied—Jenkins, Millie, and I. So life
stopped when Nevil died. At least until we could reconcile
ourselves that we had done all we could.

So, forgive me. I was a little preoccupied with the search
to locate my husband's limbs to give the proper attention
to Caroline and Trip. Call me a terrible mother, but I do
not have in my possession a manual that tells one how to
conduct oneself when something like this happens. But I
did have Millie and Jenkins, and my friends saw to the
children—Sweetie and Nancy, always there. Nancy took
Trip to Charleston for a day of visiting churches and talked
to him over lunch about how he thought the funeral should
be arranged. She was such a dear to do this. Nancy was
so modern and up on things like child psychology.

And Sweetie took Caroline to Columbia to the Happy
Bookseller to buy her summer reading. Caroline and
Sweetie liked nothing better than a good book, except to
have a stack of them, unread and waiting. Sweetie told me
she bought Caroline her first iced coffee, which Caroline
drank to the last drop. She made Caroline feel grown-up.
Then she took her shopping for lingerie and nightgowns
at Belk's. I suppose it was time for Caroline to wear underwear that matched. Leave it to Sweetie to make that
decision! It was the furthest thing from my mind, I swear.

Having them out of my hair gave me the chance to,
pardon the expression, put all the pieces together for my
husband's funeral. Jenkins and I chose a casket from wood
samples brought over from Bagnal Funeral Home in Walterboro. I simply could not bring myself to make the trip.
It would be solid mahogany with brass handles. The coroner delivered Nevil's remains to them and a time was set

aside two days later to bury Nevil in the family graveyard at Tall Pines.

First, there would be a small reception in our family's tiny chapel. Nevil's casket would be there on a platform draped in the whitest linens, covered with a blanket of flowers interwoven with flowers from my garden. Two huge sprays had been ordered for either end of it and the family's silver candelabra would be lit. Then, at three o'clock, a graveside prayer service led by the Episcopalian minister from Walterboro, where Helena Blanchard from Charleston would sing "Ave Maria" and some other spirituals that were Nevil's favorites. A grand reception would follow at the house, with the chamber ensemble from the Charleston Symphony. I was determined to send my Nevil to Glory in style. The children and everyone else would see how much I loved Nevil by the funeral I had planned. I truly hoped they would.

Millie was my well of strength. She helped with all the details, making hundreds of phone calls and taking at least that many messages. The morning after Nevil died, I found her in the kitchen, her command central, on the phone when I went downstairs for some toast.

"I managed to find five cases of Dom Perignon in the storage room at the Hibernian Society in Charleston through Mr. Moultrie," she said.

"What year?" I said, because if it wasn't a vintage year, we simply wouldn't pour it.

"Miss L?"

She looked at me with those eyes of hers, the black light through slits that said *We are damn lucky to find it at all!*

"Oh, all right. Tell them to deliver this afternoon," I said. "Did the Colony House call back?"

The Colony House in Charleston was one of our favorite restaurants. When Ray Smiley, the owner, found out about

Nevil's accident, he called immediately to offer to bring
all the food and waiters. I accepted his gracious favor and
asked him to have the chef call me regarding the menu.
When the fellow called the first time, I was appalled by
his proposal. He must have thought he was Craig Clai-
borne or somebody with all the foie gras and Gougette and
pike mousse he proposed. No, no! He had probably taken
a summer course in Paris. God only knows. His name was
Ashley. Any man named after a river could probably cook
fish and simple things, I figured, so I said, "Ashley, darlin'? You are so, so sweet to plan something so grand for
my Nevil, but I am afraid I was thinking of something less
complicated, like little pieces of goose liver and apple on
toothpicks and some hot cheese puffs people can just pick
up from a tray. And maybe some little whitefish fluffed up
in a tiny pastry shell."

"Leave it to me, Miss Lavinia," he said, "just leave it
to me."

I had decided that he had understood the subtlety of my
message so I said, "Fine. Just call me when you have it
all together, all right?"

"Yes, ma'am, I will."

That was at ten in the morning. Now it was noon and I
was famished—toast would settle me, I decided.

"Yanh's the menu," Millie said, handing me a legal pad
when I came into the kitchen.

"Roasted turkey with a creamy dijonnaise on small rye
bread rounds with a cranberry confit garnish, roasted ten-
derloin of pork on wild rice blini with a mélange of apple
to finish, Angels on Horseback with a citron dipping
sauce . . ." On and on it went with one highfalutin dish
after another. It tried my patience, it truly did.

"Millie? I can't deal with this! Yanh! Gimme your pencil!" I started crossing things out and making changes.

"Get this Ashley on the phone, please, and tell him the turkey's fine, but just mix up a little mayonnaise and mustard and use regular cranberry sauce on the top. Tell him pork's fine too, but use those little pancakes and just applesauce on top! Angels on Horseback? Does he think I never broiled bacon on scallops? Tell him a lemon butter sauce with that, please. God in heaven! Every chef thinks he's an artist! Isn't that the truth?"

This made Millie chuckle and if there was one thing we needed it was a chuckle.

"You doing all right, Miss L?"

"As well as can be expected," I said. "Did the florist call?"

"Go look in the living room," she said, "they been arriving since eight o'clock this morning."

As much as I adore flowers, these were flowers I never wanted to see. Indeed, the room overflowed with baskets, sprays on stands, glass vases and bowls—all of them filled with exquisite flowers; every surface of the room and all over the floor were flowers for my Nevil. I began to cry, the tears just came upon me in a rush of I don't know how many feelings. That I missed Nevil, that I didn't know so many people cared about us, that the sheer number of arrangements shocked me and I had had just about all the shock one woman could take.

I began taking the cards from their holders to see who had been so generous. *Miss Lavinia, If I or any member of my family can be a comfort to you, please call on us. You and the children are in our prayers. Strom Thurmond.* The next one was from Fritz Hollings: *My dear Lavinia, Petesy and I are so very sorry and send you our love and prayers. Fritz.*

That was nice, I thought, because after all, Nevil and I had entertained for our two senators during every campaign I could recall and truly, we had become the dearest of friends. Truly we had. Why, just last year, Strom's wife brought me all the sheers from their town house in Georgetown, D.C., when I was searching for fabric to decorate the pontoon in honor of Princess Anne and Capt. Mark Phillips's wedding. We covered the rails in white festoons and wrapped greens all around it. We flew the American flag and the flag of the motherland. She rode with me, drinking champagne to the music of "Rule Britannia." She was such fun.

On and on the note cards went. I wondered through my tears if all these people would attend the funeral. It occurred to me that I hadn't checked the newspaper for Nevil's obituary, which had been written by Moultrie.

I was suddenly overcome by the strong odor of so many sweet scents that I thought I would actually fall to the floor. Rather than risk breaking my hip, I opened the French doors to the verandah and went outside to collect myself.

There before me, the Edisto rolled downstream. I stood for I don't know how long and thought about how I was so awfully sad. I guess something in me always knew I would lose Nevil, that he would be the first to go. I had always found his recklessness appealing, never dreaming it would cost him his very life. I thought he'd die a more manly death—maybe a hunting accident—this was a stupid way to die. It made me mad at him for being so thoughtless. Yes, I was hopping mad.

I turned to see Millie in the doorway, coming toward me with a tissue to dry my tears.

"I know, Miss L, this yanh is a terrible day for us all. It surely is. Poor Jenkins is beside himself."

I gathered myself and took the tissue, blowing my nose, gently, as was my custom. "Tell Jenkins to pull himself together and take all those flowers down to the chapel. The men from Bagnal's are coming to dig Nevil's grave and . . ." My lip trembled and I just broke down completely, falling into Millie's arms. *Dig his grave, dig his grave. No! No! Please, God, no!*

We walked back inside together, both of us weeping, trying to stop.

"Help me, Millie." There was so much to do and I didn't have the strength for it. "We have to catalog the cards from the flowers for thank-you notes. Then they have to be moved down to the . . ."

"Miss Lavinia, you go on and wash your face. I'll call Jenkins. We gone take care of everything."

"Thank you, Millie. Thank you."

I walked back through the living room, through the jungle stench of flowers, into my hallway and faced the stairs. I am a widow, I thought. How dreadfully horrible. What would I wear to bury my husband? I didn't think I had the appropriate ensemble. I ascended slowly, holding the rail, taking each step one at a time.

28

DADDY'S GONE

1974

I woke up the morning of Daddy's funeral to the sounds of trucks outside, coming and going. Unable to face the day alone, I ran down the hall to see if Trip was still asleep. His room was empty. As quickly as I could, I dressed and went downstairs to find Millie. I found Mother instead, at the front door signing a receipt for a delivery of cases and cases of booze.

"Morning, Mother," I said, from the bottom step.

Mother looked back at me, sucked her teeth, and turned away to close the door and bolt it.

"Caroline? Please go make yourself presentable. This day is horrible enough without my child looking like an orphan."

"Mother? This is the first thing you've said to me since Daddy died two days ago. Don't you think you could come up with something nicer?"

Mother turned on her heel to face me. I thought she was gonna cross the hall and slap the hell out of me again. I would not have cared if she had. But she stared at me instead, not knowing what to say. I was furious at her because she couldn't *find* anything to say. So we just stood, faced off like two cowboys at high noon, waiting to see who would draw first. In that moment, I decided that this was a real line in the sand, so I crossed it without another word, went past her, through the dining room to the kitchen. Mother had said nothing still, and my fury grew. What kind of a mother was she? What kind of a person?

Millie was in the kitchen with a bunch of men and women, waiters, I guessed, fixing food on platters for later.

"Hey, Millie, where's Trip?" I said, taking a banana from a bowl of fruit.

"Gone out with the dog to walk. Left early this morning! You sleep all right, darlin'?" Millie said, and gave me a hug I didn't want at all. I stiffened. "What you so mad about? I see that look in your eyes. Tell me what's wrong."

"I'm okay," I said.

There were too many people in the room to discuss anything, coming and going out of the back door, bringing in crates of food and bags of ice. But, Millie read me like my brains were wrapped in Saran Wrap instead of bone. She always had.

"Get yourself out to the yard. I'll be right along. I want to talk to you."

When Millie told you to do something, it wasn't optional. So I went outside and waited. While I waited, I became even angrier with Mother. What kind of a woman would rush her children out of the house with her friends or send them to bed without a single word of comfort on the day they saw their daddy blow up right before their eyes? Hell, I was thirteen, and I was used to Mother turn-

ing her love off and on like a soap opera actress, but poor
Trip was little! And honestly, Mother's demonstration of
love wasn't winning any Emmys. I worried now how cold
our house would become without Daddy.

As soon as I talked to Millie, I had to find Trip. If he
had gone off with Chalmers, our retriever, he had the
blues. Trip was one of those kids who never seemed happy
and there was no real reason for it—just his nature. I figured he was down at the barn, talking to Ginger. Maybe
I'd let him ride her this morning. That would cheer him
up. I'd find my little brother and be as nice to him as I
could.

In a few minutes, Millie appeared with a canvas tote
bag, walking across the lawn, her stride brisk and determined.

"I know this ain't no kinda breakfast, but you need to
eat something. I put two ham sandwiches in yanh, two cold
cans of Coke, two brownies, and two apples. Go find your
brother, get him to eat, and then get on back to the house.
Now tell me what's up, missy. We ain't got all day."

Even though that sounded stern, it wasn't and I knew
it. This day would be harder on Millie than anyone, so for
her to show her concern for me by stopping working was
generous. I was looking at the ground and the truth just
rolled off my tongue.

"Mother. That's all. She's such a bitch."

She grabbed my arm and held it hard. "Shut your mouth,
you yanh me?"

"Ouch! She is, Millie and you know it!"

"I don't care! It's a terrible thing to say about your own
mother! Girl! You wouldn't be yanh without her! She de-
serves better than this from her only daughter! Shame on
you!"

"No, Millie. Shame on her. Do you know that since

Daddy died she has said not one word to me or Trip? She never came to see how we were."

My eyes filled with tears, Millie let go of my arm and her own eyes began to tear.

"Oh, Lawd!"

"She didn't, Millie. How do you explain that?"

"Got to be the shock," Millie said, knowing it was a weak explanation.

"Right. That's why this morning the only thing she had to say to me was not how did you sleep, or oh, Caroline, I'm so sorry and we're gonna be okay—no, the only thing she did was criticize what I was wearing. Nice mother, right?" My jaw was set firm and Millie recognized that it wasn't enough just to tell me to behave, but that somebody owed Trip and me more. That somebody was our mother.

"This ain't her best day, Caroline, or yours. Or mine. I ain't saying she was right. I'm just saying I ain't gonna stand for you talking bad about her at a time like this or any other time. It ain't right." Millie took me by the arm and led me down to the lawn chairs. "Sit."

I sat on the arm of a chair, kicking my heel into the ground over and over. Millie paced. "I'm so angry, Millie. I'm so angry I'd like to hit someone."

"I expect that's normal, but you listen to me and yanh me good. Everybody grieves their loss in they own way."

"Oh, brother, Millie!"

"It's true! Your mother is withdrawing, you're angry, and your brother done run off to cry in private. Me? Jenkins? We just keep so busy that we don't have no time to think about it. But everybody's got they own style. This kind of terrible tragedy shows who people really are. You want to be the person your daddy thought you were? You can start right now by putting your anger where it belongs—behind you. And be a woman today. Not tomorrow, not when you turn eighteen or twenty-one, but today."

"Daddy wouldn't believe how Mother's acting."

"Maybe so, maybe not. I'll make you a little deal, okay? You take care of Trip, I'll take care of you. Jenkins will see about me, and your momma will come around when she's ready."

"Only one problem with that, Millie. I've never had a momma; I only had a daddy. I have a mother. Big difference."

We looked at each other long and hard. If there was one moment that defined my transition from childhood to womanhood, that was it. Millie didn't disagree. She just nodded her head and said, "You go on, now. Find your brother. This is gonna be a long day and I need all the hands I can find. We'll see about Miss Lavinia later on."

I didn't know what that meant, but I took the tote bag, threw the straps over my shoulder, and ran. Trip wasn't in the barn. I scratched Ginger on the neck, and she snorted, smelling the food in my bag, nuzzling my shoulder. I pulled out an apple and gave it to her.

"Yanh, girl, I ain't hungry anyway." I spoke to her in a voice filled with a kind of sadness I'd never felt before. Millie was right. I had to be a woman that day. I'd start by trying to be nice to everybody, I decided. I'd bury my feelings about Mother and concentrate on taking care of Trip. I'd offer to help whenever I could. After those promises, I felt a little better. It didn't matter what Mother did or didn't do. I would take care of myself and Trip too. It didn't matter anymore to me what she thought. I wondered how long my wall of self-protection would stand, if Mother would ever try to penetrate my heart, let me need her. I doubted it. There was no point in worrying about that either, I told myself. Time will tell, like Millie always said.

I began to walk the old rice fields and the courses for

sporting clays, which had just been completed and hardly used. Mother and Daddy liked nothing better than to blow apart clay birds. Now, they would never shoot together again. That seemed impossible.

I was getting close to the scene of the accident and my heartbeat picked up. The sun was climbing the sky and the day was going to be a scorcher. I could smell the burned ground from Daddy's crash site, even from my distance of probably hundreds of yards. The scorched air made my eyes sting.

"Trip!"

I called his name every few minutes, hoping he would answer. Finally, in the clearing, I saw him coming toward me. His hands were dug deep into the pockets of his shorts and his head hung down. I could see he was upset and had probably been crying. I ran to his side and threw my arms around him.

"Get offa me!" he said, complaining.

"Never!" I said. "You're my only brother and I'm your only sister and we're in this together! If Mother wants to ignore us, I don't give a shit."

"You don't?" His big blue eyes were all red and swollen from crying. "Do you know what she said to me this morning?"

"Nope. Gimme a clue."

"She said she was glad you were going away to school and that if I didn't behave, she'd get rid . . . get rid . . . get rid of me too."

Trip began to bawl his eyes out, making baby noises, nose running, gulping sobs.

"She can't do that, Trip. She can't and she won't." I put my arms back around him and rubbed his back. "Just let it all out, Trip, let it all out." I was so angry with Mother now, I wanted to slap her silly. "Why would she say something like that?"

"She said I was sick in the head, Caroline, that she was gonna send me away to an institution!"

"Why would she say that, Trip? It doesn't make any sense at all!"

" 'Cause of this," he said and reached down in his pocket, pulling out something wrapped in a handkerchief. "I know it's wrong, I know I shouldn't have kept this, but I didn't want him to be gone and I thought that if I saved this, I don't know . . ."

I took the handkerchief from him and unwrapped the object. It was Daddy's finger attached to a knucklebone. I should've dropped it in horror and disgust, but I held it, understanding why he had done this—that if he had this, Daddy wasn't all gone.

"How'd she find it?"

"I was brushing my teeth and I had it sitting on the clothes hamper. She came in to say something to me, saw it, picked it up, and gasped like this." Trip held his hand to his heart and made a face of horror.

"Trip? This is serious."

"I know! I said I *know* it was wrong." He was crying again.

"It's okay, Trip, I understand."

"You do?"

"Yeah, but you know what? This ain't Daddy. And, we should bury it with him."

"Yeah. You're right."

"And Trip?" He looked up at me and my thought slipped my mind for a moment. "Man! You look terrible!"

"You don't look so hot either, you know!"

"Well, I know, but hey! What I wanted to tell you is

that bringing Daddy's finger home is maybe the most disgusting thing you've ever done."

"Yeah, I guess it is."

"But, it's not the sickest."

"Yeah? What's the sickest?"

"The sickest was the time you didn't change your underwear for a month." I punched him in the arm and laughed. He didn't even crack a smile. "Jesus. I'm sorry. Okay, look. Back to Daddy's finger. If it had been me, I'm not sure what I would've done. But I wouldn't have let it just lie there on the ground either. This is sick, but understandable. Let's go throw it in the casket."

We made our way to the family chapel. I truly thought that this was an award-winning act of mental illness, repulsive in almost every way. The only reason I didn't think he was totally crazy was that if I had found it, I would have picked it up too! Then, what would I have done with it? Thrown it in the river? No way!

"Where'd you find it?"

"Out by where the steering wheel was," he said. "It was all I could find."

We got serious when we reached the chapel. It struck me as odd that in the middle of this worst event of our lives we weren't weeping nonstop. The truth was that the weight of it all—Daddy's death—it hadn't really registered.

I had no intention of going in the chapel. Glimpsing my father's coffin through the door was enough for me.

"Okay," I said, "just go open the coffin and throw it in."

"Hell no! What, are you crazy? You do it! You're the oldest!"

"Ah, shit! Shit, Trip!" I knew I was stuck. And, I *had* made that stupid oath to myself in the barn about being nice and all. Damn. Why did I say that? It was a lot easier to be brave when you didn't have to. I looked at Trip. His bottom lip was shaking again.

"Ah, shit! Let's flip for it. Gotta penny?"

"No, I don't."

Neither of us had a coin, and we finally decided to do it together, as quickly as possible. I hated being the oldest. It was a pain in the ass.

"On three, okay? One, two, . . ." We ran like lunatics and struggled with the lid to open it. There was nothing inside but a black vinyl bag, so we threw in the finger with the handkerchief, let the top slam shut, and ran like all hell. When we finally got close to the house I stopped and turned to Trip.

"Trip?"

"Yeah?"

"Did Mother really say she was glad I was leaving?"

"Yeah. But, I think she was just upset."

Upset? That's no kinda excuse for telling my little brother something like that. Makes both of us feel real damn secure. "God, she makes me mad." We looked at each other for a minute, knowing there was no good explanation for what Mother had said about me. "Come on. Let's get showered up and dressed and see if we can help Millie."

"What about Mother? Are you gonna say anything to her?"

"She can go to hell, for all I care. And, above everything, Trip, don't let her see you cry at the funeral."

I told Trip that because if he cried and Mother wasn't sympathetic to his pain, he'd hurt even more. So would I. A bond was formed between us then, one I hoped would carry us through the trouble I knew in my bones surely lay ahead.

It wasn't as hard as I would've imagined to get through

the funeral service. After the finger, what could have been worse? Or maybe I was numbed by the amount of pain I wasn't allowing myself to feel. I watched, fascinated, as they lowered Daddy's coffin into the ground. Ms. Blanchard from Charleston started singing "Swing Low Sweet Chariot," and it gave me the chills. Boy, she had some pipes!

Then she sang "Amazing Grace" with such a passion that everyone joined in and sang with her. Now that was a killer, to sit at your father's graveside and sing his soul to heaven with everybody you had ever known. The entire crowd of several hundred people, singing and crying with all their hearts, raised my spirits so high that for a moment I thought God was there right with us, the same God who had forgotten us just days before. I felt so comforted and almost happy for those few minutes. We all stood up for that song, the Edisto River in the background over the bluff, blue against the brown and green grasses of the marsh, all against a sky so clear—hell, if that wasn't a religious experience, I give up.

> 'Tis grace has brought me safe thus far,
> and grace will lead me home.

Take my daddy home, Lord, I prayed, *take him right to heaven.*

I think that was the first time in my whole life that I believed in God. I had always attended church when Mother insisted that I go, but I had never *felt* anything until that moment. Sure, I had these weird experiences, like *seeing* Daddy's plane on fire, but there was nothing religious about that. If anything, it felt like a message from hell. A curse of a vision I'd be burdened with through nightmares every time I closed my eyes for the rest of my life.

In that moment, that moment of everyone singing together, something happened to me, something inside of me opened up to the possibilities of a real God. One that would take care of me, would listen, would advise—oh, if that feeling could last, we would all be all right no matter what! Incredible.

I was on Mother's right and Trip was on her left. I wore a navy linen sundress and sandals, Trip wore khaki pants and a navy blazer. His hair was plastered to his head with some kind of hair junk that smelled like bug repellant. I knew it was bad to discover God in one moment and criticize in the next, but it was going to take me a while to adjust to being good and all that.

In plain English, Mother was dressed like a freak, which could be another reason why I didn't break down and cry through all I was feeling. I was too embarrassed. Her hat was a huge black straw thing with a wide brim and veil that sat on her head like she was the Queen of England. Even though it was a thousand degrees and the bugs were chewing on my ankles and the back of my neck, Mother wore a black linen dress and jacket to her ankles and those damn pearls. She fanned herself with a black and pink fan brought home from some trip and dabbed the corners of her eyes with a thin black handkerchief. She never made eye contact with Trip or me, but once, during the prayers, probably for dramatic effect, she reached out for our hands to hold. Mine was hot but Mother's was cold and clammy.

I remember that cold and clammy hand because I remember thinking it was like her heart. I didn't care. I didn't need her. I was leaving in six weeks. I just kept telling myself that over and over. Soon, I'd be out of this place and I'd never be like my mother. Never.

The reception following the burial was unbelievable. I had to admit that Mother had done an amazing job to pull it off in so short a time. But that was her. Appearances were more important to her than the breaking hearts of her children. I knew I'd be angry with her forever.

Trip and I accepted her shallowness that day and held each other's attention the entire afternoon. The adults all but ignored us. Every time somebody put down their champagne glass, we picked it up, walked away, and drank it. By six o'clock, Trip and I were knee-walking dead drunk. So much for my newfound religious persuasion.

Millie found us on the docks, throwing rocks in the river, pretending to be throwing them at Mother. We never even heard her coming.

"Yanh! Take this, you old bitch! This is for not tucking me in the night my daddy died!" Trip said, throwing the stone across the water with a furious windup.

"Yanh! Stuff this up your butt, you damn bitch! This is for ignoring us!"

"Yanh! You suck! I wish you had blown up instead!"

"That's enough!" The voice of Millie shook us so hard we nearly fell in the water. *"You stop this fool! Right now!"*

"Shit," Trip said. I could see him listing and worried then that if Millie knew we were drunk, she'd be even madder. I reached over and steadied him.

"Just burning offa liddle stream," I said, twisting my words.

"Is that a fact? How much you children had to drink?"

"Us? Drink? Millie, how could you accuse us of something like that?" I thought I sounded better then.

She looked at me and I knew she didn't believe us for a minute.

"Okay, you two," she said, "I gone turn my head this

time. Go on up to my cottage and sleep it off. I come to see about you later, yanh? Now, move it!"

Move it, we did. As fast as we could. We only stopped once for Trip to water the bushes. When we got there, Trip fell onto the couch and I fell into Millie's bed, both of us sleeping through the night.

The next morning, I woke up under Millie's covers. She wasn't there. Trip was still on the couch, sacked out. Mother hadn't come for us. Big surprise. I went outside to see what the day was like. It wasn't even eight o'clock and it was already steaming. I heard a truck and thought it was probably someone picking up stuff from yesterday. To my surprise, it was a pickup truck with a horse trailer. I watched as Mr. Jenkins shook hands with the driver and as they led the beautiful gelding down the ramp to the ground. In the middle of all this hell, someone had seen about Trip's birthday. Tears of happiness and relief, tears I didn't think I had left, ran down my face. Somebody cared.

29

RESCUE ME

2000

How could I return to Tall Pines and not be reminded why I had moved away from there in the first place? I had left because there was no one who wanted me to stay. Like a mother bird, Miss Lavinia had all but pushed us from our nest. I had never looked back. And, each time I came home over the years to visit, I came with a chip on my shoulder for Mother and a longing in my heart for my daddy.

Trip had barely ever looked ahead. With only marginal planning, he had arranged his life to paint himself into corners. Raucous children, a crazy wife to justify his drinking, the lure of hunting and fishing, the beckoning call of the river sirens and all of the ACE herself. No, he was addicted to the lifestyle and it was patently clear he wanted Tall Pines for himself and his swelling brood. It would have been fine with me for Trip to have it. I had never given it a second thought, assuming all along that when

Mother went to that big Special Event in the Sky, Trip would inherit the whole shebang.

What bothered me was his unbelievable sense of self-serving timing. Who in the world was he kidding? Did he really think that Mother would move out so that he and his family could move in? Mother sit in the Presbyterian Home in Summerville or somewhere else while Frances Mae ran her house? Talk about delusional!

Well, Mother had set him and Frances Mae straight. At least temporarily.

I looked toward the barn, remembering Trip's horse, Jimbo. I thought of the endless afternoons Trip and I had spent together, racing Jimbo and Ginger across fields without a care in the world. Eric was entitled to at least that much—to have a portion of his childhood pass without a care in the world.

The sun was low in the sky and our first night at Tall Pines wasn't far away. I turned to go back to the house and Millie was standing on the back porch, watching me. I had not seen or even heard her cross the lawn. It felt so good to be in her eyes. I knew they were just blinking away and with every blink she would add something to a list of what she meant to do for me or for Eric to help us get settled.

"Hey, Millie! What's up?"

"Miss L gone be back directly. Thought it might be nice to talk to you a little bit before the house is crawling with people again."

I stopped at the bottom of the steps and looked at her. She smiled back at me.

"I don't have to tell you a thing, do I? You already know!"

"That's right, girl. Get in this house and let me show you what I did for you and my boy."

She held the door open and followed me in.

"So strange to be here like this, Millie, you know what I mean?"

"Yeah, but it ain't really so strange at all. It's where you belong and high time you came home too!" She stopped at the refrigerator and opened it, taking out a platter. "Fudge?"

"Oh, my word, Millie!" Millie made fudge that could tempt Richard Simmons to binge! "You're gonna ruin me!" I took a huge piece and put the entire thing in my mouth, licking my fingers.

"I ain't gonna ruin you; I'm gonna save you!" She laughed wide and put the fudge away. "Follow me."

Upstairs, Millie had unpacked all my things in my old room and all of Eric's in Trip's old room next door. As my eyes passed over the placement of our belongings, it looked like we had been there all along. I opened the closet door in my bedroom, trying to figure out what to change into for dinner.

"Millie, I can't thank you enough for doing this!"

"I've been waiting to unpack y'all's bags since the day that boy came into this world!"

"You always knew, didn't you?"

She smiled, looked at the floor and then hard at my face. "Why don't you get a bath and lie down for a little bit. You look tired."

I looked at the bathrobe on the hanger I had unconsciously chosen for dinner clothes. "You know, Millie? I believe I will. I am beyond tired."

"I put a CD player in the bathroom for you, because I suspect you like to have some music while you dress. You go on get your bath, I'll be right back."

The bathtub was filled with steaming water and floating gardenias. They smelled divine and I felt like taking a bath with gardenias was extremely decadent. Without a single warning, Richard flashed across my mind. Hell, I thought, I could bathe with an entire gardenia bush and not be decadent next to *him!* I undressed, hung my clothes on the empty hangers on the back of the door, and slipped on the robe. I flipped on the boom box and found she had loaded an old Joe Sample classic CD. I tested the water with my hand and it was the perfect temperature for a good soak.

Between Joe Sample and the perfume of the gardenias, I nearly fell asleep in the tub. But, I pulled my tired self out, drained the water, and dried off. I went into my bedroom as Millie was leaving, closing the door. She had opened the French doors, but turned the louvered shutters up to keep out the afternoon sun. On my bedside table stood a small Limoges pot of tea and a warm slice of banana bread. I poured with the full knowledge that the tea was laced with one of Millie's specialties and drank it straight to the bottom. The Sorceress had turned down my bed, rolling back the plissé blanket cover to reveal Mother's finest crisp white Irish linens, the ones she saved in case Margaret Thatcher stopped by. The pillow slips had been edged in a fine crochet of airy scallops years ago by my grandmother. It was no coincidence that Millie had prepared so carefully for Eric and me. No, I was on quicksand.

As I made myself comfortable under the covers, I remembered that I had wanted to ask if Trip and Frances Mae were coming for dinner. Oh, well. I was so sleepy and it didn't matter anyway. Frances Mae would just have to get used to us.

It was the breath of Eric that began to bring me from the depth of my sleep. I knew and loved his breath the way a lioness does her cubs. I didn't want to open my eyes. Apparently he was unsure of waking me. I could feel his presence next to me, the way his body took up space in the room. Then I could sense him leaving. Good, I thought, let me rest just a few more minutes. Good. Eric was safely home.

Even with closed eyes, I could sense the day slipping away by the cool fingers of the breeze. Friday? Yes, it was still Friday. Okay, I had a couple of days to figure things out. First, Eric's school. Miss Nancy was right. I should ask around about a tutor. Maybe I'd call Matthew-baby-hottie-in-a-uniform and see if he knew someone. Old Frances Mae might know someone from the Walterboro school system. A good icebreaker. I'd try to get along with her. I would.

Bam! Bam! I must've drifted off to sleep again because I was awakened by the distinct slamming of a car door and then another.

"Mom! Mom!" Eric began calling for me. Before I had a chance to get up, he opened the bedroom door. "Mom! Uncle Trip wants to take me down the river to check the crab traps! Can I go? Can I please? Please?"

"Of course you can go. Where's your jacket? Come yanh and give your old mother a kiss!"

He leaned over the bed and planted a kiss on my cheek. "On the front stairs. You're the best, Mom! You shoulda seen Uncle Trip in the courtroom! He's like Johnnie Cochran or something! He was like, *Sir, do you want to think that answer through? Sir, may I remind you that you are under oath?* Amazing! Totally amazing!" He pulled off his tie and the rest of his shirttail flew out of his khakis.

"When did you get home?" I leaned up on my elbow when I remembered that I had smelled him earlier.

"This guy was totally sweating! Uncle Trip was like, *Take that, you dog!*" He began to imitate someone in a duel, fencing and lunging across the room.

"Eric?"

He stopped and replaced his imaginary sword in its sheath.

"Just this second!" he said, finally answering my question. "You heard me, yelling for you?" I must've looked at him in a strange way. "What? What's the matter?"

My brother's voice called out for him. "Eric? Eric? Come on, bubba, let's shake a leg!" He opened the door to my room and stuck his head in. Eric's navy blazer hung on the end of his index finger. "You leave your clothes lying around and your grandmother will beat the tar outta you! You coming with me, or what?" Then he looked at me in the bed. "What the hell's the matter with you?"

"I'm having a nap," I said. "Ladies do that, you know."

"Jesus, you sound like Miss Lavinia!" He winked at Eric.

"How'd you like a black eye, buster?" I said and threw back the covers. "Wise guy. I'm stressed out. When I'm stressed out, I sleep."

"Well, you'd better get over it. Frances Mae and the girls will be yanh at six."

"Listen, Trip. I've taken an oath to be nice and try to get along with her." I stopped at the dresser and looked in the mirror. I looked like hell.

"Mom? You don't get along with Aunt Frances Mae?"

"We get along just fine, son, just fine." I smiled at Trip and ruffled Eric's hair. "Now you go change and have some fun. Just be home by dark, okay?"

"Okay!" Eric zoomed out of the room and soon another door slammed almost off the hinges. Trip and I cringed.

"I'll talk to him," I said. "You know, you could say welcome home, brother dear." I opened my eyes wide and nodded my head, waiting.

"Welcome home? Welcome to *hell,* sister dear! Yeah, boy! *Welcome to hell!*"

He grinned at me and closed the door.

"Thanks a lot!" I said to the door.

Then I remembered again. Someone had been in my room while I slept. Who was it? I could've sworn it was Eric. Maybe he was playing a game with me. Boys!

At six Mother, Trip, and I were in the living room having the requisite cocktail and nibbling on peppered cheese biscuits. The phone rang and seconds later Millie burst into the room.

"Trip! It's Frances Mae on the phone! She's pulled over to the side of the highway five miles up the road and that baby's coming! Hurry!"

"Merciful Mother of God!" Mother said.

Trip ran from the room, holding his bourbon in the air as though that would keep it from splashing, which it did not and he soaked the sleeve of his signature blue oxford cloth shirt. Mother and I followed him to the hall phone, where we stood with him and Millie trying to listen in on their conversation.

"Goddamnit, Frances Mae! Where are you? Tell me exactly where you are!"

"I hope to God my grandchild's not born in a ditch," Mother said, in a low voice.

I couldn't help thinking about Frances Mae, on the shoulder of Highway 17 south, hanging on to the car door, squatting and pushing, simultaneously mediating the bickering between her three girls, who were all strapped in their seat belts. The problem was that I remembered that Frances Mae was only in her eighth month. She had a history of delivering late, not early. Worry reared its ugly head as I remembered her fall into the Edisto and I hoped it hadn't caused this.

"Just calm down!" Pause. "Damnit, Frances Mae! Calm the hell down!" Pause. "Okay! Okay! *Okay! I hear you! I'm coming!*" Trip slammed the phone down into its receiver and began rummaging around in his pockets for his car keys. "Mother? Call the police in Jacksonboro. Tell them to send an ambulance to the side of the road to Walterboro about ten miles from the Hess station. I'll be back."

"Hold on a minute, boy! I'm coming with you!" Millie said.

"Me too!" I said.

"Me three!" Eric said.

"You stay with your grandmother!" I said.

"Mom! Come on! I don't want to miss this!"

"Yes, you do," Mother said, and swung the front door wide open. I followed Trip outside and heard Mother say, "Well, I guess dinner will be later than expected." Trip was in his Range Rover and starting the engine. I all but jumped into the front seat.

"Wait for Millie!" I said.

Millie appeared carrying a pile of things under her arm, hiking her skirt as she hurried down the steps and hopped into the backseat. "Move it!" she said.

Trip put his foot down hard on the pedal and we took off, a cloud of dust rising behind us until we reached the gate. Hardly stopping, he turned left on two wheels and tore down the road to Highway 17 at over eighty miles an hour.

"Slow down!" I said. "You're gonna kill us all!"

"You don't know Frances Mae like I do," he said, "she'll have that baby to spite me and then blame me for the rest of my life!"

"Don't say that! And slow down!" Millie said from the backseat, with a trace of panic in her voice.

"No, she'll say the fall in the river did it and blame me for the rest of time!" I said.

"Stop this talk!" Millie said. "Stop it now!"

We ignored her—an unwise thing to do. Trip cut me a glance from the side of his eyes. "That's bullshit."

"Wait and see," I said.

"All right! That's enough!" Millie said. "You're both asking for trouble! Go looking for trouble and you'll find it. Sure enough you will!"

We stopped talking for a minute to consider the possible outcomes of this drama. The best of the litany of finales? That she was just in labor. The worst? I didn't even want my mind to wander there. No, I began to say silent prayers that Frances Mae and the baby were all right. Babies were pretty sturdy, and God knows, Frances Mae was a pack mule. Still, I prayed.

The light was red at the corner, but Trip didn't care, he made the left onto 17 and took off again, tires screeching.

"Hang on, Frances Mae," Trip said, shouting to the ethers, "hold your legs together!"

Suddenly I could see Frances Mae in my mind. She had indeed given birth, and she was in shock and the baby wasn't crying.

"Hurry, Trip!" I began to shake and turned to the back-seat to face Millie. "Millie . . ."

"Don't worry, girl. Pray!"

I prayed. We all prayed. Trip was now doing well over one hundred miles an hour. We passed the blur of the Hess station and, in the blink of an eye, up ahead were a patrol car and an ambulance, lights spinning, going as fast as they could. We all raced to a stop, got out, and ran to the scene.

Frances Mae was lying on the grass of the shoulder of the road, delivering her baby. Amelia was holding her hand and crying. The other girls were in the car screaming, covering their eyes. The patrolman and the medical team were getting out of their vehicles, and it seemed to me that they weren't particularly in a hurry. But Millie was. She broke through the crowd and got down on her knees on Frances Mae's right and spread out the things she had brought.

"Where the hell have y'all been?" Frances Mae said, screaming. "Oh, God!"

"Roll over on your side," Millie said, commanding Frances Mae to do as she said. Frances Mae did and Millie slipped a quilt under her. "Now roll back to the other side. Amelia? Tell your sisters to hush before I get up and beat the hell out of them!"

"You heard Millie? Hush! Hush right now!" she said, and they quieted down.

"Is Momma all right?" Isabelle said.

"She's gonna be just fine. You girls say a prayer for her, all right?" I said. I held a sheet up at Frances Mae's feet to give the woman a modicum of privacy. Not that she seemed to care.

"Hang on, Frances Mae," Trip said, "the ambulance is here." He knelt down beside her and took her hand, patting it and looking anxious.

Frances Mae's head looked like it might blow up, she was so contorted and red. Millie pushed Frances Mae's dress up and was going to pull off her underpants. I looked away at Millie's face instead. May I say that, even given the urgency and gravity of the situation, Frances Mae's you-know-what was the last thing I wanted to see?

"What can I do, Millie?" I said.

"Tell those men to get the stretcher over here with sterile cloth, a clamp, and a sterile knife! We got a baby coming!"

"Jesus! God! Oh! God!" Frances Mae said, screaming loud enough to wake the dead. *"I'm dying!"*

The men were on their way toward us, pushing the gurney over the uneven ground. The policeman was in the road directing traffic and rubbernecks. I turned back to the scene and thought, of all the surreal episodes in my life this would surely make the top ten.

"You'll do no such thing," I said to no one in particular as I walked back.

"Push!" Millie said. "Push again! Now one more time, girl, come on!"

The baby's head appeared and Millie all but pulled the child out of Frances Mae. The child was blue and the umbilical cord was wrapped tightly around its neck. Then I saw that it was a little girl. Millie said not a word, but put her strong fingers under the cord and pulled with all her might. The medical team dropped to the ground on either side of Millie and began helping. Finally they loosened it and removed it. No cry. Blue as flagstone. Millie flushed the baby's mouth with two fingers and blew into it. The medical worker did something else—it was all happening so fast—Frances Mae screamed again, *"Why isn't my baby crying?"* Trip said, *"Hold on! It's okay!"* The silence from the tiny infant was terrifying. Millie pressed the child's chest and blew into her mouth again. *Eh! Eh!* The baby finally made a sound. One of the medical workers covered the child's mouth with an oxygen mask and slowly she gained color.

"You have a girl! Another girl!" Millie said.

Frances Mae started to cry, from relief, from joy, from pain—she was completely overwhelmed. Trip just pushed the hair back on her forehead and smiled, saying, "It's okay. It's okay now."

In a few minutes, the baby began to scream and cry. It was like music to all of us. Millie wrapped the baby in a sterile white sheet and showed her to Frances Mae, who merely nodded her head, satisfied that her child had made it into the world. The girls tumbled out of the car to have a look at their new sister, oohing and aahing at the marvel of it all. Finally, Frances Mae was lifted into the ambulance with her baby and rushed to the hospital in Walterboro. Trip would follow them in his car and I would drive Millie and the girls back to Tall Pines in Frances Mae's Expedition.

"Millie! How can I ever thank you?" Trip said. "You probably saved my daughter's life!"

"Ain't no probably about it," she said, grinning wide with relief, "but God helped. Y'all should give Him some credit, yanh?"

"You're right," I said. "God. Millie! You're the hero of the day!"

Trip shooed his girls into their mother's car, threw me the keys, and waved at us and went to his car, leaving Millie and me outside for a moment's private speculation.

"I'm the hero? I don't know about all that. Did you see that baby's angry face, crying and wailing like a wild animal?"

"Looks just like Frances Mae," I said. "Tiny and all wrinkled! Sure hope she's smart, 'cause she sure ain't pretty."

"Shoot! That ain't wrinkles! Ain't nothing at all but meanness! That baby's got a soul like her momma and a face like a bulldog," Millie said and we began to laugh. "Ugliest child I ever did see!"

30

BACK TO SCHOOL

2000

By Sunday afternoon, I had a shortlist of tutors for Eric. On Tuesday they would come for interviews. The movers were to arrive on Thursday and I had to figure out what to do with our things. It was going to be a busy week.

I had extracted two possible candidates for Eric's education from Frances Mae during her short stay in the hospital. I went by with some flowers for her on Saturday and found her packing. They had all but thrown her out the next day. She was good and cranky and even I couldn't blame her for that.

"Managed health care," she grumbled, "hell, my milk ain't even come in yet!"

"Well, I'm sure it will," I said.

What was I supposed to say? That we'd call CNN to send in a film crew to document it when it did "come in"?

Frances Mae and those breasts of hers—Mother's Milk with a provenance.

Her baby, temporarily named Chloe for a favorite actress of Frances Mae's and until Trip could convince her to give her a normal name—i.e., a family name—stayed on in the hospital. Chloe had high bilirubin numbers and so they wanted to keep her under the lights for a few days. Frances Mae would spend a lot of time driving to the hospital to feed her new infant and that would certainly be inconvenient.

But, the baby's jaundice was pale in comparison to Frances Mae's attitude toward us. When she should have been grateful that we all rushed to her side, and most especially to Millie, she was angry at the world. She stayed in bed crying and got up only to refresh her supply of tissues and to run to the hospital. When Amelia finally called Mother to report Frances Mae's frightening behavior, Mother got on the phone with her and read her the Gospel.

Now you see here, Frances Mae, you get yourself up from the bed this instant! You have three other children who need your attention and I dare say my son would like to have a pleasant partner to come home to in the evening! No woman in our family's entire history ever behaved in such a self-indulgent manner! Are you a Wimbley or not?

That was the Gospel according to Mother Sensitiva, not the apostles. Frances Mae got up and resumed living, but she was foul-tempered and unpredictable. I asked Trip if her doctor had said anything about postpartum depression and he looked at me like I was speaking Greek.

"What the hell is that? Another one of the analyst's excuses for a woman to shirk her duty?"

Mother and Trip had that sensitivity and sympathy gene

well in hand. Neither of them would let something minor like giving birth on the side of the road—while your new infant nearly died and your children watched in terror and earned another twenty years in therapy—throw them off for a minute. They made me shake my head. I'd get Millie to do something.

I drove to Charleston to find a gift for baby Chloe and a small something for each of the girls. For Chloe I found a precious Sea Island cotton dress in pale pink, all hand smocked across the front with a bonnet to match. Crogan's had wonderful pearl studs for little girls. Mrs. Ramsey helped me decide on five-millimeter pearls for Caroline, six for Isabelle, and seven for Amelia. She wrapped them in beautiful velvet boxes and while I waited, we talked about Mother.

"Tell your mother I said hello! She's so darling! What has she been up to lately?"

"Oh, the usual," I said, "she's ruining my boy by giving him everything in the world he wants."

Mrs. Ramsey laughed and said, "Well, I expect she hasn't changed much! She always was so generous with you and your brother."

"Come to think of it, Mrs. Ramsey, you're right!"

"My word, I know she's glad to have you all at home with her. Are you staying for a while?"

"I think so, yes."

"I declare, every mother is the happiest when she's surrounded by her children. You give her my best, yanh?"

I left her store slightly embarrassed because it was true. Mother had given Trip and me every material thing we had ever asked for. Now she was doing the same thing for Eric. This past Saturday, Mr. Jenkins rolled up to the house with a new mountain bike for Eric, a pair of Rollerblades, a skateboard, and a Sunfish sailboat. Eric was in hog

heaven and Mother was smiling from head to toe, tickled
to pieces with her extravagance. Mother had found a new
cause in Eric and Eric had found someone who would
lavish him with gifts like a Good Fairy. I never would have
guessed it. I hadn't even considered it. I had forgotten
about Mother's generous side because with every gift was
attached a barb. *Don't lose the pin! Now, Eric? Don't go
out there and kill yourself. Eric? Don't do anything foolhardy!*

I found books at Chapter Two on having babies in mid-
life, and herbal cures for depression and what the nature
of it was. I bought Frances Mae the prettiest gift set of
perfume and body lotion I could find at Saks on King
Street. I bought a big tube of Clinique Body Lotion for
Mother and one for Millie. After what Millie had done
for Trip and Frances Mae and after what Mother had done
for Eric and me, it only seemed right to pick up a little
something for them too. Trip was the only one I hadn't
bought something for, so I stopped at M. Dumas and
picked up a funny fishing hat for him. All in all, I thought
I had done a good thing and began the trip home thinking
of life's possibilities.

Thoughts of Richard came to mind. He hadn't called us.
How could I have been so naïve? His silence only fur-
thered my worst fear that he valued his sexual fantasies
more than he valued our marriage and family. If he was
willing to give that all away so that he could frequent
sleazy bars and have Lois handle his "public service," what
could I do?

Well, what I *could* do, I thought, was minimize Eric's
confusion and shore up his emotions—show him that
Richard loved him and always would. Just how I was going to do that hadn't come to me yet, but I could start by
putting Eric on the phone with Richard a few times a week

at a designated time. At least they could talk to each other. Maybe Eric could help Richard see what he had lost.

Once again, my heart drifted and was playing with the idea that Richard would change and want us back. I knew he would not.

Millie was waiting for me on the front porch when I pulled up in Mother's car. That was another thing I had to do—buy a car. Maybe I should take a one-year lease, I thought. Standing in the rose-colored slices of the afternoon sun, Millie looked positively regal. She had been cutting flowers and the basket she held was filled to overflowing with branches of fuchsia and white azaleas.

"Hey! Need a hand?" she said.

I reached into the trunk and pulled out the bags. "No, but thanks! Eric home?"

"Gone down the river with your brother to fish. What'd you do, girl? Buy out Charleston?"

"Yeah, almost. Mother?"

"Took Trip's car over to Walterboro to check on Frances Mae."

"Poor Frances Mae," I said, following her inside, picking up on the way six envelopes and boxes from the UPS man for Mother.

"Yanh, lemme help you! Baby came home today. Let's have us a glass of iced tea. How's that sound to you?"

I dropped my bags on the hall bench and dug through my packages to find the tube of cream I had bought for Millie.

"Thanks. Sounds perfect," I said. "I'm parched. So little Chloe is home! Why couldn't she name that child something else? Here, Miss Millie, I bought you something."

"Don't ask me," she said, "maybe she thinks a movie star's gonna make that baby better looking!" She looked at the tube, opened it, and sniffed. "Smells good! Thank you!"

"You're welcome," I said and followed her into the kitchen. Millie took a glass pitcher filled with tea from the refrigerator and filled two tall glasses with ice from the ice maker on the refrigerator door. I listened to them fill the glass, piling on each other with clinks, ice that would melt away. I took the sugar bowl from the cabinet and put it on the table. She popped some mint sprigs from a glass of water over the kitchen sink, and dropped them in.

"You got some phone calls," she said, handing me a glass. "It's already sweet."

I put the sugar bowl back on the shelf. "Right, I always forget. Millie? Is that green stuff in my tea gonna make me hallucinate?"

"It's just mint, missy. But you never know with Millie, do you now?"

She handed me the pad with the messages and I sat at the table with her, draining my glass. She refilled it.

"Thanks," I said. "No, I never know!" I looked at the list: Ruth Perretti, tutors math and science; Peter Greer, tutors language arts and English; and Joshua Welton, teaches fine arts and also does occupational therapy. They had all called to confirm their appointments for the next day. "Okay, so this is good. It's a step toward getting settled!"

We clinked our glasses in a toast.

"Yes, it is! Yanh's to you and Eric coming home!"

I took a long drink and looked at her. She was rubbing a generous palmful of cream on her hands and arms up to her elbows. The lotion gave her skin the radiance of a young woman's. Her beauty was amazing, even at her age to seem so vital.

"Millie?"

"What's on your mind?"

"Like you don't already know," I said. "It's Richard. It's me. Even though he's a screwball, I love Richard, you know? God, that's embarrassing to admit."

"You should never apologize for loving somebody, girl. Even if they's crazy as hell. There's a lid for every pot. There was a time you saw something in him that was worth your heart. Don't be sorry for that."

"I don't know. I keep trying to figure out what *was* the thing that made him so desirable. I mean, he's smart. You know I've always been a sucker for a guy with brains."

"I don't like men without good brains either. Ever since my Samuel ran off with that fool woman from Augusta, I ain't been sure about *any* man and whether they got sense at all!"

It was the first time Millie had ever admitted to me that her husband had abandoned her. I was so surprised by it that I let it slide, thinking we would get to Mr. Samuel and his departure in due course.

"Yeah, that's the truth. I mean, I look at Trip. What kind of marriage is his? You can almost pick up his contempt for Frances Mae and carry it outta the room! I don't want a marriage like that. And Mother and Daddy? The main thing they had in common was that they both loved Lavinia! I don't want a marriage like that either!"

"Didn't I tell you not to talk about your mother?"

"I don't mean it to sound that way. I mean, I thought at one time that I had something with Richard that was so spectacular, so unique I didn't need anybody else in my life. And, when Eric came along, I was absolutely positive my world was full. I just believed in it so hard. How could I have been so wrong?"

Millie reached across the table and patted my hand. "That's all right now. You want some apple?"

"Sure. You know what this is about, don't you?"

I watched her cross the room, rinse the apple, and tear off a paper towel to hold the peelings. She sat again and began to peel the apple around and around, choosing her words carefully. "I don't know why they wax these things—I ain't eating no wax! Last I heard, wax ain't food." She looked up at me finally and said, "Sure I know what it's about. He's weird in the sex department. Am I right?"

"Yeah, but the good thing is that he's not weird with me. The bad thing is he's weird with Lois."

Her eyebrows narrowed and she leaned on her elbow toward me. "You think that's good? You lost your mind or what?"

"Pretty pathetic, right?"

"Girl? Didn't I teach you better? I don't know what kind of *weird* you talking about, and I don't *want* to know either. People tell too much nowadays! You see them damn fools on the television? Whatever happened to people and self-respect? World gone crazy, that's what."

"Yeah, it's true, but I wasn't gonna give you the details, Millie. I'm not that indiscreet." I was embarrassed then because it was bad enough that I had my trouble. The nature of my trouble was humiliating. Yes, that was it. I was humiliated and embarrassed and I had come home in defeat.

Millie sat back in her chair, tapping her fingertips on the table, reading my mind.

"I smell wood burning," she said.

It was what we said to each other when one was lost in thought. "I don't know, Millie. I don't know what to do."

"Caroline? You have already done what you should do. You took yourself and your son out of a nasty situation." She looked at me and caught my eyes, holding them long enough to read my soul. "You still love him, don't you."

It wasn't a question but a statement of fact.

"Of course I do."

Millie could see I was on the verge of tears. "Get up," she said, "come with me."

Like a good dog, I followed her outside. We walked across the lawn in silence, down by the river, along the path to her cottage. Every hair stood up on my body in premonition of what would follow. Millie opened her door and turned to me on the porch where I stood.

"I'm gonna teach you a lesson," she said. She smiled as she said it. For a moment I had thought she meant to discipline me for moping and complaining.

"What did I do?" I said, in perfect ignorance.

"No, girl, it ain't what you did, it's what you can't do. That's what I'm gonna teach you—how to take care of yourself."

"You mean . . . ?"

"Yes, ma'am! Pay attention! Welcome to Millie Smoak's School of Magic!"

Miss Lavinia's Journal

Does anybody want to hear what I think? Well, someday, when this is read, they will all know what I know. That Frances Mae could not tell she was about to give birth is further testimony to her complete stupidity and bullheadedness at ignoring the signs! Dear God in heaven, now I have seen it all! A Wimbley child comes into the world on the side of the road! Is there no end to the indignities this horrible woman can heap on the reputation of my ancestors? Glory be to God! If Nevil were alive, we'd surely be crying in our cocktails! And Caroline and Millie? They keep running off to her cottage—I know what they're doing too! Playing with fire, that's what!

I think I'll just go get my Eric and play a computer game with him. Or maybe that Sony PlayStation thing he's got. I do so like that Super Mario game!

31

VOODOO 101

My life was poised for another drastic change, but I didn't know it that day. It wasn't enough that I had discovered my husband was a pervert and that I had come back to South Carolina, tail between my legs, to mull it over. No, routine was a stranger and normal had a new face.

It was Millie, the only person here who seemed sane to me, who would be the next catalyst. I had grown up on a steady diet of Millie's point of view, and it—along with her advice—had always served me well. I was to learn that those opinions and predictions were a mere toothpick in her vast forest of knowledge.

I found myself in Millie's kitchen and the subject, once again, was magic. She poured us two fresh glasses of tea, put them on the table, and took two small bottles from the shelf behind the kitchen curtain where she kept all the herbs. With an eyedropper from the drawer in hand, she came to my side, pulled a chair around, and sat.

"All right," she said, "look yanh. This is clematis water

and this is white chestnut. These are undiluted. We gonna
put two drops of each in your tea. The white chestnut is
to make you stop worrying and to strengthen your mind.
The clematis is to make you focus on your situation and
not be distracted."

"Are you serious?" All I could think was *Oh, God; I'm
not in the mood for this.*

"As serious as I can be. In addition to my herbs that I
grow and gather, I use flowers and bark of some trees.
People come to me for all kind of things, Caroline. When
I'm gone, they gone come to you. Then you teach somebody else and they do the same when they time come."

Her face was so serious she startled me. "Millie? Oh,
my god! You're thinking you're gonna die! Jesus!"

"What?" Millie started to laugh and that laugh came the
whole way from her toes and wiggled its way through her
whole body and she threw back her head and cackled like
I'd never seen her do. She got up, slapped her thighs and
shuffled her feet across the kitchen, laughing, saying, "Oh,
Lord! Oh, Lord!" Then, I lost it and started laughing too.
"She thinks I know the Lord's plan! Too funny! Too
funny!" she said.

"You mean, you don't?" I could feel a Gullah session
of working the jaw coming on any second.

Her laughter then was like rolling thunder. So much
noise from such a small person! Finally, she leaned against
her sink, held her side, and wiped her eyes with the back
of her hand. "Honey?" she said, between breaths of *Oooh!
Oooh!* "If I knew the mind of God, you think I'd be yanh
talking to a knucklehead like you? Shoot! Ain't nobody
got the right to claim they know God's mind! Iffin they
tell you that, it's blaspheme! God ain't taking me anyplace
till I pass on what I know!"

She always broke into Gullah when amused or upset.

"Millie, I always thought you knew everything!"

"Bad news, girl! I don't! No, I sure don't. Whew! That was so good! Cleared my soul!" She took a notebook and pencil from her drawer, handing them to me. "Now, we need to get a few things straight. That's your notebook. Don't lose it. Don't give to anybody to read. Understand me?"

"Understood." How had I gotten myself into this?

"Number one, you are an apprentice and an apprentice means you are learning. What Millie is gone *teach* you, *if* you can pay attention and not make her fall on the floor laughing, is how to use nature to heal yourself and others. You gone discover what the good Lord is trying to tell you through rituals. You gone talk to the Almighty God through the ancestors and, most of all, you gone dedicate your life to only do good."

"I guess that scratches your teaching me a spell to make Richard crawl down the Interstate from New York to Tall Pines, begging my forgiveness, huh? You're really serious, aren't you?"

"Ain't never been more serious in my life. Drink that tea and don't fret over Richard."

"Sure, I'll just throw him out of my heart. Just like that." I snapped my fingers for emphasis.

"That's not what I mean. I mean that, by and by, if you pay attention to all I teach you to see, the answer to your trouble with Richard will be as plain as day."

"I hope you're right."

"I'm right."

Millie sat across from me then, looking hard at my face. Seemed that she was trying to decide if I was worth the effort required. But, she had no children and I was her best bet. She sighed long and hard. In that moment she had given me, the reluctant one, a sign that she knew, once again, exactly what I was thinking and that she agreed.

"Caroline? Gone be a year, maybe two, before a lot of this makes any sense to you. Tell me what you believe."

"And it looks like I'm gonna be yanh for a while. As to what I believe? Well, Millie, that's a loaded question. I mean, I believe in God, if that's what you're asking me."

"That's what I'm asking. But tell me why."

"Gosh." I sucked in one corner of my mouth and tried to organize my thoughts. "Well, first of all, man is the most highly developed being we know of."

"Maybe."

"We can't be the end of the line, Millie. I mean, wouldn't it be the height of all arrogance to think we were? And how did the cosmos form itself? I guess I've always thought that there was something mysterious, something greater, something else, you know? When I was in school I studied world religions. Big ones, but little obscure ones too. What people hold sacred is fascinating, don't you think?"

"There ain't nothing *more* fascinating!"

She sat across from me now. The smallest relief combined with the greatest of hope was all over her face. All Millie had to give in this life to survive her was what she knew. She was willing to give it to me. While I recognized her lifetime of discovery to be an enormous gift, I had great reservations about taking it. I wasn't sure I wanted to be the new voodoo–herbalist–whatever it was she wanted of me, and I mean I wasn't so sure at all. I just felt that out of respect I had to hear her through. If something came up that I didn't believe or understand I'd just say so. The problem with the conversation was that she wanted me *to ask her* to teach me. She wanted me to *want* to learn. So far, I was barely passing the test.

All my life, her Ife gods and goddesses had been ab-

solutely enthralling to me, but I accepted them as *her* religion. I had no need of rituals in my life. I tried to find
God in other people and in myself. I wasn't descended
from African roots. I was as white as I could be. How
could I perform the rituals? I'd feel like a jerk. A phony.
And, looking at her, I knew she knew I felt that way. It
was the hurdle we had to jump.

"Caroline? I can see what you're thinking."

"I hate that," I said.

Millie chuckled and continued. "Listen, I've lived a
good many years more than you and maybe it's because
of this place that I've been able to come to understand
certain things, to know certain things."

"Yeah, this part of the world has that way of teaching
you things."

"Well, one of the most important things I have learned
in my life is this: People get sick when they fail to recognize things. People, all of us, are a part of a great and
all-powerful God. When men and women are prideful or
mean, hateful or self-centered or greedy, they get sick. Can
you see that all those mistakes are about being self-
absorbed?"

"Yeah, self-love is all those things, but I'm not so sure
they make you sick."

"All right. For the sake of this argument, let's assume
that it is. Just for a few minutes, okay?"

I must've looked reasonably agreeable to that, because
she went on. I pushed my chair back and leaned against
the wall to listen.

"Look, if there's a God, then you have to ask yourself
why are we on this earth in the first place, right?"

"Good question!" I wagged my finger at her.

"Well, yanh's the million-dollar answer. Your soul is a
part of God, right? The God in you, right?"

"Yeah, I'll buy that."

"And your intuition tells you that there's more to life than just this life, right?"

"Yes. Definitely. Take one look at the night sky when the lights are off. Makes you feel like a peanut."

"Exactly. Our soul, or the God in us, *knows* what we need. So He *puts* us where we land on the earth to get the experiences and knowledge we need to work toward being part of Him in paradise. Isn't that communion? Being one with God?"

"Well, I think I have always believed that everything happens for a reason anyway."

"That's just what I'm saying. Trouble comes when we separate ourselves from what the good Lord wants us to do. The Lord guides us by that little voice in us we call our conscience."

"Okay, for the sake of this argument, I'll buy that."

"Fine! You ain't supposed to jump headlong into something like this. You have to arrive to the conclusion in your own way. Think of it this way: God's got His plan for us. We go off all willy-nilly, half-cocked, loving only ourselves. Time pass and something's gonna come along to make you unhappy you did that, right?"

"It sure *seems* like the universe throws me a roadblock when I get too cocky."

"Or a cold in your head, yanh? When you get sick, you have to rest. When you rest, you have to think. When you are forced to think about what you've been doing, you realize you been working against what God wants for you. See what I mean? Going off the path eventually brings unhappiness."

"So what are you saying exactly? I mean, I don't disagree with anything you've said, really I don't."

"What I'm saying, Caroline, is that this life was given

us to serve God, not ourselves. By serving others through compassion, with love, with forethought—that by listening to our conscience we serve our souls, and God. In a nut-shell, life is about service. That's all there is for us to do."

"Would learning your work help me help Eric?"

"Of course it would." Millie reached across the table and covered my hand with hers. "Of course it would," she said again. "And children of other mothers, and people who worry, folks who mourn, old people who are scared—on and on the list goes! That list is as long as my hair! Mostly what I do is help people heal themselves."

"Jesus! An herbal shrink! Wait till Richard yanh about this! Don't you have something in your war chest to do something with Frances Mae?"

"That's the one problem. People got to *want* to improve!"

"And she's the happiest sicko I've ever known." I took another drink of tea and it occurred to me that I couldn't taste anything different about it. The drops hadn't changed the taste. "Millie? Did you make the drops in the tea?"

"Heavens to Betsy, no. I ain't got time for that fool! They ain't nothing but the Bach Flower Remedies!"

"The who?"

Millie rolled her eyes up to heaven and shook her head. "Ain't you never been in a health food store?"

"Sure! I'm in them all the time!" I must really look like an idiot, I thought.

"Well, they got these little racks, like spice racks. In them are thirty-eight little bottles of essences of flowers, most of them from flowers."

"What do they do? I mean, some flowers are poison, aren't they?"

"Oh, Lord, girl? All right. We can start with the Bach Remedies. There's so much to tell you!" Millie got up and pulled back the curtain again, revealing all the little bottles lined up. "Each one has a different purpose. When somebody's sick, you got to look to the mind first. You have to decide what their mental state is. That's what you treat. These work on people's emotions and spirits."

"Aren't there more than thirty-eight different states of mind?"

"Ahhhhhh! Ah, yes! That's my girl!" She came to me and patted me on the shoulder. "That's ab-so-lute-ly correct! So, you have to learn to *combine* them!"

"Okay." I was feeling slightly more pleased with myself, but I still couldn't see people lined up at my door for a cure. I got up to look at them. "How do they make these?"

"Simple. Take the flower; put it in a clean bowl of water in the sun. The water begins to take on the essence of the flower; evaporation condenses the essence. You put the liquid in a bottle with a drop of brandy to preserve it. Then you use a dropper and put it in a liquid and drink it. Works like a miracle."

"Humph," I said.

"Now you sound like me!"

Several hours passed as Millie explained the various benefits of each essence and I took notes.

"You can order them on the Internet if you don't feel like gone to the store," she said, and gave me the Web site.

She opened each bottle for me to smell, handling each one like a religious artifact. Some were sweet, some were vaguely medicinal; I suspected that if Millie owned them, all were potent.

All along the way, she told me stories of various cures. One woman had anxiety for no good reason. Three drops of aspen essence in her orange juice, three drops in her afternoon tea, and three drops in water before bed washed away her fear.

"Millie?"

She was putting away all the bottles, and making note of those that needed to be replaced.

"Need some water violet," she said. "What?"

"Remember when Daddy died?"

She stopped and turned to me. Her face was solemn. "How could I forget?"

"Remember how Mother changed overnight—how she was so mean to Trip and me? How she ignored us? How she was so critical of everything?"

"She couldn't help it, Caroline, you know that."

"Then remember when Trip and I went away to school, remember how she went wild?"

"That was my fault." A grin covered her face. "Oh, God! I was giving her enough Saint-John's-wort to drive ten women wild!"

"Oh, God! Millie! Even I know that acts like Prozac! And you knew it in nineteen seventy-four? That's amazing! No wonder!"

"Shoot, I knew it in the fifties! But, yeah, it was terrible. I didn't figure it out until I caught her in bed with the UPS man! Don't you say I told you that either, or I'll call you a liar!"

"The UPS man! Millie! God in heaven!"

"Yeah, God! They were just going to town! She was happy as a lark, but I cut back her dosage after that."

"Well, it's a good thing you did! I can't believe you overdosed Mother!" My face was scarlet. Jesus!

"Listen, she had fun and I ain't perfect."

"You crazy old woman! I gotta go—Mother's gonna think I ran away again."

"I'll be along directly," Millie said.

I walked home along the banks of the river, watching the afternoon sun sparkle and dance on its surface. Lost in thought, I wandered down to the dock and leaned over the railing. The water moved with such resolute purpose. It knew exactly what its mission was—swift and sure, never looking over its shoulder.

I toyed with and then decided that perhaps I would trail Millie's footsteps for a while and see where they led. It would be almost impossible to work as a decorator out in the country, where people prided themselves on the age of their chintz and the bagginess of their faded upholstery. No. My decorating days were over, unless I moved to Charleston. So far, aside from the one conversation with Miss Nancy, I'd not thought about being anywhere but Tall Pines. I was willingly in her grip, as comfortable as a swaddled baby in her cradle. I had a halfhearted thought that we'd homeschool Eric and move for the fall. Summer at Tall Pines was the best time of year anyway. No reason to go right away.

If I wasn't running down to Charleston to establish my independence, I knew I needed something to occupy my time once we were settled. I didn't need money, beyond what Richard had promised to provide. For the first time in my life I had no expenses! This could be very interesting, I thought.

All my life I had compared Millie to the witches in *Macbeth*. *Double, double, toil and trouble* . . . it wasn't true. She was basically a homeopath. Okay, not just a homeopath, but so far there wasn't anything really bizarre about what she had told me. It wasn't like I had to drink rat blood or something. And who knew? Over time, I might be able to settle into her faith. I didn't know enough about it to make a judgment yet.

Homeopathy. Better for Eric than Ritalin if I could make

it work. Much better. Besides helping Eric focus and concentrate, maybe I could straighten out a few family members. God knows, they needed it. Then I chided myself for the critical thought. Hadn't I, minutes before, bristled from the memory of Mother's criticism? How much of her *was* in me? How many of the traits I loathed in her could I finger in my *own* behavior?

And what Millie said about life being all about service to others. That was heavy. Very heavy indeed. It would freak her right out of her mind to feel the blast of the prevailing winds of self-centered frenzy that blew down the canyons of New York City—the ruthless deals on Wall Street, the cutthroat competition on Madison Avenue, the Seventh Avenue circle of deceit. And the monstrous law firms that defended them against each other—a virtual war between billable hours and integrity. All of it about money, status, and power. Not exactly Woodstock.

No, I had found plenty to mull over. Away from the glare and tumult of New York, the veils of denial lifted. In my heart, I knew Manhattan was no place for a boy like Eric. Sure, the museums were great, but I could take him there a couple of times a year. Charleston did have an airport, after all.

Here I could concentrate on him, make him well rounded, and teach him to do all the things unique to Lowcountry living. Even Mother and Trip had demonstrated their desire to let Eric know he belonged. Taking him fishing, showering him with breathtaking generosity.

And Richard? I would always love him in spite of everything. I wished things were different but it wasn't in my power to change them. He had given me Eric. I could never hate him. I just didn't want to be his wife and live his life of hedonism. Wasn't I entitled to pursue happiness?

Just what would make me happy? I wondered.

I had existed in my marriage like a gerbil on a wheel—
every day the same repetition of activities; this didn't serve
anyone well, including myself. Or Eric. All that running,
running. Where? I had a lot to think about. I had not taken
enough care in the way I'd allowed my life to unfold.
Maybe that was the problem—that I'd been standing by
on the sidelines of my own life too long: not really living,
belonging nowhere and to no one. Hiding behind Eric.
Trying not to be my mother.

The sky was turning red and I was feeling blue. *Jesus,
Caroline, you sound like bad country music*, I said to myself. *What would your father say?* I stood at the rail a few
minutes longer watching the sun slip behind the trees on
the bank opposite me. I'd never felt so alone and began to
examine my conscience to understand why. What kind of
a daughter *had* I been to Mother? Passable. Sister to Trip?
Fair. Never mind what kind of aunt to my nieces or what
level of sister-in-law to the whore from hell. Not so hot.
No, I'd been hiding behind motherhood all snug and cozy
seven hundred miles away. I'd drop in from time to time
and judge them. Surely I could do better than the vapid
and shapeless life I'd left behind.

Millie was right. If I embraced my duty to my family
and to myself, maybe I'd find happiness and purpose. Food
for thought. Correction. Buffet for thought.

32

SQUARE ONE

Tuesday

At one o'clock sharp the next day the doorbell rang. It was the math and science tutor, Ruth Perretti.

"Hi! Come on in!" I said, holding the door open for her.

"You must be Mrs. Levine?" she said and extended her hand.

"Yes, call me Caroline, please."

We shook hands and on the way into the living room, I got a good look at her. She was gorgeous, and I don't mean maybe. She must have stood five ten, if an inch. Her red hair was swept up with a clamp. She wore khakis, a blue shirt, and a white sweater tied around her shoulders. Thirty? Maybe.

"Well, then, you call me Rusty. All my friends do. It's the hair."

"I figured that! Would you like a glass of tea?"

"Sure, thanks."

At first blush, I liked her. A lot. She was old enough to have had some experience. Her personality was lively and she was pretty. Eric would like that. I poured and handed her a glass.

"Please sit down," I said. "Tell me about yourself. How did you become a tutor?"

"Thank you," she said, and took her seat on the wing-back with a definite grace. "Well, I've been teaching for eight years as a substitute in Walterboro. The problem is that the average age of the faculty is fifty. They're not going anywhere for a while. Supply-and-demand theory. So, I tutor. To tell you the truth, I think I like doing this better than I would being in a classroom."

Her green eyes twinkled with an honest gaiety. Here was someone who liked her life and her work.

"Why's that?"

"When you teach a child one on one, you have them in your hands. And, homeschooling is so flexible. We can use the Internet for research and build a Web page and link it all over the world. We can take field trips to the library, collect specimens from the river for science. When it's a nice day, we can study outside. When we want to study astronomy, we can have a night class with a telescope."

"Eric loves the constellations."

"How old is he?"

"He'll be twelve soon. He's adorable," I said.

She went on to tell me that she had special certification in special education for dyslexic children. Her younger brother was dyslexic, she said, and it had not stopped him from becoming a veterinarian. It wasn't a big deal, just a learning-style difference.

She got points for good attitude.

"And what curriculum of math do you use?"

"Standard math—the old-fashioned kind. There are all

these horrible new systems of math out there that confuse the kids more than teach them."

"Chicago math?"

"That's one! Lord, what a disaster it is! You see, I know from my own education that without a good solid foundation you fall apart. Once the foundation's in place, then you can go crazy and have fun."

"Do you let your students use calculators?"

"Only when they can spit out their basic math facts as well as they do their own name."

Okay, one down, two to go. I hired her on the spot. Eric would adore her. I adored her. Forty dollars an hour. I didn't care. Eric would learn something from this woman. I showed her the textbooks and workbooks Eric had been using. Rusty, the redheaded, long-legged science and math tutor, accepted and would start the following Monday. Six months with her and Eric would be Einstein.

At three on the nose, the doorbell rang again. It was Peter Greer, the language arts tutor.

"Hi!" I said. "I'm Caroline Levine, Eric's mother. You must be Mr. Greer."

He switched his briefcase to his other hand and we shook hands. He was every bit a southern gentleman, insisting I enter the door first and that he would close it behind me. He wore a perfectly pressed tan suit, polished brown wing tips, a white shirt, and a little bow tie. From behind his wire-rimmed glasses twinkled blue eyes of understanding and patience. I guessed him to be near seventy and retired.

We went through the same routine that I'd just been through with Rusty. He was a darling, darling man.

"So you were the assistant superintendent of schools in Charleston?"

"Forever, but my real love was curriculum planning."

He was about to reveal all to me when Mother appeared in the hallway. Mr. Greer just about fell over himself getting to his feet when she entered the room. Mother couldn't take her eyes away from him. He was a pussycat—even I thought so!

"Mother? This is Mr. Greer. He's here to discuss tutoring Eric in foreign language and English."

"How lovely to meet you, Mr. Greer." Mother extended her hand with a slow and deliberate movement, causing Mr. Greer to clear his throat and consider proposing marriage to her. I'd seen it a million times. When Mother flipped the Miss Lavinia switch, she was not to be trifled with. "What foreign languages do you speak?"

He still held her hand as though he were in a trance, but finally found his voice.

"Please. Call me Peter."

"Languages?"

Mother rolled her eyes at him and batted her eyelashes for good measure. I couldn't believe that a woman in this day and age could bat her eyelashes at a man without him laughing right in her face. But he didn't laugh. He went nearly catatonic.

"Mother?"

He dropped her hand, cleared his throat again, and, thank God, recovered his dignity.

"Mrs. Levine? I'm fluent in seven—"

"Peter? I'm not Mrs. Levine. My daughter carries that name. I'm Lavinia Boswell Wimbley. Please. Call me Lavinia, won't you?"

Well, the rest of that interview was shot to hell. He called her Lavinia, all right—all afternoon! They walked the yard together, her arm looped through his. I saw him wipe off a chair with his linen handkerchief before he would allow her to sit in bird squat. The last sighting?

They were on the way to the chapel on the bluffs with a picnic basket. I watched them from the kitchen window. Millie was at the desk, paying bills.

"Millie! Come yanh!"

She got up, grumbling. "What you want with me, huh? I got things to do! I'm trying to reconcile the phone bill. It's full of nine hundred–number calls and I can't imagine . . ." She looked out of the window at Mother and Mr. Greer as they ambled and sashayed their way across the lawn. "Jeez-a-ree!"

"He's a dead duck," I said.

"Humph," she said, "ain't no fool like an old fool, yanh?"

"Which one are you talking about? Mother or poor Mr. Greer?"

Millie and I had a good laugh.

"Don't make no never mind to me," she said.

"Me either!"

It was almost five and Joshua Welton, who was supposed to have been here at four-thirty, had not called. I was mildly annoyed. His résumé was so fabulous, I decided to refrain from judgment until I knew something. Hell, he could have had a flat tire. That *had* happened in the history of travel.

I was upstairs when the doorbell rang. I looked out the window and saw an old white Triumph TR6 convertible. Cool. Millie answered it and I assumed she showed him into the living room. I applied a little lip gloss and hurried downstairs to meet him, stopping dead in the entrance. His back was to me as he stood before a portrait of one of my ancestors. He had dreadlocks. Nearly down to his waist, gathered up in a ponytail. This wouldn't work. Too weird. Oh, well, I thought, I'll just interview him briefly and let him be on his way. I cleared my throat and crossed the room.

"Hi!" I said, "I'm Eric's mother, Caroline."

"Hi!" He turned to face me and for the second time in ninety seconds I stopped in my tracks. He was so handsome, I gasped. I mean, we were talking male model—and not gay male model, okay? Industrial-strength testosterone filled the air. I nearly fainted.

"Is this a Sargent?"

His voice was melodious and soft. He was probably my age. Maybe younger. When he smiled, his gold-flecked brown eyes flashed. This guy had more sex appeal in one eyeball than I could handle.

"No, he was a corporal. That's another one of our . . . Oh! You mean, did John Singer Sargent paint it! Oh, golly!" I slapped the side of my head. "How silly! Of course it's Sargent. Here, would you like to sit down? Can I pour you some tea?" I started to blather. I was mortified by my lack of control. Oh yeah, Mrs. Freaking Cool from New York is a big-time freaking ass in front of the freaking art tutor with the freaking dreadlocks.

"Tea would be great."

The pitcher was long gone so I excused myself to refill it in the kitchen. Millie was just putting away the accounting books. I opened the refrigerator and stared into it, trying to remember what I had come in here for in the first place. My breathing was uneven and Millie couldn't let it pass without comment.

"What's the matter with you, Caroline? You taking a shine to hippies now? That boy in your mother's living room looks like a drug dealer!"

"He ain't no boy, Millie. He's hot. I need tea. Please?"

"You need a cold shower, that's what! Between you and your mother today! I don't know what's come over the women of this house! Go on! I'll bring it out!"

I stared at her. A drug dealer? A hippie?

"Get! Skedaddle!"

I went back through the swinging door and heard her say in Gullah under her breath, *"Hot, my foot. Humph! Dese women ain't know hot was iffin it bit 'em in dey behind!"*

I reopened the door and she looked at me. "Oh, yes, we would!" I said and she started to laugh.

In the living room, Joshua Welton was looking from painting to painting.

"Whistler?" he said, pointing to a seascape that had belonged to my grandmother.

"Yes, he gave it to my grandmother as a gift when she got married. They were friends." Okay, it was a damn lie, but I wanted him to be impressed. He was.

"Well then, that would explain why I've never seen it. I did a paper on him in graduate school. It's probably always been on this wall."

"That's right. It has."

It felt like he was the source of all air in the room, that I could only breathe when he did. What in hell was the matter with me?

"Do you want to ask me any questions?" he said.

He had a smirk on his face that I should have slapped but all I wanted to do was lick it. Jesus! Was my estrogen out of whack?

"Of course! Let's sit for a few minutes. Millie's gonna bring some tea for us."

I sat in one of the oversized rolled armchairs and tucked a leg under me. Realizing it was an unprofessional posture, I sat up straight. He smirked again. Every move I made held his notice. He was playing with my head and I couldn't get control of myself. This had never happened to me before. Who was this guy? He wasn't arrogant. No, that wasn't it. He seemed to be as off-kilter as I was. But not quite. He sat opposite me. Waiting for me to speak.

"So! You're an occupational therapist, I see? Tell me about that." There. That was officious enough to get back on professional footing.

"Are you married?"

"No, separated. Are you married?" This was stupid. Stupid but inevitable.

"No, divorced two years ago. No kids. No dogs. I live alone in downtown Charleston on East Bay Street in the home I grew up in. Parents left it to me. I've been knocking around the world studying indigenous cultures and religions."

"You're hired," I said and shrugged my shoulders.

"Tough interview," he said. "Wanna have dinner?"

"I'll get my coat."

"I'll cook for you."

"Cool. I'll help."

I nearly collided with Millie and her tray in the hallway. Once again, I looked like an idiot.

"Where are you going in such a hurry?"

"Out to dinner with Mr. Weston."

"Uh, that's Welton," he said, "but call me Josh."

We didn't talk in the car. The top was down and there was too much noise from the wind. I had on my huge sunglasses and held my hair back with one hand. Every now and then, I looked at his arm. It was toned and tanned. All I wanted to do was run my finger down the muscle and see if the blond hair was as silky as it looked. He'd catch my glance and smile. I'd smile back. We screamed down Highway 17 north and I knew I was going to be a bad, bad girl. It was out of character, to say the least.

His house on East Bay Street, overlooking Charleston

Harbor, was nearly three hundred years old, one of the wonderful old historic pastel-colored ones with earthquake rods running through it.

He got out of his car to open the elaborate wrought-iron gates. I could tell through his clothes that he was in very good shape. His khaki trousers hung from his backside like a tablecloth. He probably worked out all the time.

All the way to Charleston, I wondered if he planned to seduce me. What would I do? When had I showered? That morning. Legs were waxed, no trauma there. *Oh, please,* I told myself, *get over it. You're just gonna have a little dinner and go home. You'll discuss the state of education and religions and you'll go home. Try to remember the part about going home.*

We pulled into the courtyard, he closed the gates and came around my side to help me out.

"Been a while since I was in one of these," I said. He gave me an arm and I pulled against his weight to get out. As gravity and nature would have it, my chest brushed his, but he dropped my arm and I smoothed out my pants. It was already dark. Too early to have Studly Do-Right throw-me-down. And please! Go inside for heaven's sake!

I was so busy talking to myself that I didn't hear him talking to me. "Oh! I'm sorry! What did you say?"

"I said, why don't we get a glass of wine and then I'll show you around. Sound good?"

"Sounds great," I said, following him up the front steps and inside.

We passed down a long wide hall with roped-off period rooms on either side, through an almost invisible door, into the kitchen.

"House tours?"

"Yeah, I promised my parents I wouldn't change anything. I figured if I was destined to own a museum, I may as well open it to the public. Pays the taxes and I don't have to work full-time, all year, which is why I tutor."

"Trust fund?"

"Yeah, thank God. The interest isn't huge, but there's not much I want. White okay?"

"Sure." I dropped my bag on the center island and thought what else could there *be* to want. He lived in a virtual palace. "May I ask a question?"

"Sure, ask away!"

He twisted the corkscrew into the neck of the bottle. I watched his muscles flex as he removed the cork. It was a beautiful thing. I forgot what I was going to ask. His eyes caught mine. He blushed.

"Got some cheese and crackers or something?" I said. "I'm starving!" Now, how stupid a recovery was that? About a two on a scale of one to ten.

"Sure! In the fridge. Help yourself."

I dug around the bottom hydrator and found a new piece of Saga. When I turned and closed the door, I caught him shifting his stare from my derriere. I started to relax. At least it wasn't just me. For a while there, I had been worried. I went through the drawers until I found some reasonably fresh crackers.

"So, does it drive the tourists crazy that their host has dreadlocks?"

"They think I'm the maintenance man. It's my cover."

I just shook my head. "Got a cheese board in this house?"

"Over the stove," he said.

I found it, took an apple from a bowl of fruit on the counter, rinsed it, and dried it with a paper towel. He handed me a goblet.

"What are we drinking to?" I said. He was standing so

close to me that I could smell his skin. He smelled slightly of musk. My heart was in my throat.

"Interesting question. What do you think we should drink to?"

My heart was now going about five hundred beats a minute. If I died from nerves and anticipation it would ruin everything and I'd never forgive myself.

"Let's drink to courage," I said, "something I'm lacking."

"Oh, God! No! Let's drink to something else. I say we drink to romance."

We clinked and I said, "No, no. Too corny. Let's drink to something noble!"

"Romance isn't noble?"

"Okay, you win. Here's to—"

"Wait! I know what! Let's get serious here. Let's drink to the feeling we had when we first looked in each other's eyes. I don't know what it was, and I don't know what you call it, but it was some very nuclear energy."

"Yes. It was." At least he gave it a name. "To nuclear energy!"

We touched the rims of our glasses once more and finally drank. Yes, he had named it. When you name a thing, I thought, it's real and belongs to you. I knew that we had to find something to talk about or else we'd just rip off our clothes. For the sake of some semblance of propriety, I took a stab at small talk, while I went back to fixing our hors d'oeuvres.

"So tell me where you've traveled," I said.

"I spent last year in Nepal, Bhutan, and India," he said.

"Take a lot of pictures? It's hot as hell there, isn't it?"

"Yeah, but it's hot as hell here. I'm sort of a student of Hinduism and I stayed at an ashram with my guru for six months. I have lots of pictures; photography is sort of a hobby of mine. Did a lot of yoga, a lot of meditation."

"What kind of yoga? I do Hatha."

"Well, this was different. Tantric. Red."

"Oh, great. I'm going home."

He may as well have said that he was rewriting the Kama Sutra. Then we both started to laugh. We were going nowhere except to bed.

Miss Lavinia's Journal

Here it is, only eight o'clock in the evening, and I am thoroughly enjoying the change in my household and just wanted to make note of it. I am propped up in my bed watching my adorable Eric construct a huge LEGO thing that has a motor and I know that any minute it's going to come racing across my room! Oh, my! If I had the strength, I'd be on the floor with him. I'm so tired these days! Maybe I need some vitamins or something! In any case, having him and Caroline here makes me so so happy! And where did she run off to tonight? Gone without so much as a fare-thee-well! What if I'd decided to fly to Lisbon with Peter? Well, Millie could've watched Eric, I imagine! Oh, that Peter Greer! They just don't make men like him anymore! So genteel! So attentive! Even though he's on the back nine, I'll bet he's an an-i-mal, if you know what I mean! He said he'd stop by around 9:30, if he could. I'll be waiting, Peter!

33

BREATHE

We took our wine, cheese, and crackers to the large study that adjoined the kitchen. He turned on music and opened the French doors to the porch and garden. Trying to be casual, I turned on a few lights, had a bit of cheese, licked my fingers, and took a sip of my wine.

"I use this as my living room. No tourists allowed."

"Well, you have to have a place of your own."

"Absolutely. You stay right here and I'll go get my portfolio. I'll show you the Ganges and the Himalayan mountains."

I walked out onto the porch and smelled the perfume of jasmine. I knew that technically I had no business fooling around with a man before my divorce was final, but that finality was still two years away. The courts in New York were so backed up, it would be a miracle to get it even then.

I decided to ignore my marital status. I was sick to death of being thought of as so correct—Richard's wife, the reliable, the predictable, the scrubbed-up and squeaky clean, quintessential southern belle. Fifteen years of the missionary position had taken its toll on me. I was in the mood for adventure.

I walked along the neat brick path, which led to an outdoor fountain. Water from the jar held on the shoulder of the ancient Greek maiden in the center cascaded and splattered drops, making music on the surface of the pool. From that center I could see the formal pattern of the garden was like a wheel, footpaths for spokes. Each wedge held different horticultural specimens, ornamental grasses, things I'd never seen, all cared for by someone who loved growing things.

I strolled all around, talking to myself—of what the night would bring. When I finally stopped arguing with my inner voice that I wasn't here to get revenge for Richard's infidelity and that I longed for the touch of a man, this man, I came to another conclusion. It was high time I started taking some risks. My father had possessed the mocking soul of a gambler. My mother was as theatrical as they came. They both did as they pleased and in the process loved their lives.

So would I. I knew then that was what, or part of what I had heard from the soul of my father. *Be my daughter! Change!* It meant to let go a little, take chances on life. Not dangerous ones, but to investigate my own wants and desires. I had bought into Richard's politics on everything for too long until I had damn nearly become a translation of him. Maybe I would reclaim myself and become my father and my mother's daughter.

I saw Josh moving in the light of the study and called out to him.

"Hey! I came outside to poke around! Beautiful garden!"

"Thanks! I thought you left me!"

"Yeah, sure." *When hell freezes*, I thought. I came up the steps to join him. "I love to garden. When you come out next week, remind me to show you our roses. They're pretty wonderful."

"Gardening is my passion. When I'm away I have this amazing woman . . ."

"You do?"

"Yeah, she's been gardening for over seventy years. Taught me all there is to know about compost."

"Oh!"

Jesus, Caroline, I said to myself, *you've known the man for* how long *and you're already possessive?* Wait until Lavinia sees his hair! I was beginning to think it was pretty sexy and wanted to touch it, in the most urgent way. We stepped back inside.

The noise of my thumping libido was momentarily quieted by my decorator's eye. The study was filled with beautiful English antiques, which stood gleaming in every part of the room. Asian artifacts were everywhere. I had hardly noticed them when Josh had been in the room the first time. The pale green walls rose to fifteen feet and the tan curtain panels flanked the French doors and long windows, hanging from a fat rod and puddled on the floor.

He just stood there, leaning against a tall chest on chest, watching me. "You think I'm going to take you to bed, don't you?"

"The thought never crossed my mind," I said, lying and smiling.

"Wanna see some pictures?"

"Sure," I said. I took his hand and he led me to the couch.

He had several black leather portfolios, stacked on the table in front of him. I picked one up and began to flip through. They were all eight-by-ten color photographs of temples, mountains, monks, and pilgrims.

"Where's this taken?"

"Oh, that! That's Pashupatinath—major shrine to Shiva. And those are young Tibetan monks at the Sera Monastery in Lhasa."

"These are so great! Why are they so blue?"

"Good eye! Thin air—altitude makes the blues more prominent."

"Is it warm in here or is it just me?" I could feel little beads of perspiration on the back of my neck. "Josh?"

"Hmmm?"

The room temperature continued to rise. "Let's have dinner. Okay?"

"Do you want to have dinner now?"

Nope, I want you to show me your whole bag of tricks and I want you to show me with vigor and enthusiasm. I want you to make me sweat!

"Sure," I said and put the album back on the table. I drained my glass and so did he. It was all I could say.

"Come on!" he said, pulling me up, "you're just a lazy feline!"

"You're absolutely right." I held up my glass. "I'm on empty."

"I can take care of that right away."

He filled our glasses and we began to make dinner in the kitchen. It was remarkable how distracted I felt.

Josh was digging around in the cabinets and I searched the refrigerator.

"If I had known you were coming, I would have shopped for something and actually planned this meal."

"Who knew is right!" I could not have cared less what I ate for dinner.

You're Caroline's dessert, Josh Welton. I'm gonna be such a bad girl with you . . .

"Hey, Caroline. Risotto?" he said.

"Sure! With what?" . . . *I want to examine your entire body! Call me Dr. Caroline. . . .*

"Asparagus and onions?"

"Perfect! I'll make salad." . . . *And then we're gonna play with your Kama and my Sutra and see what happens!*

I made the salad, set the table, lit the candles, lowered the lights, all with more enthusiasm than I could recall having for domestic duties in ages.

His silver flatware was beautiful. Everything was beautiful. He asked me about my childhood. I told him my version of the truth. He entertained me with stories of his. We alternated between cooking and thumbing through his pictures with laughter and refilling the glasses many times.

"Was this silver your mother's?"

"Yep. I try to keep everything in good shape. Well, actually, *I* don't do it. Someone comes in."

"Double her salary. Your time is not best spent polishing silver," I said and grinned.

"And what do you think is the best use of my time?" he said and smiled, biting his bottom lip.

"Talk about a rhetorical question!"

"I have other knives that match it in the bottom drawer. Those have steel blades and they rust."

He was chopping shallots on the cutting board next to the stove. I opened the drawer and sure enough when I unwrapped the gray flannel bundle, it held twelve knives—reproductions—which matched down to the last thread. The butter and olive oil sizzled when he dropped in the onions. In minutes, the room smelled so delicious that my stomach began to growl.

"So, Josh, you know I have to ask you this question . . ."
Exactly how big is it?

"Sure. Ask anything," he said and stirred the risotto around the bottom of the pot. "Want more wine?"

"Sure, thanks."

"You seem so calm to me—intense as a whole freaking town in flames, but calm nonetheless." I offered him a slice of tomato. He opened his mouth and I fed him, thinking I'd like to run my finger around his teeth. He closed his mouth on my finger and sucked it. "Jesus, bubba! Cut it out!" I said that with no conviction in my voice and he didn't stop. "Do you think we could kiss or do something remotely germane to this culture? Just to humor me?"

He released my finger and said, "Kiss? That's germy!"

I put my hand on my hip and looked at him like he was crazy.

"I'm kidding," he said, "come here."

He extended his hand, I took it, and he pulled me to him. Yeah, boy, I was about to kiss a man with dreadlocks. I wished Richard could see how unprovincial I was. He pushed my hair away from my face and neck and that's where his mouth went first. I thought I would pass out on the floor. I wanted him to push my salad out of the way and throw me on the center island. I wanted his weight on me and I kept pulling him closer. We backed into the is-land and, sure enough, the whole bowl of roughage went crashing across the floor. Who cared? He was getting very feisty and I was right there with him. Then he stopped, opened his eyes, and looked at me.

He said nothing and lifted me onto the center island.

"I hate salad," I said.

With the flick of his wrist, he turned off the stove and then all hell broke loose and it became crystal clear why women took younger lovers. I could not believe that I was on a marble slab having the time of my life and getting a chiropractic adjustment at the same time. By the time I was ready to chastise myself for doing this with my son's tutor, the cruise to paradise had begun. *Oh, well*, I thought, *too late. Hang on and enjoy the ride.*

And I did. When we finally came up for air, we had progressed from the island to the floor to the couch and to the floor again. This fellow took his vitamins. When I opened my eyes I was looking at the hand-plastered ceiling of his study, wondering what it would cost to reproduce it in today's market. What does that tell you? I looked over at Josh and smiled. This couldn't happen again. After my disastrous final episode with Richard, this had been good for my ego, to be sure. Even then I knew that Josh would have to remain on the perimeter of my life. I wasn't ready for a relationship—a friend, perhaps, but nothing serious.

"Do you want to stay the night?" he asked.

"Baby boy, I'd like to stay forever, but I think Mother would have a cow if I did. And besides, we really shouldn't be doing this. Especially if you're going to be Eric's tutor. It's not cool."

"You mean, this was it?"

"Yeah, I'm afraid so."

"Too bad, I mean, you're right, but what a bummer."

He understood. I was grateful for that.

We rode back to Tall Pines with the top up on his car. He held my hand and every so often, squeezed it. Several times I reached over and ran my hand down that lovely arm of his. His skin was smooth and cool. I had a surprising affection for him and hoped we could find a way to be just friends.

The house was almost dark when we arrived, except for the porch and hall lights and one small light in the living room. It was nearly eleven o'clock. We said good night and promised to talk the next day, and I went inside, feeling pretty groovy about life in general.

Having turned off the outside lights, I stepped into the living room and caught my breath. Mother—wearing one of her more bizarre jeweled caftans and turbans—was sitting on the couch with Mr. Greer's head in her lap. They were both snoring loudly.

The remnants of their evening—a cocktail shaker, cut-glass tumblers, rubberized cheese, strawberry greens, crackers softened from the night air, wrinkled napkins, an overfilled ashtray, and a nearly empty fifth of bourbon— were all on the coffee table before them. I didn't know what to do, so I left them and went to the kitchen to get a glass of milk and a sandwich. I was surprised again to see Millie there, reading a paperback at the table. She looked up at me.

"What do I smell?" she said, looking suspicious.

"Love Potion Number Nine, Miss Nosy. You waiting up to lecture me?" I stood before her with my hands on my hips, pretending to be defiant.

"Humph," she said. "Think I'll save my breath. Your mother still courting that man in the living room?"

"They're both out cold, snoring like a couple of bull-dogs."

"I don't know what's come over this family! Muss be the spring air." Millie closed her book, stood up, and stretched. "Yeah, God! Shoulda seen your brother when he got a eyeful of that redhead! He 'bout drop to the ground."

"Rusty?" I opened the jar of peanut butter and took out a loaf of bread.

"Didn't that man feed you?"

"Still hungry. So what about Rusty?"

Millie raised her eyebrows with the full knowledge that

I had not had a sufficient supper. "Left her sweater or some such fool. Came back. Trip got the door and that's all she wrote. Gotta wake up Miss L. Gone have a crick in her neck and be cranky all day tomorrow."

"Let me do it, Millie."

"No, girl. You go on to bed." Then she looked at me up and down from head to toe and sniffed in disapproval. "You gone sleep good tonight, yanh?"

"Millie? Do you know how annoying it is to be around somebody who knows everything?"

She cocked her head to one side, pursed her lips, and said, "Caroline? You getting to be more like Lavinia every day."

"That's not nice, Millie." Boy, if you wanted to get under my skin, that was all you had to say.

"It ain't good, but it's true all the same. Go on up to your boy. I expect he's sleeping but waiting for you all the same."

The swinging door whooshed to a close behind her. I took a drink of water and left the glass in the sink. Was it true? Like Mother? Hell no. Couldn't be. I took the back stairs up to Eric's room and peeked in. He was sleeping with a book across his chest. I removed his glasses, kissed his head, and turned off his light.

In my room, I tried to think about what Millie had said, but I preferred to let my thoughts wander back to Josh— a much more pleasant topic. I'd think about Millie's words tomorrow. Wednesday was another day. *Fiddle dee dee, Scarlett, time to go to bed.*

34

TRIPPED UP

Friday

Josh and I agreed to be pals. It was the best thing. Mother found my new friendship very amusing. She felt Josh's hair and pronounced it sponge. Needless to say, she understood the point in a one-night stand—not that I had told her. Millie still thought his hair was an indication of a drug habit. Eric was too busy enjoying himself to have an opinion. Josh and I were just *hanging out*. Occasionally.

Eric must have been born to be a Lowcountry boy, and had almost immediately immersed himself in discovering everything there was of interest at Tall Pines. When Mr. Jenkins wasn't teaching him to cast a seine net, Trip—who had a curious new sprightly spring in his step—had him on the river. Mother taught him to drink sweet tea and enlightened him on the historical significance of our family's illustrious history—Lavinia style, which is to say, greatly exaggerated and embellished. Needless to say, Millie taught him the names of her herbs and all the vegetation around our property. At least once a day Eric said, "Mom? This is hog heaven!" I was relieved and satisfied that he meant it and continued on with trying to settle us at Tall Pines.

When the movers arrived yesterday, Josh, along with Millie, Eric, and Mr. Jenkins, helped me sort through the cartons. Actually, I realized we didn't need very much. Eric wanted his toys and computer games and I wanted my books, music, and business records, but almost everything else was relatively unnecessary for the moment. All the collections of fifteen years of our life seemed unnecessary. It was strange that I felt I needed so little. All that excess would go into storage.

"Good thing you have a barn," Josh said.

"Yeah, well, too bad this stuff can't stay here. Too humid. All the pictures will curl and mildew."

It was true. Beautiful as Tall Pines may have been, everything needed some kind of climate control to preserve it. The barn was where the mission of consignment was conducted. We had a huge mess on our hands. Eric darted from the barn to the house and from the house to the barn, arms filled with comic books, plastic boxes filled with LEGOs, and his other treasures. Mr. Jenkins went back and forth to the house with the wheelbarrow, carrying the heavier things. Mother appeared every hour or so, shook her head, and clucked. "Still at it? My word, Caroline, you should have had a tag sale in New York!" Then, before she would leave, she'd shoot Josh one of her best Miss Lavinia come-hither looks. We'd both giggle like children when she was gone.

"Mother is a flirt," I said.

"Dangerous?" he said.

"Only when provoked," I said.

"I found a storage company that would pick up on Saturday, if you want to get this stuff out of yanh tomorrow," Millie said, coming out from the tack room. "Just had them on the phone. They want to know how long you want them to hold on to your belongings." She had a pencil pushed through her braid, her reading glasses on the tip of her nose, and a legal pad in her hands. "I told them I didn't know but that I'd find out directly and call them back. Time affects the rate, you know." Millie heaved a sigh—one that said, *I don't know why you are doing all of this; it's a waste of your time and mine.*

"Time is money!" Eric said, piping in. "Grandmother says that. I guess she's trying to teach me the significance of time more than money."

Not missing a beat, I said, "Well, darlin', thank God she doesn't have to worry about . . . what?"

Everyone had stopped and was staring at Eric.

"Significance?" Josh said. "How old are you, anyway?"

"He's smart like his momma," Mr. Jenkins said.

"That's my boy!" I said and ruffled his hair.

"Your grandmother's right too, boy," Millie said. "So, missy? What you want me to tell them? One month? Three months? Ten years?"

"I don't know, Millie. Let me think about it for a few minutes."

How long *would* I be here? Was my return to Mother's home a statement of failure and surrender? Did I want to move down to Charleston? Perhaps eventually.

No, it would take longer than a few minutes to decide my fate. I had toyed with the idea of staying the summer and moving in the fall. But at that point, I really wanted to see how the homeschooling thing would go for Eric and then make up my mind. I was rather enjoying being coddled by Millie and Mother.

"Well, you bess make up your mind, honey, 'cause I gots to tell them something!" Millie walked away in a small huff. The huff wasn't anything but Millie staking out her authority and a little teasing that I should use my brains and quit living in limbo.

I knew she wanted us to stay. Forever. Yes, the coddling was nice. "Tell them I want space until I let them know," I said, calling to her back. "Probably August, okay?"

She stopped, turned, and looked at me, her face the mirror of displeasure. "We'll just see what we see," she said and turned again.

Sometimes her psychic talents rankled my nerves. I let the thought pass on the breeze and turned my attention to more pleasant matters.

I was sitting on the floor of the barn, folding and stacking packing paper to recycle, looking like a perfect angel— considering the tone of Josh's butt from a safe distance— turning into Mrs. Robinson, mentally treating the man like an object, but not putting out. So what? Haven't women been objectified for eons? Goose and gander? Like a bolt of lightning came the thought that even if I wasn't Lavinia, I was sure on the slick path to embracing her sexual politics.

Josh was leaning over a carton of books, taking them out, reading the spines, flipping through the pages.

"The Joy of Cooking?" he said.

Knowing his deviant mind was thinking of the joy of something else, I said, "It happens to be extremely useful!"

"You can tell a lot about someone by their books, you know," he said.

"Keep digging. The complete works of Balzac are in there somewhere, right next to Flaubert."

"The History of Textiles?"

"Excuse me, Mr. Tibetan Book of the Dead, I worked as a decorator, you know."

"Right, and I respect that."

My alarms pinged. If Josh was going to start giving me grief about the shallow way I had earned a living, like Richard did, our friendship wouldn't last long. I looked at his face to detect traces of sarcasm.

"What?" he said.

"My work—my estranged husband thought it was shallow and therefore I was shallow. I can't take going through all of that with . . ."

He was sensitive enough that he was able to understand immediately that making fun of being a decorator wasn't going to hold much water with me. He came to me and took my hands.

"Caroline. I don't think you're shallow. Frigid maybe, but not shallow."

"Thanks a lot, hot lips." Those damnable gold flecks in his eyes were reflecting the afternoon light and I felt like a prude. A big stupid one.

"In fact, I was going to ask you if you knew of a company that reproduced historic wallpaper. We have some water damage in the dining room."

"Oh." I was further embarrassed for my fast judgment against him. "Sure. Scalamandre can do it. Just give me a swatch and we can FedEx it to them this weekend."

"Great. That would be great."

He was looking at me as though he pitied me. Pity? Yes, he was somehow sad and maybe disappointed that I was so spiritually tied to the earthly shortcomings—self-doubt, insecurity, flash temper, and the whole laundry list of human failings. I felt a little juvenile—certainly not on his plane of thought. And, I wasn't. And, so what?

I had considered myself to be pretty together when I

was living my life with Richard in the narrow confines I
had drawn for myself. My daily habits had centered around
Eric's needs, Richard's needs, and my clients' needs.
Maybe what I had done was withdraw from challenge into
denial. Maybe what I pretended was growth was in fact
resistance of any deep introspection. After all, Josh hadn't
been anything but nice to me and I was still waiting for
an ambush.

I hadn't meditated in nearly a month or done any yoga
in just as long. It was really time for me to settle down
and try to find my good habits again. Since I'd been home
I'd done nothing but drink wine, eat animal fat, and screw
Josh that one spectacular night. The rest of my time was
spent making him think it was possible somehow that it
might happen again. Not! Come to think of it, I was having
more fun than I'd had in years. The downside was that as
long as I continued this kind of behavior, I could no longer
stand on Mount Superior. Oh, to hell with Mount Superior,
I decided. What I needed was fun.

It was strange that for all the belongings I had gathered
like a pack rat over the course of my years in New York,
I could leave so much in boxes and not care if I had them
around me or not. Maybe that was a first step toward some
kind of growth. All that really *did* matter to me was that
I had Eric and I was away from the hell of Richard and
Lois.

I began unpacking another box. I looked up to see Eric
skipping along. When he entered the barn, I saw him shoot
a suspicious look at Josh. He saw that I had seen him do
it and came to my side to whisper in my ear.

"Mom? Can I ask you something?"

"Don't whisper, Eric, it's not nice, sweetheart. Whatever
you have to say to me I'm sure you can say in front of
Josh."

He bristled. I had said the wrong thing. There were always going to be things that Eric would want to be private and I had just put him in the uncomfortable position of having to treat someone he barely knew as a confidant.

He sort of looked at the floor and then back at me and said, "I was just wondering if you were going out again tonight with Josh. That's all."

At least Josh had the God-given sense to stay out of the conversation at that point. He made himself busy with boxes on the other end of the pile.

"Yes, I think we are, Eric." Eric's face fell a little. I could tell by one look that he probably wanted me to stay home that night. I put my arm around him. "Tell you what . . ."

"What?" he said, as forlornly as though I had told him I was leaving for a month.

"Mom's been having some fun. And, admit it, you have too! Now, I know it's hard for you to understand that Mom needs a pal to hang around with . . ."

"No, I don't! Everybody needs friends!"

"Okay, good. I don't blame you for wondering what's going on and, in fact, I think you're probably right that I've been gone a lot. So this is my suggestion—you don't have to say yes—just think about it."

He looked at me and I melted just like I always did when he looked at me in need.

"Okay," he said.

"Tomorrow, you and me, *just* you and me. How about if we go on a trip all around Charleston on a boat and stop at Fort Sumter?"

"Lunch too?"

"Yep, and we rent movies and pile in the bed together and eat popcorn and drink Cokes and stay up late. How does that sound?"

"Excellent bribe, Mom! I'll take it!" He threw his arms around me and hugged me. I could smell his head—the sweat of a young boy who'd been running and was over-heated.

"Great! Now, unpack this box. We ain't got all day and I'm already bored."

"No problemo!"

Josh reappeared, carrying a picture frame. Before I saw it I knew what it was. Richard and me on our wedding day. Oh, Lord.

"I never thought he'd look like this," he said.

"And he'd never think you looked like *this!*"

We laughed—all of us together—Eric, Josh, and I; it felt good.

"You know what?" I said, "I'm sick of this dusty barn and all this paper—how about I get a quick shower, Josh, and let's drive down to your place, get that wallpaper sample, grab a bite, and then come back out here for the night? Wanna come, Eric?"

"Nah, y'all go. Bring me a pizza?"

"Guest room?" Josh said.

"I should say so!" I said and shook my finger at him.

Josh and I drove to Charleston on Highway 17 north in a comfortable silence, slowing down at the speed traps and then accelerating again. Every now and then he'd look over at me. In the failing light of afternoon, the Lowcountry once more took on a mantle of romance. The groaning sounds of the engine as he shifted gears, the tiny breezes and drafts of the sweet air of early evening—it was a subtle but unfailing spell. The mood was dreamy—a time for reflection and mind drift.

I thought about Josh and how I was allowing him to take up space in my life—even as friends, it shouldn't continue. On the other hand, I couldn't see anyone suffer-

ing for my philandering around with this unlikely choice
of a friend. I didn't have much at stake in it besides the
reprieve he offered from Mother, Millie, and Eric. Okay,
it was cheap and self-indulgent. I admitted that. But right
then, self-indulgent was what I needed. Boy, could I ra-
tionalize or what?

We arrived at his home and without any particular ceremony, poured a glass of wine, snipped a piece of his
wallpaper, and dropped it in a plastic bag. I was putting it
in my backpack when I heard him from the kitchen.

"Do you want to go out, or stay in for dinner?"

It was a warning dressed like a question. It required a
certain amount of admission of involvement from me. It
was one thing to hang around with Josh and his hair in
private, but if I were seen on the streets of downtown
Charleston with a man in dreadlocks, talk would follow. I
thought about it for a second. Fact was that there were so
many tourists in town and I'd lived away for so long that
unless we went to the Yacht Club, the odds of me seeing
someone I knew were small. If I chose a tourist spot, I
could avoid the questions and stares.

"Let's go out," I said, calling back to him. *There,* I
thought, I'd jumped that hoop with ease. Didn't make him
feel uncomfortable; don't have to wash dishes either. Also,
once out of his house, I could avoid the call of the rack
monster. Perfect.

"How about SNOB's?"

Slightly North of Broad—SNOB—no good. Too many
locals.

"Magnolia's?" I said. "I'm up for crab cakes."

"Fine. Magnolia's it is."

It was seven-thirty and nearly dark. We decided to walk.
In the shadows of crepe myrtle trees, to the sounds of
slow-moving traffic, in the fragrance of jasmine, we

strolled along the ancient narrow streets to dinner. It was
a beautiful spring night, the kind you lived for in Charleston, that you tried to recall in the blistering heat of summer. Those nights justified living there; August made you
pray for relief from the relentless and withering sun and
humidity so thick you could reach out and grab it by handfuls. I remembered being a young girl as we walked along,
remembering going to the Dock Street Theater with
Mother and Daddy.

Soon we arrived. Josh held the door open for me and I
stepped into the low light of Magnolia's. It was jammed
with people, all dressed in their linen finery, ignoring the
wrinkles the fabric invariably gathered like so much Spanish moss on a live oak. The noise level was formidable,
the crowd obviously enjoying the hospitality of that pop-
ular haunt. The bar area was three people deep, small clusters of visitors from elsewhere, in light conversation,
toasting this and that.

Josh spoke to the host, a jovial fellow who assured him
that our table would be ready in ten minutes—would we
like to have a drink at the bar? I maneuvered him through
the crowd until we reached the end of the highly polished
oak ledge. I managed to wedge myself up to its edge and
order two glasses of Sterling chardonnay for us to sip,
while we people-watched.

We were in good spirits, he and I, planning to have a
plate of dinner and then drive back to Tall Pines.

"No appetizers and no dessert, okay? I don't want to
get home so late tonight."

"Understood. I think Eric might like to have his mom
tuck him in."

"Exactly," I said, grateful that he agreed with my feelings. I looked at him for a moment, knowing that in him,
at the very least, I had a friend with some soul. I decided

to go freshen up. By the time I returned, our table should be ready. "You hold the beachhead," I said, "I'll be right back."

He nodded his head and took my glass to hold. I squeezed my way through the guests to the hallway leading to the ladies' room, and I spotted the back of a familiar head. My brother. My brother, Trip, was engrossed in the company of a woman, one who was not Frances Mae. It was Rusty the tutor! His hand was stretched across the table, holding hers, as they talked.

My feet were cement. My jaw dropped and my wide eyes could only stare in disbelief. My first thought was to run. Except for my unfortunate feet, which refused to respond. Josh and I could simply leave, and eat somewhere else. Or, we could stay and hope they didn't see us. Or, I could use this as a valuable bonding experience with my brother, entering into a conspiracy of betrayal and secrets, against the despicable Frances Mae. I didn't really want any of those things. I seriously wished I hadn't seen them at all. That was the ostrich in me.

I finally moved to the powder room, where I asked myself what to do and gave myself a good lecture. It had been Frances Mae's ovaries from the beginning that had driven the wedge between Mother, Trip, and me. Trip had married her out of a sense of duty, believing at the time that it was his responsibility to parent the child he had fathered. Of course, who would have suspected the challenges his offspring would present? But, his marriage was an honorable act and I respected him for it. Still, infidelity was unbearable to me. To sleep with your spouse and then sleep with someone else at the same time, justifying it *how?* Hadn't Richard embraced the position that his needs were more important than our commitment? Was

Trip doing the same thing? No, I wouldn't believe that for a moment.

I washed my hands and looked at myself in the mirror. I needed to replace the look of shock on my face with composure, thanking the heavens that Rusty hadn't seen this as the perfect moment to wash her hands as well. I dug around in my purse for my makeup bag, thinking then about my alleged quest for truth, self-discovery, and all the things my marriage with Richard had denied me—or I had denied myself (I couldn't decide that just then)— and remembered that my original mission had been to *see about Mother*. Why couldn't I see about Trip at the same time? Wasn't there a whole family here to be rescued?

All at once, while applying Chanel's Cocoa lipstick, I started to laugh. I couldn't hold my mouth straight to cover my lips. Mother had the language tutor's number, I had the fine-motor "coach" running like a Bentley, and Trip was caught on something Rusty! Oh my, what clever irony!

"You won't believe who's here," I said, rejoining Josh, and telling him.

I was nonplussed; Josh was neutral. I couldn't fully believe that Trip had the nerve or courage to do such a thing. I knew this much, though: I didn't blame him.

"From what you've told me, there's only one thing to do," he said.

"What?"

"Be gracious. Let's get the wine list."

In a matter of minutes, we had a bottle of Mumm's champagne delivered to his table with a note that read: IT'S OKAY. MUMM'S THE WORD. CAROLINE.

Miss Lavinia's Journal

I cannot for the love of God believe that I allowed that man with all that hair to stay in my guest room last night! I never thought I'd say this, but I believe she may have been better off with Richard. Yes, she would. Oh, I know they had their problems, but Merciful Mother, he was a shrink, wasn't he? How in the world could I introduce this madman to my friends? They would think I'm joshing them! I can just see the faces at Cotillion! Although, in his defense, he is very nice. He holds my door open for me and after all, good manners can forgive other imperfections. And, he was very interesting to talk to—all that karma stuff—well, I imagine that's what he is for Caroline, a pleasant diversion. Unlike my Peter—did I say my Peter? Oh, Lavinia! You bad girl! I must remember to tell that to Sweetie and Nancy!

35

FAMILY JEWELS

Every family had its secrets, tales of our human weaknesses and how we rationalized them. Now that Trip had been caught with his hand in the cookie jar, it would be harder for him to find fault with us. Harder now for any of us to judge each other. Clearly, it was time for making lemonade from our citric indiscretions.

So, big deal, Josh slept at Tall Pines, but in another bedroom, thank you very large.

Saturday morning, I got up at six and ground Mother's latest on-line purchase—Costa Rican beans with a hint of some damn thing—for coffee.

The coffee dripped, filling the air with delicious promise. I had to admit it. Even though each day meant the onslaught of packages that nearly crippled the deliverymen, Mother had discovered so many things to buy on the Internet that made life easier.

I began sifting flour into Mother's ancient ceramic mixing bowl. This moment of self-examination needed to be

marked with some ritual to help me get my brain in gear.
I was going to make biscuits—something I hadn't done in
years. No, in New York, I'd be toasting a frozen bagel or
eating a low-fat piece of whole wheat bread. Now I was
sliding to hell on a slick road of fat grams. And loving the
trip.

I cut in the cold butter and Crisco with two forks, the
way Millie had taught me as a girl. In my yet dreamy,
early morning state of half awareness, Eric crossed my
mind. My angel, upstairs sleeping. I wondered if Eric
would ramble downstairs and what he would think about
having breakfast with Josh. He probably wouldn't like it
worth a damn.

New worries blew into town, like small-craft warnings
and dark skies—the foreboding kind. How stupid I had
been! There was a *reason* that divorced—separated—estranged—whatever the hell I was these days—people
waited until there was longevity to a new romance before
introducing the new "friend" to the children. It was just
plain uncomfortable.

And, I had to ask myself, was the puny relationship I
had with Josh worth making Eric uncomfortable? Hell,
Mother was getting it on with old man Greer, Trip was
pussyfooting around with Rusty, and I was hanging with
Rastaman! Some stable environment we were! But *was* it
worth it, this stupid game I had going on with Josh? He
was my son's tutor, for Christ's sake! No, of course not,
I told myself, and prayed Eric would sleep late. Yeah, I
had that whole pursuit of happiness thing all figured out.

I preheated the oven, poured myself a mug of coffee,
and continued making biscuits. I flipped the doughy mess
over on the floured marble slab and kneaded it. Too dry,
I decided, and sprinkled it with cream. To hell with calo-
ries. I wrapped the whole thing in Saran Wrap, threw it in

the refrigerator to chill, and took out eggs to scramble, cracking them into another bowl. I caught a sweet whiff of the ripe cantaloupes in the fruit bowl, so I peeled and sliced one, placing the wedges on Mother's Herend Rothchild platter, the one with the hand-painted birds and bugs.

When the oven was ready, I took the chilled dough from the refrigerator and flattened it, cutting biscuits with the floured mouth of a juice glass. I wondered then how many thousands of biscuits had been made by the generations of women of my family for their husbands and children. How many women got up to a cold house, heated the stoves, and began breakfast alone. Did their hands ache in the dampness of winter mornings?

I tried to imagine myself wearing a nightdress and robe, during the Civil War, maybe even a sleeping cap instead of jeans from Banana Republic and a T-shirt from the Gap. It made me melancholy for a past from which I felt such a long distance.

I would have to ask Mother if she could put her hand on my great-great-grandmother's diaries. Maybe I was finally old enough or wise enough to have patience for them.

In New York, I had opted for meals of convenience for too long, at least when Richard was present. His dinners consisted of grilled something, salad bar, and a starch of some kind. Fast everything. And while I truly had learned to enjoy cooking, our lifestyles had shortened time spent in the kitchen and time spent together at a table, so much so, that food had become little more than fuel. All the romance of cooking had been lost along the way.

At home here in the Lowcountry, I had a new vision of the possibilities of food and cooking. Eric would catch fish and clean it. He would bring it to me to cook. I would marinade it, or brush it with different types of oil and herbs. Its flavor would come to life like it was supposed to, unlike the bland fish I bought at Food Emporium in New York—fish that had been on ice for maybe two weeks! No, food would bring us closer together—the act of a shared meal would resurrect itself as an intimate family experience. It made me laugh a little to think of all the unnecessary pomp that accompanied Mother's table. I would not teach Eric that I reigned as queen, but that together we had made the meal and that's how it would be remembered—that we owned those moments together.

Finally, the kitchen door swung open and there was Josh.

"Morning!" I said, calling out in a low voice, so that no one would hear me but him. "You ready for a little breakfast?"

He wore only a white T-shirt and khakis. Bare feet, bare arms. Jesus, he was flammable. He walked toward me. Those peaceful and happy brown eyes of his were a mirror of his disposition.

"Morning!" he said, and kissed me on the cheeks. "Rest well?"

"Yeah. You know that I just realized that inside of twenty-four hours, the entire faculty I engaged to educate my son is in one way or another entangled with a member of my immediate family. I got up and did the only thing a southern girl can do in this situation."

"What's that?" He was laughing at me with his mind. I could almost hear him.

"I put 'Ironic' on the CD player, lip gloss on my lips, and I made biscuits! You have any other advice?" I pulled the baking sheet from the oven and rested it on the countertop. "I'm starving. Impending crises make me hungry."

"You shouldn't worry so much. Let's eat; it smells like heaven in here."

Indeed, the sweet air of melted butter and cooking bread

saturated the room until my mouth watered. The compulsion to scrape the bottom of a hot biscuit from the baking pan with my fingers and pop it in my mouth was more powerful than the thought of blistering my fingers and mouth. Josh scooped up two biscuits with the spatula, spread them with butter and a dollop of Miss Sweetie's TBDJOTP Strawberry, and plopped them in our mouths. We rolled our eyes and licked our fingers, steam escaping with groans of delight. Face it; there's nothing like a hot biscuit.

At around eight, we put the dishes in the dishwasher and I said good-bye to him on the front steps. I was relieved to see him leave and to know that nothing had changed between us. We had an easy rapport. For right then, I imagined, a part-time friend was all I needed or could handle.

I had half expected Trip to show up to put the boat in the river, but he was nowhere to be seen. I guessed he was trying to figure out what to say to me when we would meet and still hadn't decided. I knew I was right because only something as potentially damning as being caught as he had been could keep him from the Edisto.

It certainly would be interesting to see how our team of tutors interacted on Monday when they would begin their work with Eric. I would see what I would see. I was thinking of all these things when the phone rang. I leaped to answer it, not wanting it to wake Mother or Eric. It was Trip.

"You up?" he said.

"Been up since six. What's going on?" I wrapped the spiral phone cord around my finger, suppressing a snicker the size of Oregon.

"You alone?"

"Yes! Eric and Mother are still sacked out. Hot Lips went home."

Silence from his end.

"Trip, for God's sake! Quit acting like the Fugitive! You want my opinion? Of last night, I mean." Was I really going to tell him what I thought?

"Do I have to buy your silence, Caroline?"

"I'd cut out my own tongue before I'd tell on you."

"No, I mean, if Frances Mae knew that I had dinner with Rusty, she'd do to me what I do for my clients."

"Trip? Why don't you come over and let's go out in the boat. We need to talk."

Thirty minutes later, Trip lumbered into the kitchen, sheepish and nervous. I poured him a coffee in a Starbucks traveler and reheated a few biscuits.

"Well?" he said.

I put his breakfast in a paper towel and looked at him.

"I'd like to initiate this meeting with a general statement," I said, pulling on my denim jacket.

"What's that?"

"That everyone in this family is severely screwed up. Let's go scare the alligators."

I grabbed a bottle of water from the refrigerator and went out the back door, hoping he would realize that I was more his sister than he had probably thought.

The engine turned over easily and the smell of diesel gasoline came over us in a breeze. What should have smelled like toxin registered like perfume. Trip stuffed his mouth with the biscuits and chugged his coffee while tossing the loops of rope from the cleats. I pushed off dockside with the heel of my sneakers and put the engine into reverse.

"I'm driving! Let's ride over to the Ashepoo," I said, "I wanna see what's going on."

"Plenty's going on."

They were ominous words. I waited for him to tell me and he waited for me to ask. I slowed the boat down and turned to face him.

"Okay, Trip, spill it."

"I have a question."

"Sure," I said, "fire away."

"Do you intend to stay here on the plantation or do you think you and Eric will move down to Charleston?"

"Why? I mean, I don't know yet. I just left my husband and my head's still kind of spinning from that. I was hoping to just take the summer to think it all through, you know?"

"Eric's a great kid."

I ran my hand through the water and shook it off, wiping it on my jeans. "Thanks," I said, wondering where this was leading.

"I've been approached by some developers," he said, "real estate guys. They want to buy a thousand acres and turn it into a housing community—you know, like those gated plantations on Hilton Head?"

"Mother would never agree to that. This land is hers."

"Yeah, but we're gonna inherit it and this would be a great windfall for us."

I looked at him and narrowed my eyes, trying to read his mind. I had sensed some urgency about him earlier on the phone but this was something larger. I didn't want to pry, but maybe, I thought, I could wiggle it out of him.

"Trip. What's going on? This land is Mother's to do with whatever she wants. She might leave it to us; she might give it to the Nature Conservancy. She's pretty involved with that, you know. I wouldn't count on anything except the fact that she has taken her responsibility to hold this land together in one piece very seriously for the better part of her entire life. Did you tell her about this?"

"No, I wanted to talk to you first. It could be worth as much as four million dollars, Caroline, depending on how much riverfront we gave them. That's a lot of money. Two for you, two for me. Think about it."

I let go a long low whistle. It *was* a fortune. Ten years ago I wouldn't have thought the plantation was worth anything much. But, real estate had escalated for a variety of reasons—more people working from home, baby boomers taking early retirement—all sorts of things. He was right about that but missed the greater point. It wasn't our call to make—it was Mother's.

"Move over," he said, "I want to drive."

I gave him the wheel. "Still, Trip, this is so out of character for you. Since when have you been so desperate for money that you'd try to talk Mother into a scheme like this?"

He speeded up the boat and now we were heading full throttle down the Edisto.

"I can't talk about it."

"Slow down, Hoss, you're gonna get us killed!"

He cut the gas and we slowed down abruptly, rocking in our own wake. "I might get killed anyway," he said. When he looked at me, I saw a look of terror on his face I had never seen before.

"Trip! If you're in trouble, you have to tell me!"

"It might be better if I let them just put a bullet in my head. I've thought about killing myself a lot lately." He reached over to his cooler and took out a Heineken, draining about half of it before he took a breath.

I thought about his liver and that he was killing himself slowly. It was finally dawning on me that he was deadly serious. What had my brother done?

"How deep is the hole, Trip, just tell me that, okay?"

He looked out at the river, probably debating whether or not to tell me. The birds swooped and squawked and Trip listened and watched as though it would be his last chance—a condemned man, trying to memorize the thing he cherished most. In my fear I began to cry. What in the world had he done?

"The hole's deep. I racked up almost five hundred thousand dollars of bad gambling debt and I'm afraid of getting killed. And, while I was pondering my probable shortened life span, I finally admitted to myself that I hate my wife's guts."

"Jesus Christ! What are you telling me?" Gambling? We'd get to Frances Mae in a moment, but gambling? My brother, the hot-shit lawyer, a gambler?

"You know the poker machines at the gas stations?"

"No. I mean, it's not something I would notice."

"Yeah, well, I never noticed that I had this addictive personality either. First, it was football. Hell, everybody bets on football."

Not in *my* world, but that wasn't the time to point that out.

"You couldn't stop, right?"

"Right. Some weekends I'd win thirty thousand dollars! I mean, it's a great feeling! You know?"

"I think that's what junkies say, Trip."

"Thanks, Caroline. Thanks a lot!"

"Hey, stupid! Somehow I'm gonna help you figure this out, okay? But don't expect my approval. Now, about Frances Mae . . ."

"Yeah, Frances Mae. Okay—consider my options. A gal like Rusty Perretti—gorgeous, sexy, smart as a whip, cultured . . ."

I reached out and put my hand on his arm and said, "Trip? God forgive me for this, as much as I hate infidelity and believe it's sleazy, I don't think there's anyone on earth who would blame you. Whatever you decide to do, I'll support you. But don't run around on Frances Mae indefinitely. It's gross and Rusty's too nice a gal to drag her into some triangle deal, you know?"

"You're right, but it seems that I'm already addicted to Rusty."

"Give it a rest, bubba. Frances Mae catches you? She'll clean your clock."

36

HOLY MOLY

Trip and I rode the river for almost an hour before return-ing home to drop me off at the dock. He all but chewed the ears off the side of my head with the details of his situation before bringing me back.

I had decided to work in the garden before it got too hot. I could think things through when I worked in a gar-den. While I walked to Mr. Jenkins's toolshed, I couldn't take my mind from Trip's *situation*. He was in damn se-rious trouble. He told me that he had used the interest from his portfolio at first, then the principal to cover his debts. Wisely, he had not fully apprised Frances Mae of this. I didn't blame him for that. He was broke and half a million in the hole. He didn't need her hysterics on top of his debt. He needed a solution. One thing we were in agreement on was that a solution wouldn't come from Frances Mae. And I thought I had problems?

From the neatly lined shelves of garden supplies, I grabbed a pair of gloves, a paper bag for cuttings, a water bucket for cut blooms, and a pair of clippers and walked across the damp grass to Mother's rose garden. The bushes were filled with buds. I started pinching them off with a fury and tried to think Trip's problem through. He didn't have a lot of choices.

Apparently the fellows who ran the receivables department for the organization that collected debt and paid winnings were a humorless but diversified lot. Their other businesses were drugs and murder. They had been prudent to cut him off from sporting events. If he couldn't come up with fifty thousand dollars in one week, they said they were going to hurt him. Not good. I had to help him.

Even if I had five hundred thousand dollars to give him, which I didn't, would it really solve his problem? No, it would not, I decided. This was larger than my resources and frightening. Damn frightening. *I'll think of something,* I'd said to him when I jumped off the boat. This was not going away—it had to be solved. Fast.

I must have removed a hundred buds and cut fifty flowers to take into the house before I was aware that someone was standing behind me, watching. I turned to see Millie, standing under a live oak. What was she doing?

"Millie!" I called out to her. "Good morning!"

She started toward me and when she reached my side, she said, "You tell me. Is it a good morning?" She stared at me with eyes that held a thousand years of worry. "You want to tell me?"

Although I doubted she would have anything in her repertoire to solve this and even though I had sworn silence to Trip, I took a deep breath and told her everything I knew. She would have seen it in her tea leaves anyway. And, she was outraged.

"What kind of crazy damn fool is my boy messing with? Gambling? I got a mind to beat his behind! Switch him till he can't sit!" Millie paced back and forth, muttering to herself. "Lord, don't he know he got children to raise? And that Frances Mae, all right, she ain't no kinda nothing but a canker sore to live with, but he took an oath before God and that ain't for him to rearrange when the mood strike! This ain't no good. No good a-tall. Can't let the Ajogun have my boy. No way. No how."

The Ajogun were the evil spirits who sought to destroy humans.

"Millie? I'm scared for him." My chin started to tremble and she looked at me, shaking her head.

"Come on with me," she said. "Yanh, let's clean up this mess. Hang on to your tears, girl. Save 'em for later."

Millie and I began to gather the cuttings from the ground and tossed them in the paper bag. When we were done, I followed her back to her cottage. I dropped my things on her front porch, peeling off my gloves and knocking the dirt from them on her banister, watching it drift to her flower beds below.

"Get in yanh, Caroline!"

When Millie said *get* I *got*.

Before my eyes even adjusted to the low light of the room, I saw that her altar door was open. Millie wasn't there but came in minutes, dressed in a white caftan with a red sash around her waist, carrying bowls of herbs. She was going to pray. When Millie prayed, she got answers.

She began her ritual, lighting candles, shaking gourds, performing a genuflect on the right hip and left elbow and then one on the other side. Between incantations, her jaw was locked in a vise. Her pupils, visible under her half-closed eyes, fluttered, rose, and fell as she swayed in prayer. She was on her knees, arms outspread and going into trance. I hadn't seen her in trance since I was a little girl and my father died. Maybe she did it all the time. I didn't know. I just hung back and watched. Her urgency and the depth of her concentration held my rapt attention. A few minutes more passed and she mumbled something incoherent. Finally, she sat back on her heels and dropped her arms. The trance was over.

It took noticeable effort for her to get up; she extinguished the candles and when she closed the door, she spoke to me. "Gone root your brother for protection and gone send the hag to them men." She was as solemn as I had ever seen her. "Go on back to the house. When he gets off the river, send him to me. This ain't the time for no fish and fool. Better he make time for his breath."

"You're worried, aren't you?" I said.

"You ain't? Now, go on and leave me to work. I could use some help but you don't know enough yet to fill a thimble."

I felt a heaviness in my throat, one that blocked my words of apology for being so useless to her. Useless to my brother too. What could I do?

I worried about Trip as I walked home. What *could* I do? I could start by taking the roses to Mother and by making breakfast for Eric. Daily needs still had to be met. Jesus Christ in all His heaven! If they snuffed out Trip, the family would have to help Frances Mae raise those kids! That meant me! "Get hold of yourself, Caroline," I said out loud. And think of an answer.

I wanted to tell Mother. So much for my oath of silence to Trip. Maybe Mother would read my thoughts about Trip and then I wouldn't have to tell her anything. Maybe she'd become Sylvia Brown overnight. I doubted it.

When I opened the back door, there was Eric eating toast, drinking juice, and watching cartoons on the television. It was ten o'clock.

"Hey, sweetheart!" I said, and went over to kiss the top

of his head. "Did you get enough breakfast?"

"Huh? Oh, yeah! When I saw Uncle Trip's SUV, I just helped myself. I figured you were out on the boat with him."

"Thanks, honey," I said, and put the pail of roses in the sink. "Is your grandmother up?"

"Not so far," he said, and laughed, fully engrossed by the antics of the cartoon characters. "Mom, watch this!"

I put the roses in a vase and said, "Can't, honey. Don't sit so close—you'll ruin your eyes." He ignored me. "I'm gonna take these up to Mother. I'll be right back."

Just as in New York, he could not have cared less. All the way up the steps I thought of how natural our transition had been from New York to South Carolina.

Now this horrible and dangerous business with Trip had been discovered. Well, there had been that regrettable showdown with Frances Mae, but that paled in the light of Trip's problem. We would figure it out. Millie and I together. Somehow. Maybe Mother too.

I opened Mother's door and she was up and in her dressing room. I put the roses on her chest of drawers.

"Who's that?" she called from the other room.

"The Morals Committee, coming to discuss your most recent conquest!" I called back.

She came through the dressing room into her bedroom, smiling like a twenty-year-old sorority sister who'd just been pinned.

"*Good morning, Mother!* she meant to say! Oh, roses! Thank you, dear! Is everyone up?"

She picked up the vase and turned to go back to her dressing room. There was a black mark on her back, above the line of her slip, between her shoulder blades.

"Mother! What's that? On your back?"

She didn't stop but called to me over her shoulder.

"Nothing! Nothing at all but a pesky little mole!"

I knew it was more than a pesky little mole from across the room. I followed her to her bathroom, where she stood applying makeup under the Hollywood lights that surrounded the large mirror.

"Mother? Have you had anyone look at that?"

It was mean-looking and festering, as though she had broken the skin several times.

"Oh, Caroline, don't bother about that. When you're my age, you have things growing on your body you wouldn't believe, and certainly not discuss! Have you had breakfast? Tell me what you think of Dr. Greer!"

"Yes, I've had breakfast, I think you should not fool around with Eric's tutors, and I am definitely concerned about this growth on your back! Stand still, Mother, let me have a look at this."

The growth was about the size of an irregular quarter, reddish black with small spike-shaped feelers protruding from its edges like a weed that travels as ground cover. I was no doctor, but it looked like all the warnings I had seen for melanoma.

"Will you quit fussing so? I had the darn thing cut off last year and don't you know it grew back? Pain in the neck if you ask me, yanh?"

"Just the same, if this were my back, I'd have it looked at."

First Trip, and now this. I was unsure of what to say. Just like Tall Pines wasn't mine to sell, Mother's back wasn't mine either. She pulled her robe—pale aqua, satin finish, appliqued with rose-colored flowers—around her, blustering her discontent with me for being so nosy.

"I don't know what's come over young people today! They think they can say something about anything that pops into their mind! In my day, my mother would have pitched a fit."

Still, I was very concerned about it and decided to take some initiative.

"Mother? You are pitching a fit. However, that thing is coming off as soon as I can make an appointment for you with a good skin specialist. Who's the jerk who removed it the first time?"

"A very handsome doctor—tall and dark with the most beautiful eyes!" She squirted hand cream into her palm and began to spread it on her arms. "Want a shot of this? Magnolia! Smells divine!"

"No, that's okay." Mother arched her eyebrow at me. "Thanks anyway," I said, to preserve the peace. I decided to change the topic to Trip and fish around to see what she knew. "Have you noticed anything unusual about Trip lately?"

She went to her shoe closet and pulled out the shelf of flats. God, she was so organized. That shoe closet was brilliant! "Mother? Who designed this closet?" It was off the topic, but I didn't know why I had never thought of using something like this in the scores of closets I had designed.

"Why, I did! Don't you remember? Your father always said I should have been a decorator." She looked at me and smiled. "Like you, Caroline! Who do you think you got all that good taste from anyway, girl?"

It was the emotional equivalent of a small water balloon being dropped on your head from a window above. I had inherited Mother's appreciation of space and her eye for design. I'll be damned.

"From you, right?" I had to smile with her.

Suddenly, for the first time in my life, I was overwhelmed with desire to hug her. And, I did. We stood there for a minute, just hugging each other—the same size, the same blood, the same likes and dislikes, the same crazy taste in men and I had never realized it. Tears of regret spilled over and streamed down my face. I had a lot of making up to do with my mother and I was going to do it. When we finally pulled apart from each other, I saw that she had cried with me. For women who rarely wept, the tears were flowing too easily these days.

"Here, blow your nose," she said, in her characteristic way of half chiding us for being emotional. "You asked about Trip? I'm extremely worried about your brother, Caroline. My heart is so heavy with worry and I don't know what to do!" She sank to the end of her chaise and dropped her hands in her lap, looking to me for answers. "Is there something going on I don't know about?"

"I'm sworn to secrecy," I said, halfheartedly.

"Bull poop! You tell me! I am still the mother of this family! I have a right to know if there's trouble!"

Bull poop was as close to a curse that had ever crossed her lips, at least in front of me.

"Okay, he's got money trouble."

"Well, that explains *something* at least!"

I decided I could learn more by saying nothing—a technique I learned from good old Richard. I sat on the end of her bed and waited.

"That boy has been bleeding me dry. He must owe me a hundred thousand dollars! Is it Frances Mae's family? Is it drugs? What's going on, Caroline?"

"He's a gambler, and not a lucky one." There. It was out.

"How unlucky is he?"

Mother seemed amazingly calm, so I decided to divulge the facts.

When I told her the entire story, she clasped her hand to her heart and yelled, "Great God!"

"Mother, please don't get upset! It won't help solve this one bit!"

"He was going to throw *me* out in the street and sell *my* family's land to cover his *gambling debt?* What kind of a *hooligan* have I raised? Your father would have him horse-whipped!"

"Mother! Calm down! Gambling is an addiction! It's an illness! He needs help!"

Mother began to pace the room, thinking out loud. "We've got to put a stop to this."

"His creditors have already done that and fortunately our good governor happens to be having all the poker machines removed from the state on July first. Obviously, Trip needs to join some group for gamblers and get some one-on-one help too."

"Call Richard, Caroline. He'll know what to do. Call him right this minute! Use my phone—it's right there!" She raised her chin in the direction of her end table, as Mother never points.

I flopped back on the bed and stared at the ceiling. I'd rather have had to call Beelzebub himself. I got up and looked at her. "Let me give this some thought for a bit. Go see Millie. She's working her roots."

As I closed her bedroom door, I heard her call out, "Don't tell me what to do! I'm still your mother!"

It called to mind that sign that reads: THE BEATINGS WILL CONTINUE UNTIL MORALE IMPROVES. She meant well and I knew it.

I had betrayed Trip's confidence, but I realized that keeping it would mean possible death, as in *finito,* at the hands of thugs! Between Richard, Trip, and Mother's ne-glect of that mole, my daddy must be flipping out in his grave.

37

TRUE COLORS

I called Miss Sweetie as soon as I left Mother's room. I asked her to find out the name of the best dermatologist and plastic surgeon in Charleston. It took two minutes for her to call me back.

"You want Jack Taylor. He's the head of dermatology at the Medical University. If she needs a plastic surgeon, tell her to go to David Oliver in Savannah. He's the only one I'd trust my skin to! Not that I've had anything done, of course."

Just her eyes, chin, breasts, armpits, ears, forehead, and whatever else she could think of. She and Miss Nancy nipped and tucked on an annual basis. They were the Co-chairs of the Quilt Club.

"Of course. David Oliver?" I was writing as fast as I could.

"Yes, Oliver. Actually, he's an ENT, but a genius. No bargain, but an exquisite talent. Caroline? I've told Lavinia time and time again to wear a long-sleeved shirt when she gardens, but you can't tell her a thing! Has to wear those tank tops to get herself all tanned and for what? This?"

"I know, Miss Sweetie, I know. I'll call you just as soon as we've seen a doctor. Say a little prayer for Mother, will you? And would you call Miss Nancy?"

She said of course, she would pray like crazy, and we hung up. It would be Monday before we could see Dr. Taylor. I felt a growing urgency inside my heart.

I walked right out the front door, headed for Millie's cottage. Something made me stop at the bottom of the steps and look down the avenue of live oaks, toward the road. I saw my past in a flood of comings and goings under their umbrella of shade—driving fast, whirling a trail of dust, in the soaking rain with mud splattering our car, going to school, coming home from a date, leaving to return to New York, the day the men came for Daddy's body. Like a movie in my head, I could see my great-grandmother, twelve years old—Olivia—planting the thirty-odd live oaks with her mother, Elizabeth Bootle Kent, right after the Civil War. That every generation of my family in America had enjoyed their shelter. It was a moment of pause and reflection, striking me in a place I could not name because it brought confusion to what I wanted to believe rather than what I knew to be true. I fought to hold back the thoughts, but the thoughts came at me full force—the recognition that these were not merely Mother's trees or the road of my ancestors, but that it was my path to home. My home. Where I had every right to be.

At that moment, I knew that Mother was in more danger than any of us would have thought. She had no appetite. She was tired all the time. She complained mildly about pain in her ribs. Something was dreadfully wrong.

I ran to Millie's, passing the dock where Trip's boat

was tied up. He must've gone to her too. She probably met him on his return and started giving him hell. I wondered if Mother was there too. I would know in moments, as soon as I got there. I slipped on the wet grass and nearly fell, catching myself, regaining my balance. My heart pounded against my chest and when I finally pushed open Millie's door, I found them all in the living room. The altar door was open and the smell of burning incense was thick and strong. Millie was seated on one side of a folding card table; Trip and Mother were on the other.

"Sit on the sofa; don't say a word," Millie said.

I sat, watched, and listened. I had interrupted something. Millie held Trip's hand and massaged it, as though she were reading his bones. She was.

"Sign this paper," Millie said to Trip. "Read it out loud and sign it."

" 'I, James Nevil Wimbley III, promise before God and all that is holy, to cooperate with authorities to put an end to the gambling ring in Columbia, renounce all ties with the men I know to be involved in it, give their names to the proper authorities, and to never gamble again. If I do not comply with this oath, I stand ready to receive the consequences.' "

Now, I had heard a lot of things in my day, but I had never heard Millie make someone take an oath. Maybe it was for extra protection, and Trip sure needed it. Trip was floating in some treacherous waters. Millie cleared her throat, handed Trip the pen, and he signed. She continued.

"How many men know your name?"

"Two," Trip said. "There are about fifty guys in the racket, but just two control the names. Except for the runner—Jimmy Brown. He's the guy who collects the money."

"Write the names down here," she said, and handed him

another slip of paper. "How many men have your phone number?"

"The same two," Trip said. He was so miserable that his voice cracked. "And Jimmy."

I felt very sorry for him. Trip had never done a dishonest thing in his entire life and now this! It was stunning to all of us, but not one of us asked why or how. The focus was on an immediate solution.

"They both live up to Columbia?" Millie said.

"As far as I know," Trip said.

Millie made some more notes and then said, "Give me some coins."

Trip reached in his pocket, produced a handful of change. Millie took a penny, a nickel, and a dime. She got up and stood before her altar. She lit another candle, a red one, the candle of Oya. Oya is the queen of the spirit world, a warrior goddess and fierce protectorate of her children. She is also the patron of justice and the goddess of storms and hurricanes. The altar today held a bowl of red grapes, a large eggplant, and a bunch of dried comfrey, tied with a red ribbon. She held her arms wide and began to pray.

As powerful as the strong wind,
More fierce than the storm,
Oya, guard this man against the many fingers of evil!
Extend your weapon to protect him from destruc-
    tion . . .

Trip began to weep, his head in his hands, elbows on his knees. Mother put her arm around him and told him to shush, that everything would be all right. I remained quiet, sitting on Millie's sofa, listening and watching—thinking to myself that no, everything was not going to be all right. I knew it in my bones.

Millie finished her prayer, blew out the candles, and turned to Trip. She wrapped the coins in the paper and handed it to him. "Put this in your pocket, the one where you carry your wallet. Leave it there for three days, then give it to the Edisto. If the paper comes off the coins before three days pass, throw it in as fast as you can."

"Then what? What do I do until then?"

"You do as you promised, if you know what's good for you," Millie said. "I'm sorry for you if you don't, yanh me, boy?"

"Thank you, Millie," he said. Trip put the paper-wrapped coins in his back pocket and left the house.

Millie and Mother went to the window and watched him walk away.

"Stupid," Millie said, and added a good *"Humph!"*

"That's my only boy, Millie," Mother said.

"Yeah, but he's stupid," she said.

"Yeah, he's thick as a post. Is this gonna save him?"

"It ain't up to me," Millie said, "all depends on him."

In front of the window, Millie looped her arm around Mother's shoulder; Mother looped hers around Millie's waist. They were better than friends, closer than sisters. Their affection for each other was nearly a palpable, tangible thing—a strong force that filled the spaces between us so fully with its warmth that you could nearly grab a handful of it. I wanted what they had for myself. I have no one in my life like that, I thought, and then realized that this *was* my life and their love was there for my taking. All I would have to do would be to indicate my need.

"Millie?" I said. "You got any tea in your refrigerator?"

They stopped and looked at me. My desire to belong to

them and with them was all over my face. I stood rubbing my arms, waiting for a response.

"You pay attention to what just happened?" Millie said.

"I could repeat every word," I said, knowing that she was asking me if I was staying, if I was still interested in her legacy.

"Why don't you pour some tea for all of us?"

"I've made a decision," Mother said. "Millie, you've inspired me."

I took three glasses from Millie's cabinet and filled them with ice from the ice maker. The pitcher of iced tea in her refrigerator was jammed with mint leaves. I poured and heard Millie reply from the next room.

"What?"

"Well, short of a magic wand to make those men in Columbia forget they ever heard my son's name, he has a huge debt to pay, yanh?"

"I send them the hag, I did that, but that ain't gone solve nothing really. Just makes me feel better."

I handed Millie her glass and then Mother hers. "You're a bad girl, Millie."

"Humph! If I'm bad, what does that make them? Evil preying on the weakness of others. That's the devil himself in action, girl. Don't you forget it, yanh?"

"Caroline? Did you call Richard as I asked you?"

I shook my head.

"I figured as much," she said. "Well, I had another thought. What about that boy, that Strickland fellow who became the policeman?"

"What about him?" I asked.

"Why don't you see what he knows? I'll bet you anything he knows about these men in Columbia! What do you think?"

It was worth a shot. I drank my tea to the bottom of the

glass and said, "Millie? I'm going to go up to the house and call Matthew Strickland. Would you please look at the festering mole on Mother's back and see what you have to dry it up? I'll be back."

"I'm going to pay his debt," Mother said, announcing her plan.

"Good Lord!" I said, surprised.

"But, I'm going to make him take an oath, just like you did, Millie. It's going to come out of his inheritance, but he's going to have to join Gambler's Anonymous or something like it. I'm going to set up a sliding scale for penalties, should he fail and gamble again. And, finally, I'm going to insist that he seek professional counseling."

"God, Mother, that's incredibly generous!" I was shocked that Mother had that kind of cash at her disposal. "But, it's probably the only solution."

"It won't do for my only son to float to the bottom of Lake Murray in chains," Mother said. She sighed with a kind of sadness I'd never seen her reveal to anyone before. It was a terrible sigh of deep disappointment and stoic resignation. "Perhaps we should insist that until he's truly recovered an accountant handle all his money. Put him on an allowance?"

"Or, Frances Mae could probably do it. Hell, at least she's free."

"Free and with a brain that's got all the judgment of a little bitty cornflake," Millie said.

"Okay. Whatever you decide, I'm sure Trip will kiss your feet for it," I said. "I'll see you in a little bit."

Millie and Mother said in unison, "Humph! He should!"

The sky looked a shade of blue more bold and vibrant than it had when I arrived. I wondered if state of mind affected perception of color. It certainly affected everything else. What would I say to Matthew Strickland? *So,*

Matthew, what would you do if you had this "friend" who had unsavory "friends," to whom he owed half a million sporting dollars, who told my "friend" that they were gonna rip out his throat if he didn't cough up ten percent of it in one week? Not subtle enough. How about, *Matthew? You've seen trouble before*—To which he would offer a manly reply, *That's my life—trouble, that is*—and I'd say, *Oh, Matthew! Lord, I have a friend in trouble with some terrible men in Columbia and I swear, we—that is, Mother and I—we don't have the first clue on how to solve his money trouble. Our friend is so dear but has this weakness!* Oh, God, I thought, that's demure enough to make Scarlett and Melanie gag. No, I knew what I would do.

I found his number and called him, leaving a message with my cell phone number on his voice mail. I decided to work in the garden some more and if he wanted to reach me, he could. He did. I was elbow deep in mud, dividing hostas, when the phone rang. I ripped off my gloves and flipped it open to answer.

"You're under arrest," he said.

"Charged with?" I said, and giggled.

"Failing to call me as promised," he said, deadpan.

"Oh, fine," I said, "arrest me. Where are you?"

"In your driveway. Want some company?"

"Sure. I'm in the rose garden. Come on out."

I wiped the hair back from my face and by the time I stood up and straightened my T-shirt, he was coming toward me, across the lawn.

"Hey!" he called out, waving.

"Hey, yourself! Want something cold to drink?"

He nodded and waited until I reached him. I gave him a cheek peck and said, "Thanks for calling me back. Gosh, it's nice to see you again!" I was as nonchalant as though we were old and dear friends. "Come on, I'll make you a tomato sandwich!"

"Why are women always trying to feed me? Do I look haggard or something? Undernourished?"

"Hardly, honey."

He was a pretty thing and I gave myself two seconds of hell for what the sight of him made me think. Two seconds. Don't ever want to overdo hell.

In the kitchen, Matthew sat and I served him—two thick tomato sandwiches with mayonnaise and lots of salt and pepper and another mouthful of story. I just begged his confidence and let it roll. He listened carefully.

"Well, I'll say this. You've got timing down to a science."

"What's that supposed to mean?"

He leaned back and wiped his mouth with the red and yellow foulard Pierre Deux napkin I had placed next to his plate. His eyes never left mine.

"Okay, since we're talking confidences here, I'm gonna give you some inside skinny. Between us only, okay?"

"Of course!" I sat at the table next to him and refilled his tea glass.

"In Jacksonboro, we look like a speed trap."

"Hell, Matthew, half of South Carolina knows that."

"Yeah, but there's more to it in our neck of the woods. We're talking drugs, abandoned airports, airstrips on plantations, deliveries by water—all of that funded by illegal gambling."

"God, this is something so far removed from my life I can't even begin to tell you."

"We've been working with the FBI for a long time trying to indict the Columbia boys along with the Atlanta boys, who they suspect are tied into the Miami boys, who obviously have ties to South America. It's the same old game these lowlifes have been playing since the sixties. Just different methods of delivery, different names—but it always leads back to drugs and illegal something. Your brother doesn't understand that these fellows have less regard for human rights than the Chinese government. They'll pop a fucking bullet to his brain just for the fun of it, pardon my French."

"Jesus," I said.

He had delivered his comments with a kind of boredom I found curious. Maybe he had used this blasé tone so I wouldn't think of him as an ordinary patrolman, but see him as someone who faced mortal danger, rendering him more attractive. As if that were an issue.

"So, how can I help?" he said. "We are on the brink of indicting the Columbia guys and the Atlanta boys any day."

"Well, the good news is that Mother is going to pay his debt, but only on the conditions that he turns over all he knows to the authorities, joins a gambler's help group, never gambles again, and gets one-on-one counseling. I'm thinking you might be the authorities?"

"Caroline? You are even lovelier at forty than you were at twenty. You are clearly smarter and more unflappable than you were then. Tell me why I should save your brother's ass and not haul him down to the jailhouse and throw him in the pokey."

"Because this is a confidential conversation? Because it would ruin his life? Because Mother would be disgraced and because you and I are friends?"

He looked to the ceiling. Then he rapped his fingertips on the top of the table. Next he took a long drink of his tea and then he looked at me again. After what seemed to be years, he finally said, "Where's your brother?"

"I don't know," I said, "around here somewhere."

"Let's find him."

Matthew got up from the table and I followed him out the kitchen door, across the lawn, toward the dock. He was noncommittal about not involving Trip or taking him in for questioning. I had taken a risk on Trip's security. I hoped to God that Matthew would just let Trip tell him what he knew and let the Columbia boys just take Trip's money so we could be done with it. If Trip went to prison, he would be disbarred and then what would he do?

Trip wasn't at the dock—his boat was, but he wasn't. We walked over to the barn. Mr. Jenkins was there, at Daddy's old desk, reading a Burpee catalog. It was the first time I had ever seen him reading. Suddenly I was proud of Mother for what she had done.

"Hey, Mr. Jenkins! This is my friend, Matthew Strickland."

Mr. Jenkins stood up and Matthew extended his hand, shaking it soundly and smiling.

"Mr. Jenkins? They still got you over here working you to the bone?" Matthew said.

"Mr. Matthew Strickland," Mr. Jenkins said, "I should say, Chief Strickland! I ain't seen you since you was just a young buck! My goodness, I must be an old man if you're this grown!"

"You ain't old, Mr. Jenkins. You just hitting stride, that's all!"

They looked at each other for a long while, remembering years long gone. I was remembering too—Matthew and me riding horses, waterskiing, teasing each other, all the fun we had enjoyed so many years ago. Matthew was one of those men who exuded competence, reliability, integrity, and enough masculinity for all the men of a small town. I was struggling to remember what it was he didn't have enough of to hold my interest. I think I was so possessed with my own need for escape that he must have just disappeared from my radar screen. Yes, it had to have been something stupid like that. No, Matthew wasn't someone to be taken lightly or to play with like Josh. He also wasn't someone I could orbit around my planet either, reeling him in when it suited me and reeling him back out when I was temporarily finished with him for that moment.

"Let's go," he said.

"What?"

"Didn't you hear what Mr. Jenkins said? Trip took Eric out to shoot skeet. God, girl! Are you getting flighty on me?"

"No, I was just thinking about something else. Sorry."

We stopped outside the barn. He grabbed my upper arms and looked at me.

"First, we solve this problem for your stupid brother and then we have cocktails at a party in Charleston then dinner later at my house. Is that okay with you?"

My insides felt funny, slightly gelatinous, squiggly. He made me nervous because I thought I was sure that dinner meant sex. Was it sex in return for saving Trip's behind? Was I wrong? I was afraid to know the truth. This would not be a night where I would call the shots.

"Matthew? I'd love to spend the evening with you. I'd love you to solve Trip's problems. But, I gotta tell you, I'm nervous." Truth was the best policy, I had decided.

"You should be," he said, smiling with one side of his mouth. "Let me go talk to your brother alone."

"I'll come with you to take Eric," I said.

We walked in step, his stride and mine perfectly matched.

Later, when Eric was back in the house, and Matthew was long gone, and Trip had returned to Walterboro in a state of obvious relief, after Mother had read him the riot

act behind closed doors in Daddy's study—later when I
was in the shower, and then dressing for Matthew to pick
me up at six, I had some tiny truths revealed to me. I
hadn't allowed myself to be serious about Matthew because I had spent my entire life avoiding men like him.
Superficial was safe. Matthew was dangerous.

This had nothing to do with me growing up with privileges or Matthew growing up the son of a shopkeeper and
his wife, a bookkeeper. It had to do with risk. Would I
continue on this road of self-serving love affairs like
Mother? Was that really what she had done? Wasn't she
maybe just lonely? Was I?

I opened the French doors in my bedroom. The smells
of Japanese honeysuckle drifted in. I watched the river for
a few minutes, thinking of all that had been placed before
me in just a few short weeks. I needed to deal from
strength with all those things—Millie's wishes, Trip's
trouble, Frances Mae's attitude, Mother's suspected illness,
Eric's education, and, most important—my legacy.

Perhaps it was indeed time for me to *be my father's
daughter.* He had been a problem solver, fearless and edgy.
Up until today, when I reached out to Matthew, I had been
a freaking wimp. Now that I had taken a risk, asked an
old friend for a favor, depended on his integrity, what
seemed a life-and-death situation had been reduced to a
simpering mass of bubbles, floating away with each passing breeze from the river. No, this was good. Everything
for Trip would work out. We had worked together—
Mother, Millie, and I—worked together with what we
could offer to solve a nasty, nasty flaw in my brother's
character.

I knew then that he gambled to rebel. He was rebelling
against Frances Mae, Mother's thumb, Daddy's death, and
who knew what else? Logic told me that if he removed

what there was to rebel against, the compulsion to bet would fade. Maybe. We'd have to see.

I took a long drink of the sweet air. And then, another. For the first time in years, I was excited to be alive and I almost liked myself. I wasn't a victim and I wasn't a savior. No longer content to live in the script written by others, I was finally a woman almost worth something. Now the games would begin. Now, I would wage my mettle against fate.

Hell, I thought, Caroline? You watched your daddy blow up as a girl, you were most certainly abandoned emotionally by your mother immediately thereafter, you left home in a huff for what? You married the most bizarre of all men you had ever known in some attempt to resurrect your father. You have carried these things alone for too many years.

Now, finally, you have turned a tiny corner. You just took a small step toward your mother's care and your brother's well-being.

Yes, I had done this. What else was I capable of doing? And, was I really as clever as I wanted to be? Probably not, but maybe there was a higher force at work?

I was no magician. I knew that. Yes, I felt things and they happened. And I dreamed things that came true. And, on a rare occasion, I heard things and saw things. Don't ask me to describe them. It has taken this long to admit it. I needed Trip's trouble solved, Mother's health to be all right, Eric to find his power spot and then I could concentrate on the veils of understanding and realization that were lifting faster than I could count their colors.

I would greet Matthew with relief and gratitude. I would make him my friend again. I needed his friendship. We all did.

38

FAMILY STEW

The front doorbell rang promptly at six. I thought I looked pretty darn cool in my Manhattan armor—little black dress, hair blown out straight, minimum makeup, major CFM Manolo Blahnik low-heeled slides in leopard. Bare legs—creamed within an inch of their lives. Small black handbag holding breath mints, lipstick, house key, comb, and a twenty-dollar bill, in case of whatever.

Eric all but broke his neck getting there to answer it.

"I'll get it!" he called out all over the house.

I heard him say hello and take Matthew into the living room, presumably to grill him. That's what he did these days. Protect Mom.

"I'll be there in a minute!" I said, calling down the stairs. I just wanted to say good night to Mother.

I stuck my head in her room and she was there, stretched out on her chaise, fast asleep with a magazine on her chest.

"Mother? I'm going out now," I whispered to her.

"Perfume!" she said from her sleep.

"What?"

She opened her eyes and looked at me. "Go wash your neck! You smell like you-know-what!"

"You know what, Mother? You can be one cantankerous old bird, do you know that? Can't you just say, 'Gosh, Caroline, you look nice? Maybe a bit heavy on the cologne, but it smells good, I must say'—something like that?"

"I just want you to be aware," she said. Then she sat up. "Come here. Feel this."

She took my hand and put it to her rib on her left side.

"Feel that?" she said. "It's been there for over a year. But now it's growing. It hurts like the devil too."

It was a growth on her rib. No doubt about that. I choked up, knowing it was indeed not good to have a lump on your rib and a melanoma on your back. I wanted to ignore it. So did she. In her way, she just wanted me to know about it, but not to discuss it.

"We're seeing a doctor first thing Monday, Mother."

"I don't need any doctors poking around me at my age. Try to get in at a decent hour, all right?"

"I will, Mother."

I headed for the door.

"Caroline?"

I turned to her and waited.

"You look lovely. Have a nice evening and *tell* Captain Strickland how grateful we all are to him. Don't *show* him—never on the first date, dear—just tell him. Understand?"

"Mother? I wish we could bottle you!"

I blew her a kiss, she smiled, and I left her to go downstairs, hearing Eric and Matthew before I got there.

"So, can I pour you a scotch?" I heard Eric say.

"No, that's okay, son," Matthew said.

"You gonna marry my mom?"

"So far, we're just having dinner. Is that okay with you?"

I was purple! "Eric! Good grief!"

Eric turned to me, decanter of scotch in his left hand and his jaw set firm. He was aggravated.

"I just want to know what's going on around here, that's all. We were supposed to go to Charleston today and we didn't."

God, he was right. "You're right," I said. "I'm sorry."

"You have time for this guy but not for me, is that it?"

"Eric! Where are your manners?" I was mortified by Eric's outburst. He had never acted like this before!

"Eric," Matthew said, "would you like to come with us? We're going to a cocktail party down in Charleston for some old friends of mine and then we're going out to my house on the Ashepoo to cook dinner. You're welcome to join us. You can help me grill the steaks."

"My mother's a vegetarian," Eric said. As if to say, *Shows you what you know!*

"Not anymore," I said. "I'd love a steak."

"Want to come?" Matthew said. "Last chance! Not gonna beg you."

"Nah, I'm all dirty. Maybe next time." He looked to me.

"I'd love to have you along," I said. "Just take a quick shower and throw on some khakis and a clean shirt."

"Really?" His blue eyes started to dance.

"Yeah, really. Now, move it! You have exactly ten minutes or we're outta here without a chaperone!" Matthew said.

Eric took off running up the stairs, stomping every step like a herd of elephants.

"He's never acted like that, Matthew. I'm sorry."

"He's perfect. Now about that scotch? A light one?"

In fifteen minutes, we were on our way in Matthew's Buick. I had thanked Matthew profusely in the living room and in the car for whatever it was he had done for Trip—which he obviously wasn't prepared to discuss. Fine with me, I thought. Just end it. I don't need the details. All I knew was that they were going to mark the money that Mother was giving Trip and that would help them trace the hands it crossed.

Eric was in the backseat fully absorbed by his Game Boy. Very soon, the traffic became heavier as we approached Charleston, and then slowed, as we passed the Citadel Mall. He took Highway 7 over to the Cosgrove Avenue Bridge, then to Interstate 26 and we exited at East Bay Street.

"Faster than going downtown," he said.

All along East Bay Street, we pointed out things to each other that we remembered.

"Ever sneak into Big John's?"

"What self-respecting underage person didn't chug their first beer in there?" I said.

"I heard that, Mom!"

"Well, just because I did it, that doesn't mean you should."

"What about my self-respect?" Eric said. "Nailed you on that one!"

"The boy's sharp," Matthew said.

I just rolled my eyes over Eric's giggles. It occurred to me that I had no idea where we were going.

"Whose house are we going to?"

"Susan Hayes on Queen Street. Know her? She's a bit older than us. She's giving a party for the daughter of a friend of mine who's getting married. Should be fun."

"No, don't think I do. I've been gone so long, who remembers anything?"

We turned right on Queen Street and pulled up behind a line of parked cars, taking the last available parking place on the street.

"It's up there on the left," Matthew said. "You'll like Susan. She's hilarious!"

"Yeah?"

"Yeah, husband dumped her for another woman; she's a single parent."

"Sounds frighteningly familiar," I said.

"Well, her ex got prostate cancer, nearly died but didn't. They say he was cured by a miracle. Who knows? He and his new girlfriend moved to California. Susan took it up with her childhood sweetheart. He's a pussycat of a guy. Simon. Rifkin, I think. I've only met him two or three times."

"Well, this sounds like fun. Eric, leave your Game Boy in the car, okay?"

"Okay," he said, with a groan, and tossed it in the backseat.

I combed his hair with my fingers and gave him instructions, "Now, remember your manners. Look at people in the eye and shake their hands, all right? And just stay with me like a good boy."

We rang the doorbell of the old Victorian and were ushered in by a teenage girl.

"Hi! I'm Beth Hayes," she said to us. "Who are you?"

"I'm Eric," my son said, completely moonstruck by her young beauty.

"Wanna play Sims?" she asked. "My cousins are upstairs in my room going nuts with it."

"You got the Sims game? Cool! Yeah! See ya, Mom!" Eric looked at me and took off up the stairs.

"All the children are upstairs, eating pizza and having

their own party," she told us. "The bar's in the living room."

This made me giggle, as she couldn't have been over sixteen.

"Thanks, Beth," I said and followed Matthew into the next room.

It was a good-looking crowd of people—mostly in their forties, some slightly older, some younger.

"White wine?" Matthew said.

I nodded my head.

"How did I know that? Be right back."

I made my way through the shoulder-to-shoulder crowd to the side of the room and found myself with my chest pressed against the back of a navy blazer. When he turned to me I saw he was one of the most gorgeous men I had ever seen. I gasped.

"Excuse me," he said, "the enthusiasm of this crowd can be dangerous to your health."

"Are you a doctor?" I said, like an idiot. His eyes were like molten chocolate. He was my height. He had the most adorable salt-and-pepper curly hair.

"Do you need one, ma'am?" he said and grinned at me.

"No," I said and tried to step back only to be pushed into him again, this time chest to chest. I blanched eighty ways to hell and back in pink, then red, then crimson. "But my mother does. Do you know Jack Taylor, by any chance?"

"He's my tennis partner three times a week," he said. "Do you want to go somewhere to talk? Or should we stay here and get crushed ribs?"

"If you can find a safe place, that'd be great."

He took my hand and worked his way through the crowd. Then he stopped in the kitchen, where the caterers were in full force, moving around and in between each other, stacking appetizers on silver trays and taking racks of glasses over their heads back out the door. It was organized, professional bedlam. He grabbed two glasses, a corkscrew, and a bottle of wine and I followed him out to the backyard.

"Whew!" I said. Another very intelligent remark, guaranteed to impress this man.

"Well put," he said. "White okay?"

"Sure," I said.

He popped the cork, poured two glasses and handed me one. "Cheers! Now tell me about your mother and why she needs Jack Taylor."

"Shouldn't we be inside?"

"In a minute. I hate crowds."

"Me too. So here's the story . . ."

I told him the history of Mother's suspected melanoma and also about the lump on her rib. The whole time I spoke, his eyes never left my face. He was too handsome to be real. All I wanted to do was touch his hair to see if it was as soft as it looked. No wedding ring. Good sign. *What about Matthew, you little slut,* I asked myself, not giving a damn.

Originally, I thought he had brought me out here to check my hormonal waters for the tide, but from the morose look on his face I finally got it through my thick head that he was not in the phallic mode. When I stopped running my mouth like the Chatahoochee, he put his glass of wine on the picnic table and pulled a cell phone from his pocket. He dialed a number and held his finger up to me—a signal not to speak.

"Jack? It's me. Yeah, can you come out to the backyard? Sure. I have someone I want you to meet. Bring a glass. Yeah. Okay." He closed the phone and smiled at me. "He's here at the party."

"Oh. Good." It was another poetic response that would take his breath away. "So, what do you think? About my mother, I mean? Are you married?"

It just slipped out. God, I was so uncool. What a jerk I was. He smiled at me.

"You know? I don't think I even introduced myself! I'm Simon Rifkin—your host for the evening. No, I'm not married. I'm worse than married."

The back door opened and a man, who I assumed was Jack Taylor, came down the steps with a beautiful woman on his arm.

"Hi, sweetheart!" Simon Rifkin, the one who didn't call me an ass but should have, said. "I want you to meet my fiancée." He said this to me, and extended his hand to her. "This is the woman of my dreams, Susan Hayes!"

He pulled Susan to his side and kissed her cheek.

"He only says that when he's done something naughty," she said and winked at me.

"And you must be Jack Taylor," I said.

After hellos all around, Susan turned to me and said, "Now, do I know you?"

"No, I don't think so," I said, "I came with Matthew Strickland. You have a beautiful home."

"No, I have a falling-down disaster of a home, but I have a beautiful man. I'm sure it's my usual paranoia, but if I thought you were out here flirting with my man, I'd have to take those shoes right off your feet and put one of the spikes in your ear! Where did you get them? They're fabulous!"

Her blue eyes twinkled and she smiled the entire time she spoke, but I knew she was serious about this guy Simon and I couldn't blame her. I had an instantaneous admiration for her way with words. She probably carried a stick in the backseat of her car to beat the women off of

him when they went out in public. I decided I wanted her
for a friend. I sure as hell didn't want her for an enemy.
She also had an engagement ring on that was big enough
to choke a Great Dane.

"What size do you wear?" I said. I looked down at my
favorite mules and knew they were up for adoption.

"Gunboats, honey. I wear a nine and a half."

"Jesus, me too!"

At this point, Simon had taken Jack aside. Jack's face
was serious too. He looked over at me when Simon
stopped talking. Susan stopped talking too when she saw
how serious Simon was.

Jack spoke first.

"Caroline?" He pulled his wallet from his back pocket,
fumbling through it. "Here's my card. You bring your
mother to me at eight-thirty Monday morning. In case you
get there before I do, just tell Trudy, she's my head nurse,
that I told you to come. Don't worry about your mother.
That's my job. Whatever it is, we will get her the best
talent we have and take it from there, okay?"

"Okay. Gosh thanks, Jack."

"Don't mention it. This happens all the time."

I looked at his face for the first time. There wasn't anything remarkable about it, except that it was almost perfectly symmetrical. He had nice green eyes and blond hair
mixed with gray and amazing eyelashes. Even though
there was hardly a line on his face, I guessed his age at
around fifty. No ring. He was also taking inventory of me.
Not in a leering way like Josh or in a wave of testosterone
like Matthew. Just a nice way. He was tall but not lanky
like Richard. He was solid and looked like he had probably
played football most of his life. When he smiled at me, I
felt shy. For me to feel shy is a helluva thing. I liked him.
Better yet, I trusted him.

Susan spoke up. "Um, y'all? We have a party going on?"

This woman did a *lot* of speaking up, I decided. When I left with Matthew and Eric at around eight, I positioned my shoes on the front hall table with a note.

Susan, great meeting you and Simon. If the shoes fit, wear them! Call me for lunch! Caroline Levine 843-890-4499.

"I'm sure there's a good reason why you're barefoot," Matthew said.

"I like that woman," I said. "We'd better get going."

Eric slept in the car. He had enjoyed himself thoroughly. I had to promise to buy him this Sims game for his computer the next day to get him to stop talking about it.

"It's like you're God, or something, Mom! I swear it is so cool!"

"Don't swear, Eric. It's not nice."

"But it is the most unbelievable game! Completely mind-blowing!"

"That's nice, Eric. We'll look for it tomorrow, all right?"

"But, Mom, let me just tell you one thing. I built this house, right? And then—"

"Eric?"

He got the message. I looked over at Matthew as he drove the car, his face in a smirk.

"Boys," I said.

"Boys are great," he said and smiled at Eric in the rear-view mirror.

Later, after dinner at his house—grilled steaks and plenty of wine—we had a walk by the river, and then Matthew drove us home. Eric ran inside the house, slamming the front door behind him. I'd have to remind him not to do that. I looked over at Matthew and shrugged my shoulders. Matthew stood a safe five feet from me.

"Well, thanks for a nice evening, Caroline."

"Oh, Matthew, it's wonderful to see you again and I can't begin to thank . . ." I tried the front door. It had locked itself.

"Not another word about your brother, okay?"

"Let's walk around to the back door," I said.

I went up the back steps and he waited at the bottom. He just stared at me. No moves, no kiss, no feels, no nothing. I was beginning to wonder if I should change my toothpaste.

"Okay, mister," I said, and walked back closer to him.

He cocked his head to one side and said, "You want me to kiss you, don't you?"

"Not unless you want to, Matthew." Jeesch, I thought, is he studying to be a minister in his spare time? "Are we saving it for something? It's perishable, you know."

He obviously didn't know what I meant, because he said, "Wha . . . ," and then, "Why don't you just come here?"

Then, in a glorious moment of moonlight and pheromones, Matthew Strickland pulled me to him, laid his lips on mine, and went to work. Good Lord! I thought I had left the earth! He couldn't have kissed like that in high school or I would have remembered! My knees were weak and my stomach fluttered. Sweet Jesus! What a man! I would have melted his clothes on Mother's back porch, except that the kitchen light went on. We stopped and looked toward the door. It opened slowly and out came Mother's broomstick with an alarm clock swinging from its end. Eleven o'clock. I started to giggle.

"Decent people need to be asleep!" came the voice from an unseen source.

I turned to Matthew, who was now practically eating his lips, suppressing laughter.

"Good night, Matthew, thank you for a wonderful time."

"I'll call you tomorrow," he said, and walked away toward his car.

39

MR. M.D.

Convincing Mother to get in the car wasn't easy. It required the full cooperation of Millie and Trip and a big, fat slice of guilt. Eric's tutors, "the family lovers," were coming within an hour. Millie agreed to orchestrate their day. It was just one too many complications for me and I gladly took her help.

We were all gathered in the kitchen slapping together a little breakfast. Over coffee, toast, and scrambled eggs, Mother bickered with us.

"I don't understand why in the world you think my body is your business! I'm perfectly content to live as I do and perfectly content to let y'all live as you do. And if anybody around here has the right to point fingers, it's me, not you or you!"

"Mother," Trip said, "look, I know you hate doctors. I hate doctors. But if you've got something growing on your rib and a big nasty mole on your back, don't you think someone should look at you?"

"Not necessarily," she said. "The whole problem with doctors is that, at my age, they will most assuredly find something wrong! I'd bet my last dollar on that!"

"Oh, come on now, Miss L, you lost your mind or what?" Millie said.

"If this was me, wouldn't you make me go to a doctor?" I said.

"That's different. You're my daughter, Caroline. I couldn't stand by and see anything happen to you."

"Well, Grandmother," Eric said, piping up from his plate, "I'm just really getting to know you, and even though I'm just a kid and you'll probably tell me I'm out of line, I don't want to stand by and see anything happen to you either. I love you."

That clinched it. The room fell silent. All eyes were on Eric and he shifted in his seat, nervous that the big ax of the matriarch executioner was about to reshape his Abercrombie & Fitch haircut.

"Eat your eggs, son," I said, hoping the moment would pass. "It's brain food."

It didn't, but the ax didn't swing either. Mother rose from her place and went to Eric's side in the gliding, graceful move of an Olympic ice-skater coming to the close of a gold medal dance routine.

"For you, darling, I will see this charlatan of a doctor. For you." She kissed him on his head. "You dear, sweet, darling little boy," she said to him in an audible whisper, and then to the rest of us, "Did you hear that? My grandson loves me! I'm going to dress. We leave in fifteen minutes."

She left the room with all the flourish that Loretta Young used to descend a staircase in the fifties. The swinging door, as alive as any costar, swooshed behind her on cue. Each of us stared at each other and shook our heads.

The door swung back open and she poked her head inside, looking at me with an arched eyebrow.

"How old is he?"

"Who?" I said.

"This doctor, of course. Is he handsome? Should I wear something exciting? A hat perhaps?"

"Mother? Please! Just wear something normal. A St. John knit. It won't wrinkle in the car. Yes, he's very handsome."

It was impossible not to smile. Mother had only wanted someone to tell her why she should submit to the intrusive eyes and probing hands of a stranger. She hated doctors. But she sure loved men.

By eight–forty-five, we were in Dr. Jack Taylor's office. He took her right in as though she were the queen. At nine-fifteen, he called us into his office while Mother dressed in his examining room. I was filled with dread. In the tradition of our family's emotions, I wanted to dislike him and decided in advance that anything he said would be reexamined by a second opinion.

"Please sit down," he said, motioning to the two leather occasional chairs in front of his desk.

While he shuffled through his papers, I looked around his office. It looked exactly as you would expect a male doctor's office to look. His mahogany desk was nicked and dulled from years of abuse, but the top was neatly organized with a pen set, blotter, and pencil cup. His cards rested in an old clamshell, which had probably been painted and decorated by one of his children years ago. His walls were covered with diplomas and citations and photographs of what appeared to be open-air-market people in Istanbul and Greece. He apparently liked to travel. And to read. In addition to bookshelves of reference materials on various skin diseases, he had a small collection of leather-bound old books—classics—probably first editions. He treasured books. He couldn't be all bad.

He made a few notes on his prescription pad and cleared his throat.

"I want you to take your mother to this clinic at the Medical University for blood work, when you leave this office. I'll have my nurse make the appointment." He cleared his throat and looked from Trip's face to mine. "There's nothing good to report."

"What does that mean?" Trip said.

"I'm sorry to be the one to tell you this, but I've been practicing medicine for twenty years and I can predict and recognize with certainty your mother's condition and the prognosis."

It still wasn't sinking in with me—that Mother was seriously ill. "I'm sorry," I said, "it's early and I'm just not sure what you mean. Is Mother in danger?"

"Ms. Levine . . ."

"Caroline," I said.

"Caroline," he said, "look, the mole on your mother's back is melanoma. No question about it. The lump in her side is almost definitely related to it. I'd say her cancer began to metastasize more than a year ago. She has all the classic symptoms—loss of appetite, loss of balance, numbness, and leg pain—the blood work will be the definitive clue. So I'd say, go get the blood work, I'll rush the lab for results, and as soon as I know for sure, I'll call you. In the meanwhile, I'm going to call my friend Jim Thompson—he's the best oncologist I know—and tell him to open his calendar for us tomorrow."

"Thank you," I said, and a numbness crept through me. I didn't even know what questions to ask. I looked at Trip and his face was a mask of shock.

"Can you have her at Dr. Thompson's around four to-morrow?"

I lost it and tears spilled over my lids. I got up and leaned over his desk. "Are you saying this might be fatal?"

He reached his hand out and covered mine. Then, he squeezed my hand with a kindness and sympathy for which I was completely unprepared. Trip got up and put his arm around my shoulder.

"What can we do?" Trip said.

"First, we get the facts, then we decide," Dr. Taylor said. "It may be that there is a course of action which would at least put her into remission. How old is your mother?"

"She'd shoot me if I told," I said, wiping my eyes with a tissue and cracking a halfhearted grin. I blew my nose with a frightening sound. "Sorry."

Jack Taylor and Trip smiled, all of us at once having a moment to honor Mother's feminine mystique and my emotions.

"She's young enough to fight," Trip said.

"I thought so. She's quite a lady," Dr. Taylor said.

"What did she do to you?" I said and knew it was none of my business to accuse her of anything, but I knew her.

"Oh, the usual personal questions. Was I married? I said, no, I was a widower. Did I have children? I said, yes, one boy at the Citadel. Did I want to remarry, and I said, I was too busy to think about it. And, finally, did I know she was single."

"Oh, my God! When will she stop?" I said, but had to giggle. Mother was an impossible flirt.

"Yeah, boy, she's something, yanh?" Trip said. "There's only one of her."

"What should we tell her?" I said.

"That you're taking her for some blood work. No reason to alarm her. Even if the news is as grave as I suspect, even then, you should wait for her to ask you. She will."

The office was suddenly filled with a weight that made my ears pound. It was my blood pressure. I was going to lose Mother. Not today, but soon. I knew that was what he was saying. I couldn't fathom it in a million years. I didn't want to acknowledge the depth of his diagnosis, what it meant in the end. That there would be an end. Soon. It was too horrible to accept. It was the same for Trip. When I looked at him, I could see he was having an even more difficult time digesting the news. We did the cowardly thing. We thanked him, met Mother in the waiting room, and left.

Mother knew. Don't ask me how, but she knew. She didn't bring it up; neither did we.

"After the vampire takes a snack from my arm, why don't we drive over to Shem Creek and have lunch on the water?" Mother said.

It was a suggestion she would have made on any ordinary day. Not on the morning of the first peal of her death knell. We were entitled to our denial. We would face the inevitable if and when we had to face it. Not a moment before.

Later, at our waterside table at the Shem Creek Bar and Grill, our favorite spot for seafood, we watched the seagulls swooping down and around as the shrimp boats came in from a night's work and docked. The air was filled with the healing smells of salt suffused with an undertone of slightly decomposing marine life. Sunlight playing on the silver ripples of Shem Creek had a hypnotic effect on us. We watched the waters, picking at our platters of deviled crabs, fried shrimp, and flounder, silently dreaming. Mother hardly ate at all.

I didn't know what rattled around in their heads, but I was remembering summers with Daddy, waterskiing on the Edisto, picnics on Otter Island, laughing in the blistering glare of summer's midday light, sunburned and sticky and adoring my daddy. He was my world when I was a little girl. Good things, fun, loving moments of praise and encouragement flowed from him as easily as instructions and corrections rolled from Mother's tongue. Never again had I loved anyone like I had loved him. Except Eric. I had locked it all away and saved it for my son.

For her own reasons, probably to ensure our permanent proximity, Mother had made us afraid of living, of taking chances. She had railed against New York. I realized now that Richard had been like Mother—that somehow I always came up short in their eyes. Over time, that had become familiar for me—to be short something that would have made me whole, by their standards. What were my standards?

Trip drove us back to Tall Pines. I pretended to nap in the backseat, but all the while, I worked to make sense of our personalities, the qualities and deficits that drove us.

It had appeared to me that Mother had no fear of risk for herself, only for us, second-guessing every choice we had made. After Daddy's death, we accepted her authority without question. We knew too that she wanted us gone then. Without Daddy, she didn't want to be a parent. It was too much. So she became Attila the Hun, and we yessed her to death, all of us keeping an emotional distance from each other that ultimately served no one well.

True, Mother had her moments of being a wild woman, classic parental defiance after Daddy was gone, but only within the confines of Tall Pines. On closer examination,

I could see she had been practically agoraphobic, refusing to fly after Daddy's death.

She had become her mother, who had beaten a disdain for the outside world into her, creating an environment of postures, propriety, and gentility which was a self-selecting process of elimination for most things life offered, such as risk and adventure.

Daddy had taken her everywhere, but once he was gone she lived in a warp of sorrow, reverting almost to the life her parents had lived. Had it been necessary for her to have shunned the world to preserve the past? To keep Daddy alive? Did Trip and I owe her that kind of blind obedience? Was I to take up where she left off?

Indeed, over the years, her world had dwindled to only a few locales—her friends' homes, King Street to shop, downtown Charleston and Shem Creek for restaurants. Her garden shows, her work in conservation of the ACE. She was comfortable in that narrow alley of places and trusted faces. They threatened nothing.

There had been a time when she lectured on American paintings at the Gibbes Art Museum in Charleston and at the University of South Carolina in Columbia. I couldn't remember the last instance of her calling me to tell me of her successes and acclaim. It had been years.

And, most onerous of all to consider, if she had been closed-lipped about sharing her sorrow and phobias because of some locked-away fears, would she be afraid to die, if that was what we were facing? I felt blindsided by her illness, alleged or true. I wasn't ready to let her go. I wasn't ready to face my own needs. Something told me I had no choice.

It was nearly six o'clock when we turned into the driveway at Tall Pines. As we passed under the umbrella of live oak shade, I reminded myself to put my anxiety aside for

Eric's sake. I would tell Millie; although, Millie had probably already seen it in her mind. I was right. As our car pulled around the circular drive, the front door opened. Out stepped Millie.

40

STARDUST

Millie had iced tea, a platter of carrot cake squares, a wedge of Jarlsberg, and water crackers waiting for us in the dining room. She called Eric in and we stood, eating and drinking, making light talk about Mother's doctor visits and inquiries about Eric's first day of homeschooling.

"I'll tell you, Millie, that Dr. Taylor was a very manly man!"

"Lord, please, no," Millie said.

"What?" Mother said. "If I were twenty years younger? Ooh-hoo! Yes, sir! What musk!" Her voice twinkled but her eyes were clouded. She wasn't fooling Millie or me.

I stuffed a square of cake in my mouth. "Mmmm. Millie! This is tho gud!" I garbled, then swallowed and said to Eric, "So, sweetheart? Which one of your tutors did you like the best?"

"Rusty," he said, licking the cream cheese icing from his fingers, "she's so cool. Everybody else gave me homework except her!"

"Please use a napkin, son, okay?" I really didn't blame him. It was so delicious I wished I'd been home to lick the bowl myself. "Well, you have a snack now and I'll help you with it in a little bit, okay?"

"Sure," Eric said and turned to Mother. "Grandmother? Are you sure you're all right?"

"As sure as I am of my own name! Wait here! I brought you a little sursy!"

"What's a sursy?" Eric said, his voice cracking slightly—puberty already?—and looked at me for translation.

Mother slipped out to the hall for her purse.

"A little surprise," I said, wondering what she had for him.

"I reckon I'd better get a move on," Trip said to no one in particular and didn't make a move to move on anything.

Mother returned with her hands behind her back.

"Guess which hand?" she said.

"That one!" Eric said.

To Eric's delight, Mother produced a huge Hershey bar.

"Don't eat it all at once; you'll spoil your supper!" she said. "I picked it up at the cashier counter at the restaurant!"

It was an old custom of ours, but it was Daddy's, not Mother's. Like the hand reaching from the grave, Mother gave Eric what Daddy had always given Trip and me when he was in a good mood. A plain Hershey bar. It was a small symbol of his large indulgence of us.

Trip's eyes met mine and I imagined we both had the same thought—that Daddy was calling through Mother, and telling us it would all be all right, not to worry. Sure.

"Supper's gonna be around eight o'clock," Millie said. "I made collard greens and fried chicken."

"Collard greens?" Eric looked at me with a gag, rolling

his eyes. Under his breath, he began to mumble. "Well, I'm not that hungry anyway."

"You're gonna eat 'em and like 'em," I said. "It's food of the Gods."

"Jeesch," Eric said, "this morning I ate brain food. Tonight I gotta eat God's food. Can't I just get some regular food? Like Chinese?"

"Come on, boy, help me carry all this mess to the kitchen," Millie said, ruffling his hair. "Iffin you don't like my collards, I'll make you some kale!"

"Kale? Augh!" Eric said, grabbing his throat. "Mom?"

"Help Millie," I said. "Nobody ever died from Millie's greens. Folic acid. Good for you!"

Eric continued groaning, alleviating some of the tension we tried in vain to disguise. Arms filled with glasses and napkins, he followed Millie to the kitchen.

Trip didn't know whether to stay or go. He hemmed and hawed around for a period of time until Mother finally excused herself to freshen up, walking him to the door. After some small talk and promises to call each other right away when the doctor called, Trip left to go home to Frances Mae and his children. His reluctance to leave Mother and me hung in the air like so much humidity. Even big old Trip felt the need to sit with her until the phone rang.

Millie returned and we stood in the hallway together, watching Mother ascend the stairs. She moved slowly with resignation; even from her back—the way she held the rail and the position of her shoulders—we could sense her weariness and disappointed resignation. Disappointed that her time on earth was to be truncated by what she had loved about life most—to feel the sun, to garden, to be on the river. The very things that had made her feel alive would in fact, cost her this life. Betrayal of the worst sort.

She knew. We knew. None of us were talking.

After dinner and long after I had tucked Eric in, I decided to call Richard. It was after eleven. I dialed him on the pretense of asking him to seek another opinion from some of his colleagues, but the truth was that I was worried and yes, afraid. Something in me, that asinine inner child who was never quite silent, wanted someone to assure me it was all going to be all right. He answered on the fifth ring, his groggy voice filled with sleep.

"Hello?" he said, and cleared his throat. It was a habit of his to clear his throat when he was ready to reprimand someone. I could hear the lecture before it came. *Do you know what hour of the night it is?* "Hello?" he said again.

When I knew he was about to hang up, I spoke. "Richard? It's me. I'm sorry to call at this ungodly hour . . ."

"Not at all," he said, "I'm so relieved to hear from you, Caroline. I thought you'd never call. Is something wrong? Is Eric okay?"

I could visualize him rolling over, reaching for his glasses, turning on the lamp by the bed—that had been our bed. Since when did he worry about Eric?

"Eric's fine." And then the story rolled out as the tears came, choking, sobbing, nasty, tears of female weakness. I was looking for his strength, something I thought I lacked and my gulping tears were proof of it to me. "I'm just not ready to lose her, Richard! I'm just not ready! I'm sorry to be such a baby!"

"Hush, now, Caroline. Dry your tears. I don't blame you for crying. She's your mother! I feel like crying myself! I adore Lavinia! Damnation. There must be *something* that can be done. Let me get on it in the morning, all right? First thing! I promise!"

"All right. Thank you, Richard. I mean it."

"Now let's get some rest, shall we? I'll call you before ten."

I pressed the End button and rolled over into my pillow, allowing myself an episode of the most sorrowful scenario. Mother would grow weaker and weaker. The vile indignities of terminal cancer would descend like Satan's punishments for having lived too happy a life. She would become Job, her skin torn open with oozing sores while every earthly pleasure was taken from her. I would witness it all, having my heart broken with each new pronouncement of her doom. I would see her suffer until she died from it. Unless something could be done to save her.

I rolled over again and opened my eyes. Hell, I didn't even know these things for sure. We didn't have the results of her blood work! I was paying the toll before I crossed the bridge! Stupid! Self-indulgent! I got up to wash my face and undress for bed.

I was turning back my covers when I heard her voice. She was talking to someone.

"I know, I know. It's all right. I'm not! How can I be afraid if I have you to guide me? Why would . . ."

The voice trailed off. I looked at the telephone. No lines were lit. I thought that perhaps she had called Miss Sweetie or Miss Nancy. But, no. She was talking to someone else. I crept down the hall to her room as quietly as I could. Her door was ajar.

Oh, dear . . .

I pushed the door open. There she stood before the mirror, dressed in her wedding gown, the same one worn by her mother and her mother before her.

"Mother?" I must admit, it was a shock.

"I want to be cremated in this dress, Caroline. Is that understood?"

"Yes, but you're not going anywhere just yet." I stepped inside the room in my nightshirt and bare feet. "Besides, don't you want to save it for Trip and Frances Mae's girls?"

"Maybe. Maybe not. And, I want my ashes strewn along the bluffs while everyone drinks champagne. Can you manage that?"

"Of course! But why are you talking this way? I don't like it, Mother. It's creepy."

She turned and looked at me with an anger I hadn't seen on her face ever.

"No. If you want to know what's creepy, I'll tell you what's creepy. Fear. It's the worst demon in Satan's hell. Come with me. I'm in the mood to talk."

Obedient girl that I am, I followed her, down the hall, down the stairs, and outside into the moonlight. I walked behind her as she crossed the lawn on the river's surging breezes, gown whipping and gusting around her legs. I watched her all but float toward the dock. Mother in her wedding dress and I in my nightshirt. We must have been some sight.

We stood at the rail for a few moments, her feet planted in my favorite spot. I didn't care. I could smell her breath, the night air was so dense; or maybe it was that she owned the air around us. Lavinia's air, fogged by the smells of honeysuckle, gardenia, and her soul. Lavinia's night, warm and steadfast like cashmere blankets, wrapped around the baby girl held close in her mother's arms. Lavinia's golden moon and sky of navy flannel shot through with billions of diamonds for her and her daughter's amusement, finery, and wealth of spirit. That moment was too gorgeous for the frail and dying. No, that magical stardust falling all around us, the river pounding and pulsing with its own power, the voices of promise hidden in the swaying and swooshing of limbs of the live oaks all around us—that threshold to the infinite belonged to us, the living.

The poignancy of the moment was not lost on either of us. It was a time for truth, the variety that sometimes arrives with the necessity of facing one's mortality, with your own intellectual and spiritual legacy. If Mother would have one, if I would find something of worth to give to help her, we needed to be candid and literal with each other.

"Caroline? There are so many things I see now that I couldn't understand when you were little. Why did I have to come all this way to see?" Her voice drifted off, like someone thinking a thousand concurrent thoughts, seeking a starting point.

I remained quiet, sure that it was better to let her find her own words into the unburdening of what she carried in her heart.

"You know, I've been a foolish woman . . ." she said.

"Sorry. I don't think you're foolish, Mother."

"Oh, not now, but years ago, when you were little, I was a very foolish woman." Her mood became pragmatic; she was going to be straightforward and sensible. "I'm dying, you know—"

"We know nothing of the sort—"

"Do you think you could stop interrupting me before I lose my train of thought?"

"Sorry."

"That's another thing. Stop apologizing all the time." She looked at me, tight-lipped, and shook her head. "Now, pay attention to me. I am not going to die like some pathetic Camille. No, sir. I intend to expire in a blaze of glory, celebrating every good thing I can think of to celebrate. For too many years I was afraid of my own shadow. When your father died in that horrible accident, I couldn't get on another airplane for fear I'd die in it. Without him, I was afraid of you and your brother turning out to be God only knows what. I was afraid you would see how afraid I was, so I packed you off to Ashley Hall and your brother to St. Andrew's. And then, and I admit this, I went off my rocker a little bit. I probably drank too much; I know I kept company with certain gentlemen who were somewhat less than the measure of your father. . . ." She paused then and rolled her eyes at me, making me giggle, and then she giggled as well. Her light laughter tinkled like tiny bells. It had been a long time since I had heard her laugh that way.

"Well, anyway, Caroline," she continued, "I've made my share of mistakes and I may die from this villainous mole or lump on my rib, but I'm bound to go from something and I just want to be in charge of it. Do you know what I mean?"

"Sort of like you've spent too much of life living up to what others thought you should be instead of just being who you are? Sort of like taking too many instructions from others? Like being afraid of your own shadow?"

"Yes, exactly, and worse. Your father, God rest his gorgeous soul, was a wonderful man, but do you realize that, for all my life with him, I did everything exactly as he wanted? I didn't have an opinion or a thought or a plan that wasn't his!"

"Like Richard and me?"

"Your father left me in a lurch! And I mean, a lurch! When they carried him away, they took my brains with him. I had no idea how to be a parent or how to start over. So I did as I pleased and, in the process, forfeited my attachment to you and Trip. For years it was impossible to even look at Trip; all I saw in his eyes was my Nevil. And you were so needy! Do you see that if I allowed you to need me, and I got so close to you and if I lost you that I would've gone insane? The same thing for Trip but made all the more worse because he's the spitting image of your father. I wanted to make you strong. So you wouldn't be afraid like I was. But I see now that all I did was make you wonder if I loved you and send you searching through life for parents!"

It was true, but I couldn't agree with her.

"And your brother? I turned him into an idiot, married to someone who would cost him little if he lost her—and I don't mean financially, I mean emotionally—and someone who looked to fill the void in his heart with gambling. Because if he was powerful and independently wealthy, he wouldn't need me either!

"I was so afraid of letting you go but I was too afraid to keep you. You see, if I let you down, I couldn't live with that. I had already been so let down by Nevil's death. I had no control over it. Over anything. So, I have to at least be in charge of my last days."

Mother stood there, in the cobalt silhouette of late night, on the same dock where I had once stood, spinning beautiful fantasies of my future and solving my suspected nightmares of my young tomorrows. She stood there in my spot and opened her heart to me for the first time in my life. I was lost for words, trying to make sense of what she was trying to explain about herself.

"Are you saying that you really do love me?"

"Oh! My dear child! Did you ever think I didn't?"

My tear ducts were about to get another workout. And hers. There I was, child of today's generation of far-flung family, disconnected, disoriented, so convinced of my own truth that she had given our care over to others because she didn't want to get her hands dirty with us. I cried. I had been wrong too.

The truth was that she had tried to make us hard and cold so we wouldn't be shattered the first time our hearts were broken. She had tried to give us tough skin, not splintered emotions. She had failed and recognized that with obvious regret. Mother was weeping, actually asking for my forgiveness.

"So you see? All those rules I imposed on you and your brother, all the times I was demanding of you the way my parents had been to me, it had served me well to get me through life, but I don't think now that it helped you and Trip. I think I hurt you more than I understood I could. I never intended to hurt anyone."

"It's all right, Mother. Really it is. I never thought you were diabolical. I think every child feels some bit of being misunderstood by their parents. And, you did your best. I *know* you did."

"Well," she said, and sniffed, wiping her nose with the back of her hand, "I love you, Caroline. I truly do. And our little Eric is the most precious gift to me. Yes, the most darling boy. I don't want you to worry about him, Caroline. He's going to be just fine. I know it. So do Millie and Trip. Millie said his tutors all said they were greatly impressed by his aptitude. Trip said he's a natural outdoorsman."

"It's okay, Mother. I love you too. Very, very much. And, I'm going to help you face and get through whatever is before us."

"You mean you won't abandon me the way I know you thought I abandoned you?"

"Mother? You never abandoned me. I abandoned myself. But I'm here now." Then I said to my mother the words every child wants to hear. "It's all going to be all right." I put my arms around her frail figure. "It's all right. I'm here."

Later, when I was about to turn out her light, after I had

pulled her covers over her shoulders, she said to me, "I was talking to your daddy."

"Hush, now," I said.

"I talk to him all the time."

I closed her door quietly, whispering *I love you, Mother.*

As I plumped my pillow, on which I intended to rest my very weary head, I noticed that someone had placed an old Bible next to the light. I picked it up and opened it. It was Daddy's Bible, well read over the years and inscribed to him by Mother as a wedding gift. Lavinia gave him a Bible? My mother? What a shock! Where had this come from? This hadn't been here an hour ago! I'd have to discuss it with her in the morning.

I flipped through it, hoping for some words of consolation to fall before my eyes. Sure enough, a passage important and relevant enough to scare the pants off of me stood out. It was a passage in Mark, about a leper coming to Jesus. He said, "Thou can make me clean." Jesus touched the man and he was immediately healed.

"Oh fine," I said out loud, as every hair on my body stood on end, "now I'll never sleep!"

Indeed, how would I? Was that some weird sign? No, it was your basic karmic, New Age synchronicity. Sure. Leper? Skin cancer? Close enough for me. I was going back to church. Okay, I would start sooner. Right then, in fact. I was going to ask, no, beg, God's forgiveness for ignoring Him for the past couple of decades and go from there. Maybe, I thought, you lazy, self-serving, cynical, arrogant, no-good sinner, maybe it's time you used your knees. Hell, millions of Catholics couldn't be wrong. And, if God would indeed cast His eye in my direction after my self-imposed absence from the flock since my daddy's death, it couldn't hurt for Him to find me on my knees before Him.

I prayed my guts out—for Mother, for Daddy, for help, forgiveness, understanding, patience, compassion, acceptance, and, of course, I prayed for Eric. As long as I was in the mode, I prayed for Trip and Frances Mae, and yes, I prayed for Richard. For good measure, I threw in Lois and Harry. And Josh too. Couldn't hurt.

There was no answer, no psychic message and no miracle. But, it was after one in the morning and the prayers had actually made me feel some better.

I don't know what possessed me to do this, but I called Josh. The phone rang several times before a sleepy voice answered.

"What?" he said.

"Josh? It's Caroline. I'm sorry . . ."

"What time is it?"

"Late. Listen, Josh, I found out today that Mother's dying. She's dying, Josh, and I just have to talk to someone."

"Hey, Caroline. That's her karma, okay? Call me tomorrow."

He hung up on me before I could say a word. Her karma? Call me tomorrow? Okay, Josh could tutor Eric until I found someone to replace him. Karma. I'll karma him!

In my bed, the last thought I had before falling off to sleep (after I thought of a thousand things to say to Josh) was that we—my whole family—were all very busy telling each other everything was fine. It wasn't. Not one bit. Desperate prayers. How perfectly pathetic. I'd have to do better than that. In the end desperate calls to God may not change the outcome, but they might change me.

41

THROUGH THICK
AND THROUGH THIN

Through the early morning stillness, I heard cars arrive, banging on the door followed by more banging. I rolled over in my tangle of sheets to look at my clock. Seventen. What in the world?

I ran down the stairs before the whole house was awakened. I saw Miss Sweetie peering through the window on the left of the front door, and Miss Nancy on the right. Why so early?

I opened the door and they rushed in.

"Is Lavinia up?" Miss Nancy said.

"No, at least, I don't think so."

"Of course she's not up, Nancy, look at Caroline! I told you it was too early!"

"No! It's fine! Really!" I said. "Do y'all want some coffee?"

I started toward the kitchen and they followed. I fingered the Start button on the coffemaker and opened the refrigerator looking for juice.

"I wanted to wait until nine to call but Sweetie thought you might go out or something, and to tell the truth, Caroline, we didn't sleep a wink all night! Please tell us what happened at the doctor's office!"

It all came flooding back—that Mother was ill and dying and even though it hadn't been confirmed, I knew it and so did they or else they wouldn't have come so early in the morning.

I put three mugs on the counter and three juice glasses, shaking the carton of orange juice and filling them. Where should I begin?

"English muffin?" I said.

"Thanks, sure," Miss Sweetie said.

"No carbs," Miss Nancy said. "So?"

"Well, we don't know anything for sure," I said. I leaned over the coffeepot—it was still dripping. "But, we don't suspect anything good."

They were silent; the occasional blink of their eyes was their only movement.

"She had blood work done and a CAT scan at the Medical University yesterday."

I didn't tell them about Mother and me and our conversation down at the docks last night or how I was feeling about the whole issue at all. I was frank but my words were spare. It just seemed that this was a time to let it sink in and besides, nothing was confirmed yet. They were Mother's friends, after all, not mine.

The kitchen door swung open and Mother sailed in.

"Smelled coffee and heard the ruckus! What are you old birds doing up at this hour? I have a grandson to educate, so I have to get up! Have you come to borrow a cup of coffee or to hear the latest predictions of the medical world?" Mother came to my side and kissed my cheek. "Good morning, sweetheart. Sleep well?"

"Lavinia?" Miss Sweetie said. "Why didn't you call us? We've been worried sick!"

"She's right, Lavinia, you should have called us!" Miss Nancy said.

I poured Mother a cup of coffee and a glass of juice and put them on a small tray.

"Oh, brother!" Mother said. "If there was anything to tell you, I would've called! But, there's nothing to worry about!"

The English muffins popped up from the toaster and I put them on a plate with butter and jam on the side and handed it to her.

"Mother? Why don't you take Miss Sweetie and Miss Nancy upstairs or into the dining room and then I can make breakfast for Eric. I'll join you as soon as I'm finished."

"*C'est une excellent idée!*" Miss Nancy said.

"Good one, Nancy," Mother said, on her way out, "thank God you're not interested in Romania!"

"That was French for 'that's an excellent—' " Miss Nancy said to me as she rose to follow Mother.

"She knows! For God's sake, Nancy, she's been living in New York!" Miss Sweetie said.

"Sorrrrrry!" Miss Nancy said. "I didn't know they spoke French in New York!"

The door closed behind them.

The closing of one door, the opening of another— Mother's friends here, drawn by some instinct, filled with disbelief but knowing that something was terribly wrong with their friend. And if something was that wrong with her, then maybe something was that wrong with them.

This was what real friends did for each other. They came without being called. They laughed and made light while they still could. They stood ready to shoulder part of anything that would happen. Three heads were better than one or two.

They were not going to be shut out. They would be as much a part of her death as they had been of her life. They wouldn't let her be alone should she have the slightest need that they could fill. And if they couldn't, they'd find someone else to fill it.

I sat at the kitchen table and sipped my coffee. It was warm and rich. I was so glad that they had come. There was never an inappropriate time for a rescue or for a shoring up. They would keep Mother on her toes, reminding her to think positively. They would reminisce and exaggerate the past.

Soon, Millie would open the back door and another day would begin. Soon, I would have to wake my little boy— my little boy so fast on the way to growing up and becoming a man. I had not told him about Mother. There was time for that—after Dr. Taylor had confirmed what he found—time to choose the words, the moment, and the manner in which I would tell him.

No, I had only told Richard. Richard had promised to help. And Josh, who was now, in my book, a major rectal opening. I no longer had a stick of guilt over anything that had happened there. Somehow Josh and I were even.

I got up and went to the back door and outside on the back porch. In the distance I could see Millie coming toward the house. I looked over to the river and it was strong, blue, and powerful as always. The sky was filled with huge clouds traveling by and the song of birds was all around me.

An outsider would never have known a thing in the world was wrong. Things looked the same as yesterday. *Coming to you live from the ACE Basin of South Carolina, here we are! Nothing ever changes here! Except our hearts.*

I waved at Millie and went back inside.

Miss Sweetie and Miss Nancy had arrived to prop up Mother and to be present when the sentence was read. Did I have a friend like that? I should have called Matthew. I should have told him everything. I took a shower instead.

42

SKIN DEEP

The morning would have been solemn if we hadn't had a little boy in the house to feed and get ready for his tutors. And, for some unknown reason, I felt I had the strength of a gladiator. It was probably that Miss Sweetie and Miss Nancy were upstairs with Mother, leaving me to concentrate on Eric for the moment.

Eric and I were alone in the kitchen, pulling breakfast together, talking about his homework. We had both developed a new fondness for cornflakes and sliced peaches with any number of squeezed or pressed juices. Mother may well have been the queen of kitchen gadgets. The pastel yellow KitchenAid standing mixer that sat on her counter had more attachments than I knew what to do with.

But Eric did. Probably stemming from his fascination with Transformers and LEGOs, he had figured them out, one by one. By pure hands-on trial and error, he had discovered out how to press watermelon into a juice that tasted like nectar. And, peaches, blueberries, strawberries and combinations of berries, herbs and vegetables.

"Try this," he said, handing me a glass filled with something almost black.

"What is it?" I said.

"It's good for you," he said.

Headline: CHILD BECOMES PARENT—POISONS MOTHER! I held the glass and waited for him to tell me what was in it. After my intestinal experience of his spinach and garlic cocktail, I wanted no more surprises.

"Well?" I waited.

"Okay, okay. It's blackberries, blueberries, and apple with a little mint! I think it's my best one yet! See?" He took my glass and drank. "Ah! Delicious! Didn't kill me!"

It was, in fact, fabulous. "You know what, son? You should be Millie's apprentice, not me. You've got a natural knack for her style of chemistry!"

"I'll take that under advisement," he said.

"You sound like your Uncle Trip, kiddo."

"Aw, Mom."

We smiled at each other and I felt compelled to say, "This is as good a way to start this day as there could be."

"Yeah, these peaches are awesome."

"So are you, baby, so are you." I ruffled his hair on the way to the sink to start cleaning up a little and looked up at the wall clock. "It's almost eight-thirty; you better go brush your teeth."

"I brushed them yesterday," he said, knowing my response would be *Eric!* Then he said quickly, sliding his glass across the table to me, "I'm going! I'm going!"

The swinging door closed behind him and I looked at the clock again. Dr. Taylor could call anytime. Maybe Richard would call too.

Millie and I had missed each other when she arrived earlier. I knew she was in Daddy's den, paying bills.

Maybe she had a plan. I went to offer her a smoothie, but her face told me she had bad news.

"Morning!" I said.

"Humph, I wish my mother were alive," she said. She got up and picked up a stuffed brown grocery bag from the floor beside the desk. "She'd know what to do."

It was a half-finished statement that required no finishing, but I did it anyway.

"Because you can't do anything?" I said.

"You got coffee left?"

"Only a little, but come on. We can make another pot. Miss Sweetie and Miss Nancy are upstairs with her."

"I knew that."

"Psychic message?"

"No, I saw their cars out front!"

Millie smiled at me as she opened the kitchen door, but she wasn't herself. She seemed tired, more so than usual. She dropped her bag on a chair and poured herself a mug. I handed her the container of milk from the refrigerator and took out more beans to grind. Silence. I didn't need to wait for Jack Taylor to call and confirm what we already knew. Millie sat down at the table, blew steam from her coffee, and took a careful sip. I refilled my mug with the remains of the old pot of coffee and turned the fresh one on. I sat across from her. Silence. Then she cleared her throat.

"See, here's the problem," she said. "The medicine I practice and the spontaneous healing I'm able to get with my herbs depends on certain things. The body's immune system responds to lots of things—happiness, love, laughter—those are the good things. But it also acts the same way to negative feelings—sadness, worry, stress, and so on. By the time somebody's disease has gone on like Lavinia's, it has passed by so many safeguards in the immune system that would have turned it around. Then you can't fix it."

She called Mother by her name. It was the first time I had heard her do that. Maybe it was something she did unconsciously to separate herself from her relationship with Mother. I sighed, considering that. "Well, why don't we wait until Dr. Taylor calls before we get depressed."

Millie ignored what I said and began to babble in an agitated way. She began at normal pitch, as though she were thinking out loud, and then became excited and clipped her words.

"I went through everything! I brought everything I got that might help. When I see Miss L's back the other day I 'bout to drop. I say to myself, *Millie? How you gone fight God's plan?* Then I say, this ain't God's hand; this is Mr. Evil who put that mark on Miss L. And, Mr. Evil stronger than this woman. Then I say, yeah, but he ain't stronger than the Man Upstairs! So, we gone use what we got and then we gone see what we see by and by. If God already got Miss L on His list to come home to Him, we can't do nothing. So we gone pray and we gone see." She blew her cup again and took another sip. "We gone see. That's all."

She stared into space as she spoke. It frightened me and spoke volumes about Millie's concern.

"What's in the bag?" I said.

She finally looked up at me. "Where's the food processor? Mine's on the blink. Otherwise, I could have mixed this up at home."

I opened a cabinet under the counter and lifted it up to the counter. Pale yellow again. KitchenAid again. They must've had a helluva sale. Millie emptied her bag, laying out little Ziploc bags all across the counter.

"First, we gone make a poultice to draw out the poison

from her back. I got pine tar, olive oil, tallow, comfrey, red clover, chickweed, and a piece of poke root. Got some other stuff too." She continued to unpack and organize her herbs.

"Where do you want this?" She shot me a look that said she didn't care one bit. I put it on the counter next to her and plugged it in. "Which blade?"

"First, we gonna grate this root and then we gonna liquefy it all together, using olive oil to make a paste."

"No garlic? Doesn't that cleanse the blood?" I said.

" 'Course I got garlic! Garlic goes in everything!"

She seemed irritated and militant and very unlike the Millie I adored.

"Hey, Millie. You okay?"

She looked at my face and her chin began to quiver. I had not seen Millie cry since my daddy died. She must have been terrified that she could lose Mother. Sure enough, tears began to slide down her cheeks.

"No, I am not okay one bit," she said. "I was up all night worrying and fretting about your mother. She's my best friend on this earth and I am so afraid right now that I can't help her. How come God lets me help all kind of fool people with they love life and nonsense and my Lavinia is under my nose needing me and I don't know it?"

I pulled a tissue from the box by the phone and handed it to her, resting my hand on her arm. "This is not your fault, Millie, you know that."

Her face was a rack of stress. Little lines appeared in her forehead and around her eyes that I had never noticed before. "Millie," I said, "look. I'll help you. We will do everything we can. Both of us. I even called Richard to see if he knew of anything. He should be calling us back this morning. Please don't cry."

"That man? You call him?" She took a deep breath and blew her nose. Her eyes opened wide and she finally grinned. "You *must* be worried!"

"I am. Look, she's your best friend, but she's my mother. I'd like her to stick around long enough to be my best friend too. You know?"

Millie relaxed and shook her head, looking at the floor and then the ceiling. "I just feel like I should have known! Why didn't I know?"

I leaned against the counter and crossed my arms over my belt. "I don't know. Usually, you know everything. But maybe this is the good Lord reminding you that He's in charge, not you and not me."

This caused her to squint at me in suspicion.

"You gone back to Jesus?"

"Millie? I don't know, Buddhism and Hinduism are one thing, but I do know that this whole New Age thing is a load of crap. I don't believe in God because somebody told me I have to or I'll burn in hell. I believe in God because I do. And if I can accept the whole concept of God, and I do, then why not Jesus too? I mean, we are the lousiest bunch of undedicated agnostics in this family I ever heard of. One sniff of a trauma and I go running for my Bible. Well, actually it came for me."

"What are you saying?"

"It was there on my bedside table where it hadn't been a few hours earlier. It just materialized."

Millie tightened her lip to me and shot me a look. It was all right to make jokes with her, but not about God. No, sir.

"Don't ask me! There it was! Poof! I spent the next who knows how long on my knees begging for guidance! Somebody in this family needs to take a position in times of crisis and there's not exactly a line of volunteers outside the door, is there?"

"You are one hundred percent right. Come on. Let's get them cleaver flowers in a pot to boil. Roots and all. Make some tea. Makes tumors shrink."

I shot her a look, like the one she had sent me.

"What?" she said, and put her hands on her hips.

"Shrink tumors? I thought you always told me it was a diuretic."

"Rinse the dirt off the roots. It's a diuretic too. Good for what ails you. Can't hurt."

"Oh," I said, and put the pot under the spigot, giving it an inch or so of water.

"Yanh, put this in too," she said and tossed a handful of ivy in the pot.

"Ivy? Isn't that poisonous?"

I knew the minute I said it, hell would reign.

"You know something, girl? You gone drive me crazy, yanh? We gone add some honey to the mix and it stops cancer from growing. Also opens the liver, gallbladder, and spleen to flush out toxins! Now, go on answer the door!"

I hadn't even heard the knock! Millie was right. I should just leave her to her business and let her tend to Mother. By the time I reached the door, Eric was there and was welcoming in Rusty. I could almost see his heart pounding under his T-shirt and he reeked of mouthwash. Young love. Nothing like it.

"Morning, Rusty! So good to see you!" I said. "Would you like some coffee? Hot tea?"

"Oh, no, Mrs. Levine," she said, "I brought a thermos. But thanks."

"You go on, Mom. If she needs anything, I'll get it for her," Eric said, beaming at her like Alfalfa at Darla. He followed her to the living room where Millie had set up a table for them to use.

"Oooo-kay!" I said and returned to the kitchen.

The phone rang. I watched it with Millie and then picked it up on the fourth ring. It was Dr. Taylor's office. Could I come in with my brother? She wanted to know if that afternoon was convenient.

"No, I'm sorry, it's not. Can I just speak to Dr. Taylor?"

"He's with patients," she said, politely and firmly.

"I'll wait," I said. Okay, that was a New York City, ballsy thing to say, but I had every intention of holding until he picked up the line.

"That's not possible," she said, taking an Am-I-Not-Special? thrill-pill to mark her tiny and insignificant amount of power.

Yesterday, I hated doctors. Today we could add nurses to that list.

"Oh, but it is!" I said, sweetly, assuring her I'd be a gargantuan pain in her ass if she pushed me.

"Hold on, please," she said.

I held. And held, and held, and held. Millie looked at me as though I'd lost my mind.

In a moment of ingenuity, I placed her on hold and redialed Dr. Taylor's office on another line. She answered.

I said in a very even tone, the kind I used with Eric's old teachers when I talked to them in my bathroom mirror, "If you don't put Dr. Taylor on this phone right now, I'm going to call you every five minutes and drive you insane."

She put me on hold without a word and Jack Taylor picked up the line.

"Caroline?"

"Oui! C'est moi! Qué pasa?"

"God. And she's multilingual. Listen, Caroline, I don't like to talk about these kind of things on the phone but I understand your anxiety so I'll come to the point and then if you want to, you can come in and we'll discuss any questions you might have."

"Good," I said, "thanks."

"It's what I feared. The CAT scan shows enlarged liver and spleen and tumors in the bones and brain. The blood work indicates that your mother's liver is already failing. She has fully metastasized cancer. She probably has about six to eight weeks to live before she begins to shut down. There is no course of treatment—just to keep her pain-free. I want you to stay in touch with me and call me every day if you want to. I'm sorry, Caroline. I truly am. I'll call Jim Thompson myself. There's no point in putting her through more tests."

I couldn't speak. Life drained from me, the room went black, and I sank to the floor. The next thing I remember is Millie kneeling down by my side.

"I told him we'd call him later," she said and wiped my face with a cold cloth. "I've had my cry and you've had your swoon. Time to call Trip, put our heads together, and figure out what to do with this information."

She pulled me to my feet. My face was locked in a scowl.

"What you thinking, girl?"

"That this is a big mistake," I said, sticking my chin out and shaking my head back and forth, my eyes brimming with tears again, never leaving hers. "This just can't be so."

"Go on, honey, let's let 'em roll."

Millie and I went out to the back porch and sat on the top step together. Sat like we had sat stringing bushels of beans and shucking corn when I was a teenager, sat like we had sat when I was younger, pulling heads off shrimp—like two old friends, anchored together, and we wept and wept like children.

43

A Doctor in the House

Friday afternoon

Richard called me on Tuesday night. His colleagues had nothing to offer that Jack Taylor didn't know. Same procedures, same prognosis, same predictions.

"Oh, hell, Richard. It's bad," I said, after I told him about the test results. "I am just so broken from this. I feel like I'm falling apart."

"Of all the rotten things. Do you want me to come down?"

What? Want him to come down? Advice, sure. Visitation, of course. But, come down here and sleep in my bed? Was that what he meant? Was he insane or did he find death titillating? Did he think I was implying that I needed him? I did, I admitted that to myself. But for comfort as a friend, not as a husband.

"Come *here*?" I said. It was the best I could manage. I'd had enough shock for one week.

"Caroline," he said, "you left me, darling. I didn't leave you. I still love you. If you need me, I'll come."

I hardly knew what to say. In just a few weeks, I felt that I had struggled and rearranged my life to go on, perfectly well, thank you, and that that new arrangement had only occurred as a result of his outrageous infidelity and his bizarre erotic tastes! Was he crazy? Or was I?

"What are you saying, Richard?"

He sighed deeply, the way he always did when he was searching for words. "That I've had sufficient time to think and sort things out. I realize that I took you outside the boundaries. You are perfectly entitled to your opinion. I know that seeing Lois and me together was very upsetting to you. I know I was wrong, Caroline. Not wrong to want what I want, but wrong in that my desire hurt you."

"What? Now desire is different than infidelity?" Not wrong to want what he wants, but wrong to hurt me? Or what? More head games! He had been leading a double life and the only reason it was wrong was because I caught him? Because Lois was nearly strangling Johnson under a tent of linen?

"I'm saying that I'd give it a go again, if you wanted to, that is."

"What happened to Lois?"

"She's dating an oral surgeon."

"A root canal doctor?" I had to snicker. A perfect Freudian coincidence.

"Apparently," he said. "They seem to be rather serious."

"Gee, that's too bad." I felt a fleeting droplet of sympathy for him. All alone in New York with no one to wrestle his Willie under a napkin in a restaurant. Puhhhhleaaase. "Sometimes a cigar is just a cigar."

"Very funny," he said.

"Well, then, try the personals in the back of *New York*

magazine. Sure—MWMDRPHD seeks F for SMBDHJ. Like Eric says, do the math."

"I imagine that on some level, I deserved that."

"Yeah, my inner child felt like a drive-by."

Silence. Followed by sighing and more silence.

"Oh, hell, Richard. I'm just not, I don't know, I can't think about . . ."

"There, there, darling. You're right. Now is not the time. You just remember that if you need me, I'll be there in a few hours."

I thanked him to give the conversation a cordial end and gave the phone to Eric for them to chat. I walked away feeling my stomach roll.

The past few days had been that way. Mother had been suspiciously quiet all week—locked up in her room, on the phone. She took it upon herself to call Dr. Taylor Tuesday afternoon and invite him for dinner Friday night. She said she preferred to talk to him on her territory, that she'd be more comfortable asking questions in her living room while knocking back a bourbon and branch than in his office where she could smell medicine. *Surely he could understand that?* Poor Dr. Taylor was no match for Mother's disarming charm. He accepted and Dr. Death would arrive within the hour. She was upstairs dressing and primping as though her lover were about to knock on the door with flowers.

Okay, I'll admit that Jack Taylor was a nice man and it wasn't his fault that Mother had skin cancer that would kill her. And it wasn't his fault that he had to be the one to deliver the bad news. Still, he was Dr. Death.

Eric and I had decided to help prepare the dinner, with Millie's supervision.

"I ain't so crazy about you coming back yanh and trying to take over my kitchen!"

"It's a good thing I am back! You and Mother would buy every gadget available on the Internet if I let you!" As soon as I said it, I wanted to take it back. Mother wouldn't be buying gadgets any longer. No, Mother's "dotcom" days were countable. I pushed the thought aside and went over the menu with Eric once more.

"Did you put soup spoons on the table? The round ones?"

"Yep, to the right of the teaspoon, just like you showed me," he said. "What's the soup anyway?"

"Cream of tomato with lump-meat crab, finished with a shot of sherry."

"Hold the sherry in mine," he said, "I don't drink."

The edges of my lips turned up and I looked up at Millie. She was shaking her head, testimonial to witnessing another precious statement from Eric.

"Lemme check that crab meat. Might have some shell in them," Millie said.

She was determined to have a role in everything we did all week. I couldn't blame her. The reality of Mother's certain demise had hit us all, shaking us up. Even Frances Mae had appeared on Wednesday, her right arm filled with flowers and that ugly redheaded baby of hers on her left hip.

"Hi! Come on in!" I had said when I opened the door.

"No, I can't stay. These are for Mother Wimbley. How is she feeling?"

"Well, she won't discuss her health. But she's been in her room a lot and on the phone a lot. Are you sure you don't want a glass of tea?"

"No, thanks," she said. I took the flowers from her and she shifted my niece, Little Red Rottweiler, to her other hip. "The girls have ballet this afternoon, so I'm driving all over hell's half acre again! I swanny to Saint Pete, all

I do is drive!" She was already halfway to her car. "Bye! Tell Mother Wimbley I send her a big kiss!"

I thought about Frances Mae as I chopped tomatoes for the soup. Even she had been uncharacteristically generous and congenial. We had all been seeing less and less of her. A small blessing given the hurricane we were feeling in our hearts.

Trip and Frances Mae were not coming for dinner. We would be just four at the table—Mother, Jack, Eric, and I. Somewhere during the week I had decided to throw myself headlong into the kitchen and cook away my grief.

As bungling and out of practice as I was, every technique I knew resurfaced slowly as I called on them. Actually, what I did was buy *Gourmet* and copy the presentations as well as I could—that and other things I downloaded from the Web. Having pictures helped.

I counted portions of meat and realized I had overcooked again. We had tomato soup, grilled baby trout on a bed of greens, sliced medallions of pork over garlic mashed potatoes, and homemade peach ice cream for dessert. We didn't need four pounds of pork, even if it did shrink when I roasted it.

"Your potatoes smell good!" Millie said, lifting the top of the double boiler and inhaling the steam. "Garlic?"

"You betcha! Learned that from you! Sautéed and then smashed and chopped. Everything's ready—just have to quickly reheat the fish. Roast is done too. What did the world do before garlic?"

I turned to see her stick her finger in the potatoes and quickly lick it off.

"Mmm!" she said. "Whatcha got for appetizers? This doctor is single?"

"And why would I care if he was? Appetizers? Oh, Lord, Millie! I completely forgot about that! Yeah, he's single but he's the messenger of doom. You know I hate doctors."

"You stupid too, yanh? He's pleasant to look at, I suspect?"

"Pleasant enough. If you like the undertaker type."

"And you think you don't need me?"

"Millie? I need you now worse than ever!"

We eyed each other for a minute of serious thought and we were either going to start crying again or make dinner before Dr. Taylor arrived.

"I'll go to the freezer. I got raspberries and brie in phyllo. Turn that oven on to four hundred degrees and go on and get dressed. You look like something the cat dragged in! Where's Eric?"

"I don't know; I'll find him. Where did that boy go?"

I called all around the house and when I went upstairs, I heard his voice coming from Mother's room. I stood in the doorway and watched them. They were completely oblivious to me. Mother was on her chaise in a kimono, hair and makeup perfectly done. Eric was enthralled, curled up on the floor at her feet.

"Yes, that's how they caught bugs in my great-grandmother's day!"

"With sugar?"

"Oh, my, yes! Here. Look at her diary." She showed him the cracked yellow pages. "They would soak the sponges, squeeze them nearly dry, sprinkle them with cane sugar, and put them on the windowsills. Those stupid ants lined up like fools! Then some poor fool would lift the squirming sponge and drop it into a pot of boiling water. Dead ants!" She reached down and tickled Eric's ribs, sending him into peals of laughter.

"Stop! You're killing me!"

Eric laughed and laughed. So did Mother. It was the

kind of moment I hoped he would remember and one that would give her strength when she needed it. I went in the room then and picked up the leather book with its yellowed pages.

"Where have you been, young man? Up here talking fool with your grandmother?"

"Yep!" he said. "Did you ever read this, Mom?"

"No, I never did, but I'd like to." I looked at Mother. She had held those diaries and journals in safekeeping all my life. "Can I? You go help Millie, son."

Mother smiled at me like she was seeing me truly for the first time. I knew what she was thinking, that I was acting as a parent should, moving the children along to their responsibilities. As she had done a thousand times. And that I sounded like her. And that part of her lived in me, as part of me would live in Eric.

"What?" I said, wanting her to confirm my thoughts.

"It's impolite to read other people's minds, Caroline," she said and smiled again. "I know you think you're like your father and not like me, but every time you open your mouth to direct Eric, it's my voice you use."

I sat down on the end of her chaise and she leaned forward to me and took my hand. "It's true," she said, and patted my hand. Then she held hers next to mine.

"I have your fingernails," I said.

"Isn't that miraculous? I mean, the whole reality of re-production? The more I can see of me in you, Caroline, the easier this will be."

"The easier *what* will be?" I knew she was going to talk about dying and I didn't want to hear it.

"Caroline, listen to me. I'm not a fool. I have called my lawyer this week and we are discussing some changes in my will." Her eyes searched mine and then she fell back against the chaise. "Oh! So many things trouble me now!

I cannot leave this earth with Tall Pines up in the air. And, I cannot bequeath it to my son. I'm too afraid that he'll gamble it all away. And you? What about your life? I can't have you tied down to a place you don't love. I don't know what to do about all of this. I wish things were different. I truly do. My illness just comes at a most inconvenient time, don't you think?"

"Mother, we can discuss your future when Dr. Taylor arrives. I'm not an expert on these things, he is. As to Tall Pines, it's yours to give away. Not mine. You have to do what you think is right. And, it's true, you know I've got these vagabond shoes. I might tire of all this, but I don't know that yet. Who has had the time yet to even think about that?"

"Well, I know one thing. I'm not going to have it ever turned over to a bunch of real estate developers. I'd rather see it used as a museum or a bed-and-breakfast. But condominiums? On the land my ancestors shed their blood to keep? I think not! I'll haunt these halls until kingdom come!"

She was working herself up to a snit and I knew that couldn't be good. Especially with company coming. I leaned over and kissed her on the cheek and brushed a few strands of unruly hair away from her face.

"Mother? I'm here. No one is going to do anything stupid with Tall Pines now or ever. I promise you that." That seemed to relax her a bit. "Dr. Taylor is going to be here in thirty minutes and I look like I've been working in the fields all day."

"Yes, you do. Would you please take a shower? And put on some lipstick?"

I smiled at her, thinking how much I loved her cantankerous side. "Yes, I will, Miss Lavinia. To make you happy, I'll even put on a dress!"

"That's my good girl. And, one more thing."

"Yes'm?"

"The diaries. You should have them. I want you to promise me you'll take care of them."

She extended the single volume to me, with a look of pride and surrender. The passing of the diaries. As symbolic a gesture of complete trust as I had ever received from anyone.

"You can rely on me, Mother, not only to take care of them, but to treasure them."

"I know that, now go fix yourself up. It's cocktail time!"

I showered, put on some makeup, pulled my hair up in a twist, and sprayed some cologne on my neck and wrists—Chanel No. 5—the only one mosquitoes didn't seem to drink. When I got downstairs, Dr. Taylor and Mother were in the living room, chatting like old friends. She had poured him a generous drink and was enjoying her bourbon, sipping away like a debutante. She was in costume. Pucci. Vintage 1970. Neon paisley with turban. Feather-toed matching mules in lime. A thousand bracelets and, of course, her pearls.

"Here's Caroline!" she said, "Don't you look pretty, dear! Come say hello!"

Dr. Jack Taylor got up from the wing-back chair, the one my father always sat in, and I got a good look at him. He looked very nice. I went to shake his hand and could smell his aftershave. Very nice, I thought. Masculine.

"Hi!" I said, "nice to see you again."

For the second time I noticed his eyes. Green. Nice. Didn't he have on glasses in his office and at the party? Maybe not. He wore a navy sport coat, a white silk T-shirt, and khaki trousers. Polished loafers. No socks. Updated Lowcountry look. Pretty cool, even if he was a doctor. Actually, he was gorgeous, but I would have called anyone a liar who said I thought that.

"It's nice to see you too." He smiled, but it wasn't a flirt smile, it was an *I know this is gonna be a rough night for your mother and I'm glad you're here* smile.

He was pretty much all business. That suited me fine.

"There's a bottle of wine in the cooler, dear. Corkscrew's in the drawer," Mother said. "Caroline prefers wine, you know. In New York, they drink wine. Very chichi!"

"Oh, Mother!" I started to open the bottle and Dr. Harbinger of Doom stepped in.

"Here, I can do that for you," he said.

It wasn't sexist or a defensive takeover; it was just a nice offer. I let him have it.

"Thanks! I'll see about the hors d'oeuvres," I said.

Of course, as soon as I turned to leave the room, there was Eric with a round silver tray. Millie's plump, steaming, and toasted brown phyllo pastry nibbles were arranged in a circle on the outer edge and a bouquet of chives, rosemary, and lemon mint (all of them blooming tiny flowers), tied with kitchen twine, rested in the center, pretty enough for a bride. How did she even think of these decorations or garnishes or whatever you called it if you were in the food business? I thought I was being old Julia Child herself to conceive of crab meat in a tomato soup! Hell, when I moved up from Waverly crackers to Carr's Table Water crackers I thought I was a freaking gourmet!

"Watch your fingers!" Eric said, "they're hot as Hades!"

"Thanks for the warning!" Jack Taylor said. "Are you Caroline's son?"

"Yes! He's my precious grandson, Eric!" Mother said. "Always offer the ladies first, dear, starting with the eldest, then the men."

She took one and then Eric turned to me with his eyes rolled up in his head.

"Live and learn," I said, taking one.

"Like I'm gonna be a waiter when I grow up?" Eric said, in a whisper to me that everyone heard.

"Don't be a wise guy," I said, before Mother could throw in her two cents again.

"What are you going to be, Eric?" Dr. Nosy said. "Any plans?"

"Yep," Eric said. He put the tray down on the coffee table and stood, feet apart with his hands on his hips. "I'm gonna be a pediatrician. Or else a paleontologist."

"My word! I never even heard such a word!" Mother said, grasping her bosom. "You are so smart, Eric! I declare! Paleon . . . what?"

"I'd go for paleontology, if I were you," Dr. Career Counselor said.

"How come?" I said, just to be polite, wishing that dinner was ready.

"HMOs. Used to be that medicine was a lucrative field. HMOs have taken all the fun out of it."

"Shouldn't healing people be the incentive? Not money?"

"Caroline!" Mother said. "What an appalling thing to say to our guest!"

"I'll be in the kitchen," Eric said and gave me a private thumbs-up on the way out.

"Sorry," I said. But I wasn't sorry at all. I hated this man who had told me my mother was so ill. I knew it was juvenile behavior, but I couldn't help it.

"That's okay," Dr. Jack Shit said. "It's a legitimate question, to which the answer is no. I didn't go to school for twelve years and live like a dirtball for another five to spend my time arguing with insurance companies on the necessity of tests patients need to determine their course of treatment! Used to be that doctors thought they were God. Now it's the HMOs."

"I've heard horror stories," I said, conceding an inch. "My ex-husband used to have patients badly in need of extended therapy, but the HMOs wouldn't cover it. And half the meds they needed too."

"My point exactly," Dr. Greed said, "these days physicians practice at the mercy of big business and what some soulless, not-medically-trained creature at a desk thinks my patient should or should not have. It's outrageous. And, not very effective."

Millie appeared at the door. "Dinner will be ready in two minutes," she said. She eyed Dr. Available up and down, then shot me a look that said, *You are even more stupid than I thought. This is a nice man and you don't like him 'cause he gave you bad news? Ain't that like shooting the messenger?*

"Let's go in to dinner," Mother said, "shall we?"

She stood and her caftan billowed slightly. Dr. Jack Ass offered her his arm, which she took, winking at me to say, *You see? I haven't lost my touch! Take notes, my moron of a daughter.* I followed them to the dining room like a good girl, thinking to myself that he was taller than I remembered. And that I liked the way he touched Mother's hand. It was sweet, like he was handling something rare, a tropical flower.

He was.

Dinner began with Mother's usual flourish of protocol. Eric seated me and Dr. Manners seated Mother. The conversation was pleasant enough throughout the soup course. Eric and I got up, cleared the plates, and took them to the kitchen.

There, Millie was plating the next course.

"How's it going?" she asked.

"Mom doesn't know it, but every time she looks at me or Grandmother, that guy has his eyeballs glued to her!" Eric said.

"What?" I said.

"That's what I wants to yanh!" Millie said. "Eric, you stay with me, boy. Let the grown-ups have their boring talk. You can help me whip cream!"

"Cool!" Eric said, and looked at me for permission to leave the table.

"All right," I said, "but come join us for dessert?"

When I returned to the table and took my place again, the conversation had turned grave.

". . . believe in God?" Mother was saying to him.

"Oh, yes, ma'am, I surely do," Dr. Biblical Prediction said.

"You do?" I said, "Don't you think that most of what people describe as religious experience can be explained by science? Apparitions? Voices?"

He looked at me and saw that Mother and I were borderline in the "accepting" department. If he knew how I flip-flopped back and forth, he'd surely think I was a woman incapable of convictions at all, not that I cared what he thought at all.

"Yes, science explains a lot, but there is a lot it doesn't explain and even more that defies explanation. I've seen too much over the years not to believe."

"Such as? Can I get anybody anything?" I said, waiting for him to shoot himself in the foot.

"I'm fine, thanks. Well," he began slowly, "when I was an intern, I practiced emergency room medicine. I had the privilege to be with many folks at their last moment of life. I have seen dying patients claim to see Jesus. Many times."

I took a bite of my fish and salad and mused for a moment on that. "Don't you think people project what they want to see?"

"By the way," he said, "this fish is delicious. Maybe, but not when they're comatose."

"Comatose?" Okay, he had my attention.

"My word! My grandson caught the fish himself! But, let's not change the subject. This could be useful to this woman I know who's dying."

We all stopped breathing for a moment. Here was the moment.

"And, she claims not to believe in God," Mother threw in for good measure.

Eric rambled back in and took his place at the table. He all but went unnoticed.

"Mrs. Wimbley?"

"Please call me Lavinia, Dr. Taylor."

"And you call me Jack. Lavinia? Anyone who doubts the presence of a real and living God should spend a few days with me. I see people of great faith heal from life-threatening diseases and people of little faith die from minor illnesses."

"Mind-body connection," I said, the cynic in me rearing up on my hind legs.

"No," he said, and blotted the corners of his lips with his napkin, "it just isn't that simple."

"What's simple about the mind-body connection? Have you seen Bill Moyer's stuff?"

"Caroline! You are particularly contentious tonight! What on earth is the matter?"

"Mother? Dr. Taylor?"

"Jack, please," he said.

"Eric? Please ask Millie for some more bread, dear." I

waited for him to leave the room. "Mother? Eric hasn't been told anything yet, has he?"

"Yes, he has. He asked me if I was going to die and I said, not if I could help it. He seemed perfectly fine about it. I would never frighten Eric. You should know that."

"Jack?" I said, and lost my train of thought, thinking that the news about Mother should have come from me. So, I just said, "This conversation is upsetting to me. You say that Mother is so desperately ill, yet she seems perfectly fine to me. You're here at our table and even though I know this is completely irrational for me to think this, I want to hate you. You're a perfectly nice man, a gentleman in fact, and I can't bear it—to be in the room with you. And, you're talking about God. The other night this Bible appeared out of thin air on my table . . ."

"Please forgive her, Jack. Caroline's been under tremendous stress lately," Mother said and shot me a look of ice cube daggers.

"It's all right, Lavinia." He got up and poured more wine for me and for himself. "What do you mean—a Bible appeared from thin air?"

"Exactly what I said." I turned to Mother and said, "Unless you put it there?"

"What on earth are you talking about?" Mother said.

"Daddy's Bible—the one you gave him when y'all got married? It was by my bed the other night. On the table."

The color drained from Mother's face and she began to slide from her chair. She was fainting and it wasn't drama. It was real.

"Mother!"

Jack jumped up from his place and caught her as she melted on the floor. I dunked my napkin in my water goblet and squeezed it out to wipe her face. I screamed for

Millie and she came through the dining room door in a blast.

"What?" she said.

I said, "Get water! Hurry!"

Jack held Mother's head in his lap and tapped her cheeks. In a moment she opened her eyes.

"Can't be," she said in a whisper we could barely hear.

"Are you all right?" Jack asked.

"Can't be . . . I buried . . . I buried that Bible with his remains," she said and began to cry real tears of fright and worry.

To say this put a damper on our dinner party would be the understatement of the year. I got goose bumps as big as golf balls and even Jack Taylor was unnerved. Millie helped Jack get Mother upstairs. He gave Mother a mild sedative. I took a nightgown from her closet and Millie helped her undress. I pulled back the covers and Mother all but slid between her sheets. Millie volunteered to sit with her and I went downstairs with Jack.

"Can I offer you something? Coffee? Tea? Booze?"

I decided it was time to shape up. Something weird was afoot.

"How about ten milligrams of something for you?" he said. "You all right?"

We were standing in the hallway, by the front door, debating whether to say good night or if he should hang around for a while. I felt like talking.

"Let's see. Mother just informed me that I got a Bible from my dead father's grave. . . ."

"I've seen stranger things."

"And, according to statistics, she'll be gone in six weeks to—"

"That's up to God, not us."

"Okay. My ex-husband called a few days ago, suggest-

ing a conjugal visitation, which I declined. With enthusiasm. . . ."

"Thank you for sharing."

"My most recent liaison ended in karmic hell. . . ."

"Been there. . . ."

"I don't know where I'm going to be living in the next
few months. . . ."

"What's the matter with right here?"

I had ticked these things off, counting on my fingers,
deciding to keep Trip's problem to my myself. Then I
stopped listing my troubles and counted my fingers again.
"Yep, five. That about sums it up. How about you?"

"Let's see . . . aside from your mother's illness, the rest
of that stuff seems pretty fixable."

"If I could get a grip on it!"

"Sounds like you could use a friend. What about that
guy who brought you to the party where we met? Where's
he in all this quagmire of indecision and confusion?"

"Quagmire of indecision—good one. Matthew? Oh,
hell, he's just an old friend from high school. There's not
much going on there. Just a nice guy from eons ago."

"A-ha," he said.

Alone together, standing in the dim light, there was obviously the beginning of a pheromone sizzle, despite the
fact that my dead father's Bible was floating around. We're
not talking about fireworks, no, the chemistry between us
was more in the realm of a sparkler. I could tell by the
tone of his voice, which was slightly lower—the kind lovers use when they exchange secrets.

"And, what does 'a-ha' mean?" My voice became qui-
eter too.

"That maybe you'd like to go for dinner? I don't know,
just seems like you are gonna need someone who knows

what's up, you know? I mean, a friend or something like that?"

His face was sincere. His words were honest and true. He was right, but you know me, I couldn't resist the urge to torture him a little.

"Doctor? Don't you know I hate doctors?"

"Yeah, I got the drift."

"It's because they're always looking for something to be wrong with you. In my case, I'm divorcing a psychiatrist. Also a Jungian analyst. In his world, people are rarely, if ever, cured."

"Ninety percent of my practice is reconstructive and cosmetic. Only ten percent is devoted to melanomas. I cure bumpy noses and things that sag."

"Ah! I feel more pleasantly disposed to you now. Were you saying you'd like to take me out somewhere, sometime—for the purposes of friendship? Or something?"

"Yes." He smiled wide.

Why hadn't I noticed his dimples? "Okay. Yes. I'd like that."

Why did I feel like I had known him all my life?

44

LAVINIA SAYS,
Y'ALL DEAL WITH IT

The very first thing I did when I woke up was to pull my laptop into my bed and get on the Net. I was going to the Vatican to see if I could find a priest or maybe even a cardinal to tell me why Nevil's Bible was out of his grave. No luck. I signed the guest book and asked for their prayers. That was the whole problem with being a Protestant. We didn't have a Vatican, not that it did me much good. After I'd been there and had no luck, then what did I do? Got in a chat room and asked directions to Web sites that would give me some clues as to what was going on with my body and soul, that's what!

Well, it was not very smart of me to expect to find the crème de la crème on the Internet at seven-thirty on a Saturday morning. Nothing but whackos. I gave it an hour and then decided I should call Sweetie and Nancy and tell them to get over here and distract me. I was a bundle of nerves; truly, I was. Before I logged off, I went to BN.com and ordered every book Elisabeth Kübler-Ross ever wrote and got the Bill Moyers tapes too. If I was going to Glory, I would travel as an informed citizen. I even paid for FedEx charges to ship them. It wasn't as if I had time to waste!

I realized I had to tell Sweetie and Nancy that I had been given a sentence, but I just couldn't bring myself to do it quite yet. I would just simply tell them that I had to have more tests. They'd buy that; I was sure of it. Who wanted to talk about all this dreary stuff anyway? Ah, me. Oh, well. All I seem to do is sigh and sigh. I'm so tired I could go back to sleep for ten more hours!

That nice Dr. Taylor seems to have taken a little shine to Caroline. I hope so. I hope he's not the kind of doctor who's a tightwad with the morphine! I'll just start to scream as soon as I feel the first twinge of pain, that's all.

I exited Windows and let my laptop slide to the floor. To hell with it.

Oh, God, Nevil, can you hear me? Are you coming for me? Is that why your Bible is floating around here like a spook?

I must stop this at once! I'll get myself into a state of depression and that just won't do.

I reached for my phone and called Sweetie. She picked it up on the fifth ring.

"Sweetie? You old slugabed! It's the Queen of Tall Pines calling. What are you up to today?"

I could tell I woke her, but she would never have given me the satisfaction of letting me know she liked to lie in bed like the Queen of Siam.

"I was just getting ready to get on my treadmill, why?" she said, lying like a cheap rug.

"I'm in the mood to play cards," I said as sweet as I could, "care to join me?"

"Sure. Why not? I can exercise anytime! Want me to call Nancy?"

I said that I did. She hung up and called back to say they would be over by ten. I decided to rise and make myself presentable. I didn't know how many good days I had left and that made me a little afraid. As I rolled over to sit up, my head started to spin. Oh, fine, I thought, here we go. Well, take it slow, sister, I said to myself and took my sweet time standing up.

My legs felt funny—pins and needles. I'd have to call Dr. Taylor and ask him what that was from. Probably because I spent too much time in bed. Hell, what time did I go to sleep anyway? I know it was before ten. Oh, yes, I remember now! Dr. Taylor gave me a shot to calm me down. I was in a highly agitated state and who wouldn't have been?

Dressing seemed to take forever. I kept staring at my face in the mirror and wanting to cry. I didn't look sick; I looked scared. I was. Then and there I decided that it wouldn't do at all for a woman like me to go around all hangdog, looking pitiful. I mustered my strength, put on my makeup, and went to greet the day.

When I entered the kitchen there they were—the Tribunal! Trip, Millie, and Caroline. They fell silent the second they saw me.

"Good morning, everyone! Talking about something I'm not supposed to hear?" I knew that was rude, but sneaking around, talking about me behind my back just seemed inappropriate! At least Trip had the decency to get up and give me a kiss! His eyes were all red.

"Oh, dear boy," I said, "save your tears! I feel fine!"

"I love you, Mother," he said.

He hugged me so hard I thought he'd crack a rib, mine

not his. "Great jumping Jehoshaphat! You're hurting me, son. I love you too!"

When he finally released me, I moved away as quickly as I could so that I might at least get a cup of coffee! I poured myself the dregs. I hate that.

"Morning, Mother!" Caroline said.

"I'll make a fresh pot," Millie said.

"Blow your nose, son. Thank you, Millie. Good morning, Caroline, where's Eric?"

"Fishing with Mr. Jenkins," she said.

I looked at them, going from face to face at a deliberately slow pace so they would get the message loud and clear. Then to make sure they understood, I told them what I was thinking.

"I am well aware of my condition. I do not wish to discuss it. I do not wish you to discuss it. And, when I'm good and ready to discuss it, I'll let you know. Is that understood?"

They nodded their heads and cleared their throats and looked at me like I had two heads.

"Nevil's Bible is not floating around here for nothing. I know that. But for the moment, I'm fit as a fiddle. Now, Sweetie and Nancy are coming at ten to play bridge and, Caroline, I want you to play fourth. Can you manage that without going to pieces and spilling the poop?"

"God, Mother, about the last thing I want to do today is play bridge!" she said.

I leaned on the table and widened my eyes at her. "Given my delicate condition, Caroline, it's the height of all conceit to refuse me this one little favor!"

"I'd love to play bridge, Mother, just love to," she said, with a small grunt.

"Please do not grunt, dear. Pigs grunt," I said.

Caroline rolled her eyes all over her head in complete

exasperation, so much so I wanted to kiss her face! She's more like me every day! That girl!

"Now, Millie? Shall we make some egg salad for the girls?" I said.

"No, *I* shall make some egg salad!" Millie said.

That was just fine with me.

The doorbell rang promptly at ten. I loved it when people honored the hour of my invitations by being prompt. Caroline and I answered it together.

"Sweetie, darlin'! Nancy, darlin'! Y'all come right on in!" I said.

"Lavinia? What on earth are you so happy about?" Sweetie said.

"Aren't we bright-eyed today, Lavinia," Nancy said.

"Oh, you old poops! It's a beautiful day! The sun's shining! I'm with my two dearest friends in all the world and my only daughter! Why shouldn't I be happy?" I said. I spread my arms and turned on my heel.

They followed me into the living room where Caroline had set up the card table. I poured sweet tea for everyone and Caroline passed the sandwiches. Although it was early for lunch, no one refused them. We chatted about this and that and finally Sweetie asked the big question of the day.

"All right now, Lavinia, tell us what the doctor said."

I was poised for her. "If you must know, Sweetie, he said that I had great legs for a woman my age!"

"Well, that's just perfect," Nancy said.

"He's adorable," I said. "I just wish I had the energy for him!"

"You're so bad, Mother!"

"And, you're a priss, honey," I said to Caroline, taking the wind right out of her sails. "No, seriously, y'all, he did some tests and we should have results on Monday. I suspect he'll want to dig on that mole some, but we'll see."

"Well, if that's all there is to report, let's shuffle and deal!" Nancy said.

And we did. We played two hours of some of the most exquisite bridge I'd ever played in my life. When they left, we all kissed each other in midair and they looked deep in my eyes and Caroline's too, trying to find out what we knew. Caroline was an impregnable wall of resolve and so was I.

I knew good and well that my best friends knew I was lying to them about the doctor's news. We all knew it. When I felt they were ready to hear, I'd tell them. But just for that one morning, I just wanted everything to be normal. I thought that was perfectly understandable. The very fact that they *didn't* pry told me that they knew.

In one way it was selfish not to share my horrible news with them, but then I would have been in the unfortunate position of having to deal with their feelings too. For right then, it was all I could do to handle my own.

45

THIS IS FOR REAL

For the next week, Mother was reasonably fine. I had begun to worry that I'd find her on the floor—that she'd crack her head open, give herself a concussion—who knew? But no, the only changes I noticed was that her skin was distinctly yellowing—not every day; some days more ochre and some days less—and that she seemed a little wobbly in the mornings. In addition, her appetite and energy were truly fading away. I called Jack to see what it all meant and he confirmed my suspicion that it was jaundice and liver failure that was turning her complexion yellow. Appetite and energy loss were a part of the progression of the disease.

Jack brought another doctor in—a guy named Dr. Harbin from Charlotte, North Carolina. He was an oncologist, specializing in skin cancers and in particular with geriatric patients. If Mother ever heard that her name and geriatrics were linked, she'd have shrieked! This Harbin fellow prescribed enough pain medication to last for a month. Jack would check on her periodically and monitor her dosage.

Mr. Jenkins was Mother's full-time driver now, taking her back and forth to Jack's office and the Medical University, and Millie looked over Mother like a mother hen. I looked over Millie and Eric, and Trip stopped by once a day to look over us. We were quite the vigilant team! The extra attention we were all giving each other was warm and reassuring. Not that things would be all right, but that we would all do our best.

Of course, Mother had yet to tell her two best friends what was going on. She said she just wanted to think about it for a while. They surely suspected because they called her every day and when she was napping, I spoke to them, trying to assure them that Mother was doing fine. I longed to tell them, but it really wasn't my place to do it, especially given that Mother had clearly asked me not to.

I was to have dinner with Jack on Tuesday night. That morning, Mother called me to her room. She didn't look well at all. But her spirits were as they always were—lively and full of the devil.

I brought her a glass of one of Eric's concoctions—carrot, apple, celery, and parsley juice. She was resting in her bed, reading Josephine Humphreys's *Rich in Love*.

"Good! You're here!" She sat up and removed her reading glasses, accepting the glass. "Rat poison?"

"Yes. Good for you!" I said and sat on the side of her bed. "How are you this morning?"

"Did you deadhead the roses?"

"You know I did." I patted her leg. "Eric's downstairs with Rusty, making big eyes at her. She's got him building rockets and calculating the volume of cylinders. I think he'd eat fire if she asked him to and make a graph to chart the pain."

Mother smiled at that. "So sweet." She looked at me for

a moment, once again evaluating my skills and strength. "I need your help."

She told me her plan of how she would break the news to Sweetie and Nancy and it was the most outrageous and wonderful idea. We would have an event. She could supervise, but she was feeling more tired than usual and did I mind doing all the work? I assured her that I didn't mind in the least—that her little surprise was the most splendid, appropriate, and sane thing I'd ever seen her envision.

I simply called Miss Sweetie and Miss Nancy and arranged for them to come Saturday morning at nine with their cameras and tape recorders. I enlisted Millie and Mr. Jenkins to help with the rest of the details. It was to be a great secret.

I drove to Charleston to meet Jack at his office at six. We were just going to grab an early bite and maybe stop by the home of his friends, Simon and Susan, for a drink.

His office was empty of patients and staff. I found Jack at his desk, answering e-mail.

"Hey!" I said, in a quiet friendly voice, so I wouldn't scare him out of his skin. "How goes the war?"

"Oh, Miss Caroline! Hi!" He got up and kissed my cheek.

It was nice. So, I don't know, normal! I was *not* used to normal!

"Hi, yourself, Rhett Butler! How was your day?"

All right, I liked him. A lot. There was nothing not to like. He was so genuinely nice and pleasant.

"Let's see now," he said, rubbing his chin and looking at the floor, "I removed six warts, fourteen moles, and a broken toenail this afternoon in the office. This morning I had a stubborn case of acne—all around, it was a decent day. How about you? How's our Lavinia?"

"Well? She matches her lemon-colored sheets. That can't be good."

"Did you call Harbin?"

"No, she's not complaining, so let the man be. She's got plenty of pain medication."

"Okay, good." He took off his lab coat and slipped on his jacket. "Caroline, at some point, she's gonna feel this—once it gets in the spine. And the more it progresses into the brain, she may act out of character."

"Pain, I'll recognize. Mother out of character? You don't know her when she's *in* character!"

I laughed a little and Jack shook his head.

"You be nice now, Miss Caroline. You're too pretty to talk ugly."

Somehow that kind of distinctly southern, infinitesimal but polite chastisement had a warming effect on my heart for him. He was sensitive and, still, he was a doctor. In my experience, that made him a contradiction. Of course, my experience of intimate relationships with doctors was limited to Richard.

He was turning out lights and closing doors to set the alarm system and I followed behind him.

"Let's stop by Susan and Simon's first, okay? I think they want to see you again—Susan said something about some shoes?"

"I left my shoes at her house," I said, remembering.

"Oh, well, I'll remind you to take them." He pressed the numbers of his code into the keypad and I stepped outside the back door with him. He double-locked the back door.

"No, they were a gift. I left them on her hall table with a note."

"Don't most people bring wine?"

He looked at me like I had a large void between my ears.

"It's a sister thing," I said. "Girls do things like that."

His eyes danced in the gold light of late afternoon. "Sounds pretty generous; must be a good thing. Leave your car here; we'll take mine. Come on."

He pulled out his cell phone as we walked across the gravel in his parking lot. He dialed their number.

"Hey, bubba! I got this woman here with me and we're coming over to take advantage of your hospitality. That okay with you?" Pause. "Dinner?" Pause. "Yeah, you better do that." He put his hand over the phone and looked at me, smiling, "He's checking with the real boss."

It was adorable—the way he became animated when talking to his friend. I liked that careful quality of not giving away too much of himself to me, but that there was more warmth and obvious good humor under the top layers of his staid personality.

"Okay, yep. Can do. You got it!" He hit the End button and dropped his phone in the pocket of his jacket. "Wants us to pick up some vino. He said Susan's got enough food for a block party. I don't understand how they stay so skinny! Susan's been cooking all this weird stuff—things in puff pastry with antennas coming out of them. Her pastry obsession reminds me of my mother when she got a hold of cream of mushroom soup! It was everywhere except the breakfast table!"

"That's funny," I said. "I've been trying my hand in the kitchen lately too."

"You like to cook?"

"Well, I like to eat. I cook with cookbooks, pictures, and exact recipes. I'm not exactly a gourmet or anything."

"Me either, but I have to cook for myself if I want to eat. When my son comes home on the weekends, we usually go out to eat."

It was true; Jack was positively the all-American,

charming guy. Innocent and clean-cut. What a radical change for me.

He had a great car, a 1998 Mercedes, S Class, 500—black, with deep luggage tan interior. I liked it that he drove a sedan. It was sort of welcoming, like a tweed sport coat, unlike Josh's sports car, which was the fashion equivalent of a strapless dress worn with a huge hat. Josh, that ass. I had carefully avoided him all week. Still, I had no replacement for him and the truth was, he was a good occupational therapist. He had Eric catching a baseball, something I thought he would never accomplish. But he was too out there for me.

Yeah, step-by-step, Jack was becoming more soothing and comfortable.

I waited in the car, listening to Ray Charles, while he went into Harris Teeter's for wine. Fifteen minutes later he came out carrying three huge shopping bags.

"I thought you were just getting a bottle of wine!"

"Yeah, well, I figured as long as I was in there . . ."

"God, I do that all the time."

He cracked a smile and I grinned too, finding a weakness in common. We drove down East Bay Street to Queen and turned right, passing wonderful old houses, many of them probably still inhabited by the families that built them when Charleston enjoyed an economic boom from trade in the 1700s. All of them were lovingly restored. The sagging pitch of the ancient porches, the low entrances of the street doors, and the overgrown live oaks, roots kicking up the sidewalk—all of it proof of the property's authenticity and historic value.

We pulled in the narrow driveway and drove slowly around to the backyard. Simon was working on the grill, stoking the coals.

"Hey!" Simon called out. "How y'all doing?"

I started to open my door and Jack reached across, put his hand over mine, and said, "Caroline? No lady should have to open her own car door."

"Will you carry me inside too, suh?" I said, oh, smart mouth of mine, unaccustomed to any sort of male gentility, embarrassed by my lack of memory on the subject.

"If you'd like me to, I'm sure I can manage," he said.

Now, if this had been any other man, I would have thought I was being corrected once again for some sort of behavior that "came up short," but Jack didn't even have that kind of criticism in him. No, he didn't. He was just a guy, a southern gentleman, whose momma had trained him right. I had forgotten that southern men treated women with a kind of lovely deference, reserved for those considered or assumed to be ladies. It was a compliment, not a kick in the sexist head. It was damn romantic.

I struggled, fooling around with my purse and hair, waiting for him to open my door, trying to make myself busy so I wouldn't appear to be embarrassed, ungraceful, unappreciative, or a big-ass klutz. When he opened my door, he had been calling some remark over his shoulder to Simon, but he took my hand to help me out, looking in my eyes. It was the strangest feeling. While I was in his company, I was in his care. Very strange to realize this, I noted, strange, but sort of nice. I stood up next to him; he smiled and closed my door, releasing my hand.

"I'm going to get the bags from the trunk," he said, walking around to the back of his car.

"I'll help you," I said.

"No, no," he said. "My mother always said, it was enough that she had to unpack the groceries. Men carry the bags, ma'am."

"Wow," I said, standing there like an idiot, "what a woman she must be."

"Eighty-three, still gardens, drives to church, and knits," he said, piling the bags on the ground. "She lives in Monck's Corner. Spry as ever! You'd love her."

"I'll bet I would."

Jack hauled the bags into the kitchen, through the back porch, and Simon and I exchanged hellos across the backyard.

"Susan's in the kitchen!" he said, calling out to us.

"Great! See you in a few!" I said.

I opened the kitchen door and it took a moment for my eyes to adjust to the low lights. Susan was headfirst in the refrigerator, looking for something. When she heard us, she popped up, smiling to greet us.

The first thing she did was say, "Hey, Jack, you old dog, you been behaving?" But she passed him by and threw her arms around me. "She's here! My shoe fairy! Oh, my God, I can't tell you how those mules have changed my life!"

Sure enough, they were on her feet. She had on a black linen sundress to her ankles, hair up in a knot at the back of her neck, and if I'd ever seen a happy woman, she was the one.

"I am so thrilled you like them!" I said. "Can I help you cook?"

Jack reached in the refrigerator and took out a beer. He popped the top and said, "I'll be in the backyard with Simon. Y'all holler if you need help, okay?"

He winked at Susan and went outside.

"He's adorable," Susan said, "and nice."

"He's awfully nice," I said, "in fact, I can't remember meeting anybody that nice in a long time. Where's your daughter? My boy, Eric, was crazy over her."

"What do you mean *was*? She's at the movies so we can have an adult night."

"Oh! Eric's just twelve! What can I do to help?"

"That's right; I remember now! Okay, here, you can take these salads out of these deli containers and put them in bowls to make it look like I made them—there's tomato, cucumber, and red onion; tortellini salad; and some crab dip I need to put out with crackers. I can't cook worth crap."

She was rushing around, banging cabinet doors and cussing under her breath when she couldn't find what she wanted. She was a whirlwind and hilarious to watch. I began scooping salads into bowls and then dug through the groceries that Jack had brought. One bag had two six-packs of beer, the next had three bottles of red wine from California, and the third had taco chips and chocolate frozen yogurt.

"Well, we got ourselves a real gourmet treat here!" I said, and lined everything up on the counter. "Would you look at this?"

"Good. I can't find the crackers."

She ripped open the bag of Doritos and poured them in a basket. Then she handed it to me with the bowl of crab dip. "Tell the boys I made the dip, okay?"

"Why would I tell them? Admit nothing!" I said and took it outside to the chefs, thinking that Doritos and crab dip was about the worst possible combination of foods on earth.

I could smell something burning and when I got to the grill, I saw that the chicken was completely black. I put the chips and dip on the picnic table and went for a closer inspection. Jack handed me a glass of wine and I took the long fork from Simon. I stabbed a piece of the chicken, which was all but unrecognizable and inedible.

"I think it's done," I said, trying to be polite about its condition, "what do you think?"

"A few more minutes," Simon said, "it's Susan's specialty. Hand me the basting brush, will you? She likes it crispy."

Jack rolled his eyes at me and I laughed.

"Okay! Whatever you say!" I said and went back to the house.

Susan was leaning against the kitchen counter, smoking a cigarette, sipping a glass of wine, looking out the window at the boys.

"Isn't he great?" she said. "He lets me pulverize, marinate, and kill that chicken a thousand times and he still eats it just like it's food. God bless 'im."

"He loves you," I said.

"He must," she said and looked at them, musing, and turned to me. "I knew Jack's wife. She was sort of a halfway friend of mine."

"What was she like? Can I set the table?"

"No, already done. Want some more wine?"

"Sure," I said and held out my glass. "Thanks."

"Are we friends?"

"Are you kidding? You're wearing my Blahniks!"

"Okay, seal of confession?"

"You got it; what was she like?"

Susan stubbed out her cigarette and took a deep breath. Then she sort of sucked in her cheeks. "First of all, I know it's a thousand years in purgatory to speak ill of the dead, but if meanness were a disease, that woman woulda been dead years ago."

"That bad?"

"Honey, you and I don't know any bitches like this woman. She was in a class all by herself. She ran around on Jack, spent his money like she was crazy, lied to him all the time, and treated his momma like hell. I couldn't stand her and neither could anyone else. I know it's horrible to say this but when we found out she had throat cancer, it was like justice had been served."

"Jesus! Susan! That is a *terrible* thing to say!"

"Listen. I know it is. But you didn't know her. What kind of mother leaves her five-year-old son at home on Christmas Eve when her husband's at the hospital for an emergency so that she can go get drunk and screw one of his colleagues? They got so crocked, they wrecked the car and wound up in the emergency room where Jack was on duty!"

"Holy hell!" Damn, I thought, she *was* bad!

"That ain't the half of it! You smoke?"

She offered her Marlboro Lights to me, but I waved my hand, declining. "No, thanks," I said, "I quit."

"Yeah, well, me too. I only smoke at night and never in front of Simon!"

She lit another one and blew the smoke, checking the yard to make sure the guys weren't on their way inside. "Yeah, old Valerie! She must have gone down with half the staff at the Medical University before Jack would believe it. He was devastated. It was a good thing she died because I don't think Jack would have divorced her under any circumstances."

"Why? Are you kidding?"

"Nope. He loves his son so much; I guess he was afraid she'd get custody and take him to another state."

"Well, that's exactly what I did to my husband, but it was okay with him."

"Oh, God, Caroline! I am so sorry! I had no idea! I didn't mean to say . . ."

"It's okay," I said, "it really is!" I laughed because she was so upset that she had offended me. Then she laughed too. We could hear the men coming. She quickly drowned her cigarette under the faucet and threw it in the garbage can.

"Me and my big mouth," she said. "Why don't we open another bottle of vino? It's gonna take a lot of grapes to digest my cooking!"

She wasn't kidding. We drank three bottles of wine on top of the beer the guys had. The chicken was torched and unchewable, so I pushed it around the plate, eating salad, which did not absorb the alcohol. That explained my extreme state of inebriation. I was so busy listening to them talk and tell stories, I just continued to drink.

I was very sleepy and just wanted to close my eyes. The next thing I knew, Jack had me over his shoulder like a sack of potatoes, and was telling them good night. Everyone was giggling and I knew it was because of me.

I don't remember a thing about driving anywhere. All I knew was that I woke up and he was tucking me into a bed and saying, "I'll call your mother and tell her you've decided to stay over. Don't worry. Just sleep. You're gonna need to get in shape, Miss Caroline, if you want to run with this crowd."

I slept so hard, I sat up with a jolt from the morning light. I was in a man's pajama top. Jack's. Shit! What had I done? I looked around. It was a very nice room, although it was covered in posters of race cars and sports trophies. I must have been in his son's room. Okay, I haven't been raped, I thought. I still had on my bra and panties. Thank God. And, I didn't put out. Oh, sure, there I was commending myself for my high morals when I had been carried out of a dinner party over his shoulder.

I fell back against the pillows, cursing myself for being such a damn fool. Jack was a nice man and I liked him a lot. Now, I'd never see him again. The door opened and I had no place to hide.

"You alive?" he said. "Want some coffee?"

I groaned, dove under the pillow, and pulled the covers over my head. "I'm so embarrassed I could die."

He sat on the side of the bed and fished around under the covers for my hand. He took it into his and leaned over the layers of cotton and duck feathers that covered my head and whispered, "If you *could* drink like those characters, I'd have serious doubts about your character, Miss Caroline. The fact that you caved in is a good sign."

"It is?" I said, from under the pillow.

"It is. Now come on out like a good girl and drink this. Doctor's orders."

I know I looked like a shameful thing—if I didn't, I sure felt like one. I took the mug from him and drank. It was delicious coffee.

"Thanks. What is this? Guatemalan roast with a touch of Colombian, ground by Juan Valdez's own little hands?"

"Maxwell House," he said, smiling. He smelled so good.

"Figures. Jack? I'm sorry." I said this trying not to breathe my funky breath in his direction.

"Don't be silly, nothing to apologize for."

I rolled over and sat up. My head was a little squirrelly. "I need a shower."

He stood and pulled me to my feet. "Aspirin's in the medicine cabinet."

Twenty steamy minutes later, I was dressed and smelling bacon. He was making breakfast. What a doll! I made up his son's bed and wandered out into his kitchen. It was beautiful—state-of-the-art everything. I glanced at my watch. It was eight o'clock.

"Don't you have to work today?" I said, munching on a piece of perfectly fried bacon. I knew I should call home and speak to Eric.

"Show me a doctor that works on Wednesday, and I'll show you a desperate man. In Charleston, Wednesday is golf day."

"Ah! Do you play golf?" I said.

"Nope." He motioned for me to sit at the table and I did. My mouth watered at the scrambled eggs and grits before me.

"God, this looks good," I said. "Thanks! This is so nice of—"

"You look good," he said.

In the cold light of day, sun on the rise, heat climbing and stone-cold sober, we took a long hard look at each other. This was it. Yep, that was just about all it took. I was about to be taken back to bed by Jack Taylor, and we had no intention of sleeping. He took my hand and I followed him.

He was amazing. The whole thing was amazing. We fit. I loved the way he looked, he smelled and tasted. His skin was cool and smooth; his arms and chest were firm and beautiful. I was stunned. It was real. Right there and then, we were falling—together—into something that felt very much like real love. The kind you can't deny and can't fake—the kind that lasts forever. The genuine article. I was transformed. I knew real love was out there, but not out there for me. Or so I had thought. I rested my cheek on his chest, listening to his heart, and he stroked my hair. And, it wasn't just the sex. Hell no. It was me letting my defenses down, letting him into my heart, him letting me into his. For whatever reason, it seemed we had chosen the same moment to surrender. I knew he could take care of me and I knew I could take care of him. I could love him more and more.

"Where have you been all my life?" he said, lifting my chin to him.

"Ah, Dr. Cliché, obviously in the wrong places," I said.

He smiled at me again and said, "I mean it."

I said, "Amazing."

46

ROLLING! ROLLING! ROLLING DOWN THE RIVER!

Jack, Trip, and Eric had all gone out on Trip's boat Friday afternoon while Mother, Millie, and I put the final preparations on Saturday morning's party. I had pretty well exhausted myself running around gathering all the things we needed. It was to be a pontoon party—a flotilla of three, closely joined, slowly traveling the Edisto—to mark Mother's life as a celebration.

I had rented two pontoons from a company in Summerville and borrowed one from a friend of Trip's. Millie and I set about decorating them while Mother, reclining in a lawn chair on the dock, gave out liberal advice, to which we said, "Yes, yes!" and then promptly ignored every word.

The railings of all three were festooned in navy and white sheer fabric for the colors of South Carolina's flag. The lead boat would fly the flag of the United States, the second, the state flag, and the third, the flag of England—

in recognition of our ancestors. No Confederate flag, thank you.

Boat one would have music and speakers; boat two, the ice bucket, refreshments, and a microphone for sending messages to the shore. All three boats would have fake palmetto trees and huge bouquets of fresh roses to signify Mother's love of this place and the flowers she grew with such care and pride. A cameraman hired for the occasion would be on boat three with Mother (in her fan-back rattan chair) to film the others.

"I don't see why you're not on the lead boat," I said.

"Because I want to watch my family and friends, that's why. Is Frances Mae coming with the girls?"

"Yes, and she's making ham salad sandwiches," I said.

"Dear heavenly Father, please ask her not to put olives in it. I hate olives."

"My pleasure. Any excuse to tell Frances Mae she's screwing up is a welcome invitation," I said. The wounds weren't healed completely.

Mother arched her eyebrows at me. "Claws in, Sheena. I don't want any trouble tomorrow. Did y'all invite Reverend Moore?"

"Yes, Lord, I did," Millie said.

"Good; see that he gets enough food and booze. The clergy love to drink and they are always starving," she said. "Everyone knows that."

"Like she's the expert on clergy," I said to Millie.

"Don't make jokes, missy, your mother has changed her heart about many things lately. Many things. And it's all good, yanh?"

I knew that meant that Mother was praying. Hell, I was praying, especially since that Bible kept showing up on my night table. If I put it in my closet, it was back by nightfall. If I put it in the drawer, it was out again. You bet I was praying.

I was praying Mother wouldn't suffer, I prayed my affection for Jack was going to grow and that he wouldn't turn out to be another freak from sex hell. I prayed that Eric would come to understand his grandmother's illness and death without a painful trauma, that Frances Mae would somehow become civilized, that Trip—recognizing her complete metamorphosis—wouldn't dump her, that Trip would never gamble again, that Millie would live forever, that we would all be all right. And, I prayed that my daddy would be there to take Mother's hand. I was praying with all my might that somebody, God, somebody was listening.

It was mind-boggling to me. Mother was dying before my eyes and there wasn't a thing in the world I could do. And, not a single complaint from her either.

By Saturday morning, the world had changed. It was the day of the beginning of Mother leaving us, and in her own way. She seemed pretty much the same, except that she refused the tray of breakfast I brought to her. She didn't appear to be in any pain—at least, if she was, she didn't say so.

"Is it a crime if I don't feel like breakfast?" she said.

She was brushing her hair in front of the mirror over her chest of drawers. I turned around, looking for a spot to place the tray, stepping by Shiva and her shoulder bags hanging from his arms.

"This is actually rather practical," I said, adding, "weird, but practical."

I could feel Mother's smile without looking at her, but when I raised my eyes to meet hers in the mirror, I caught her in a grimace of discomfort. She leaned forward on the chest of drawers, holding on to its edge for balance.

"I'm all right!" she said.

"No, you're not," I said, "where's your medication?"

"In the bathroom medicine cabinet, third shelf, on the left."

I hurried to find the bottle, and saw that she was taking Darvoset. Jack told me that the time would fast approach when Darvoset wouldn't do the job, that she'd need morphine.

I handed her two pills and a glass of water and noticed she was clammy, that her forehead was wet with perspiration.

"Come on, let's sit down." I led her to the side of her bed and she sat. "You okay? Want to talk about it?"

"What is there to say? That this hurts? Yes, it hurts, but as long as it hurts, I'm still alive."

I was silent. She searched my face and my eyes and then she took my hand.

"My darling daughter," she said. The tears began to flow. "I don't much like the idea of this, you know. I mean, I've had a wonderful life and I'm grateful for that. But I finally find you again and now I'm the one who has to leave. It doesn't seem fair."

I began to cry silently. She continued talking. As she spoke I found myself trying to memorize her words. I was racked by a terrible fear that this would be our last conversation, knowing that our parade of pontoons was the last. All prior river exhibitions, the ones I swore humiliated me, were now treasures. As were her costumes, her outrageous behavior, and everything else that was a part of her. My anxiety increased as I realized then how precious these moments were. She was going and I couldn't follow. There was a limit to something I had never considered would truly end. I knelt in front of her and put my head in her lap while she stroked my hair. She was giving me

the comfort I had longed for as a child when Daddy died.
I only cried and tried to listen to her.

". . . oh, I know I wasn't everything you needed, but I
loved you, Caroline. I always loved you so. Everyone has
moments of complete stupidity! Well, I certainly had my
fair share! Maybe more! You were my little girl and I just
hated it when you grew up. Do you understand that?"

"Yes, ma'am, I do," I said.

"Well, it does my heart good to see you with Eric.
You're a better mother than I was and I'm so proud of
you, Caroline."

"Oh, please don't say that. Mother? Maybe you weren't
all goopy and touchy but you're Miss Lavinia! How is the
world going to manage without Miss Lavinia? I just don't
know."

She lifted my face and although we were a sopping sight
with our red eyes, when she smiled at me, I smiled right
back.

"It's going to be all right, they'll have a Miss Caroline,
dear girl."

"No, there's only one of you!" I wanted to cry again.

"And thank God for that, yanh? You'll just have to figure out on your own how you'll go about it!"

That made us giggle like old friends.

"Reach in my top drawer like a good girl and hand me
the blue felt sack with my pearls."

I did and I took them out, handing them to her. "Thank
you," she said.

Their luster was brilliant in the morning light and she
fingered each one, then stopped. I knew she was thinking
about Daddy.

"When I see my Nevil, I'm going to thank him again
for these." She put them on as she had a thousand times

before. "And, I'm going to tell him what a wonderful daughter we have."

I began to choke up again.

"Will you please not cry? If you use your tears now, you won't be able to sob at my funeral! I'm counting on that, you know."

Her eyes twinkled. Mother's wicked humor would be the thing that got us through the coming weeks.

"You kill me," I said.

"Good. Now, for the love of God, go put on some makeup. There's a photographer coming and I don't want you to look like a scrubwoman!"

"Miss Lavinia?"

"Yes?"

"You're impossible."

She shooed me away and I left her to do as she said. I went to my room and the Bible was on my bedside table. I decided to test the Good Book once more and shoved it under my pillow, locked my door, and went into my bathroom to put on my makeup.

I forgot all about it while I flossed, brushed, rinsed, gargled, washed, applied fruit acid, moisturizer, and antiperspirant, and creamed my legs. I brushed the dickens out of my hair and looked in the mirror. She was right. I needed makeup. It was nearly nine when I finished the old *daily toilette*. While I was digging through my closet for something not black to wear, the phone rang.

It was Matthew.

"Long time, no hear," he said.

"Oh, Matthew!" I flopped on the bed and tried to think fast. I knew I owed him some explanation of why I wasn't returning his phone calls. "You wouldn't believe what's been going on around here."

"Try me. You're Miss Lavinia's daughter and Trip's

sister. I know there's an outrageous story in there somewhere."

After I thanked him a million times for getting Trip's
butt out of trouble I told him about Mother.

"Please don't tell me this," he said.

"It's true and this morning she's going to break it to her
two best friends while we float down the Edisto on three
pontoons."

"Seems like a crazy way to ambush your best friends
with bad news, but nobody's asking me, I reckon."

I was quiet at his words. He was right.

"Matthew? You are an angel. No, an archangel.
Thanks."

"You're welcome."

"You know? It seems like all I ever do is thank you for
something."

"Yeah, seems that way, doesn't it? Listen, Caroline, I'm
awful sorry about your momma. If I can do anything, it
would be an honor."

"I'll call you, Matthew. I swear I will."

We hung up and I made a mental note to call him.
Maybe I'd make dinner for him. Yes. That would be nice.
God knows, he had the patience of a saint with me. The
least I could do was cook something for him. And, keep
the information on Jack to myself.

The doorbell rang. I knew it was one of Mother's
friends—either Miss Sweetie, Miss Nancy, or both. I had
to stop her from telling them this way. On the way out of
my door, I glanced at my bedside table. There it was. The
Bible.

I had no time to waste on the supernatural. I ran to
Mother's room. She had left and was going down the
stairs, wearing a billowy white silk caftan and South Sea

pearl earrings to match her necklace. She looked positively virginal and angelic.

"Mother!"

Eric was running from the kitchen, sliding in his socks across the glossy heart pine floors, to answer the door too. She stopped and faced me.

"What? Come on, we have a parade in my honor to attend!"

"Mother, please! Eric, get the door."

"Going there anyway!" he called out. I was momentarily amazed by the fact that three people could simultaneously inhabit the same space—all with different realities.

I pulled her back into my room to talk to her. After I said my piece, she took a deep breath, sucking in the air supply of Charleston County, and then released it.

"Oh, fine!" she said. "I'll tell them later."

As it turned out, she didn't have to. We—Mother, Miss Sweetie, Miss Nancy, Eric, and I—proceeded to the docks, where the photographer waited with Frances Mae and Amelia. Trip was already on the boat with Millie, Reverend Moore (who had very skinny legs in his madras Bermudas), and Mr. Jenkins.

Frances Mae rushed toward us and threw her arms around Mother. "Oh! Mother Wimbley! When I realized I was making ham salad for your last river parade, all I did was cry!"

Miss Sweetie and Miss Nancy looked at each other and then at Mother.

"Have I said something wrong?" Frances Mae said.

"Frances Mae? I swear to God, I could just wring your neck," I said.

At least she had the brains and humanity to flush deep red. Amelia hid behind her. Mother took her friends, looping her arms through theirs, and walked to the lawn chairs.

"Oh, God damn," Frances Mae said, "I've done it again! Why do I always put my foot in my mouth?"

"Because you're an ass, that's why," I said, not giving a hoot if she exploded.

The breeze was coming from the river, blowing my hair in my face, but I stood and faced her, thinking that I might just slap the hell out of her. Little Amelia stepped forward to break the tension, or so I thought at the moment.

"My momma's not an ass, Aunt Caroline, *you* are!"

My eyes shot open to the size of saucers and I bent over to get very close to my niece's face. "Oh. No, I don't think I am, Amelia. But your mother is," I said, throwing caution out with propriety, "she's an *ass* and *so are you!*"

"Well! I never!" Frances Mae grabbed her daughter, the one with enough meanness in her to scare all the alligators on the planet back to the Everglades, turned on her heel, and rushed toward the dock, shouting, "Trip? Darlin'! Trip? Darlin'! Your sister . . ."

"Oh, blow it out your ass, Frances Mae."

She didn't hear me, but I felt better for having said it. I wasn't even sure what it meant, but that didn't matter.

I joined Mother, Miss Sweetie, and Miss Nancy.

". . . and I just wasn't going to do this without y'all," Mother was saying. "Here! Take a tissue!"

Both women were crying and took them, wiping their eyes. I put my arm around Miss Sweetie, whose chest rose and fell with heavy sadness.

"Well, we knew it anyway, Lavinia," Miss Nancy said, "we just didn't know it for sure."

"We've been knowing you all our life! Of course we knew!" Miss Sweetie said.

"I told Frances Mae something bad," I said. They looked at me. "Real bad. I've been reported to my brother."

"Good!" they said together.

"Frances Mae needs a good whipping, if you ask me!" Miss Nancy said.

"She doesn't have a sensitive bone in her entire body!" Miss Sweetie said.

"Or a smart one," I said for good measure.

"Gee," Mother said, "I'm really gonna miss her, yanh? Maybe I'll haunt her ugly self."

With that they began to laugh, releasing the tension and some of the sorrow. They still had their friend and I still had my mother. We would not waste a moment of it wallowing around in self-pity.

I heard a car and turned to see Frances Mae leaving in a cloud of dust as fast as she could. We giggled again.

"I hope she took her nasty ham salad with her," I said.

"Don't worry," Miss Sweetie said, "I've got enough food for a hundred men."

"And, I brought my special chicken, Lavinia. Fattening as hell."

"Good! Come on," Mother said, "the river's calling! Let's go, yanh?"

Matthew's car pulled in. He got out wearing shorts and a knit shirt, looking very good.

"Would you look at what I see?" Miss Nancy said, with all the slow phrasing of a construction worker ogling a pretty girl on a hot summer's day.

"He's a big one," Miss Sweetie said, as Matthew got closer "Yessireee!"

"Yeah, look how he walks. I'll bet it's eight, no, ten inches," Mother said.

"Mother!"

Jesus, these girls were terrible! It was sweet of him to come by.

"Morning, ladies!" He nodded to them and then gave

me a light kiss on the cheek. "Thought your brother might
need a bartender!"

"I'm sure he'd appreciate the help," I said.

Matthew and I walked away toward the boats. I turned
around to make sure Mother and her friends were following. They were clucking, high-fiving me and measuring in
the air as though Matthew's britches held an eel. Honest
to God. They were some bunch.

We boarded the boat and Mr. Jenkins and Matthew took
each lady's hand to be sure they didn't fall in the drink.
We pushed off from the dock. Trip put on his sunglasses
and barely spoke to us; certainly he made no reference to
Frances Mae's departure. Good. I didn't want to hear it
anyway.

The day was glorious—sun shining, no humidity, a perfect breeze. The sounds of birds blended with "La Vie en
Rose" sung by Piaf. We drank champagne—mimosas—
and munched on Miss Nancy's barbecued chicken, deviled
eggs made with shrimp that were the most divine I'd ever
tasted, ever, asparagus with the perfect crunch wrapped in
proscuitto, and Miss Sweetie's mondo strawberries with
whipped cream. Would you believe Mother had requested,
and received, a Sonny's shredded pork barbecue sandwich
on a hamburger roll and one large onion ring.

"Mother! Where on earth did you get that?"

"Mr. Jenkins went down to Charleston for me!"

Mr. Jenkins looked up at Mother and grinned so wide I
could count his back teeth. He loved Mother and I was
sure he knew everything that was going on.

"You're a doll, Mr. Jenkins," I said, "did anybody ever
tell you that?"

"Nope, but I wouldn't have been able to read that menu
without my Miss Lavinia. I reckon I'd go to hell for her
iffin she ask me, yanh? Yes, sir, I would."

"Well, let's hope you don't have to come there to find me!"

Now that the bad news was out in the open, Mother fully intended to horrify us with gallows humor. But, we just shook our heads instead. Even in the face of her own demise, she was irrepressible. And amazing, gracious, and very beautiful.

Mr. Jenkins turned his watery eyes away from her as she left our pontoon to hop on another. He looked over the expanse of water, marsh grass, tiny creatures all over the small shores, and out at the cloudless blue sky. I could tell his thoughts were a million miles away. I put my hand on his shoulder and gave it a squeeze.

"It's okay, Mr. Jenkins," I said.

"We don't truck with Gawd's will, Miss Caroline, no sir. That don't mean you have to like it. But you got to accept it. Ain't that right, Millie?"

"I hear you, Jenkins! You gonna spoil Miss L!" Millie said, teasing him. "Oh, yeah, Jenkins got his philosophy book out now! Y'all better watch out!"

"It's the Bible—not just some old book, Millie! The Bible!"

"Don't talk to me about Bibles," I said, "I've got one with legs!"

I told them the strange story and they threw their heads back, laughing good and hard.

"It's not funny, y'all!" I said. "It's seriously strange!"

"No, it ain't!" Mr. Jenkins said. "It's just your daddy coming to get your mother!"

"Yeah," I said, "that's what your girlfriend says too."

Millie raised her eyebrows at Mr. Jenkins and they laughed again. It was true, I decided to believe it. There were many worse things than that which could have been going on. And, hell, it was the Lowcountry.

Millie, Mr. Jenkins, and I were alone on the lead pontoon.

Matthew, Reverend Gold Digger—who was there for some spiritual good measure for Mother—and the fellow with the video camera were on the second boat with Trip, talking and nodding their heads. Matthew looked up at me every now and then, smiling. I never was worried that Matthew would be angry with me over seeing Jack, but suddenly I began to fret that Jack wouldn't be happy to see me with Matthew. I should have invited him, but I hadn't invited Matthew either. It had just worked out that way.

People on their docks and in passing boats smiled and waved. The infamous Miss Lavinia was at it again. And her daughter was up to it too!

Matthew got up and came to my side with a bottle of champagne, refilling my glass.

"You're seeing someone, aren't you," he said.

"Yes. Yes, I am. I was going to tell . . ."

He held his hand up for me to be quiet. First, he looked out over the water and then he looked back at me. "Caroline, I loved you when we were children and I'm probably gonna go on loving you until I die. But, this time, we started out as friends. That's not the worst thing—to be friends. You know?"

"Oh! Matthew!" I threw my arms around his neck. "I would love to be your friend!"

I guessed that Trip had told Matthew about Jack. It was alright. Matthew was a sweetheart, but he wasn't Jack. There I was, on a pontoon, drinking champagne in the middle of the day, and realizing I was truly in love, more deeply than I had ever been in my life. Mother's crazy parade had made me see it.

Mother's plan to be a voyeur at her own party had

failed. Miss Sweetie and Miss Nancy sat on her either side in folding chairs and Eric curled up at her feet. Her left hand never left Eric's head or shoulder. I watched her explain the stories they recounted to him. He was completely enchanted by her and she by him.

She might have been wearing one of her dramatic outfits, and yes, we played every song with the word *rose* in it we could find. And, okay, it was a corny tradition, these parades of ours. But when the red ball of the sun slipped under the Edisto River that evening, I was pretty sure that life didn't get much better than being in the place you loved most, surrounded by the people closest to your heart.

47

THE SECOND TIME AROUND

Jack called the next day. It was Sunday, around ten in the morning. I was getting dressed for church.

"Hey, how are you doing?" he said.

"How am I doing? Good question. Not so hot, I think. I'm on the way to church to beg God's mercy."

"Want company?"

"Sure. Why not?"

I promised to save him a seat and sure enough, about fifteen minutes into the service, he appeared at my side. Eric and I moved closer to each other to make room for him in the small pew. He smelled and looked good enough to nibble.

Mother had stayed home. The festivities of yesterday had worn her out and she wanted to sleep. Miss Sweetie and Miss Nancy sat behind us.

The small choir was in full form that morning and Reverend Moore's eyes swept the congregation, surprise in them when he saw me next to Jack.

I was so upset during the entire service. I remained composed, but inside I quaked. Thoughts of losing Mother crawled up my spine and down again. There was no escape from what we were all going to have to face.

There in that tiny church, I admitted to myself that I was waffling—one day falling apart and the next as strong as I could be. How could this upheaval occur in this sliver of time? Everything was different now.

I had finally finished the two pending decorating jobs in New York by giving them over to another decorator I knew. I didn't care. That had been easy enough to do, but it was also the final chapter in my life there. Another closure. Another relief.

I had established a nice friendship with Matthew and was also terrifically happy that I hadn't blown that apart by my relationship with Jack. I was determined to find him someone wonderful to love. Matthew was one of the sweetest men I had ever known.

Some nights I'd rest in the folds of deep slumber and others, I paced the floors, reading that Bible, trying to communicate with Daddy, asking him to ask God to leave Mother with us for a little while longer.

As though he could read my mind, Jack reached over and put his hand on mine as it rested on the pew in front of us. From the corner of my eye, I could see Eric's notice of it and the smallest of smiles crept across his face. He liked Jack. Jack listened to Eric's thoughts and never talked down to him. If anything, Jack was thoroughly delighted to be around a little boy. His own son was in his last year at the Citadel and I guessed it was nostalgic for him to have a young boy around again.

That wasn't true and I knew it. Why was I always trying to protect myself? Well, I had good reasons. I had to admit,

Jack was genuinely great. He liked Eric for Eric. It made me love him more. Yes, it did.

When the ushers came around with the collection plate, Jack gave Eric a five-dollar bill to contribute. Eric looked up to me for approval and I nodded my head. It was the first time I had been in a church with my son and a man I loved. I couldn't help but feel sentimental.

Outside, when the service was over, we milled around a little saying hello to people. Eric ran around with some children he had gotten to know and inside of no time, his shirttail was out and he had grass stains on the knees of his trousers. Across the yard, I saw Miss Sweetie was all dressed in red linen, with gold jewelry and a large straw hat. I saw her with Miss Nancy, who wore a white silk tunic over pants with slides; both of them were wildly flirting with Reverend Moore. Reverend Moore just gobbled them up, smiling broadly and waving us over.

"Morning, Miss Caroline!" Reverend Moore said. "Do I know your friend? Welcome! Welcome!" he said to Jack, shaking his hand until I thought it would fly off into the hedges.

"Great sermon, Reverend! I'm Jack Taylor."

Miss Sweetie and Miss Nancy were all a-titter.

"Dr. Taylor! I'm Nancy, Lavinia's oldest friend! It's so nice to have you here with us!"

"She is not Lavinia's oldest friend, Dr. Taylor, I am! I'm Sweetie! And I've known Caroline since the day she opened her eyes in this world."

"Oh, fine, Sweetie, you've known her six months longer than me. Big deal," Miss Nancy said and turned to Reverend Moore. "Here we are, straight from Sunday services, already bickering. Do you have plans for breakfast, Reverend?"

"No, ladies, I don't. Shall we meet . . . where?"

Miss Sweetie and Miss Nancy looked at each other, awash in the thrill of entertaining Reverend Moore.

"Let's go to the country club!" Miss Sweetie said.

"Done! Meet you ladies there in an hour? I just have to tidy up here."

"That's fine, Reverend. Caroline? Do tell Lavinia that we'll be around to see her later?" Miss Nancy said with a wink.

What she meant was *Tell Lavinia we bagged the preacher!* Well, Reverend Moore was a big boy, and he was walking into this with his eyes open. After all, I was sure he thought he would be safe at a country club!

"I'll tell her, don't worry," I said and gave them both a peck on the cheek.

I turned to Jack and said, "Have you seen my boy?"

"Let's go find him," he said.

I could almost hear Miss Nancy and Miss Sweetie sighing in relief, approval, and happiness that I had a man in my life again. Between Miss Lavinia, her friends, and Millie, I had a surplus of mothers. We walked away from them, arm in arm, in search of Eric. At the side of the church, Jack stopped and spun me around.

"What?" I said.

"Is this possible?"

"What?"

"That I feel this way about you?"

There wasn't a shred of guile in his voice. It was a serious question. A breeze came from nowhere, a gentle reminder from Mother ACE to pay attention to the moment. We looked into each other's eyes and saw each other. We began to laugh.

"Are you gonna go all mushy on me, Doctor?"

"Yes, ma'am, I am."

"Good. I don't want to be the only mushy one around here."

For a few more moments we stood there. It was one of those infinitely stupid times when you size the other guy up, try to predict the future, calculate the risk, and decide whether or not it was worth it. As though you could help yourself from falling into the void anyway.

"I want you to meet my son," he said.

"Oh, God, the ultimate test," I said. Images of an angry cadet with a gun crossed my mind.

"He's gonna love you," Jack said, smiling wide, eyes dancing.

"What makes you so sure, Dr. Genius?"

"Because *I* do."

"You do?" I couldn't believe it! Jack was in love? With me? How could he be so sure? I mean, I was in love with him, but I hadn't said it.

"Yeah, I do."

"Don't say *I do*. It makes me nervous."

The sun was all over us; we were dazzled by it, by each other. In my peripheral vision I saw Eric running toward us.

"Time to go?" Eric said. "Mom? You okay?"

I struggled to peel my eyes away from Jack's beautiful face. He looked like something from a Greek coin. How was it that he became more handsome every time I looked at him? I just wanted that moment to last and last.

"Mom?"

I put my arm through Jack's and offered my other one to Eric. With Jack on my right and Eric on my left, I could take on the world. I'd read about levitation in Tibetan Buddhism, and I could have sworn that on the walk across the lawn to the parking lot my feet never touched the ground. No lie.

48

FREE AT LAST

August

In the coming weeks, all focus was on Mother. In an odd way, her illness seemed to cure everyone around her of what ailed *them*. Millie continued to plaster her with herbal ointments that seemed to impede the violence of Mother's now-frequent nausea. She prayed with Mother and sang to her, filling Mother's final days with friendship and love. She became Mother's gatekeeper, regulating her visitations from her other friends. She'd call Miss Sweetie and Miss Nancy with daily reports.

She's having a good day today. Why don't y'all come on over and play some bridge with her? And, for God's sake, please keep her out of the chat rooms, yanh?

They would arrive and for several hours, there would be riotous laughter and muffled whispers followed by more laughter as they entertained her and themselves—Mother propped up in her bed, her laptop computer up and running.

Their cards were dealt for bridge, but I knew they remained untouched—they were all in LoveChat@aol.com. We were all sure that they were still up to their old games—impersonating twenty-year-old college students with insatiable sexual appetites. The laughter had to do her a world of good.

I would walk them to the door when they left.

"This is breaking my heart, Caroline," Miss Sweetie said.

"Mine too," Miss Nancy said.

"It's a nightmare," I said, "but at least she has y'all. She's not alone."

We stood at the door in the foyer, no one sure of what to say next, when the real question we all wanted answered was, *How much longer will we have her and what can we do?*

Mother's lawyer paid her several visits and we all gave her total privacy for those meetings. We knew she was clearing up some details of her will. And, she consulted with Richard, who kept offering to fly down here and be with her.

"I'd like to see her while she's still well enough," he said to me.

"It's up to you, Richard. I'm sure Eric would like to see you too."

It seemed that once I had given him permission to come, he lost interest. "Well, I'll have to check my schedule. I'll get back to you."

He never called to confirm a visit.

Jack was now a fixture in our lives and after several weeks of Mother's not leaving the bed, he insisted we hire a nurse and put Mother on a drip to administer low dosages of morphine. It was increasingly difficult for Mother to walk—she was losing the feeling in her legs, and had to be helped to the bathroom.

"I will not be a drug addict!"

"I won't let you become a drug addict, Miss Lavinia," Jack would say. "You're too fine a lady."

We all knew the truth was that she wouldn't live long enough to develop a habit. We wanted her out of pain, and although she still didn't complain, her protestations against pain management were weak. Morphine it was, administered by a wonderful nurse named Carolyn Nelson who claimed it was her privilege to care for Mother. She was an older lady possessed with a quiet nature and sat by Mother's side doing cross-stitch for her grandchildren in between dosages. She gave Mother sponge baths, changed her gowns, brushed her hair and, most importantly, didn't get in Millie's way.

The pecking order was well established and maintained. Millie would continue bringing Mother her favorite foods on beautiful trays and cajole Mother into taking a few bites.

Eric continued to study, even though he had officially completed the required work for the year. Rusty had him hooked on science—astronomy and botany in particular. The early summer skies offered fabulous views to the naked eye, but boggled the mind with a telescope. Rusty had a portable telescope with a ten-inch lens that she set up on the docks for their enjoyment. And gathering specimens for study couldn't have been easier between Millie's gardens and the habitats of the riverbanks. Under her tutelage, Eric could name most of the flora and fauna and recognized all the major constellations in the night sky.

Rusty and I had become friends of a sort. She volunteered to be Eric's companion during Mother's illness, but

we all knew she was deeply in love with Trip. And that
he was with her.

That would have been objectionable, but given the
change in him when she was around, we all had to agree
that she was bringing out his better side. She attended
Gambler's Anonymous meetings with him. There was no
evidence of him gambling—on the contrary—and he frequently thanked Mother for getting him out of trouble and
me for having Matthew do the hard part.

Matthew? Well, Matthew came by once or twice a week.
We had a few dinners together in the kitchen with Eric
and Millie and on occasion, Jack was there too. Matthew
and Jack got along fine.

It didn't seem right to sit at Mother's table without her.
Most of my energy went toward trying to will Mother's
recovery. Sit in her dining room? No. Either her seat would
be empty or someone would fill it. It was like sacrilege
and we continued our days in denial waiting for her to get
well, watching her die.

Frances Mae tried to attempt repair with us, sending
Mother homemade cards and letters from her girls, photographs to be placed around her bedroom, and hard can-
dies to keep Mother's mouth from getting dry.

But, Mother slept a lot then, unaware of all the activity
around her. Sometimes for two or three days straight. I
spent a lot of time in my room, reading the Bible that had
now progressed to following me from room to room.

"I get the message!" I said to the air in the living room
when it appeared on the coffee table. So I would open it
at random and read. I kept stumbling on passages about
God's mercy, and came to understand that Divine mercy
was about forgiving our imperfections and His understanding of our weaknesses. Boy, I had plenty of those!

Jack called Saturday and wanted to see me. Mother was

asleep. Millie had gone to Charleston with Mr. Jenkins; Eric was fishing with Trip. Frances Mae was coming with the girls for dinner. Seeing her was unavoidable. At least she was bringing a casserole. I said to Jack, okay, I want to take a nap first, so why don't you come out around four, and we can all have dinner outside?

"Fine," he said. "Caroline?"

"Mm-hmm?"

"You okay? Can I bring you anything?"

"No, thanks, Jack, but you're a sweetheart to ask."

"Susan and Simon send you their best."

"Tell Susan I'll call her soon, okay?"

"Sure. They wanted to come out with me, but I told them it was just too much with everything going on."

"Thanks, I appreciate that."

Jack knew that this wasn't the time to look for a commitment from me. Yes, I loved him, and more each day. He knew it too. When love was like ours, no one had to make any great announcements. Our growing love was a given. But, right then, Mother's comfort was my first priority. I was exhausted from stress and climbing the steps was almost like climbing a mountain. My legs were heavy and I could hardly hold my eyes open. My French doors were open to receive the fresh air, and I slipped between my sheets, sleeping almost immediately.

I woke up to the sound of rain, a constant rapping of drops on the roof. I had been dreaming of Daddy. He was young and handsome and had come for a visit. Was that it? Yes. In my dream, I knew there was a reason he didn't live with us anymore, but I couldn't think of what it was. He gave me a Hershey bar. *This is for you,* he seemed to say. *But I'm grown up, Daddy,* I said. *Then give it to Eric.* We were in the hall by the front door and Daddy stopped looking at me and looked up the stairs. His face was filled with wonder. Mother was coming down, face beaming, and radiant—her delight at seeing him so powerful, so apparent. Then I woke up. *It's just a dream,* I told myself. I knew that it wasn't.

I rolled over and looked at my bedside clock. Three in the afternoon. I decided to check on Mother.

"Is she sleeping?" I asked Mrs. Nelson.

"Indeed, she is. Why don't you sit with her and I'll go get us some iced tea."

"Sure, thanks."

She left the room and I pulled a chair to Mother's bedside. She looked so tiny and fragile. I took her hand in mine and just looked at her. Time passed and she stirred a little, smacking her lips from dryness.

"Do you want some water, Mother?"

She nodded her head, so I poured some water into her glass and put the straw to her lips.

"Ice," she said.

I dug into the bucket and put small slivers of ice on the end of a spoon for her.

"Here we go," I said, slipping the spoon between her lips.

She sucked on the ice chips and I went to the bathroom to get a cold cloth. I wiped her face, carefully and slowly. I don't know why I did that except that I remembered she did it for me when I was little and sick with a virus. It always made me feel better.

"How are you feeling today, Miss Lavinia?"

She opened her eyes and looked at me, recognizing me.

"Caroline?"

"Yes, ma'am?"

"Caroline?"

Her voice was weak. "Yes, ma'am?"

"Pearls. Get them. Call me Mother. Still Mother."

"Always," I said and I choked on tears. I couldn't help it.

I went to her dresser and took the pearls from the drawer. Maybe she wanted to wear them and so what, I thought, why shouldn't she?

Her eyes were closed again, so I put them in her hand. Silently, she felt them and a smile crossed her face.

"Put them on," she said. "Don't need them anymore."

"Oh, Mother, I don't know . . ."

"No," she said, "put them on."

By now I was sobbing, realizing this was the last conversation we would have. There was no one to call—except the nurse. Selfishly, I guess, I didn't want to share this moment with her. Or anyone. I put on the pearls.

"I'll take good care of them, Mother, thank you."

She opened her eyes again, looking at me with such love and intensity, the tears just streaming down my face; she patted my hand.

"Don't cry, baby," she said, tenderly and almost whispering, "I'm just going home." It was a strain for her to find her words and a struggle to speak them.

"Please don't leave me, Mother, I'm not ready." I put my head on the mattress next to her.

"Eric," she said in a whisper.

I raised my head and tried to understand what she meant. "What?"

"I wanted to see him grow." She sighed and closed her eyes again. "Regret. My only one."

"I'll pray for you. Every day."

"Caroline?" She spoke louder, as though she thought I had left the room.

"Yes, ma'am?"

"My roses! Smell them?"

"No, Momma, I don't."

"Momma. I like that. Momma."

She sat straight up in the bed and looked at something I couldn't see.

"Oh!" she said. It was an exclamation of surprise.

"What? What is it?"

"Mother!" She stopped staring in her state of . . . was it hallucination? She looked at me, then laid her head down again. "Fertilize the roses for me, all right?"

A full sentence, whispered, but spoken nonetheless. She drifted off to sleep. Or at least I thought it was sleep.

By three-thirty, Mrs. Nelson had called Jack and he was already on his way. Millie and Mr. Jenkins returned and joined me at Mother's bedside. Trip and Eric came back, triumphant with a cooler filled with fish. When Trip got the word, he kept Eric out on the docks on the pretense of cleaning their haul. Frances Mae and the girls came and Millie let them poke their noses in for a moment and then shooed them downstairs.

When Jack examined Mother, he intimated that it wouldn't be long.

"Days?" we asked.

"Hours, I'm afraid," he said. His sympathy was genuine. "I'll be right here."

Mother's breathing became labored and loud. It frightened me and Millie.

"We'd better call Miss Sweetie and Miss Nancy," I said.

"I'll do it," she said, "you stay with your mother."

Hours passed and Millie lifted the sheets to look at Mother's feet.

"What are you doing?" I said.

"Feet stiff and blood pooling," she said and pointed to the dark marks on Mother's lower legs. "Dear Jesus, it's almost time."

I was so unnerved, that I called Richard. Maybe it was

some last-ditch effort to let him redeem something of himself.

"Dr. Levine," he answered the phone with his name. I decided to ignore this.

"Richard?" My voice broke for the zillionth time that day. "Mother's dying."

"I know, Caroline, I'm sure this is difficult for you."

"No, I mean she's dying now. Today. Tonight. Can you come?"

"Sweetheart, I appreciate your anxiety, I truly do, but today is out of the question! It's already dark, and I have a seven-thirty breakfast meeting . . ."

"You said to call you if I needed you. I need you."

"Caroline, I'm sorry. I just can't. When she's dead, I'll come."

I hung up the phone without saying good-bye.

Our vigil lasted until around midnight. Everyone had come and gone from Mother's room except Frances Mae, who thought it was best to keep her girls downstairs. She was probably right.

Millie made coffee with all the caffeine she could and we drank it. Miss Sweetie passed around slices of strawberry pound cake and Miss Nancy passed through the rooms, picking up glasses, cups, just doing whatever she could to stay busy.

Trip poured liberal douses of bourbon into his coffee and offered it all around. Most of us declined it and he began to drink himself into a stupor. For once I couldn't blame him. His manliness was not required. Jack and Mr. Jenkins could perform whatever was required. The awful truth was that there wasn't anything anyone could do. Nature was taking its course.

At about one o'clock in the morning, I was alone in Mother's room with Jack and Millie.

"Why don't you ladies get some sleep?" Jack said. "I'll wake you if there's any change."

"Not me," Millie said, "I ain't leaving."

"Me either. How could I sleep anyway?"

"Well, I'm gonna go on down and fix myself a cup of coffee," he said.

"Humph," Millie said to me as he left the room, "think that man's gonna mess up my kitchen? I'll be right back. Lavinia? Don't go nowhere!"

Mother's breathing was so loud; it sounded like croup. And then, it stopped. Just like that. One minute she was here, the next minute she was gone. Like somebody pulled the plug. Just like that. I was stunned. I didn't know what to do, so I waited. I tried to hold her hand. When there was no reflex from her, I put it to rest by her side. I knew I should tell the others.

It took all my strength to get up and do this. I leaned over Mother first and kissed her forehead.

"Love you, Miss Lavinia," I said, "I love you."

I looked at her for a few more seconds and then went to deliver the worst news since my father's death. For some reason, almost everyone was in the living room or the foyer when I came down the stairs. I imagine the look on my face told them what I hadn't said.

"Oh, God," Miss Sweetie said, "she's gone, isn't she?"

"Yes," I said.

Jack ran up the steps and hugged me.

"Oh, God."

"I'm going to see about your mother," he said.

I wanted to kiss him for that. My eyes traveled the room for Millie, whose eyes met mine, and I saw Mr. Jenkins put his arms around her for comfort. Trip was in the chair with Frances Mae at his side. They were both weeping.

She stared at my neck. The pearls. I had forgotten that I even had them on.

"She ain't even cold and yewr already grabbing! Shame on you!" Frances Mae said.

"Shut your trap, Frances Mae," Trip said. "Just shut up!" He got up and came to my side.

"She gave them to me," I said evenly.

"I know she did, honey," Trip said. He put his arms around me and I cried like a baby, the same way I had when Daddy died, making sounds I didn't know were there inside me.

"Let's go outside," he said.

We passed Eric in the kitchen.

"Come on with us, baby," I said to him, "I've got something to tell you."

"Grandmother's dead, isn't she?"

"Yes, come on."

We left the house—my brother, my son, and I—and we did what we had always done when the pain was too great. We went to the river to listen to her song and searched the sky for signs of peace.

49

DETAILS

This may sound strange to say, but my mother's wake was one of the proudest moments of my life. I cannot put words to the feelings I had as hundreds of people came and went, telling me how they had loved my mother and my father too. I was their daughter. I made another oath with myself to live up to their name.

The noise level of the wake was deafening, people talking and telling stories. Somehow I knew Mother was there, listening, with Daddy. Every now and then I could feel her objection to a story or an event as they were described by her friends.

"I remember when she told me that Jackie Kennedy had called her to see if she and Nevil wanted to spend the weekend at the White House to discuss protocol," one friend said, "and she said, 'Ma'am, if it's an advisor on etiquette you seek, surely there is a book you can find in the Library of Congress!' Oh! She was something, all right! Can you imagine telling Jackie Kennedy no?"

I could feel Mother's spirit bristle. She had gone to Washington and advised Mrs. Kennedy; and a picture of the two of them stood on a table in the living room for as long as I could remember. She had told that story over and over. But it was funny, I had to admit.

Mother was truly larger than life, and if Mother's friends had turned out by the score in her honor, so had mine. Richard had flown in that morning, heart filled with apologies and arms filled with flowers. He felt terrible about not coming the day I had called. It didn't matter to me anymore.

Eric and I were in the front hall. Richard had just arrived.

"Caroline? I didn't know you meant she was dying right then! I just misunderstood, darling. Can you forgive me?"

"Sure, Richard, why don't you put your things in the guest room? Eric? Help your father, okay?"

That had taken care of that.

I spotted him now across the room at Bagnal's, talking to Jack. Susan and Simon were there too. Oh hell, I thought, let them talk. What harm could it cause? Then I saw Josh joining them and hurried to them to try and run a little damage control.

"Josh! How nice of you to come!" I shook his hand and then kissed his cheek.

Richard, Jack, and Simon stopped talking, watching to see who this man with the hair was.

"Hey, Caroline, I'm so sorry about your momma," Susan said.

"Thanks," I said, "y'all are so sweet to come."

Simon gave me a light kiss on the cheek and Josh wedged his way in between us.

"Hi! You okay? I mean, I'm real sorry. Your mother was a very cool lady," Josh said.

"Thanks. She thought you were pretty cool too!" I looked up at Richard and Jack. "Josh is one of Eric's tutors and very talented too!"

"Ah!" Richard said, "I've heard all about you from my son! Good to meet you! Thank you for coming!"

They shook hands all around and I took Richard by the arm. "Come with me, will you? Frances Mae needs a sitter."

Frances Mae was curled up on a couch, breast-feeding the Jackal, Chloe. If Mother could have, she would have gotten up from her coffin and buttoned Frances Mae's blouse. She couldn't, so the onus was on me.

"Frances Mae? Here's Richard! Oh! You're busy! Sorry. Maybe you'd like to go to the ladies' room?"

She looked at me without a shred of embarrassment, pulled Chloe from her breast, the loosening of the suction making a loud pop, and looked up at Richard.

"You and me, darlin'—we ain't ever gonna fit in with these people!"

"There, there," Richard said, helping her to her feet, "let's not be unpleasant at Lavinia's wake. Come with me, Frances Mae, tell me what's . . ."

They walked away. Thank God.

I had to see if Josh was filling Jack with the inappropriate details of my little fling with him. No, he was talking to Matthew! Right there and then, I started to laugh! The room was overflowing with people and I was in a very strange position. Oh, hell, I thought, let them all talk. I could not have cared less!

I turned to see Peter Greer signing the book on the lectern at the door of the room. He looked so sad. I couldn't get to him as he worked his way over to Mother's casket. He stood there, alone, and looked down at her. He was talking to her. When I finally reached his side I heard him say to her, "You were a helluva gal, Lavinia Boswell Wimbley, and this old fellow is going to miss you."

"Hey! Mr. Greer! Thanks so much for coming! You made Mother's last days so happy, do you know that?"

"She made me happy too, Miss Caroline. She made me young again."

"And you thrilled her too, but I'm sure she told you that."

"Better yet, she showed me, Miss Caroline! She did so many nice things for me, I haven't ever known anyone like her before and I know I never will again. She was very special."

"Thank you, Mr. Greer. You'll join us back at Trip and Frances Mae's, won't you?"

"Dear lady, your mother won't rest until each of us has toasted her. Do you think I want to be haunted by a lady in a paisley caftan?"

He chuckled and so did I. He was right. The reception would be packed.

After the prayer service, people began to leave. I was one of the last to go. Jack had waited for me. I was glad of it.

"Hey," he said, "you tired?"

"Yeah, God, but I sure am glad you're here."

"No place I'd rather be than with you," he said. "Come on. I'll drive you to Trip's. Eric went on ahead with him."

I couldn't blame Eric for wanting to get out of the funeral home. "Sure. In a minute. Just want to tell Mother good night."

He waited for me at the door to the large viewing room and gave me a moment alone. I walked up to the edge of Mother's casket and looked down at her. It wasn't her. There, in front of me, was a shameful imitation of who my mother was. There was no other truth. Mother was

gone. Still, out of respect for her and knowing she was on
my shoulder or somewhere very close, I moved a stray
hair from her forehead. She wore the most simple of jewelry, just her wedding band and tiny pearl stud earrings.
Her dress was her favorite caftan, the lavender and blue
paisley Pucci one from the sixties. She had decided to save
her wedding gown for Frances Mae's girls after all. She
looked glorious.

Too many things went through my mind and at the same
time, it was blank. I was standing before my mother's casket and there were her remains, but not her. That was all
I could think. Where had she gone?

I turned to Jack, thinking I may as well leave because
there was nothing I could do. I took his arm and he walked
me to his car, opening my door and seeing that I was safely
inside. He came around his side, got in, started the car,
and looked at me.

"Hold on, girl," he said, "I promised your mother I'd
keep an eye on you and that's what I intend to do."

He began to back up from the parking space and I felt
myself smiling. He picked up my hand from the seat and
kissed the back of it. I hoped I'd never forget that moment.
I'd never known a man to be so tender and so strong at
the same time.

"You are so wonderful, Dr. Taylor, do you know that?"

The reception at Trip and Frances Mae's was the most
beautiful party I had ever attended. A valet service from
Columbia parked cars. Waiters in black tie met us with
trays filled with goblets of champagne and tumblers of
mint juleps. People wandered in and out of the crowd, their
plates piled high with roast beef, barbecue, and classic
southern dishes. There was no stone left unturned in Trip

and Frances Mae's quest to ensure a successful and memorable night. I was so tired I could barely stand to be on my feet for another minute. But I had to speak to Trip and Frances Mae and give them the compliments they so deserved.

I saw Trip at the bar. Big surprise. I worked my way over to him, thanking people every three feet for coming.

"Hey, Trip! Ya done good, bubba! This is a great send-off for Mother, it really is."

"Think she would have approved? I couldn't have done it without Millie though."

"She would've loved this, Trip. Really. And where is Millie?"

"Look over there," he said and pointed to the back porch.

There was Millie with her arms around Mr. Jenkins. I loved it.

No, the night was a success from start to finish. I even kissed Frances Mae on the cheek before I left and told her so.

"Mother would've been thrilled, Frances Mae, really."

"Well, I did my best; that's all I can say. And tomorrow we all gather to throw dirt on Miss Lavinia!"

"Throw dirt?" I said.

"Yeah, that's what they call it, don't they? When them monks up at Mepkin die, they just pull the hood over their face and put them in the ground, don't they? Then all the monks pass by and put a shovel or two on the one in the hole? Isn't that right, Trip?"

"She's being cremated, Frances Mae, right now in fact," I said.

"That's horrible! Trip, honey? Is that true?"

I just walked away, but not before giving Trip the eye. Millie and Mr. Jenkins drove Eric and me back to Tall

Pines. I couldn't wait to lie down and rest. I gave Richard a house key, since he wanted to remain behind, saying he was doing what he could as a host to help Trip and Frances Mae. Since when did he care about them so much? Maybe he was gathering material for a book.

I faced the next dilemma—being in Tall Pines without Mother and tucking Eric in bed after he'd seen his first dead body. All the way back, he slept with his head on my lap in the backseat of the car. His breath, slow and even, was reassuring and all I could think about was that he needed me.

Millie and Mr. Jenkins talked quietly about the evening and how Mother would have been so surprised to see what they had put together in her honor.

When we arrived, I shook Eric awake and we went inside through the kitchen door. Millie and Mr. Jenkins said good night and I thanked them for all they had done. Eric clopped up the stairs, moaning about being tired and please let him sleep late the next morning. I locked the doors, left a few lights on for Richard, and followed him.

He was under his covers, turned on his side toward the door.

"Good night, baby, I love you."

"I can't sleep," he said.

"Wanna sleep with me?"

"Definitely," he said. He headed toward my room.

"Wait!" I said. "Go to Grandmother's room, I'm sleeping in there."

"You be Miss Caroline now, girl!" he said and smiled from ear to ear. We were finally home.

"Go on git, fore I buss yo lip!" I said, laughing. "My ma wouldn't hab she no utha way!"

It was a Lowcountry lullaby, sung in pitiful Gullah. We slept like angels.

50

Day Clear

The high sun of midmorning flooded Mother's room. The sound of van doors slamming—the caterers—woke me; I turned to find Eric's head next to me in my mother's bed. I assumed I would sleep there indefinitely.

Richard was in my old room. I could hear him snoring all night, like a foghorn in the distance. At some point, he had put his nose in Mother's room, but seeing Eric there must have kept him at bay. I was glad for that. The last thing I needed the night of Mother's wake was a drunken ex-husband in my bed.

Eric had protected me. Fact was, we all needed someone to give us shelter. It was his first and only experience with death. I kept my arm over his side all night so he'd know I was there to protect him.

I knew I had to get up and face the day. I was beyond exhaustion. The wake had taken place without a hitch. It just went on too long. Trip ignored Frances Mae the entire night and spent his time at my side or with Richard, Jack, and Josh.

And the preparations for the funeral were well under way. I looked out of my window and saw that the entire yard around Mother's rose garden was tented. It was where we would gather after we spread her ashes. The funeral service was to be small; immediate family, her two best friends, and, of course, Mr. Jenkins and Millie would attend. It would be as she had wished. Some of her ashes would be spread next to Daddy and a marker would be placed there as well. Another reception would follow and the reading of her will would take place after that.

I washed my face in her bathroom and looked in the mirror as I patted it dry. Heavenly days! I could feel her looking at me through my own eyes! My eyes began to take on her twinkle without my permission! I stared at my reflection for what seemed like an hour. Every time I tried to deny that part of her had taken up residence in me, the feelings grew in intensity!

It was very confusing, to say the least! I dressed quickly to go to Millie and ask her what she thought. Was I losing my mind? I began to laugh as I dressed. Suddenly I didn't want to wear jeans or shorts, but pulled a sundress from her closet and decided it was more appropriate. It wasn't even black! It was red! It wasn't even mine! I didn't have shoes to match so I did something I thought I'd never do in a million years. I went to her closet and searched the Polaroids for a pair of sandals and found several choices.

A little poem ran through my head:

> *When I die,*
> *Please wear red,*

> *'Cause there ain't no sense,*
> *In me being dead!*

Where did that come from?

When I finally finished gleaning my mother's closet and went downstairs, I checked my face in every mirror I passed. By golly, there she was! Looking right back at me! It made me laugh like a fool!

I composed myself to enter the kitchen, knowing Millie was probably bustling all around, giving instructions to chefs and waitstaff. She was. She didn't even look up from the table where she worked, going over lists and lists.

I poured myself a cup of coffee and sat beside her.

"Give me a job," I said, "what can I do to help?"

She finally looked at me and her eyes got wide, traveling from my dress to my shoes.

"What . . . ?" Then she stared deeply into my eyes and I twinkled at her for all I was worth. "Gee-za-ree! Lawd! Lemme have a good look at you!"

"Weird, right?"

"No, chile. We all become our mothers. We all do."

"She's just visiting," I said.

"Let's hope not!"

"Wants to be sure we don't screw up her funeral!"

"Humph!" Millie said, followed by, "Glory be!"

And so, we had a prayer and music ceremony for Mother. I stood at the family chapel, dressed in a red suit of Mother's, with a large red straw hat and sandals, wearing the pearls, with my arm around Eric on my right. And Trip stood on my left, his arm around Frances Mae. The girls were next to her and she held the squirming baby in her arms. Richard sat behind me with Miss Sweetie and Miss Nancy. Across the grave marker, Millie held hands with Mr. Jenkins.

Helena McKay sang more beautifully than I imagined anyone could. She had come with her husband, Fred, old friends of Mother's from Charleston. Then, when Helena finished, Millie and Mr. Jenkins sang a song of their own.

> *I see a world of spirits bright,*
> *Who taste the pleasures there;*
> *They all are robed in spotless white,*
> *And conqu'ring palms they bear.*
> *Oh, what has Jesus done for me,*
> *Before my ravished eyes;*
> *Rivers of life divine I see,*
> *And trees of paradise!*

Mr. Jenkins pulled out his harmonica and played and Millie hummed. It was clear to all of us that Mother wasn't going to paradise without Millie and Mr. Jenkins helping her make the trip. *Rivers of life.* Wasn't that our river too? The Ashepoo, the Combahee, and, of course, our Edisto?

They sang that first song slowly and then gave us another more lively one to show to the Lord and all of us that going to God's heaven—and they were sure Mother was there already but still watching us—was a happy and joyous occasion.

> *Why don't you sit down?* Mr. Jenkins sang out.
> *Can't sit down!* Millie replied, shaking her head.
> Then, *Sit down, I told you!*
> *Go 'way don't bother me,*
> *I can't sit down*
> *'Cause I just got to heaven*
> *An' I can't sit down!*

Every one of us clapped along with her and she repeated the lyrics again. On the third round, we joined her, singing with all our hearts, knowing somehow that Mother made it to the other side.

Now, Mother's wish was to have her ashes spread over the river and that was the next thing on the agenda. The pontoon waited, decorated with white sheer fabric, white lilies tied with gold ribbons, a champagne bucket, and Mother's finest Lalique goblets.

I got ready to leave and Miss Sweetie tapped me on the shoulder. "Can I say something?"

"Gosh! Of course!"

She walked to the top of Mother's marker, a temporary one, but something to mark her place in history that day next to Daddy. Miss Sweetie cleared her throat and spoke.

"Lavinia Ann Boswell Wimbley was my dearest friend in this world and I shall miss her deeply, as we all will. Lavinia? If you can hear me I just want you to know that I love you and I'm going to pray for you. My life was richer for your friendship in every single way." Miss Sweetie's eyes filled with tears and Miss Nancy went to her side, pulling a tissue from her pocket and handing it to her, putting an arm around her shoulder. Poor Miss Sweetie began to sob.

"Lavinia?" Miss Nancy said, looking up at the blue sky. "See here! Do something to let us know you're not gone! We just *can't stand this!*" And then she broke down.

Just then, out of nowhere, came a shower. The rain was short, warm, and if you asked anyone who was there, they would tell you it was Mother's tears, at having to leave so many people she loved. The rain stopped as quickly as it had begun and when it did I looked from face to face; all of them were incredulous, mine included.

Millie was the first to speak.

"Devil's beating his wife behind the kitchen door!"

It was what we said when it rained with the sun out. An old Gullah saying turned sorrow to faith—faith that there was more to life than us: God in His heaven waiting for us when we died.

"All right then," Millie said, "let's go make Lavinia Boswell Wimbley happy one more time!"

"Not yet," I said, "gotta leave a little bit of the Queen of Tall Pines." I opened the box and let some ash fall on Daddy's grave. No one said a word. I simply closed it, smiled, and carried the box to the docks. Everyone followed. We walked quietly, thinking our thoughts.

"Where do you think she is?" Eric said to me.

"I think she's all over and inside of each of us," I said, "can't you feel her spirit?"

"Yeah," he said, "you wanna hear something weird?"

"Sure, but you're gonna have to have a whopper to tell me something that qualifies as weird, sweetheart."

"No problem," he said, stopping.

We let the others pass.

"I had a dream last night, only I don't think it was a dream."

"Continue," I said.

"Grandmother was sitting on the end of my bed. She said, *Eric? I love you.* I just stared at her and said, *I love you too.* Then she stared at me and said, *This is your home, son.* I thought, *Shit!*"

"Eric? Do you think it's appropriate to say that word when I'm standing here with her ashes in my hand?"

"It's just her ashes, Mom, it ain't her."

The breeze picked up and all the leaves of the trees rustled in a song. I looked up to see the others in the distance.

"You're right, baby, but we have a job." He looked at

me and waited. "Besides letting her ashes fly in the wind, we've got to figure out how to pick up where she left off. Come on. They're waiting."

We walked in the very back of our procession, reaching the dock. Mr. Jenkins had started the motor, Trip had opened and poured the champagne—Dom Perignon, of course. Millie began to hum again and soon she was singing as we made our way down the Edisto.

> *Oh, Jordan bank was a great old*
> *bank!*
> *Dere ain't but one more river to cross!*

We toasted each other and said, "To Lavinia, Queen of Tall Pines! Queen of the Edisto! We love you, Lavinia!"

"These glasses were an anniversary gift to Mother from Senator Hollings, you know," I said. "I remember the day she received them. Mother was so thrilled!"

"Caroline?" Trip said. "She got them from the Ross-Simons catalog."

"Whatever," I said and laughed. And then Trip looked at me, his face all funny. I gave him the "Miss Lavinia twinkle" and he shook his head in disbelief, laughing.

Then I opened the box and Millie continued.

> *We have some valiant soldier here,*
> *Dere ain't but one more river to cross!*

I turned to Trip and said, "Come on, do this with me."

We stood at the back of the boat with the small urn in our hands and let Mother's ashes fly in the wind.

> *Oh, Jordan stream will never run dry,*
> *Dere ain't but one more river to cross.*

Dere's a hill on my left and he catch on my right,
Dere ain't but one more river to cross!

It was a grand ceremony. A fitting tribute to a great woman. Mother had crossed the River Jordan by way of the Edisto and we all knew she was never going to really be gone.

I was deep in thought, thinking about the nature of eternity, as we walked from the dock back to the house. It was close to the time that guests would arrive.

"Do you think that shower messed up the grass?" Frances Mae said. "I mean, a lot of people will be on the grass, you know? Not just under the tent."

It was actually a good point, but the sun was climbing in the sky and it would surely be dry by one o'clock when guests were due to arrive.

"I don't think so, but if you want to check, I'd appreciate it."

She looked at me, eyes filled with confusion. "I don't know why I said that about the pearls, Caroline. I know she would have wanted you to have them. Sometimes my mouth just has a mind of its own."

That was as close to an apology as I'd ever heard from her. I looked at her, trying to find a comeback that wasn't hostile.

"Frances Mae, just forget it, okay? Mother asked me to get them and then she said please take them; she didn't need them anymore. You can't imagine how hard it was for me to do that."

"Oh! I'm sure it was!"

Okay, the bitch's voice dripped sarcasm and even though I wore Mother's pearls, and even though everything, I was going to skewer her. I stared at her hard and let Mother come through.

Lavinia and I said, "You just can't help it, can you? That Litchfield genome just cannot be denied."

I turned away and even though I knew it was a crummy thing to say, it felt good.

Millie and I went to the kitchen to make sure the caterers had everything under control. Eric ran off to play with the girls, Richard and Trip were somewhere, and guests started to arrive early. I rushed out to greet them.

When I got to the tent, I passed Mother's roses. Every bush held full fragrant blooms. Another gift from the other side. Until three o'clock, we drank champagne, mint juleps, mint iced tea, and punch. Waiters passed trays of petit fours, smoked salmon, marinated shrimp on skewers, lobster in puff pastry, and Sonny's Barbecue on tiny hamburger rolls—in Mother's honor. People told the same stories we had loved all of our lives, children ran around, shirttails and hair flying, until their faces turned red, adults offered sympathy and promised to visit.

When the last guest pulled away, it was time to read the will. We gathered in Daddy's study with the attorney— Richard excused himself on the pretense of taking a walk with Eric. We all found a seat and waited.

Mother's lawyer, Frederick Babbit, cleared his throat and began.

"Mrs. Wimbley made some changes to her will in her final days. What I'd like to do is read the division of properties and then ask you to meet me downtown sometime in a few days if there are questions."

"That sounds fine," Trip said, throwing his hands in the air. He was drunk again.

"Yes, please, that's fine," I said.

"Well, first to Mr. Jenkins, she has given him his cottage for the rest of his days and his salary with a five percent increase each year, all the books in her library, and the sum of two hundred thousand dollars in cash. She also asks that you spend two hours a week reading to her grandson."

Mr. Jenkins stood up and clapped his hands together. "Oh, Jesus! Oh, Miss Lavinia! Thank you so! Thank you so! Yes, God, thank you!"

We all smiled. Mr. Jenkins was thrilled. Millie reached over and patted his shoulder.

Mr. Babbit continued. "Mrs. Smoak? Mrs. Wimbley has left you your cottage and five acres around it, your salary with a five percent increase annually, her silver tea service that she knew you loved so dearly, and the sum of three hundred thousand dollars in cash."

"That's Tiffany!" Frances Mae said, a little too loud.

"Shut up, Frances Mae!" Trip said.

"To each of her granddaughters, she has left the sum of two hundred thousand dollars and the desire that it be placed in trust until their thirtieth birthday, using the interest from the principal for education. That trust will be managed by an appointed manager employed by Merrill Lynch."

"She never did trust us, Trip! Did you hear that?"

"Will you please, for the love of God, shut the hell up?" Trip said.

"To her son, James Nevil Wimbley III, she leaves the sum of three million dollars in cash, stocks, and bonds. This will all be held in trust by Merrill Lynch with an appointed manager, principal to be untouched unless he is free of all alcohol and refrains from gambling for a period of five years."

"Son of a bitch!" Trip said, yelling.

"We'll hire us a lawyer and contest this, Trip. Trip? Trip?"

"Anything else?" Trip said, ignoring Frances Mae.

"Yes. Invested conservatively at seven percent, this fund

will yield an average income of two hundred and ten thousand dollars. She also leaves you your father's watch and all his personal effects, including their letters to each other. In addition, she grants you lifelong use of the docks here at Tall Pines."

Trip got up to leave and then Frances Mae got up as well.

"I suppose the rest goes to my sister?"

"Yes, but only if she remains in residence here. If Caroline leaves the plantation for a period of more than three years, the property is immediately given to the Nature Conservancy. In addition, Mrs. Levine, the contents of the house, your mother's jewelry, and all her personal belongings are yours. Your mother also set up an endowment fund of sorts to provide for the care of the house and all the outbuildings, that upkeep to be overseen by Mr. Jenkins and Mrs. Smoak. She also leaves you the sum of one million dollars in cash, and two hundred thousand dollars for your son, Eric."

It knocked the wind from me. I mean, Mother must have made a killing in the stock market! I knew she wasn't broke, but God's holy word, I had no idea! I was speechless!

"In trust with a manager from Merrill?" Trip said.

"Actually, no. Mrs. Levine is free to use the money as she wishes."

"I'm getting out of this house and away from this family for once and for all!" Frances Mae said. She stomped out of the room, hissing and muttering as she went. All of us, including Trip, were quiet as we listened for the front door to slam. *Bam!* She was gone. Forgive me, but it was the sweet sound I'd waited years to hear.

"You know what?" Trip said.

"What?" I said.

"Mother was a smart cookie."

"Yes, she was," I said, "and a rich one too. I had no idea."

"Me either. Helluva lot more than I expected!" Trip said and smiled at me. "Guess I better go get Miss Litchfield and take her home."

"Yeah," I said, "I reckon so."

I walked him to the door, said good-bye, offering my sympathies for what was surely waiting for him, and went to the kitchen to make some hot tea. I was exhausted. Richard was there with Eric. Richard's suitcase was packed and on the floor by the back door.

"Well? How did that go?" he said.

"Better than expected," I said, telling him nothing.

"Eric? Why don't you run along for a few minutes and let me talk to your mother, all right?"

"Sure," Eric said and ran out the back door.

He stood up and came close to me, putting his hands on my shoulders.

"I have an eight o'clock flight to Newark," he said.

"Well, I appreciate you coming, Richard." His eyes were searching mine and the old Caroline was still there, just fortified. "I truly do."

"I guess that means you'd rather I go?"

"I think we'll be fine," I said. "This has been so difficult; I think I'd just like to have a good swoon for a week or so."

He picked up his bag. "All right then. I understand. Do you want to proceed with the divorce?"

"Is that a fair question on a day like this?"

How the hell should I know? Jesus. Hadn't I been through enough for one day? The day I scattered Mother's ashes would be remembered as the day I gave my husband permission to file final papers? The day I inherited Tall

Pines? How insensitive could he be? In fact, maybe this would be the time to cut him loose. Let *him* remember that it was *his* insensitivity and *his* proclivities that ruined what we had!

"Just want to keep a tidy life, that's all," he said and sort of smirked.

I opened the back door for him to leave—his rental car was in the yard. I just stood there.

"If you want to say good-bye to Eric, just call for him."

"Okay," he said and opened the screen door, "well?"

"File 'em, Richard," I said, "and keep things tidy. After all, tidiness is next to cleanliness is next to godliness. Right?"

He looked surprised and I couldn't for the life of me imagine why. "I enjoyed meeting your friends—that Tantric fellow, Josh? He's quite something. Very talkative. And Jack? Seems nice. Certainly thinks *you're* special, Caroline."

"Is this some kind of a threat, Richard?"

"No, Caroline. I just thought you'd like to know they gave me an earful at the wake." Suddenly his face looked mean.

I held the palm of my hand in front of me and worked my fingers up and down the way a child does. "Bye-bye, Richard. Thanks for coming."

"Caroline? Know what? Looking at you is like looking at your mother."

I said nothing but watched him go. Seeming to be like her was the highest compliment I could imagine. And, he surely meant it as an insult.

He didn't call Eric to say *Good-bye, son.* He just got in his little tin can car, the smallest, cheapest, ugliest rental car I'd ever seen, and drove away. I watched his dust and

said out loud to no one, "Y'all come back now, yanh?"
Right.

About eight-thirty that night, I was tucking Eric in bed.

"Is Daddy coming back soon?" he said.

"If you want him to, I'm sure he will. Or I could take you to New York to see him too, you know."

"Nah, let him come here. It's more fun here. The city sucks."

"Eric!" I said in mock horror. I scratched his back, smiling. It was true.

"Think Grandmother's in heaven?" he said.

"I know it! Honey, she did so many good things in her life, don't you know the Lord was happy to have her? And, you know, I think that in her last days, she had an honest conversion."

"What do you mean?" He rolled over and looked at me.

I wasn't sure either what I had meant by that, but in retrospect, she had asked forgiveness, she had shown remorse, and she had tried to mend her fences. In addition to all that, she was somehow changed, in that she had reconciled her soul.

"Well, I'm no expert on this, son, but I guess you could say she came to terms with God."

"How come we don't go to church?"

"Because there was always a question of bringing you up Jewish or Christian."

"So you brought me up nothing? Am I agnostic?"

I could see this was not going to be a simple tuck-in so I stretched out on the bed next to him. Every bone in my body screamed at me to rest.

"No, I have tried to bring you up aware of all religions and thought that when you expressed an interest or a preference, then Daddy and I would guide you."

"Well, I'm picking Christian."

I rolled over and looked at him. This child never ceased to amaze me. "How come?" I said.

"Better action," he said.

"What?"

"Yeah, see? I found this Bible next to my bed—"

"Oh! Here we go! Young man, you go to sleep tonight! There will be plenty of time to discuss it tomorrow, okay?" I got up and pulled the sheet up over his shoulders and he settled into his pillows. "Love you, Eric."

"Love you too, Mom."

We were all turning in early as it had been an impossibly emotional day. I thought of calling Jack. I had seen his face in the crowd and we had spoken for a minute or two. I was just too tired to dial the phone. I'd call him in the morning.

I went downstairs to turn out the lights and saw headlights coming up the driveway. I squinted in the light, trying to make out the car, and saw it was Trip's. He pulled up to the front door, got out, and went around to the back and lifted the door. His SUV was packed to the roof with stuff. When he saw me, he stopped, put his hand on his hip, and called out.

"Hey! You got a room for a nondrinking, nongambling man?"

What in the world? "Want your old room back?" I called out.

"That'd be good," he hollered to me, "gimme a hand!"

"Forget it! We'll do it tomorrow!"

He thought for a minute, then slammed down the door and came up the steps.

"I couldn't stand her another minute," he said.

"We're even," I said, "Richard couldn't stand me another minute either."

"Do you have a boy in this house who needs a full-time uncle?"

"Yep, and a woman who needs a good brother!"

He put his arm around my shoulder and squeezed. I threw my arm around his waist and squeezed back. The lights in the house blinked off and on again.

"Good night, Mother!" I said and laughed.

"What a woman," Trip said.

He followed me around, turning out lights.

"I'll sleep well tonight," I said, "yes, I will."

I climbed the stairs with my brother, never feeling more protected or happier in my entire life. Even though Mother was technically dead, everything was right with my world.

EPILOGUE

With Rusty's support, Eric began public school in Jacksonboro right before Labor Day. He finished the first marking period and brought home a report card of all A's. I was so proud of him I thought I would burst. He was playing junior varsity football, loving it and leaving whatever frustrations he had on the ball field. Yes, there was a woman in his life, a very young woman of thirteen named Tracey, with freckles and transparent braces on her teeth. She did nothing but giggle and turn cartwheels whenever he intercepted the ball. She was a cheerleader. Rusty continued as his tutor in all subjects, twice a week. Between Tracey and Rusty, my young man's confidence was a spiral of sure and steady growth.

Once the ink was dry on his separation papers, Trip and Rusty were inseparable. She adored Trip and Eric. Their feelings were the same.

By October, I decided that the house was too small for Trip, Eric, and me. It wasn't just Trip; it was Trip, his

romance, his dogs, and visitation from his brood that was
doing us in. Frances Mae's frequent calls, the dogs yelping
under my window with every sunrise or rabbit that ran
across the yard—it was too much of Animal/Frat House
for me. Eric and I needed a steady quiet environment. Trip
realized it and was sorry for it but with Mother only gone
a few months and all of our lives turned upside down, it
was just one issue too many for him to solve.

I took that horse by the reins and called Mother's lawyer. We had a great discussion and together we studied a
land survey of the entire plantation. I had him draw up
some papers for me.

I told Eric about my plans and he all but jumped in
happiness.

"If he says yes, can I have my own dog? I mean, not a
giant Lab, but maybe a Lab puppy?"

"Lab puppies grow to become big Labs, Eric," I said,
but when his face fell I said, "Let's see what Uncle Trip
says first, okay? But no dogs in the house! Remember the
Aubusson!"

When Trip came in from the river that afternoon, Eric
and I met him at the dock.

"To what do I owe the honor of this greeting committee?" he asked with good nature.

"Well, brother, I thought we would have drinks on the
verandah and discuss the future of the world. Catch anything?"

"Didn't catch anything but the breeze," he said. "Here,
Eric, grab this line like a good fellow, okay? Wanna help
me wash down the boat?"

"Sure!"

"I'll meet y'all up at the house in an hour, all right?" I
said.

"Fine," they both said.

Eric was helping his uncle put up the boat for the night. I loved it. In the few short months we'd been at Tall Pines, so many things had occurred—most of them wonderful, the kind of changes that made you look forward to each new day. We were clearly taking root.

I watched Eric and Trip for a moment and then turned to go back to the house, filled with satisfaction. Their relationship had given both of them something neither one had—understanding, devotion, and loyalty. Pretty darn key to happiness, if you asked me. All these they gave each other and more, as naturally as day turns to night and then day again. Trip never missed a ball game of Eric's and Eric never failed to meet Trip at the door or the dock. Eric was fast becoming Trip's surrogate son and Trip, Eric's surrogate father.

I had finally cleaned out Mother's closets, donating a lot of what she had to the Costume Collection at the Metropolitan Museum of Art in New York. For all her zany-isms, Mother had been a serious collector and preserver of fashion history. Her collection of Worth, Chanel, and Balenciaga from the fifties gave the estate a whopping tax deduction when combined with unworn shoes and barely used handbags, not to mention boxes of handmade hats and trunks of costume jewelry.

I had kept some things—a few robes, some sweaters—mainly because they smelled like her. When melancholy took over, I'd throw her sweater over my shoulders or nap in her robe.

In any case, that fall afternoon, I was wearing my own clothes again, black trousers, a tan sweater, and loafers, and walking toward the house, thinking of the new role I had assumed—that of mistress of Tall Pines. Soon, I would change her history, as Mother had when she deeded Millie and Mr. Jenkins's property to them.

Halfway to the house, I stopped to give her another look. God, she was bold! Perched on the rise of the ground like a fortress, she beckoned me from the distance to embrace her. It was impossible not to want to love her every brick and board. All I could think of was the hardships suffered over the years to keep her going. My ancestors, all the men and women before me who had lived and died between her walls. The house pulsated with invisible storytellers to be discovered through Mother's collection of journals. I had barely touched them. Too many things had blocked their path.

The whole business of me becoming Millie's apprentice had gone by the boards. Even she thought that Mother's death had changed me and redirected my personality.

"Just give me that boy of ours! He's twice as smart as you ever were anyway!" She said this to me one morning over coffee.

I banged my hand on the counter and looked at her with squinted eyes. "You think you're gonna turn my boy into a voodoo medicine man?"

"No, I'm gonna help him learn to be a healer and a scientist!" She grinned a little too wide for me, meaning a zinger was coming. "Anyhow, Miss Lavinia, you're too busy being Miss Caroline! Or is it the other way around?"

"Millie Smoak! My mother would've had a fit to hear you say that!" Sometimes she said the most hurtful and peculiar things, truly she did. "You mean old woman!" I said, hand to my heart. "You have cut me to the quick! Truly you have!" In fact, I felt a little tweak in my chest muscles. I did! Lord! What next?

"Mm-hmm," she said, her eyebrows in the vicinity of the ceiling.

We both started to laugh. Lavinia still ruled. Sort of.

"And what about you and Mr. Jenkins?"

"Don't you know that old fool come around my house last night to read me poetry by some man who calls himself Amiri Baraka? What kind of a name is that? I like Sonja Sanchez and Paul Genega's work better." She was smiling and looking at the countertop, running her fingertip around in a little circle. "Yeah, we drank some wine and sat on my porch until the moon was up and high. Who would've thought that at our age . . ."

"Humph!" I said. "You ain't dead yet, girl! Go on and have some fun!"

Go on and have some fun, I had said to her, and she took me at my word, rarely showing up around suppertime in the past weeks, unless Jack was coming for the evening. Even then, I wasn't sure if she came to help or to listen at the door. Probably both!

The kitchen was deserted when I arrived there. Millie had taken a casserole of lasagna out of the freezer, and left me a note on how to reheat it. Don't you know I knew perfectly good and well how to do that? What did she think, that I was so incompetent that I could kill a frozen casserole? No, she probably had a date with Mr. J!

The dining room table was preset for three; a salad and sliced bread—both covered with plastic wrap—waited on the sideboard. A pitcher of sweet tea was chilling in the refrigerator. Dinner would be a snap.

I put the oven on to preheat (per Millie's instructions) and went upstairs to Mother's room, where I was now fully installed. I loved everything about the space; the only change I made was to move one statue, of Lord Shiva, to the attic. It freaked me out, to say the least.

I brushed my hair in the vanity mirror, gathering it at the nape of my neck with a gold barrette. I decided to change for dinner. I slipped on a pair of black silk pull-on pants, red suede flats, and a black cashmere tunic sweater. Without even thinking about it, my hands reached for the pearls. I smiled at myself in the mirror and saw I needed lipstick. It was almost as though Mother had told me to apply it! Satisfied with a second look, I picked up a journal, intending to read on the verandah while the lasagna baked.

I did just that, and found myself completely absorbed by the words of Elizabeth Bootle Kent. She was in her midtwenties at the time of the Civil War. Her daughter Olivia was a little girl of three.

April 1863

Little Olivia and I spent the morning in prayer for our valiant troops and then I kept her by my side as I gathered eggs for our lunch. She likes them cooked hard and then the yolks chopped with a little butter, salt, bread crumbs and parsley. Sometimes I add a little cream to the yolk mixture and then refry them for a moment to heat them. Food is scarce and other things scarcer still. The storehouse still holds sweet potatoes, some barrels of flour and corn but they cannot last forever. It is by God's grace and the intelligence of the servants that we painted the warnings of smallpox all around the property, fending off the troops which would surely arrive after the fall of Columbia. We fear that this wretched cause is far from over. Many of our servants have gone off with General Beauregard's army to build barricades on James Island. There is talk of an armada of Union ships, gathering at Port Royal. If that horrible Sherman marches to the seas of Charleston, Charleston will never surrender! Never!

Her words were powerful and I admired her bravery. It must have been horrific to be surrounded by the Union troops, having heard all the stories of rape and plunder from the fall of Vicksburg! So many Charlestonians had sent their silver and valuables to Columbia for safekeeping in the vaults of banks Sherman looted and then burned, losing everything of real and sentimental value. By 1865, there were accounts in her journals of Union soldiers bursting into her home, stealing everything they had, frightening them until they wept. All the time she held a pistol, hidden under her skirt on a belt, and a bag of bullets, vowing to herself to use it if they laid a hand on her little Olivia. I had no doubt that she would have done it too.

I would see my family through as well. Well rid of Richard and, God forgive me, of Frances Mae, my brother and I could rebuild our lives as a family. I had been given the opportunity to stabilize our future and I would do it.

The hour drew to a close. I knew that soon Trip and Eric would appear. I brought out three glasses, an ice bucket, sliced lemon, and the pitcher of tea. I put cheddar cheese and crackers on a plate with sliced apple and Goldfish crackers in a little glass bowl and waited for them to arrive.

The French doors opened and here they came, Trip and Eric, all showered and dressed in fresh shirts and khakis for dinner.

"How do I smell?" Eric said and leaned into me.

"Good enough to smooch!" I gave him a kiss on the cheek and turned to Trip. "Putting aftershave on my son?"

"Drives the women wild," Trip said.

"Great," I said, "just what I wanted to hear."

We chatted about every pleasant thing I could think of to chat about in our new alcohol-free cocktail hour.

"Just because I'm not drinking doesn't mean you can't have a cocktail, Caroline."

"Oh, I don't know . . . it's not import—"

"Bourbon and branch?" Trip asked.

"Maybe a small one," I said, somewhat relieved that his resolve to stay sober wouldn't impinge on my right to a little indulgence.

He returned in moments, handing me a tumbler filled with crushed ice, bourbon, and a splash of water. Oh! It was so delicious! I decided right then and there to make my announcement.

"Here! Got you something today," I said, and handed him the envelope. "Hope you like it!"

"Yeah, it's very cool," Eric said. He now said *cool* almost every other word. To tell you the truth, I was delighted to hear him use the slang of his peers. Sounding like a little professor wouldn't help him make friends with the boys in school.

"What? What's this?" Trip said.

His mouth was filled with a cracker piled high with cheese. He opened the envelope slowly and read the deed.

"I think Mother would approve, don't you?"

"Caroline! Great God! Thank you so much!" He got up, yanked me to my feet, and swung me around. *Smack! Smack! Smack!*

He planted three gloppy wet kisses on my face—one on each cheek and one in the middle of my forehead. Eric laughed and laughed.

"Quit it! I'm gonna throw up! Put me down, you big jerk!"

When he finally stopped, the world was going around and around.

I had deeded Trip one hundred acres with plenty of waterfront for a dock. He was thrilled.

"I can't believe it!" he said. He was completely overwhelmed.

"It's true, Uncle Trip! I can help you design a house or

a fishing cottage or whatever you want! I've got software for it!"

"Don't expect much for Christmas," I said, deadpan.

"Amazing," Trip said. "Why did you do this?"

"So that we could all live happily ever after, Trip. And, because I love you. I really do."

"And here I thought you loved Jack," Trip said.

"We'll see about old Dr. Jack as time goes on, and yes, I love the good doctor to pieces. It just occurred to me that if I felt like *I* owned the Edisto, *you* must feel the same way. You need your own place. We can build a little road, and pave it with oyster shells. I've already marked off the land. Want to go and see? One hitch. You can't sell it."

"Hell, who cares?" Trip said, still stunned and very excited. "Come on!"

"Want me to turn off the oven?" Eric said.

"Yes, thanks sweetheart," I said.

Eric ran in and back out while Trip paced, shaking his head in wonder. I took another sip of my drink and stood up next to my brother, looking into his eyes, feeling more like Mother than I ever had.

"Don't pace so, Trip. It rankles the nerves."

"I just can't imagine what came over you to do this."

"Dear brother," I said, "what's the point of being the Queen of Tall Pines if the subjects of my realm aren't happy? Besides, I promised Mother on her deathbed that I'd keep tabs on you."

"Get in the truck, Your Majesty, and let's go see the future."

"If I'm to be Queen of Tall Pines, then you must be King of the Edisto!"

"You're insane," he said.

"What does that make me?" Eric said.

"It makes you one lucky kid," I said.

All the way across the land we bounced and smiled. We passed Millie's, Mr Jenkins's, the barns, the family chapel and graveyard, the old smokehouse and the fields. When we came to the woods, my gift began to be marked off with orange plastic ties on branches, and we walked. In the thicket, we saw deer, who looked at us with astonishment that we were coming through the trees like invaders. Eric's uncle would live two minutes away. He was thrilled.

Soon the trees gave way to a clearing and another bluff over the water. By leaning right, you could see our dock where Trip's boat was tied up.

"This is beautiful, Caroline. Tell me why—seriously, tell me why."

"Because we're Wimbleys, Trip, and our hearts don't beat right unless the Edisto is pumping in our veins."

"I wish Mother had lived to see this day," he said.

"Don't you doubt for a minute that she doesn't know *exactly* what's going on," I said.

We stood at the edge of the bluff, the three of us. It was getting late, starting to get dark. We watched the red sun sink in the purple bands at the bottom of the evening sky. We turned to go home for dinner together, knowing should the rest of the world forsake us, this unconventional tiny family would remain true to each other, to Tall Pines, and forever to the Edisto River.

AUTHOR'S NOTE

The inspiration for this story came from visits to two plantations, one of them owned by longtime friends—Florence and Lucius Fishburne (Flo and Boots). On a visit home, at one of so many social gatherings, Boots took me by the shoulders, looked me square in the eyes, and told me I was a *bush baby*. I suspected the term had pejorative origins, but flowing from Boots, it sounded like a welcome home. It was. He proceeded to share with me his marvelous collection of out-of-print books and indeed, his own writings and remembrances of Lowcountry life. To see this magical and surreal place through his eyes was an unforgettable experience, and one that shaped much of this book.

The second plantation where I was so congenially welcomed was Ravenwood, owned by dear friends of my family—Frank and Nina Burke. Their enthusiasm for this story was a hailstorm of stories, tours, explanations, late nights on my sister's porch—the air filled with sweet olive, jasmine and words. Frank went to great lengths to help me understand all the hows, whys and details of sporting clays. Nina opened her doors and graciously explained the buildings of her antebellum plantation, the materials used and showed me how they had adapted it to modern life. They also had much to do with the origins of this book.

I am profoundly grateful to both families for their generous support.

To fully comprehend the importance of the ACE Basin takes time. It's not a theme park but rather thousands of acres of wetlands where a true public private partnership exists to preserve and maintain the habitats of thousands of wildlife species and the overall purity of the waters, marshes and surrounding land. This goal is accomplished through education, public and private funding, and good old-fashioned heartfelt love of an astoundingly beautiful place. It's where anyone can go if they question the existence of a higher power and come away in awe, humbled and forever enriched.

I hope I told this story well enough to satisfy my southern mentors and if I didn't, this *bush baby* will try harder next time.

If you'd like to know more about the ACE Basin, or to take a vacation there or to make a contribution to their many projects in conservation, preservation and education, contact these good folks and get a little bit of the Lowcountry to reward your soul.

To learn more about the ACE Basin visit www.walterboro.org/ace-basin/ or write to ACE Basin National Wildlife Refuge, P.O. Box 848, Hollywood, SC 29449. If you would like to make a contribution toward preserving the ACE Basin, send donations to the ACE Basin Fund, Bank of South Carolina, P.O. Box 538, Charleston, SC 29402.